Diamonds on the Bottom of the Sea

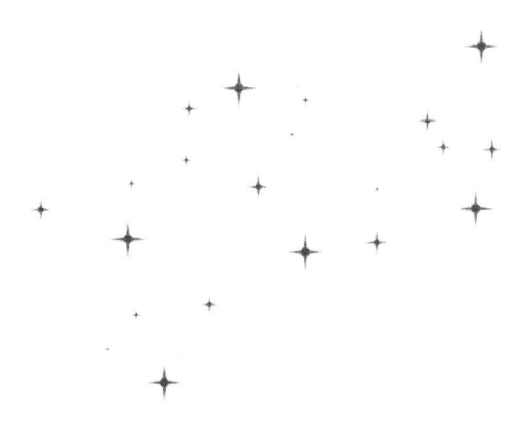

GREGORY BROZEK

Copyright © 2015 Gregory Brozek

Second edition: 2016

All rights reserved.

ISBN: 1514746328
ISBN-13: 978-1514746325

> "He not busy being born is busy dying."
> Bob Dylan

CONTENTS

	Acknowledgments	i
Act 1	**Inertia – Toronto Loka**	
1	Freewill	1
2	The Supernatural	9
3	One Master	14
4	A new drummer	20
5	Nothing in the fridge	24
6	Astrology is not easy	26
7	Time and Space	36
8	Awareness	40
9	The 8th House	52
10	River Djallon	65
11	Prediction	72
Act 2	**Passion - New Orleans Loka**	
1	Routine New Orleans	87
2	Shared Dream	94
3	Penises & Property	108
4	The Guestroom	118
5	Six feet under	120
6	Jesuits & Rock Stars	133
7	Inside Joke	143
Act 3	**Illumination - Jyoti Lokā**	
1	Diamonds on the Bottom of the Sea	161
2	Paxil	172
3	Ego is Identity	188
4	Karma, 9/11 & Hitler	197
5	Kindness is not weakness	209
6	Perspective	221
7	Meet Market Adventures	233
8	Astrology 101	250
9	Satsang	261
10	Bugs	272
11	Namaste	285
Epilogue	Guru Loka	305
Appendices		309

ACKNOWLEDGMENTS

This novel, based on a true story, is a window into a tradition whereby a student under the guidance of a Master comes to understand the universe through the meta-physics of astrology. Astrology is often dismissed by so-called scientific, or rather, materialistic thinkers whose knowledge of it rarely extends beyond newspaper horoscopes. But to anyone with any real knowledge of astrology, these horoscopes are recognized for what they are: entertainment. However, beyond these crude depictions of an ancient and noble art, there is a beautiful, complex and comprehensive system of knowledge (common to all great civilizations) that is both poetic and profound.

Whether you 'believe' in astrology or not, it is a fascinating subject when approached without bias. It is, after all, the oldest science. Having said this, nearly all the predictions, insights and readings in this book are based on real instances.

In the appendix you will find a comprehensive list of terminologies, a brief tutorial on how to read an astrological chart, a short explanation of the difference between Indian (Jyotish) and Western astrology, and a list of attributable proverbs.

I would like to thank Leena Patel, Malgorzata and my mother for their support, encouragement and love while I was composing this work. Additional thanks go to Andrea Olivera, Carmela Savoia, Davis Batson, Maha Mirza, Marion Brozek, Noam Sahar Mamane (cover design) and especially Simon Chokoisky for his editorial input. Most of all, thank you Mantriji for being my Socrates and the inspiration for this story.

Gregory J. Brozek

Act 1 – Inertia

♄

Toronto Loka
(Tamas)

1 FREEWILL

"This looks interesting." Poem pulls a book from the shelf. "Tantra."

"It's not what you think," Carmela says.

"What do you think I think?"

"Everyone thinks Tantra is about sex. But it's not."

"What is it then?"

"It's really about transforming yourself."

Poem looks at her sitting lotus position on the floor. She is petite and attractive with flowing brown hair and bright Mediterranean skin. A long time yoga instructor, Carmela is forever trying to enlighten Poem to the mystical ways of India. Her apartment walls are adorned with prints of a radiant blue Krishna in battle, giving counsel, playing flute. A picture of a kind-looking, stubbly-headed Indian man sits prominently on her shelf.

"I *am* interested in this stuff." Poem returns the book to its slot. "I just don't have the time right now." He browses a few more titles, "I do like philosophy though."

"Philosophy is for those who don't have faith."

"Yeah, but it also makes you smart," he pokes his head. "Hey! You wanna hear a philosophical joke?"

"Sure." She leans back.

"Okay, so there's these three guys walking down the beach when just ahead of them they see this golden lamp lying in the sand. All of them make a beeline for it. One guy gets it, the other guy grabs it, all three of them are in there when POOF!!" he raises his arms like billowing smoke. "A genie appears and says, 'Hmm… Usually I grant the person who finds me with *three* wishes, but I'm not sure which one of you got to me first, so tell you what, I'll grant you each one wish.'"

Carmela begins to smile.

"The genie looks at the first guy and says, 'You, what do you want?'

The man thinks and says, 'I want all the money in the world.' POOF! The beach is suddenly littered with stacks of currencies, gold bricks, and precious gems. It is quite a scene. The genie looks at the second man and says, 'What do you want?' The second man says, 'I want all the most beautiful *women* in the world.' POOF! Suddenly the beach is frolicking with gorgeous, exotic women, just hanging out with the money."

"Very funny."

"The genie looks at the third man and says, 'You, what do *you* want?' The third man thinks a moment and says, 'I want all the *knowledge* in the world.' POOF! Suddenly he has all the knowledge in the world. And his friends are looking at him like, yeah, yeah…?

"He looks at them and says, 'I should have went for the money.'"

Carmela laughs sarcastically, "Ha, ha, ha."

"What? You no like?"

"How is that a philosophical joke?"

"There's a lot of truth in that joke." Poem glances at the kitchen clock, "You know what? It's past 4:30. I should get going. Your lesson's at five, right?"

"Yeah, but you still have time." She gets up off the floor. "You sure you don't want to meet him? I thought you liked astrology."

"Yeeeah," he hesitates. "But he does Indian astrology, right?"

She nods.

"Maybe some other time." He picks up his mug and walks to the kitchen while drinking the last of his tea. The intercom buzzer suddenly splits the room. Carmela looks at it and walks over to the wall-mounted device. "Yes?"

A crackly man's voice says, *"Mantri."*

She buzzes him in and unlocks the door. "Strange. He's never early. It's not even twenty to," she looks at the clock.

Poem hastens to put on his boots, "Okay, I'm outta here."

"Well you may as well meet him!"

He stands there reluctantly with one boot on as the door opens and in walks a friendly-looking elderly man with an Indian face, a puffy grey parka, and a red-striped tuque. He greets them with a buoyant "Hello!" and Carmela helps him with his jacket. He slides off his hat and Poem recognizes him as the man in the picture.

"Sir, this is Poem," Carmela gestures. "He's the one who designed my business cards."

Mantri responds in a thick accent, "Oh? Nice to meet you. Do you like astrology?"

Poem is taken by his directness, "Uh, yeah. Yeah I do. I think it's an interesting subject."

"Mm hmm," Mantri mumbles.

Poem enunciates slowly, addressing the foreigner, "I under-stand you teach astrology."

"Mm hmm."

"Well, nice to meet you." He bends over to put on his other boot.

"Would you like to join us?" Mantri asks.

"Um, I should get going."

"Come. Come join us," Mantri insists. "Let's see who we're dealing with." He sits on the cream white sofa like it's a done deal and Poem concedes.

Carmela grins, throws him a cushion then says to Mantri, "I have good food for you, Sir. I'll warm it up." She scoots to the kitchen as Poem kneels at the centre table.

Mantri stares at him, wondering if he heard right, "What is your name?"

"Oh, it's Poem."

"Poem?"

"Yes."

"Why Poem?"

"Because 'Ice Cube' was already taken," he laughs.

Mantri doesn't get it. "Did your parents name you this?"

"No. It's kind of a stage name."

"Are you a poet?"

"Yes."

"Hmm…" Mantri thinks a moment. "Poem is not a good name. It sounds weak. No shakti."

"Really?! Well, the full name is 'Adi Poem.'"

"Ahhh," Mantri brightens. "*This* is good one. And do you know your time of birth?"

Poem gives him the April day and year.

"And your *time* of birth?"

"Oh right, umm… 4:30, in the afternoon. I am told."

"In Toronto?"

"Yes."

"Hmm…" Mantri calculates internally and looking Poem up and down, surmises, "Virgo lagna."

"What's that?"

"Virgo rising."

"Ah yes, that's right. I know a little. I remember my ascendant is Virgo."

"And do you know what this means?"

"Not really."

Carmela returns with a cup of tea which she places in front of Mantri, then gathers her books from under the table, sits and opens one. Poem sees it filled with handwritten diagrams, equations, notes and symbols and he asks Mantri, "How did you know I was Virgo rising?"

"I can see it up here," Mantri pokes his head.

"Are you psychic?"

"Oh no," he laughs. "This is not fortune-telling. This is mathematics."

Carmela is ready for her lesson and Mantri instructs her to look up Poem's birth date in the ephemeris. She finds it, nods, and Mantri begins, "This man is Virgo lagna."

She sketches into her notebook a square diagram divided into diamonds and triangles, which she numbers.

"Put Sun in 8th house," he says.

"In Aries?"

"That's right."

She writes it in and Mantri asks, "Tell me, is your father still alive?"

"No," Poem says. "My father died when I was really young."

"Uh huh," he is not surprised. "That year Rahu was in Aries," he looks to Carmela to confirm.

"7 degrees Taurus. So yes, it's in Aries."

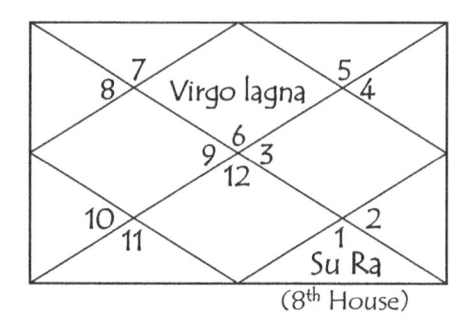

(8th House)

"Rahu ate your father when you were a child," Mantri says.

"What-who?"

Mantri again looks to Carmela who explains, "Rahu is the dreaded serpent's head, the north node of the Moon."

Poem looks confused. "So why is it in Taurus and you put it in Aries?"

"Because this is *Indian* astrology," Mantri says. "We use *sidereal* zodiac. Do you know what this means?"

Poem shakes his head.

Mantri again cues Carmela who says, "Western astrology is your Sun-sign, right, Sir? It's based on the seasons, or what they call the Tropical Zodiac, whereas *Indian* astrology is based on the stars and has nothing to do with the seasons."

"I don't get it," Poem says.

"In Western astrology," she continues, "the Sun goes into Aries on

March 21st, the spring equinox. It always does and it always will. But in *this* astrology, the Sun enters Aries on April 13—at least for now. It shifts about one full day every 72 years because of the precession of the equinoxes. Right, Sir?"

Mantri nods and Poem is perplexed, "So what's the difference?"

Mantri interjects, "If you are interested, I can teach you."

"Teach me what?"

"Jyotish."

"Jo…?"

"Vedic astrology," Carmela says.

"Vedic astrology?" Poem winces. "No thanks, I'm poor enough."

Mantri laughs. "Where is his Moon?"

Carmela checks the ephemeris, "Let's see. That's hard because it moves so quickly, but at noon it was… 14 degrees Gemini."

"We will say Taurus," Mantri says. "Put Moon in 9th house. Do you have a degree?"

"Yes," Poem says. "In music."

"So you are an artist. Where is his Venus?"

Carmela looks. "Taurus!"

"Ah hah! You *are* an artist. You have sisters, right?"

"Yeah, two."

Mantri looks at Carmela, "You see? Two female planets aspecting 3rd house. But they are *older* sisters, right?" he looks at Poem.

"Yes."

"Moon rules the 11th: older sibling."

"And benefactor," Carmela adds.

"Your sisters help you out," Mantri says.

"Yeah. It was largely my sisters who raised me."

"Mm hmm. And where is his Mars?"

"Just a second." She looks it up. "Libra, 2nd house, which puts it with Ketu, the south node."

"You can't have brothers then," Mantri shakes his head. "But very fond of pork."

"Uh right. I don't have any brothers and I do like my bacon."

"Do you smoke?"

"Uh, yeah."

"You do drugs?"

"I have."

"You like to swear?"

"Hell yeah."

"Where is his Mercury?" Mantri asks.

"Just a second." Carmela looks, "Mmm… Pisces!"

Mantri recollects, "That year, Saturn was in Pisces. Put Mercury and

Saturn in 7th house. You had back problems in '99."

"You're right! I nearly broke my back in... September 1999!"

"In '96 you ended one relationship and started another."

"Uh... yeah! How'd you know that?"

"Where's his Jupiter?"

"It would be in Cancer." Carmela jots it down.

"The 11th house..." Mantri thinks a moment. "You will not prosper until you marry."

"What?!"

"See, Poem," Carmela presses him, "You need to settle down. Why don't you marry your girlfriend?"

"Uh, because, uh..." he is caught off guard. "To be loyal to one would be to deny all the rest."

"Yeah right!" Carmela smirks. "He has a girlfriend, Sir. She's really nice."

"Why don't you marry her?" Mantri asks.

"I don't know. I guess she's not what I imagined I would marry."

"What's wrong with her?"

"There's nothing wrong with her. It's just kind of personal. We have good chemistry for some things but not for others."

"Sun with Rahu in 8th house and you want more sex," Mantri states flatly.

"Um, yeah... I guess you could say that."

"It is very difficult for you to get what you want because you won't allow yourself to have it. Saturn is very strong in this chart." He looks at Carmela, "It aspects his lagna, his main lord, *and* his Moon—what degree is his Moon?"

"Well, it's 14 degrees Gemini at noon, and he was born at 4:30..."

"Minus 23 and the Moon moves one degree every two hours. That's Mrigashira. Mars star. You're life changed in '91."

"Uh..." Poem thinks. "Yeah! That's when I sorta finished school and started gigging. How do you know all this?"

"Dasa system," Mantri says. "You have a deep mind. Do you like philosophy?"

"Yeah. In fact we were just saying—"

"But not religion."

"Well, I find it interesting but I'm not religious."

"You see?" Mantri says and Carmela nods. "Saturn aspects his 9th lord *and* 9th house."

"He's a heretic!" she declares.

"Do you believe in God?" Mantri asks.

"Well, it depends on what you mean by God."

"You see?"

Poem looks at Carmela, fascinated and confused.

"And with Mars aspecting from house of speech, he will fight about it," Mantri adds and Poem scratches his head,

"I didn't know you could tell all this with astrology."

"Oh yes. The whole life of the native is right here," Mantri points to the chart.

The smell of curry now suffuses the room. Carmela gets up and goes to the kitchen.

"But how does it work?" Poem asks.

"First, mathematics," Mantri points to his head. "Next, understanding," he points to his heart.

Poem thinks a moment. "Well, I'd be interested in learning more but I have a lot on my plate right now."

"Sun in Aries."

"Yeah… right. Well, it was very nice to meet you—"

"Stay," Mantri insists. "We're having food."

"Um, I really should go. I told my mom I would stop by for dinner."

"Ahhh, lord of the 4th is exalted."

"Right…"

"But she has problems with health. In Cancer, we will say with shoulders and women's things."

"Yeah. Yeah you're right," Poem stiffly gets up off the floor and walks to Carmela in the kitchen. "Well, thanks for the experience but I'm gonna vamoose."

"Oh all right. You can't stay?"

"Um, I would but I'm kind of freaking out right now."

"He's amazing, huh?"

"Yeah…" he sounds lost. "I'll call you, okay?" He returns to the living room. "Well, it was very nice to meet you, uh, Sir. You gave me a lot to think about. Do you do readings?"

"No. I just teach."

"Oh."

Carmela walks in with plates, utensils, and tin foil takeout containers which she arranges on the table. Poem migrates to the door, observing her servile respect for this elderly man. She helps Mantri tuck a large white napkin into the neck of his shirt and proceeds to spoon various portions onto his plate. He thanks her, beaming with anticipation. Poem gets ready, opens the door and waves goodbye, cracking an awkward smile. They nod and he leaves, closing the door behind him.

It is twilight when he emerges from the red brick building as if walking on a cloud. *What just happened?*

The air is crisp and sobering and he cautiously descends the embankment stairs, feeling outside his body, pre-occupied, his legs hollow and uncertain. He shuffles through the gold autumn leaves that litter the street, down the row of cars, looking at the sidewalk, vaguely aware of a woman passing by. *How did he do that?*

He steps into the road, to his faded black Camaro, unlocks it, eases into the seat and pulls the door shut. The hyperbaric silence isolates him and he stares at his finger moulds in the worn leather steering wheel. *Has my life been predictable?*

Turning the crank, the engine roars to life. Revving it three times, he puts it into gear, eases out onto Heath and towards Bathurst Street. Stopping at the red-light intersection, he waits and wonders, *Do I really have freewill?*

2 THE SUPERNATURAL

Poem arrives home to the ground floor apartment of an old duplex, still in a daze over Carmela's teacher. Monique is in the kitchen washing dishes. He walks in and she turns, smiles, and accepts a kiss on the cheek.

"Smells good in here. What're you cooking?"

"What?" she reacts in her cute French accent. "Oh no, that's just my socks on the radiator," she laughs.

"Very funny."

"I just ate the last of the cabbage rolls."

"That's okay. I ate at my mom's."

"How is she?"

"Good. I think. Her shoulder's acting up again."

"She needs a massage."

"She needs to retire," Poem laments.

"How's Carmela?"

"Oh, she's fine…"

"Did you get paid?"

"Yeah, and I have more work. She wants copy for her website." He eyes the pack of cigarettes on the table, "I thought you were out of Marlboros."

"That's my last pack."

"I can't believe we smoked a whole carton in—what, a week?" he shakes his head, looking downcast.

"Are you okay, Poem? You seem distracted."

He thinks a moment. "I met a very interesting man, Monique, at Carmela's."

"Oh?"

"Yeah. He's an astrologer. Very nice man. In his sixties, I think. He read my chart."

She's intrigued.

"I was the subject of their lesson. Apparently she's learning astrology now," he rolls his eyes. "It was pretty wild though, what he was able to see."

"Like what?"

Poem hears Mantri's voice:

"You will not prosper until you marry."

"Uh… He knew I injured my back a few years ago."

"How?"

"I don't know. He just said, 'You hurt your back in '99.'"

"Was that '99?"

"Yeah. That's when I tore my back up, in September, remember?"

"Okay," she recalls the day he barely made it up the stairs.

"He knew when I broke up with Sabrina in '96 and started dating you that same year."

"Did we meet in '96?"

"We met in '95, but we started doing it in '96," he grins. "Or was it 69?" he grabs her and she yells "Stop!" playfully resisting him.

He lets her go and sighs.

"What else did he say?"

"He said a lot of things, Monique, and…" he looks down, trying to figure it out. "It was freaky."

"Why?"

"Well, think about it. My birth chart hasn't changed. It's been the same since the day I was born. And there he was telling me when I had a back injury, when I ended one relationship and started another, that my life changed in '91? That's when I finished school, met Rosita and started gigging. It's also when I became interested in philosophy—oh, and he said I *can't* have brothers. That's how he said it."

"Hmm…" Monique wonders about her own situation. "Well, why does it surprise you?"

"Because I always thought astrology was like, personality types, y'know? Your *character* will determine your destiny."

"So?"

"So, he didn't say anything about my character. He just listed things that happened in my life: he knew my father was dead, he knew I smoked, that I have two sisters. What does that have to do with my character?"

"Maybe he's psychic."

"He said no."

"Does he do readings? Maybe *I'll* go."

"No, he just teaches."

"Hmm... How does Carmela know him?"

"Well, you know, she's into the whole Vedic thing. She's got his picture on her mantle."

"Is he Indian?"

"Yeah. Nice man. Thick accent. I couldn't make out everything he said; he went pretty fast, like chop chop chop!" he snaps his fingers.

"What's his name?"

"Uh... Manny or something. She called him 'Sir.' He was really nice, Monique. It kind of blew my mind though. I feel like my life just changed somehow."

"What d'ya mean?"

"Well shit, it means my life's been predictable! All this philosophy I'm reading, thinking I'm enlightening myself, like I'm a 'self-determining human being,' and then *this*?! Meet a friggin astrologer and he's got me pegged? What kind of freewill is that?!"

Monique shrugs, "I dunno. All the people *I* know are pretty predictable. I think *you're* pretty predictable."

"Like what?!"

"I know you, Poem. I know when you're gonna say yes, I know when you're gonna say no. I knew when I put those Marlboros out that you would want one."

"Yeah, that's cuz you can't get 'em here, and the power of suggestion being what it is..." he leans in for the pack.

"No!" she grabs it and he approaches her, playfully looking for a fight.

"So what'cha gonna do?"

"*I'm* gonna have a smoke!" She bolts down the hall to the rear entrance of the house.

"Hypocrite!"

"He's my favourite philosopher!"

He pursues and grabs her from behind, laughing, and they wrestle until she agrees to share one, so he looks for his pullover sweater while she fetches her coat. "Pepsi?!" he yells.

"Of course!"

We are creatures of habit.

Poem opens the door and steps down the side stairs. Monique brings a tumbler of black soda topped with ice cubes that she hands to him then sits on the doorstep halfway inside the house. She ignites a long frost white cigarette and exhales the smoke. It billows before shattered by the cool night breeze and Poem remarks, "Ya know, this is pretty predictable what we're doing here."

"I know and it's terrible." She takes another satisfying drag and hands the cigarette to Poem who thinks out loud,

"I just don't understand how he could know all the things he said. That means all my mistakes, decisions and regrets are all sort of," he pauses, "my destiny; even the accidents. They all led me here, to you, to this place," he looks up at the house. "I'm really interested to know if it's true, Monique, if we can really predict the future."

"You've never been to a psychic?"

"Not really. I know people who *are* psychic, but I never got a reading. I remember one story though…" he tilts his head, "It freaked me out at the time, this séance that happened up north."

"Oh yeah?"

Poem takes a sip. "Well, you never met my cousin, Mike, he's like 15 years older than me. He was married to this woman, Wendy, and apparently some years before their wedding her father caught her mother cheating with some guy at a drunken party and stabbed her to death right on the spot."

"Oh wow!"

"Yeah. So one night Wendy's sister, Mary, and her cousin—I forget her name—they did this séance in the cottage where the murder took place. I still get chills because they told us right out front of where it happened. Anyway, we were sitting around the campfire when Mary told us this story."

Monique stubs the butt out on the stairs.

"What happened was they set up in the basement—it's one of those raised cottages—and they lit candles and turned out the lights—I think there were four of them. Anyway, one of them knew how to do a séance. So they all sat around with their hands on the table and this woman started the ceremony to contact the dead mother. At first they were taking it only half-seriously but then they got into it and the woman who was leading it *really* got into it. Then all of a sudden the candles went out and they heard this CRASH!"

"Oh my God!" Monique holds her legs up to her chest.

"Yeah. So they all freaked and ran for the light switch but the lights wouldn't go on. So they ran outside."

"Wow."

"Yeah. So after an hour or so the lights suddenly come back on and here's the uncle driving up the road."

"No way!"

"They didn't tell him what happened but they discovered the loud crash was a mounted jigsaw puzzle of a woman that had fallen to the floor and cracked into pieces."

"Wow!"

"Yeah, and they got shit for it but no way were they gonna tell him what happened."

Monique shakes her head, amazed.

"That's why I know even to this day Mary still gets spooked every time she has to go into that basement."

"I don't blame her," Monique pictures the scene in her head. "So then you believe in the supernatural."

"I never said I don't believe in the supernatural."

"So why are you so bugged about astrology?"

"That's different because the chart never changes." He examines her face to see if she gets it. "That means theoretically you could predict everything about someone's life from the moment they were born."

"Well, I don't know about that."

"But that's what I'm saying! That's why I'm freaked out because it wasn't a psychic reading where this guy's tapping into my energy field. He told me based on my *birth chart!* And he just met me!"

Monique is silent.

"And that's what really makes me think, Monique. The *when* of it."

"That sounds really interesting, Poem. I'd like to meet him. Are you gonna—"

"I'll call Carmela and see if she'll give me his number."

"Maybe you can find out whether you'll be famous."

"Of course I'll be famous!"

"Well, you've been at it a long time, Poem," she looks down.

"Monique, don't start. I get enough pressure from my mom."

"You're just so talented, babe. I wish you could catch a break."

"*You* wish?"

"For both of us," she looks at him tenderly.

"I know."

Monique drains the last of the soda leaving three mollified ice cubes. "Come on," she gets up and goes inside while Poem looks up at the meek points of light in the urban night sky,

It's all nature.

3 ONE MASTER

Poem is parked out front of Marcus's place tapping his steering wheel to the Prelude of Die Walküre. Marcus emerges from his grey dilapidated house; a dark-skinned, youthful-looking Trinidadian with threaded dreadlocks, jean jacket, hooded sweatshirt, sunglasses and faded black baseball cap, visor pointing back. He looks up at the sunny sky like he hasn't seen it in days then struts down the walkway and hops inside. "Damn! Sorry, man, sorry," he is agitated. "Man those fuckin' squirrels were keeping me up all night!"

"In your roof?"

"Yeah, man! In my roof, in my walls, just runnin' up and down all fuckin' night!"

Poem starts the car. "I guess they're getting ready for winter."

"Yeah but in *my* fuckin' house?!"

"That's what they do."

"Aw man," Marcus groans.

"Hey, at least it's a beautiful day." Poem raises the volume on the stereo.

"Yeeeah," Marcus says cynically then hearing the music, "Hey, this is cool. What's this?"

"Wagner."

"Wagner'n'shit," he grooves along with the double basses.

"Hey, so you ready? You know what you gonna ask?"

"Aww, not really. I just wanna see what happens. You said 20 bucks, right?"

"Yeah, we're just checking it out. 20 bucks is a donation."

"Why don't we split it?"

"No man! We're not gonna be cheap. He's a very wise man and we're just paying him a little visit. You know your time of birth, right?"

"Yeah, I got it from my mom—Man, I can't believe these fuckin' squirrels!"

"Hey, did you talk to that drummer?"

"You mean Curt, or Burt? Yeah he's into it. Hey, maybe this Master G—"

"You mean Mantriji?"

"Yeah. Maybe he can tell us when we're gonna make it big."

"Yeah I hope so." Poem looks in his rear view mirror, "I don't know what to expect, Marcus. Only that he blew my mind when I met him."

They head up Lansdowne, turn onto St. Clair and up Raglan Ave. "It should be here somewhere, number… 39! There it is." He parks the car and they saunter up the walkway, enter the building and dial his code.

A gravelly voice answers, *"Hello?"*

"Hi, Mantriji, it's Poem, Carmela's friend. She said we could come by at one o'clock. I brought my friend Marcus."

"You are downstairs?"

"Yes."

"Okay."

The buzzer sounds and the glass door clicks open. They take the elevator and step out onto Mantri's floor where Poem knocks and Mantri opens the door. "Come on," he waves them in. They follow him and the incense hits them like a sack of dried flowers. They wonder if they should remove their shoes. Mantri says don't worry so they proceed through the tiny kitchen to a faded linoleum table littered with books, pens and papers. Mantri positions himself on the opposite side next to the open balcony and invites Poem and Marcus to have a seat. They sit across from him and take in the scene.

The apartment is sparsely furnished. There's a large white bookshelf brimming with an incongruous collection of books, a small desk with an ancient computer, an old TV on a long black table next to an office water cooler and wooden box. A thin stripped mattress covers the floor with feeble-looking pillows and a red fleece blanket, while a curtainless window spans the room, the only privacy being the top part of a maple tree with branches growing onto the balcony.

The kitchen table is piled with books and loose papers. The covers and bindings reveal a collection of Western and Indian philosophy, English grammar, various manuscripts, dictionary, a magazine in Hindi, a New Testament, Bhagavad-Gita, and coiled notebooks. Pens and pencils are stuffed into a tourist coffee mug and the chalkboard on the wall has Sanskrit and mathematical calculations scribbled on it.

Poem looks at Mantri with great interest, "I called Carmela because I was really uh, impressed with how you read my chart. She said we could come visit you here at one o'clock. I hope that's cool with you."

"Oh yes," Mantri says. "Carmel is good girl."

"So I was telling Marcus here how you read my chart and we're both interested in learning more. Carmela was saying we could give you a donation, y'know, to meet with you. I was hoping maybe you could look at Marcus's chart."

Mantri laughs jovially. "I don't need his chart." He looks at Marcus, "I can tell by his face."

Marcus smiles bashfully and Poem says, "Well, me and Marcus are in a band and we've been working really hard to get a deal. We both wanna know if we're gonna make it, if it's 'in the stars' sort o' speak."

Mantri listens attentively, eyeing Marcus, and says "This man is very curious. But he is impatient so he becomes jack-of-all-trades."

Poem struggles to understand him through his accent, "Uh... How can you tell that?"

"His big eyes," Mantri says dramatically and Marcus is uncharacteristically quiet. "But you can serve only one master," Mantri warns.

Poem feels the need to defend him, "Well, he *is* focused on one thing: music. Right, Marcus?"

Marcus hesitates, "Yeeah."

"You cannot focus if you cannot be still." Mantri looks at Marcus, "You like people. You like to laugh. You are a child, man."

"Yeeah."

"But you can serve only one master. Your versatility weakens you."

Poem is confused, "Don't you want to see his chart?"

"When were you born?" Mantri asks and Marcus tells him. "Really? You are that old?"

Marcus smiles, "I get it all the time."

"What *was* the time?"

"My mom says about 3 p.m."

Mantri looks upward and calculates in his head, "Hmm... Your eyes are white like a Virgin's. It must be Virgo lagna, like you!" he looks at Poem. "But so much energy. Sun in the 8th. Are you masturbating?"

Marcus shifts uncomfortably, "Yeeeah."

"You have too much energy. Your eyes want to pop out of your head. You are hungry."

"Naw I'm all right, I ate before—" Poem elbows him "—Oh right. No. I just wanna get on with it, y'know, and *live* already!"

"But you *are* living," Mantri says.

"Not like that. I wanna live righteous!"

"Are you a holy man?"

"Uh yeah. Yeah. I'm very spiritual."

"You smoke marijuana?"

"Oh yes!"

"You like to get high," Mantri pantomimes a smoker inhaling and drifting away.

"We call it 'erb. It's a very spiritual movement."

"But you drink."

"Oh yeah, I like my beer."

"But I thought Rastas don't touch alcohol," Mantri alludes to his dreadlocks.

"Well, I'm not really a Rasta *that* way. I believe all religions are good."

"Uh huh."

"Anyway, I just wanna live! Can you tell me when I'll be successful?" He thumbs between himself and Poem, "If what we got goin' on here is real."

"You have to stop thinking about yourself and find the *Master* you wish to serve. I will tell you a little story—" he stops.

Marcus is distracted by a black squirrel that has just appeared on the balcony doorstep. No doubt a cousin to those tormenting his sleep, he shoos at it but the squirrel is not intimidated. "Hey ya got a thing there on your door."

Mantri looks down and says, "Oh," like he recognizes it. He gets up, steps round the table to the kitchen drawer, reaches in and grabs a handful of dry shelled peanuts. Poem sees that peanuts are all this particular drawer contains. Mantri flings the nuts out onto the balcony and the critter leaps after them gleefully. Marcus and Poem look at one another amazed.

Mantri sits and starts nonchalantly, speaking slowly in his difficult accent, while Poem and Marcus concentrate to make out the words, "One day, a Brahmin is walking in the forest when suddenly he is confronted by a thief. The thief asks for all his money, but the Brahmin begs him not to rob him as he barely has any money at all. The bandit doesn't care and he attacks the holy man. The Brahmin—a sworn pacifist—cries out to Vishnu, 'Oh Lord of Justice, please protect me from this violent criminal! I am a Brahmin and he is beating me!'"

Poem and Marcus listen, amused.

"His cry goes all the way to heaven where it reaches Vishnu who is lounging at home with his wife." Mantri mimes taking the call, "Vishnu answers and moved by the Brahmin's plea, says to his wife, 'I must leave you now, dear woman, for a wise man is in trouble and I must save him.'

"Now the Brahmin—who was resisting the thief—rises up to protect himself and begins to punch back so that both men are now fighting. Vishnu arrives and witnessing this scene of two men beating each other, he is confused, so he turns around and flies back home.

"When he returns, his wife asks, 'Why do you come back so soon? I thought a wise man was in trouble.' Vishnu says, 'I arrived at the scene and saw two men fighting. I could not tell who was the wise man and who was the thief."'

Marcus and Poem are suspended in Zen.

Mantri summarizes, "You must serve *one* cause, *one* master, and not falter, otherwise you are a hypocrite and no one will recognize you. This Brahmin was a pacifist until he started fighting. Now there is no difference between him and the thief."

There is a profound silence before Marcus says, "Oh I get it. Just give up everything and focus on just… one thing."

"Right," Mantri nods. "If you serve more than one master your efforts will be watered down and nothing will work."

Poem muses as the conversation continues, Mantri elucidating this and that while Marcus, raptured by his surprising eloquence, struggles to understand:

"…But I am serving one master…"

"…Yes, but it is yourself…"

"…Why do I sometimes feel invisible…?"

"…You are living in a cave, hiding from the world. You cling to your poverty…"

"…Will I ever be successful…?"

"…Not if you refuse to compromise. Opportunity is in people, not in things…"

"…I sometimes do coke but I believe all religions are good…"

"…You are running while remaining in one place…"

"…How can you tell all this from just his face…?"

"…Up to thirty you have the body your parents gave you; after thirty you have the body you made…"

"…When am I gonna get laid…?"

"…When you stop thinking about yourself and serve something else…"

The hour passes leaving Marcus bemused and enlightened. Poem is in awe of Mantri's power to penetrate the character of his closest friend. With a concluding cadence Mantri stands and says thank you in a gracious yet firmly final way. He smiles benevolently at Poem who says, "Thank you, Mantriji, Sir, for your time." He takes out his wallet and elbows Marcus who comes out of his trance. They each offer a twenty.

Mantri protests in the typically half-hearted Indian way, "No, please. It is too much."

"It's okay," Poem says. "We got jobs and everything!"

Mantri laughs then hints with his eyes that he does not accept money directly so they place their notes on the table in front of him. Poem asks if he can call him some time and Mantri says, "Yes, just ask Carmel. She will give you my number."

Poem nods and the two grab their jackets and make for the door, saying thank you and nice to meet you.

They exit the apartment, enter the elevator and walk out into the October cool without saying a word, re-living what has just transpired. Marcus is particularly pensive.

Inside the car, Poem finally says, "Sorry he didn't get to your chart, man."

"That's okay."

"He said some stuff about you that I wouldn't have guessed."

"Yeah, he was pretty good—I mean, not *everything*—but he was pretty good."

"But you're not a jack of all trades."

"Well, I kinda am," Marcus shrugs.

"I know you're versatile. You play different instruments."

"I think he was talkin' 'bout somethin' else."

"Oh."

"Man, I couldn't believe that squirrel! I wanna kill mine and he's frickin feedin' his?!" He shakes his head. "Reminds me of something my old man once said."

"What's that?"

"He came over one time and noticed I had a couple mouse traps out so I told him, 'Yeah, these stupid mice are keeping me up all night, scratching, scurrying around, gettin' into the bread.' He just looked at me and said, 'Yeah, them mice gotta eat too.'"

Poem laughs and shakes his head. They continue along St. Clair West, the first act of Die Walküre on the stereo.

4 A NEW DRUMMER

Inside the ground floor rehearsal room of Cactus Studios, two Ikea floor lamps illuminate the lame November sunlight poking its way through dusty warehouse windows. A hanging Canadian flag casts its red spectre onto the opposite wall. There are Marshall ampheads on speaker cabinets, a blue Yorkville bass amp, chrome microphone stands, a beat-up drum kit, an old Peavey mixing board, exposed wooden beams stuffed with nicotine-coloured foam pads, and large colourful posters of drum accessories and the gods of Rock & Roll.

Marcus on cherry red bass and Poem on white Stratocaster groove to an aggressive 6/8 beat, working in their new drummer. Poem sings,

"You tried to ruin me, destroy my world.
But it's your deceit that really hurts.
Lies! All Lies!"

The drummer is barely keeping up with Marcus's crunching bass line when he loses the beat and Poem waves, "Whoa! Whoa! Whoa!!" The music screeches to an undignified halt. "You lost the beat, man!"

The drummer says sorry unapologetically and Marcus scowls, "Listen, Burt—"

"It's Kirk!"

"Kurt, Burt, listen. Just stick with me, okay? I'm just doin'…" he gets into the groove. Kirk joins in and does an overly ambitious drum-fill. "Naw naw naw!! Forget the fancy shit! Just lock into the pocket!" Marcus lays it down again and Kirk comes in, Poem joins them and they groove until Poem solos and the drummer again loses the beat.

"What happened?!" Marcus yells.

"His solo threw me off."

"Man, you the drummer, Man! You have to drive the shit!"

"Hey, when's our first gig?"

"Listen, Squirt—"

"It's Kirk!!"

"We ain't doin' nothin' till the songs are down, y'hear? We have a reputation," Marcus postures.

"I think it's coming together pretty good," Kirk says.

Marcus and Poem look at one another incredulously. There's pounding on the door and a muted call, "It's four o'clock, man!"

"Shit, we gotta pack up," Marcus says. He looks at Kirk, "Okay, so you listen to the tapes and we'll pick it up next time. And make sure you have the shit down, y'hear?"

"Got it!" Kirk salutes and bolts for the door. Marcus and Poem watch him, wondering if they should hit him up for money but the next band is already in.

"Sounds good, man." "What up, man?" "How you doin', man?"

Marcus collects the empty beer cans while Poem packs up. One guy gets on the drums and busts into their 6/8 groove. Marcus hollers his approval while Poem hoots. They finally exit the room into the starkly lit hall where they put their guitar cases down and lean against the wall.

"So what d'ya think?" Poem says.

"I don't know, my man. He kept losing the beat on a couple tunes and I don't think he really knows how to play reggae. It's gotta be…" Marcus slaps air bass while thumping his foot to a one-drop beat.

"Yeah, and he seems overly eager about money and gigs. Notice how he split again without paying for the space?"

"Well, cuz it's your band, man. He ain't gonna put his money down till we start *making* money, y'hear?"

"Like you?"

"Hey, I brought beer. That's *my* contribution."

"I don't know if I can go through another drummer, Marcus. Just as things were gettin' good with Francis, he up and finds God in a smelly finger."

"Yeah… Hey, so whatcha doin' now?"

"I'm gonna drop off my stuff and go see Mantriji."

"Oh yeah? You've seen him a few times now, huh?" Marcus lights a cigarette.

"Yeah, I'm seeing him every Sunday for lessons, I guess, maybe five times since that time we went."

"Mm hmm," he takes a long haul off his smoke. They pick up their gear and start walking through the maze of halls.

"I just find him really insightful, man. And I'm curious to know how he does it, like, how the fuck does he do it? He just says things and they're mostly bang on."

"Yeah, he's good," Marcus nods. "So what's *he* sayin'?"

"Well, last week he looked at my chart and said because of my Mars I just don't have the 'courage' to be successful right now. That's how he said it."

"What?! That's ridiculous!"

"Yeah. He said," Poem wags his finger, "'You'd be very successful in life if only you knew how to *use* people.'"

"Well, that's true, but you're brave. I've seen you stand your ground. Remember that girl you helped when those guys were giving her a hard time? That took balls, my man."

"Brave just means doing the right thing, Marcus. Courage is doing it regardless of whether it's right or wrong."

"Yeah, I guess," Marcus reflects. "And I'm like that too, too fucking sensitive." He takes another drag.

"But y'know, I thought about it and such a simple thing. It never would have occurred to me to think about it this way but I kind of know what he's saying. Like I'm not being assertive or I don't wanna put my neck on the line. I guess I like my cozy anonymity."

"Not me, man. I wanna be famous!"

"I know. I do too," Poem reassures him and they stop at the entrance. "I just don't want all that attention," he winces.

"Ha!" Marcus blurts and looks around, "I'm kind of that way too."

Poem pushes the door open to the cool invigorating air. They step through and see the Toronto skyline jutting up against the wintry blue. "Weird, huh Marcus, you and me, wanting success and yet, not the responsibility. And so this is where we at," he scans the industrial street, its abandoned tracks curving into former factories. The windows behind them rattle with grunge.

"Listen, I've been doing this my whole rass life," Marcus says, "and I haven't seen one red nickel, know what I'm sayin'?"

"And you're one of the most talented musicians I know."

They walk to the car, downcast, load in their guitars, get inside and Marcus says, "So what else he sayin'?"

Poem looks at him frankly, "He said I should marry Monique."

"Really? Why don't you?"

"I don't know, man. I love her but, I just don't know." He starts the car, lowers the music and turns down the fan, "She doesn't wanna have sex, man."

"Oh man." Marcus rolls down his window. "But she's French."

"I know," he sighs. "I mean, she'll please me, do whatever, but somehow if she's not into it then how can I be?" He looks at him, "I go to touch her and she just pushes me away."

"Oh man." Marcus flicks his cigarette.

"Yeah, and yet she keeps asking when are we getting married? And I'm like what?!"

"Ho, man."

"She says the sex will be better *after* we're married."

"How long you been with her?"

"Four years."

Marcus peers above his shades, "Dude, the sex ain't gonna get any better."

"I know," Poem grumbles. "And I love her, Marcus. I really do. I just don't wanna be stuck in a sexless marriage, y'know?"

"I know. And I don't blame you. But she's a sweet thing."

"Yeah, and I love her like a sister."

Marcus is 10 years Poem's senior and reflects on his own dilemmas. "Why's he say you gotta marry her?"

"So I can prosper. The lord of my House of Marriage is exalted in my House of Gain, which means I'll benefit through marriage and… I guess it'll get my mind off other women."

"Yeah, I don't know about *that*, my man, but it'll settle your ass down, that's for sure."

"But I don't know if I wanna settle down, Marcus. I just don't know if I'm ready. I feel like I have a lot of living to do."

"I know. Me too," he looks away.

"He thinks I should study philosophy, that I have the mind for it."

"That's true. You like that shit."

"I mean, I've read stuff and I like talking about it but I can think of only one thing less practical than music, and that's philosophy."

"That's true."

"He's telling me I should do it, teach it, write about it; all kinds of things and… I don't know…" Feeling heat now coming out of the vents Poem puts the car into gear and pulls out into the street.

"Well it sounds like he's making an impression, my man."

"Yeah well, he's making me think about a lot of things."

"Tell him I say hi."

"Sure." Poem checks his mirror, "So what *you* gonna do?"

"Man, I'm checkin' out the game. Cowboys are in Denver."

"Cool. I wish I could join you, but to tell you the truth… Sometimes I think watching sports is just a colossal waste of time."

"Yeah well, what else am I gonna do?"

Poem's not sure what to say. They turn south onto Dufferin Street.

5 NOTHING IN THE FRIDGE

Poem arrives home and stepping up the side entrance stairs he sees through the window Monique on the phone. She is holding her head, laboured by the conversation. He opens the door and hears her in the living room say, "Okay, Mom, gotta go. We'll talk later. Bye." She comes to greet him as he bangs his guitar case through the unwieldy door. "Hi, Poem," she forces a smile.

"Hey baby," he kisses her on the cheek.
"How was rehearsal?"
"Ugh," he groans tiredly. "Just let me drop my shit off."
Monique steps aside as Poem squeezes by and walks to the back room. He puts down his guitar, empties his knapsack and loads it up with books then comes back to the kitchen where Monique is waiting. "I don't have much time," he says. "I'm just grabbing my stuff and heading out again. The new drummer, Kurt, or whatever his name is, I don't know. He's into it but I don't know how good he is. He can't play reggae and he struggles with 6/8."

"Well, what're you gonna do?"
"I dunno. I feel like I need a vacation. How are you?" He opens the fridge door.

"There's no food. I'm okay. Hey, when are we getting married?"
He looks at her, "Were you just talking to your mom?"
"Yeah."
He closes the fridge. "Does she wanna be a grandma again?"
"She's hoping."
"So you wanna have kids to please your mom?"
"That's not the point! I want to get married and move to the next stage of our lives, Poem. We've been living together for four years. It's time!"

"That's your mom talking."

"No it isn't!"

"Okay, look, I just came home to grab my stuff and I have to get going. I have a lesson with Mantriji."

Monique shakes her head.

"I'm sorry, Monique. I'm just tired."

"It's okay. I know you're not the marrying type," she rolls her eyes. "I don't wanna be a downer, Poem. I just see Adele and she has a house with Claude and we're still here. We should at least think about buying this place before it's sold. I don't wanna just keep renting."

"I know. And I'd like to but… Can we talk about this later?"

"Sure. You'd rather see Mantriji."

"Can we just be cool? I don't have time right now."

"You never have time!"

He touches her shoulder and she looks into his eyes. They pause before hugging.

"I love you, Monique."

"I love *you*, Poem."

They rock back and forth; Poem kisses her forehead and they let go.

"I spoke to Lynette," Monique says. "She's inviting us to New Orleans over Christmas.

"I thought we were going to Texas."

"I was thinking we could spend Christmas with my parents then drive to Louisiana for New Year's Eve."

"Hmm…" Poem is intrigued.

"I was there once for Mardi Gras in high school. New Orleans is an awesome town. You'll love the music. What do you say?"

Poem smiles, "I like it. Let's go! But we'll talk about it later, okay?" He looks at the fridge, "I gotta go grab some food before my lesson."

"What are you getting from this, Poem, from studying astrology?"

"He's really amazing, Monique. I'm learning so much about human nature, about myself, how people are the way they are, about karma. I just feel like a whole new world is opening up to me."

"I know it's interesting but you need to think about money. How are we gonna afford this place? It's a good investment, you know?"

"I know. And I'll be okay with money, once we get the right drummer—"

"Poem!" she stamps her foot. "Sooner or later Jean is gonna sell this house and I want to buy it!"

"Okay! We'll talk about it. But I really have to go."

He starts for the door and Monique grumbles to herself, "That's what *I'm* beginning to think."

6 ASTROLOGY IS NOT EASY

Poem steps out of the elevator to Mantri's door held ajar by an old red brick. He opens it, walks inside and steps through the small kitchen to the always cluttered linoleum table. Mantri is standing next to the balcony door with red dusk outside.

"Namaste, Sir."

"Namaste," Mantri nods and the two settle into their customary spots. "How are you, Poem?"

"I'm okay," he unpacks his books. "We're breaking in this new drummer and it's not easy. He's not as good as we thought."

"Oh?"

"Yeah, it's getting a little frustrating."

"Okay, but how are you making money?"

"Oh I'm driving."

"Driving?"

"Yeah, I drive a truck for a costume company."

"But I thought you are a musician."

"I am, but I have to make a living."

"You don't make money playing music?"

"A little, but not enough to make a living so I have a day job."

Mantri looks down, shaking his head, "If you are driving a truck then you are not a musician, you are a truck driver."

Poem is taken aback, "Well, we do original music so it's difficult to make money unless you have a record deal."

"Oh?"

"Yeah, the only musicians who make money, really, are the ones who play other people's music, y'know, like in cover bands, cruise ships, this sort of thing."

"Mm hmm. And you don't teach?"

"I used to but I didn't like it. The school I worked for kept pushing curriculum but my students wanted other things. Plus it didn't pay well and the commute was too far."

"Uh huh."

Poem looks at him curiously.

"In India a musician is someone who makes his living playing music, otherwise it is just a hobby."

"Yeah well, that's why it's been a struggle."

"You are not a truck driver. You only settle for this. What kind of people will you meet driving a truck?" Mantri gets up to the blackboard and draws a square natal chart. He fills in the diamonds and triangles with 6 on top, indicating Virgo rising. Poem copies it into his notebook and Mantri begins, "You are Virgo lagna. This is the maiden. She is clean, analytical, discriminating, and no doubt loves music. She is a sensitive being. But maidens rarely do what they would like. This is why she is a virgin. She will work hard but when it comes to doing what she loves, it will be only a hobby."

"Like my music."

"Right."

"Why is that?"

"Because Virgo is the mother of Christ, and she is sacrificing herself for a higher cause. She is in service like you, driving a truck, working for someone else. And you have Saturn aspecting lagna," he writes it in, "with Mercury, lord of lagna, so it is very difficult for you to do what you want. Saturn is stopping you."

"But *why*?"

"Because Saturn is the planet of hardships; it signifies delays and obstacles. The whole of your life has been delayed."

"Ya got that right."

"You are like a virgin, cautious and clean, but at the same time you like to get into the mud. Saturn is darkness. It is the furthest planet we can see. It marks the boundary of time, the end of things. Death!" he wipes an imaginary slate.

"So because Saturn is with my ruler, I get into the mud?"

"Low class people, bars, billiards, hanging out front, smoking. What are they talking about? Who won the hockey game, why the boss is a dick."

Poem laughs. "But they still have lives, they love their children, they can be good people."

"No one is saying they are bad people, no. But what are they doing with their lives? Anyone can say 'I am a good man,' but *is* he a good man?"

"Hmm…"

"It is true that without Saturn nothing would get done. Saturn signifies toil and suffering. The pyramids were built by Saturn."

"By slaves."

"Yes, by Saturn, the shudra."

"What's a shudra?"

"Someone who works with his hands, cleans floors, scrubs toilets, construction, mechanic, a servant. It is the working class."

"Okay. And this makes him a slave?"

"Oh yes; a slave to his boss and to his paycheque. Saturn is the death planet and we are all slaves to death. Some work their whole lives readying themselves for it, others do everything they can to try and forget it. 'Live it up, man!' 'Have a good time!'"

"So I should stay away from these people?"

"Unless you want to be one of them."

"But I'm a musician. When I'm out there playing, that's what I'm in: bars."

"Where they serve alcohol it is very difficult," Mantri shakes his head.

"But they're not bad places. I mean, where else do you get to hear live music?"

"It is not the bars, Poem. It is what you do with the rest of your time. Every warrior must go where it is unpleasant, but if you carry that energy to the rest of your life then you are caught."

"I just find that most people are just talkin' shit and it's not like this. We're discussing ideas, philosophy, spiritual things, meta-physical things. Most people *say* they're interested but they don't talk about it and they have no real understanding of things like astrology."

"To understand takes great effort. It is not easy. First you must memorize, then you will understand."

"I have been memorizing."

"Speak," Mantri commands.

Poem recites the signs and degrees of planetary exaltations followed by the 'natural indicators' of the 12 astrological houses. He makes a couple mistakes and Mantri gently corrects him, but he gets through and Mantri smiles, "Good."

"Why do some of the houses have more than one indicator?"

"The 12 houses signify the 12 major areas of life."

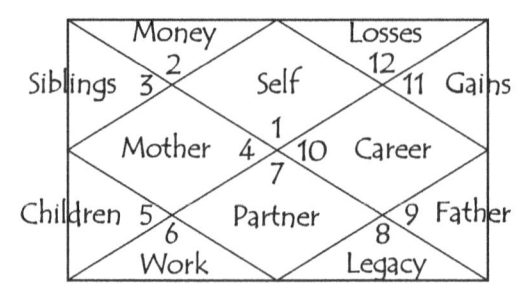

	Money 2		Losses 12	
Siblings 3		Self 1		11 Gains
	Mother 4	7	10 Career	
Children 5		Partner		9 Father
	6 Work		8 Legacy	

Mantri writes as he speaks, "Your Self, money, siblings, mother, children, work, partner, legacy, father, career, gains, and losses. Each one of these houses is divided into its related parts. Take the 4th," he circles it. "It rules 'mother' and thus 'conveyances,' 'education,' and 'peace of mind.' All these things are related to mother and to one another but how do we tell them apart? All the books say that Moon and Mercury signify the qualities of the 4th house because the Moon is mother and Mercury is education."

"I thought Jupiter is education."

"Jupiter is *higher* education: philosophy, law, medicine, PhD, scriptures. Mercury is *mundane* education, like high school, college, becoming an accountant, scientist, these things, comparative things. But Venus *also* is an indicator for the 4th house because Venus rules vehicles, conveyances, luxuries, the things that bring us comfort as our mother comforts us. The Moon nourishes but Venus provides sensual, bodily comfort."

"So why doesn't the book just list Venus as an indicator for the 4th house?"

"There is the written word and there is the spoken word. You will learn only so much from books. In India it is assumed that a teacher will be there to guide the student. This man," he points to the textbook, "is a Western man. He is going by the book. You will see if you stick with this subject that not all is written down, sometimes on purpose. The oral tradition must be preserved."

"But why not just write it down?"

"The book is there for a general idea but the guru is the true guide. You will learn why later."

"So the 4th has three natural indicators."

"Right."

"And the 10th house has four."

"That's right, because the 10th is career house and there are many careers to choose from. It used to be there were only five or six professions; you could be a lawyer or seller or policeman or doctor, but nowadays there are so many careers it is very difficult to narrow it down. If Saturn is ruling the 10th, no doubt this man will be hard-working but will he be a manager or a construction worker? If Saturn is exalted he is managing people, telling them what to do. If it is debilitated he is scrubbing toilets. If Saturn is poorly placed but his Sun is strong he could be the *supervisor* for those scrubbing toilets, you see?"

"Yeah... That's a lot!"

"Astrology is not easy, Poem. We must blend all these things and the strength of the 1st house before coming to final conclusion."

"Why the 1st house? What does this have to do with career?"

"The 1st house is the most important house in the chart. It is the Self, the body and personality of the native. If these things are weak in a person then he can do only so much. If the 1st house is strong then he has the potential or personal resources to do well because it is the *lagna* around which the rest of the chart revolves."

"How's my 1st house?"

"In your case it is mixed because lord of the 1st is weak, but it also *aspects* the 1st thus fortifying it."

"Which is good."

"Right. But you have Saturn aspecting as well. This is why you are driving a truck."

"But my Sun, the indicator for the 1st, is exalted."

"Right. But it is in the 8th, the cave house. You do not want to be seen," he shakes his head.

"Why?"

"Because the 8th signifies death, and no one can see beyond death. Your Sun, your light, your life, is in the death house."

"Is that why I'm finding it so hard to make it in music?"

"In time you will be recognized because your Saturn is strong and it is in Pisces, a good sign, and Jupiter aspects this combination. But you will always feel a touch of this debility. It is hard for you to feel worthy."

"Hmm."

"Saturn delays but it does not deny. It is the planet of experience. You will gain confidence and recognition through your experience. Saturn dasa will be better for you."

"What's a dasa?"

"Slowly, slowly," Mantri raises his finger. "We have to take all these and other things into consideration before we make final judgement."

"So it's like blending colours to come up with a new one or stacking notes to make a chord."

"Right. You are a musician, a writer, so you understand that you cannot create something from nothing. There must be a foundation, an *understanding*. Before you improvise you must first know the notes, the keys, *how* to play, *then* you can play."

"And improvise."

"Intuition is very important, knowing how to blend, but from *experience*. You must study many charts to understand what I am saying. This is not an intellectual exercise. You take an intellectual approach in the beginning but many things you study in books will not work in the actual chart because there are so many factors to consider."

"So how should I approach it?"

"You need to read more philosophy."

"Why? Isn't philosophy an intellectual exercise?"

"Not if you understand it. You have exalted Jupiter! You need to open up that lazy mind of yours. You have creativity but what are you doing with it? Playing in a band, smoking, drinking, hanging out after the show. You are a virgin, man! You want to be clean. You want to *dispel* the darkness. These people will ruin you!"

Poem can't believe it. Mantri's words ring true. He is so dissatisfied with the music scene that it makes him wonder about his life, if he is truly free. "Mantriji, are we totally subject to the influence of the planets or do we actually have freewill?"

"One has to work very hard to be free. It is not easy."

"But everyone thinks they're free."

"They think, but they are not. They may learn something but their behaviour does not change. Learning is easy, *change* is hard."

"So what we learn is not important."

"Not if the behaviour is the same. To truly learn something is to change your behaviour because once you know, you *know*, and your life is forever changed. There are many people who say 'I am a changed man' but when the opportunity comes he acts the same."

"And there's nothing we can do about it?"

"Only awareness can make you free."

"What about mantras?" Poem flips through the book, "This author says we can change our energy through mantras and gemstones."

"You need bhakti for mantras to work."

"What's bhakti?"

"Devotion. If you have no devotion, no mantra will work for you."

"So you have to believe it works."

"Right."

"So why wouldn't it work for me?"

"Because you are on the *Gyan* program! You are a philosopher, not a devotee."

"What's Gyan?"

"Knowledge."

"How can I become a devotee?"

Mantri laughs. "You don't need faith, you need knowledge. You do not believe anything you cannot see. This is why you like astrology because it is mystical and yet you see it works. But there is no explanation for astrology, only ideas. People say this, they say that, but no one really knows so you are curious."

"Yes!"

"But you cannot understand from books. All astrology books are cook books. This planet in this sign and the native is romantic; this planet in this sign and the native is successful. Nonsense! This is all just cook books. You must learn how to fuse these things. It is not A-B-C. Astrology is a very difficult subject."

"Well I want to learn it."

"You *can* learn it, but it will change you," Mantri warns.

"I don't know, Mantriji. I'm just curious."

"How does this saying go? Curiosity kills the cat," he grins. "Once you know, you *know!*" he points. "And you're life will forever change. But it begins with awareness."

"But I think I'm aware."

"We will see."

Poem reflects. "So until we develop awareness, we are at the whim of the planets."

"Right."

"The planets then are effectively our gods."

"Gods or no gods, everyone can change, Poem, but my experience is that most people, 99 percent of people, don't change. They are the same people their whole lives. Only circumstances change and they build up more personality, more property, more ego."

"And this is bad."

"Oh yes. Ego will make you suffer."

"Why?"

"Because you think this is who you are."

"So?"

"Well it won't last. Today you are a young man, nice face, good shoulders, but you will one day be an old man like me. What happened to your face? What happened to your body? You say, 'This is not me, what happened to *me?*' You are attached to your body, your name, your history. But it won't last."

"So the ego, or personality, dies with the body."

"Right."

"So what survives?"

"Awareness."

"Is that why people are so afraid to die, because of ego?"

"Ego is everything. Without ego nothing gets done. Amazing this concept," Mantri shakes his head. "There is no accomplishment without ego because there is no sense of 'I'."

"So what exactly is the part that survives death?"

"Only the atma, which is that part that belongs to the Absolute."

"Which we have in us."

"Oh yes."

"But everything else is gone."

"Right. So long as there is individuated consciousness, or that sense of 'I' that you have with your cognition; as long as this remains, so will your lives continue."

"You mean reincarnation."

"Right. This is what we study. Astrology is understanding karma, previous lives, their accumulated effect, the auspiciousness of your birth, what to expect in this life. How will this character unfold over time? Can he rise above his nature? Can he be less greedy? Can he give up milk, alcohol, smoking? Will he get money or run from it? Can he be married? Will he have brothers? These things are revealed in the chart. It shows what karma will allow and at what time."

Poem nods along, taking notes.

"If this man's chart says he's a millionaire, that's fine. The question is *when* will he be a millionaire? If it is when he is 10 years old, he will get it through the prosperity of the parents. If he is a young man, it could be through some ingenuity of his own. If a middle-aged man, it is from a project he has been working on a long time. If he is an old man, it will be through inheritance. If wealth is predicted for his 60th year but his longevity indicates early death then he will not be a millionaire in *this* life even though it is there in his chart."

"And this is because of the Moon?"

"That's right. In Jyotish the Moon is everything. It is used when timing events because it is the most dynamic element in the chart. Time is ticking and every karma is different."

"What about people born at the same time, say, two people born in the same town, or twins? Will their lives be similar?"

"They will no doubt be similar but it could manifest very differently."

"How so?"

"Take Aries for example," Mantri erases the chart and draws another with 1 on top, indicating Aries rising. "Aries is the Ram, a martial energy, male, fiery, mental. It is a warrior, just like a little child. It can be a child or it can be Commander in Chief. One man from a good family becomes CEO; another from a poor family does some heroic deed; a woman becomes a dancer or athlete and eventually a coach; someone else born at the same time wins a bowling tournament and this is *his* great accomplishment. These different lives are all manifestations of Aries and its ruling planet Mars, but what commonality would the layman find here?"

"I guess he'd have to look for it."

"Before you judge any chart, you must first ask yourself four questions," Mantri writes, "The age, sex, status, and position of the native."

"What's the difference between status and position?"

"Status is whether people like him, whether he has respect or standing in the community, what kind of family does he come from. See this man?" Mantri points out the window, "The Jamaican food, what's his name?"

"Oh, you mean Albert?"

"Right. He is a very nice man. Everyone around here knows him. He is always smiling. People like him. He has some status but his position is that he is running a takeout. Outside his community he is nothing. He is not the mayor. If he lost his business, what would he be?"

"So then what's his position?"

"Position is what he does for work, what is he? A doctor, a thief, carpenter, astrologer, manager, president... What's his *position*? Is he unemployed? Can he be promoted when he is unemployed? You cannot predict promotion for a man who is unemployed."

"Right." Poem thinks. "I still don't get it."

"Status is who he is, position is what he does. Depending on these factors *then* you look at the chart and make prediction. If he is rich, he sells his stock and makes a hundred thousand dollars. If he is working, he gets bonus, or a lottery ticket wins him a hundred dollars."

"Such variance."

"Ahhh. This is the art of astrology. It is not easy. It is a very, very difficult subject."

"To make predictions?"

"To *understand* to make predictions."

"Hmm... That's deep."

Mantri smiles and sits. "There are 12 houses in the natal chart. Each house signifies a major area in your life. Every house has its own ruler depending on the ascendant or lagna. For you, Virgo lagna, lord of the 1st is Mercury. We look to see where Mercury is deposited in the chart to determine its strength and disposition. We must also consider the Sun, which is the karaka, or 'natural indicator,' of the 1st house.

"Your Mercury is in Pisces in the 7th house. It is with Saturn aspected by Jupiter. No doubt you have a deep, poetic mind, a *profound* mind, but with Saturn afflicting, it is best that you cultivate Jupiter. How? Do philosophy, scriptures, higher learning, to grow your understanding and lessen this affliction, this critical dispersion of Saturn."

Poem nods, slowly getting it. Mantri's English is becoming clear.

"You have your Sun in Aries in the 8th," Mantri points to the board. "This is the death house, the occult. You want to understand hidden things, the inside of things. Aries is the head so you will take a mental approach. You will intellectualize. We must blend all these factors to understand the 1st house."

"Wow."

"But we will discuss more next week."

"What's next week?"

Mantri picks up the book and flips to a page. "Read this chapter. Chapter 5: 'Lordship of the houses.'" He stands up to formally end the lesson.

Poem pulls out his wallet, picks out a twenty dollar bill and slides it under the tourist coffee mug. "Thank you, Mantriji. I really enjoyed it. You taught me a lot."

"Thank *you!*" Mantri responds graciously.

Poem gathers his stuff and leaves the apartment, feeling lighter than when he had arrived, as though a lamp were lit inside. It is a feeling of knowing that everything has its place, that there is cosmic order. He walks down the stairs, through the lobby and to his car, past the everyday people who go on about their lives, working their jobs, feeding their children, falling in and out of love. A time and place for everything. It is a great comfort to him, an assurance that comes with every lesson, every insight.

Am I here for astrology or for Mantriji?

It doesn't matter. The two are linked.

He thinks about his job, his place in the world, his desire to be invisible. He is pursuing a public profession but doesn't want the attention. He wants only to understand in order to create, like a monk trapped inside a hedonist's body. He is looking forward to seeing Monique, to sharing his new insights into the higher order of things. He feels unperturbed for the first time since his last lesson.

7 TIME AND SPACE

Poem is lying in bed reading lesson notes from Mantri's class. A cold January wind knocks at the window. He looks out at the glowing streetlight and recalls New Year's Eve. *What a fun time we had.*

It was just three weeks ago, over the Christmas season, that he and Monique drove from San Antonio to New Orleans to stay with her cousin Lynette. He remembers their drive in at twilight along lush green lawns and trolley-tracked boulevards with majestic oaks hanging down like a bohemian canopy. This very big small town captured their hearts with its restaurants and speakeasies nestled into sub-tropical communities. The vibe is European but with a swampy feeling that makes you hear jazz on the inside.

Their 'Official Welcoming' to the Big Easy came via Trey, Lynette's friend, who showed up like an apparition only an hour after they'd arrived. He walked in with two stuffed paper bags of booze, ice, chips, to-go cups, tonic, celery, and Bloody Mary mix.

A charming Southerner with an attractive drawl, Trey relished playing host to the Canadians, insisting they bring their drinks for the ride. So they drove in his '66 red Buick, smoking and drinking freely, Trey and Poem each with a beer in the front seat, the girls with vodka tonics in back. It was like being in some highly civilized bygone era. They ended up at the Maple Leaf, drinking with stragglers outside before squeezing into the club for the countdown to midnight. Monique and Poem had the time of their lives partying to Papa Grows Funk with a mixed crowd of friendly locals and Georgians in town for the Sugar Bowl.

What a good time we had.

He remembers New Year's Day, finding Trey downstairs on the couch, asleep in upright position, party hat still on. He simply would not go horizontal.

Poem laughs. He recalls Trey's eyes rolling open and like coming out of a minor setback, he sprang to the kitchen to load up the blender. Half an hour later the four of them were in the Buick again, sporting Bloody Marys on route to some famous breakfast joint. The rest of the day was spent nicely baked on a steady intake of fruity Hurricanes, strolling place to place, like in some surreal outdoor museum.

He hears Monique enter the house. She is singing and he smiles, anticipating her warm body. She and her cousin Adele were out at some salsa club again. It's her latest thing, dancing all night like it's an aerobics class. He lies back and listens to her downstairs, at the closet door, getting a drink of water, using the washroom and finally walking up to their bedroom. Poking her head in, she lilts, "*I saw the light on.*"

"Hey babe," he smiles.

She steps into the room, beaming. "How are you, Poem?" She's a little drunk.

"I'm great." He can smell the nightclub on her clothes. "I was just reliving New Year's Eve."

"Oh really?" she says flirtatiously, her body swaying. "We had such a fun time!" she toasts him with an invisible martini.

"I hope we can go again someday."

"You can go any time you want. Lynette's father's always looking for an excuse to fly back to France so she's always looking for an au pair for Julien." She is referring to Lynette's difficult son, the by-product of a nasty divorce.

"How am I gonna go there when I'm working here?"

"I'm just saying," she blinks and Poem rubs his goatee, pondering the possibilities.

Monique unbuttons her dress and lets it fall to the floor then slides off her pantyhose and dumps it into the hamper. Poem admires her long muscular legs and purple underwear. She manoeuvres out of her bra and slips on a flannel shirt while he watches her. She suddenly turns, picks up the crumpled dress, pirouettes, and tosses it into the closet.

"Bravo!" Poem salutes and she takes a diva's bow. "So, how'd it go tonight?"

"It was fun," she begins then changes her tone, "Claude was a drag."

"Really?"

"Yeah. And he dragged Adele all the way home."

"What happened?"

"He refuses to dance! He just lurks in the corners watching her with different partners."

"He doesn't see different partners. He just sees other men."

"Well it's ridiculous! There should be more trust in a marriage."

"I agree. But how do you stop jealousy?"

"Jealousy is a disease of the heart, Poem. Only where there's no trust is there jealousy."

"That's true. So what, he dragged her outta there?"

"She wasn't having fun so they left early. He crushed her toe doing this stupid twirl. The man can't dance!"

Poem laughs and Monique stares out the window, "Do you ever get jealous of me, Poem?"

He thinks a moment. "No."

"Does it mean you don't want me?"

"No, it means that I trust you."

She smiles and turns, "Well I trust you too."

"I know." Poem puts his notes aside. "So how'd it go for *you* tonight?"

"Oh I'm getting good, Poem. I'm teaming with this one guy, Fabian," she goes into pose, "He's very good, especially at tango."

"I do like tango."

"Yeah, so he's the best dancer in the club and I think we're gonna," she breaks it to him slow, "team together for a competition."

"Really?"

"You should come see us!"

He looks at her doubtfully, afraid of what he might see, "Yeah, I'd like to go sometime, but y'know…"

"Yeah I know. You hate Latin music," she rolls her eyes.

"I don't 'hate' it. There's stuff I like, like tango, but the other stuff is just too happy. Like, what's everyone so happy about?"

"It's just fun music, Poem! You're too serious."

"I can have fun. But you're not into *that* kind of fun," he grabs her around the thighs and she resists.

"Poem, stop it! I'm tired. Let's just cuddle."

He sits up against the headboard, frustrated. "Monique, how come you never wanna have sex with me?"

She rolls her head and sits next to him on the bed. "Look, we have some things we have to work out. I don't give my heart up as easily as you."

"What's that supposed to mean?!"

"I just need some time, Poem."

"You mean time *and* space?"

Monique sighs then reasons with him, "I just think if you have the chance to go and Lynette is willing to pay you, you should seriously consider going to New Orleans."

"What about my job?"

"You're driving a truck, Poem. You should be playing music. You can quit that job anytime. New Orleans is a good place to meet musicians, y'know? It'll give us a break too."

He stares at the floor, "Look, I'm sorry, Monique, that I don't have my career more together and you wanna buy this house and all I think about now is astrology. I don't know what's happening to me but I really like what I'm learning from Mantriji. It's giving me deep insights that are becoming… musical."

"It's escapism, Poem! You wanna know your fate when it's right here in the moment! If you stay with Lynette this could be your break. You saw how it is down there. Live bands everywhere!"

"Sounds like you want me to go."

"Don't you?"

This question has many layers. She wants to buy a house, he wants a record deal. Perhaps this is their bridgehead to another life.

"Well, I guess we could always use a break."

She looks at him consolingly, "I think we *could* use a break, don't you?"

He ponders before giving in, "Yeah. I guess we could use a break."

"Good. It won't be till summer anyway, but I'll tell Lynette."

"I'm not making any promises, Monique. I wanna see how things pan out for me here."

"It won't be till summer, Poem. But New Orleans?!" she gets in his face, "Remember New Year's Eve?!"

"Yeah," he recalls fondly. "We had fun didn't we?"

"We had such a good time. And houses are really cheap down there." She gets lost in the dream of it, "I wish every night could be like New Year's Eve."

"You mean a new beginning?"

"Yeah. We could use a new beginning."

"Yeah. Again," he sighs.

At least their friendship is intact. Poem reaches up and turns off the light. They get under the covers and kiss goodnight.

8 AWARENESS

It is a cool winter day. Poem arrives at Mantri's door with snow still stuck to his boots. He tries the knob then enters the warm, incensed apartment. Peeking through the kitchen, he sees Mantri standing at the table. He bends down to take off his boots but Mantri says don't worry and motions for him to just come on in.

Poem obeys and lets his knapsack slide to the floor. He removes his coat, scarf and hat. "Namaste, Sir. How are you?"

"Namaste. It's cold out there," Mantri shivers. He is wearing a beige sweater over his customary button-down collared shirt.

"Have you been out today?"

Mantri shakes his head, "Too cold."

Poem reaches into his knapsack.

"Have you been memorizing?" Mantri asks.

"Oh yes." Poem places his books on the table. "Very big program," he says like Mantri who smiles approvingly. "I ordered that book you wanted me to get, 'Message of the Stars?' Man, it's like 30 bucks!"

Mantri shakes his head, "Poem, this man put his whole life into writing this book, and you are complaining it cost *you* 30 dollars?"

Poem sighs. "You're right, Mantriji." He looks at the blackboard filled with calculations, "Sir, is astrology purely mathematical? I mean, does it really all come down to math?"

Mantri wonders whether to get into this. He looks at the table, nods to himself, gets up and walks over to the bookshelf. Poem examines the haphazard stack of books and papers, spotting one manuscript jutting out with 'Lisa' and 'Homer' written interchangeably in the margin. He slides it out of the pile. It's a manuscript to an episode of 'The Simpsons.' Mantri returns with an ancient looking book which he hands to Poem who accepts it with his left hand while holding the manuscript in his right. "Is this The

Simpsons?"

"Oh yes."

"Why?"

Mantri laughs. "Oh I like to study this to improve my English."

"But this is *The Simpsons*!"

"Oh yes. They are very good. I don't know how they come up with this stuff," he bobbles his head. "Who comes up with this stuff?"

Poem laughs. "Yeah, it's a funny show but why a script?"

"This is something my student brought me from California where she lives. She knows I like Simpsons," he smiles boyishly, "because the English here is the English people speak. These books," he picks up a grammar book, "No. They are no good for everyday English."

"Really?"

"I like Simpsons because they are clever and funny and I want to speak *this* way," he puts his finger on the script. "I like the way *you* speak. You speak like a musician. 'Hey Man.' 'Cool Man,'" he imitates Poem who laughs.

"Uh… thanks, man."

"That's it! Thanks, man," he chuckles. "I want to learn some good English, how you say, 'vena-cular.'"

"Vernacular?"

"That's it."

"You like vulgarity?"

"Oh yes. Swear words are good. They have shakti!" he clenches his fists.

Poem can't believe it. This kind guru, astrologer and wise man, a teacher of philosophy and Sanskrit, a man who hung out with Jehovah's Witnesses for eleven years just to learn the Bible. "Why vulgarity?"

"Because it is the way people speak. These words have power. They are good words, funny words. They can create or release tension."

"I guess it's better to have swear words than not."

"Oh yes. A good word can release a lot of energy, a taboo word. There is great power in words and names."

"I've heard that every word has its own vibration."

"That's right."

Poem looks at the book in his left hand. The archaic looking cover reads 'Horary Astrology by Krishnamurti.' He flips through the stiff yellow pages, suddenly out of his element. What little he knows of astrology is no use here. It is written in English but reads like code, dense with numbers and stark descriptions: 'Division of the constellation into subs,' 'Whereabouts of father,' 'To lay a foundation,' 'Can I gain in the lottery?' 'Will I get admission in the college?' 'Will my wife deliver twins?' 'Promotion & overseas,' 'Will this gem suit me?' and so on. There are about a hundred questions and the methods to answer them. Sanskrit transliterations abound.

"This," Mantri points as Poem flips through the pages, "is purely mathematical astrology. There is no need for interpretation."

"How can that be?"

"Once you know this system, you will predict."

"Is it difficult?"

"Oh yay," he bobbles his head. "You are not ready for this. One day we will see."

"Well ya know it does bring up a good question." Poem reflects on something he's been meaning to ask. "One thing I just don't get is why *scientists* aren't more interested in astrology. I mean, I see how it works. I've seen you read charts of people that *I* know that *you* don't and somehow you nail them in a profound way."

Mantri smiles.

"You remember my friend John? I showed you his chart last week and you said right away, 'This man likes to eat and criticize.' I never would have described him that way but when I told him what you said, how you said it, his eyes lit up. He said no one had ever summed him up so perfectly."

Mantri laughs. "I remember. Lord of lagna in the 6th."

"Food?"

"No. 2nd is food. 6th is restaurants. He is Aries lagna with Sun deposited, right?"

"Yes."

"So he feels superior to those around him. The Sun is King and it is exalted in his 1st house of Self. Mars is a weapon, aspecting Sun from the 6th, so he likes to cut others while sitting in a restaurant. He is a good man, but with Aries lagna he is a child. And no one can tell a child what to do or he will lash out. Where's his Jupiter?"

"In the 4th."

"So he has *education*! He is a lawyer, right?"

"He's the director."

"That's right. He will do well with Jupiter in kendra house."

"So this is what I'm talking about. You have a way of summing people up based on their chart that is so insightful that how could any scientist observe this and say that astrology is bullshit? I mean, you nailed him!"

"I have experience, Poem."

"I know astrology isn't perfect, but science isn't either. I mean, how much of it is based on speculation or a model? How many things do we take to be factual that are still just theories? I mean, Evolution is a theory. You can't observe it in a lab. You have to infer it, like gravity, and if you can't observe it directly then how do you know everything it's doing and what it's *not* doing?"

Mantri winces. "You are thinking too much. Good thinking, yes. Big philosophy."

"Well for instance, I know this girl; she told me about this psychic she went to. She even made a tape of it. This psychic told her that the name 'Sasha' would soon be meaningful to her, right? So a couple months later she meets this guy who's now her boyfriend and his dog's name is Sasha! How do you explain this?"

"It is anecdotal. You cannot put this in a laboratory."

"But where is the scientist to explain this or to at least give it its props? Where is the interest? I mean, even if she got *half* the things she said wrong, something like this, a unique name, even if it wasn't important information, still, this psychic was able to *see* something of the future. How can it be argued otherwise? I mean, 'Sasha?!'"

"Science is science, Poem, and science relies on certainty. Psychics are too unstable, too unpredictable," he gives a sour expression.

"But the point is that it *can* be done and it speaks to something else that exists in us, around us, that connects us, but people just ignore it because they've never directly experienced it so they think it doesn't exist. I mean, how often do they get the weather wrong and yet meteorology is still considered a science, right?"

"Everyone can see the weather, Poem. It is meaningful to them. But the mind is like an idea: no one knows its true worth until it is too late. But let us begin our lesson." He clears his throat. "You have been learning how to calculate a chart using the ephemeris and Book of Tables."

"It seems that's *all* I've been doing."

"Right. But now you know how to do it."

"Yeah, and y'know by doing it over and over again, somehow my whole perception has changed."

"Ahh," Mantri approves. "Speak."

"Well, my sense of place in this world has, I don't know, I really see that we live on the surface of a sphere. I know we're taught to be linear thinkers but I can feel now, it's intuitive, that we live not on a flat surface but on a ball floating in space. And all of space, the zodiac and so on, it surrounds us, envelops us, not in four, six directions, up, down, east, west, but in *every* direction. It's continuous and it keeps moving around us in a circle. I mean, I know it doesn't move around us. We rotate and it only appears to."

"Astrology is a geo-centric system. We use the Earth as the centre so yes, the zodiac and planets move around us in this instance."

"Yeah I see that. It's relative. We may not be at the centre of *the* universe but we are at the centre or *our* universe."

"Very good," Mantri smiles.

"My whole perspective has shifted. It's hard to explain but I feel a change. We live on the surface of a sphere, and the signs, the Sun and so on, rise at different times according to where we are on the sphere. For people closer to the poles, they experience longer days in summer because they become more exposed by a sharper angle to the Sun. North of the Arctic Circle in fact, one day lasts six months!"

"Good."

"I always knew that *intellectually* but somehow I really get it now, viscerally. It's not an intellectual exercise. It's been very interesting to do these calculations over and over again."

"Very good. So today we will focus on the 1st house." Mantri looks in his book, "The 1st house is what?"

"The sign that rises on the eastern horizon at the time of birth. It signifies the *Self* and *personality* of the native."

"Very good. And what else?"

"Being the *Self*, it signifies the disposition and tendencies of the native and therefore his 'prosperity,' 'vitality,' 'happiness,' and 'ability to be recognized.'"

"Ahah! And what else?" Mantri gets up to the board and draws a chart with one on top, indicating the natural zodiac.

"His body, build, appearance, confidence, and in particular, his head!"

"Very good. The 1st house is *you*, the *Self!*" he circles the lagna. "It is where you are continuously born, where day is born, where the Sun rises, the present moment. It is your birth. It is called lagna because this is where time is tied down. This is where *you* began. The whole horoscope revolves around the lagna."

"Right."

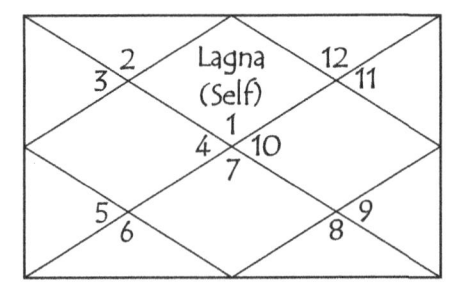

"The 2nd house is your face but the 1st is your head as a whole, your body as a whole. The rest of the houses and signs designate specific body parts but the 1st," he taps the board, "signifies the whole, the constitution, complexion, health, and so on."

"Why would the 2nd be the face?"

"Because it signifies your family, and so, your family resemblance."

"Riiight."

"Whatever influences the 1st house, whether the sign or planets deposited or aspecting, this combination of factors will determine not only the overall appearance of the native, but his temperament, disposition, and personality."

"What's the difference between these things?"

"Temperament is the *temperature* of the native. Does he run hot, cool, dry, warm, chilly. This will influence his behaviour and success in the world. He may be smart…"

"But if he's a hot head."

"You understand."

Poem writes in his book as Mantri speaks, "The *disposition* of the native will be his behaviour, how he acts, what company he keeps, whether he is confident or weak. *Personality* is what he radiates into the world. He may be a hot head, but if his *disposition* is to get along, he will be a reasonable man."

"Or he'll be repressed."

"Right. If Mars is in lagna then this man will be, how you say, 'Megolo-maniac.'"

"Ahah! Why?"

"Because Mars is the penis, and every man worships his own penis. Mars is the Commander in Chief. It is a hot planet, so this man will have too much heat to stay still. If he is an athlete, he will defeat his opponents; if he is boss, he will intimidate his workers; if Mars is fallen in the lagna, he will lash out at others out of weakness or petty self-interest."

"Why is Mars the penis?"

"Look at it." Mantri draws its symbol on the board.

♂

"This is a penis. It is penetrating, aggressive, masculine, ambitious, a weapon! If Mars is strong, he is a hero, a natural leader, content in his strength. If it is weak, he will not apply force so much as react in a violent, roundabout and cowardly way. But first always check the sign in which it sits and any planets occupying or aspecting it. If Jupiter aspects, it makes him more even-tempered."

"So how does it work? I mean why is the eastern horizon the native?"

"It is *not* the native. It is only the *Self* of the native, how he appears to the world."

"What else is there?"

"There is the Sun, which is the atma, or soul of the native, the karaka, or 'natural indicator' of the 1st house."

"But what's the difference?"

"The soul is the driver whereas the body, or personality, is the chariot."

"So when people say their Sun is in say… Leo, and they say how perfectly this describes them, what they are in fact recognizing is their 'soul' or innermost nature."

"Right."

"Which is why, I guess, people relate to their Sun-sign."

"Right."

"Even though it is not their outer Self."

"Right. People appear to others differently than their Sun-sign unless they were born near dawn, which puts their Sun in the 1st house, otherwise they will show more the attributes of their lagna."

"But in Jyotish the Sun is often in a different sign, so doesn't this speak to suggestibility in people?"

"Slowly, slowly," Mantri raises his finger. "They may still have something important in that sign, like Mercury or Moon or lagna, or the character of their assumed Sun-sign is found in their ruling planet or elsewhere in the chart."

"Like what?"

"A man thinks he is Leo. He says I am fiery, passionate, individualistic, but he is born in *early* degrees of Leo and therefore his Sun is in Cancer. So where do Leo qualities come from? Maybe he is Leo lagna, or Moon in Leo. Maybe Mars and Jupiter aspect lagna. Jupiter makes him magnanimous, Mars makes him self-serving."

"Like a Leo."

"Right. And if Mars is aspected by or conjoined with Venus, this describes his passion. We cannot consider only one factor. Astrology is blending many things into a cohesive whole. Always look for confluence."

"And if this is not the case?"

"Then he will read his Sun-sign and say astrology is bullshit. 'This is nothing like me,' he will say."

"But sometimes, like in my case, I always considered myself an Aries, but other people would guess I was either a water or earth sign."

Mantri draws Poem's chart and circles the 1st house. "You are Virgo lagna. This is earth." He writes the planets in as he speaks, "Your Moon is here with Venus, a watery planet, in Taurus, an earth sign. Your ruler, Mercury, is here in Pisces, a water sign. No doubt your Sun is in Aries but you have more water and earth than fire."

"Amazing. So a skeptic would miss these nuances."

"A skeptic wouldn't look."

"So… The lagna is the Self, the Sun is the soul, and the Moon is the mind."

"Right. The Moon is the most important planet of all. It is manas, the mind, but not the mind that most people here in the West think."

"What do you mean?"

"Most people equate the mind with the intellect, but it is Buddhi, or *Mercury*, that is the intellect. The *mind* is the perceptive faculty that reflects what is coming from the soul as the Moon reflects the light of the Sun. It is the emotions, feelings, memory, and mother of the native as you are a reflection of *your* mother through the life she has given to you from your father. The Moon is what determines the extent of your happiness on this Earth."

"Mine's in Taurus."

"Oy yay!" Mantri bobbles his head. "It is exalted!"

"That's good," Poem smiles.

"Very good."

"And it's in the 9th, a good house."

"This is the *best* house, the house of luck and fortune."

"But I'm not thaaat lucky," Poem demurs.

"You ruin your luck with desire."

"Why do you say that?"

"Your Moon is with Venus, which is also very strong, but look here." He draws as he speaks, "Mars aspecting Venus and you cannot control your passions. Saturn aspecting and you will go with widows, divorcees, older women. You are running the sex program."

"Well, I do like their company. I guess that's what older women are in India: widows and divorcees."

"Right, and *here* they are cougars," Mantri laughs. "But you at this time will go for a younger woman because Mercury flavours Saturn in this chart. Saturn can mean older partner or that *you* will be the older partner, but you will not marry your own age, no. Saturn is the servant, but in this case they are not low women because your Venus is strong, in its own sign."

"So how does that ruin my luck?"

"You either have no patience and rush in or you lay back until the opportunity is lost. In both cases your luck is ruined. Mars is hasty. From the house of speech it ruins your luck by speaking before you think. It is with Ketu, the outcast, therefore you will speak in-a-propriately. At the same time, Saturn aspecting makes you hold back and you lose opportunities by thinking too much. Saturn is vata, or air, and it is with Mercury, the intellect. You think too much, man, and before you know it the opportunity and your luck is gone," he gives a dismissive flourish. "The hardest step to take is the one you anticipate. Stop thinking!"

"So I have no luck," Poem looks down.

"You *have* luck, but you are ruining it."

"I thought the planets are ruining it."

"These are aspects, not conjunctions."

"What's the difference?"

"If the planets are conjoined, it *will* happen; if they are aspected, it *may* happen. Here's how it works. If I am in a bar and I see a beautiful woman who I want to meet and I am with a friend who knows her, then definitely I will meet her. If I am not with someone who knows her then it may happen, it may not. It is up to me to make it happen, or in your case to make sure it doesn't, you see?"

Poem nods.

"The planets are your karma and some things you can change, some you cannot. It is up to *you* whether you will curb your passions."

"But how can I control my passions?"

"By not doing it."

"Just like that."

"Right."

"So if I want to have sex with another woman?"

"Don't do it."

"And this will stop my passion?"

"Passion is attachment to the object of your desire."

"But how can I stop desiring it?"

"Don't think about it."

"But it's not that easy."

"Ahhh," Mantri sighs and Poem is silent. It seems too simple when he's looking for complicated answers.

"So how do I do it?"

"Awareness."

"Isn't there just some mantra?"

"Awareness, Poem."

"So how do I quit smoking?"

"Just don't smoke."

"Riiight. But if I want to smoke then how can I stop what I want to do?"

"Just *do* what you *don't do* and *don't do* what you *do*. This is the only way to change behaviour."

"You make it sound so easy."

"It is not easy. It is very hard. But it starts with awareness."

"But there's a chapter in this book about gems and how gems can alter your energy."

"Can you afford a 10 carat emerald?"

"Probably not."

"Then awareness, Poem."

"So the rich get it easy once again."

"Gems work with the right intention. If there is no awareness of their properties, how can they affect the individual?"

"So you're saying you have to *believe* it works."

"That helps but no. If the individual is not vibrating mentally with the notion that inert objects emit fields that can influence one's behaviour or luck, then how could he possibly reap the full benefits of a gemstone? For most of the world gems are for vanity, not enlightenment."

"But they do have real energy."

"Oh yes."

"Why does science not recognize this?"

"How do you know?"

"I don't hear any doctors or scientists talk about the healing power of gems."

"Do you know any doctors or scientists?"

"No, but I acknowledge the bias. I mean, I'm assuming."

"In India they grind certain gems into powder that is used for medicine," he points to his open mouth to indicate where it goes.

"Really? That seems odd."

"Why, when you ingest iron and copper every day. There is an energy associated with every element, whether earth, water, fire or wind. Everything in the universe has its manifestation and emits a field, or gravitational pull, however slight, unto the objects around it. Foods have their own field and influence. So do people."

"And this is astrology?"

"Astrology is a very big subject," Mantri bobbles his head. "Green emerald is the equivalent vibration of Mercury in a gem. It is a highly compressed form of Mercury. Why this is we don't know but it is what the ancients tell us."

"How did the ancients know this?"

"Poem, this world was once the domain of wise men. But where are the wise men of today? The pace is too fast, the environment too polluted. What is natural anymore? The only Rishis you will see today are in the Himalayas. They are not concerned with this world."

"But surely we are more advanced than the ancients."

"Oh ho," Mantri disagrees. "There has been no intelligence, no *real* intelligence on this Earth for five hundred years!"

"What?! How can you say that, Sir? We put a man on the Moon!"

"This is not intelligence."

"I don't understand."

"Once everything became literal, there is no poetry left. Where is there another Shakespeare?"

"There's Wagner."

"That was a long time ago and there is only one. When the world became material is when we lost our intelligence. People don't want truth, they want facts, they want to measure things, they want to talk, speculate, but no one talks truth anymore. They say this is 'my truth.' They will say justice is truth, but justice is not truth. Truth is justice, but justice is not truth."

"Hmm."

"It used to be the quest of Western civilization to find 'the Truth' but now it is said there is no Truth, just people speculating ideas, making things up. Everything now is just gap-shap."

"Gap-shap?"

"Gossip. Everyday things. 'Hello.' 'How are you?' People speak but they don't say anything. People write books but nothing is new. It is all from the Bible or mythology, recycled. There are no *real* new ideas. They just switch around words, change names and call it new. What does this Ecclesiastes say? 'Vanity of vanities, all is vanity.' People speak all the time but what are they saying?"

"Hmm."

Mantri sits down. "The only thing worth talking is scripture. Everything else is gap-shap."

"What about technology, computers, vaccines?"

"These are material things built by monkeys *for* monkeys. Material things. I am talking *ideas*, new things, what makes us *human*. Not sending a tin can into space."

"But vaccines help people. They save lives."

"There is no difference. They live only to talk more gap-shap. There would not be the diseases we have today if people did not mix. But this started a long time ago."

"You mean mix races?"

"Races, castes, the whole world is mixed up now. No one knows their true dharma. This man is a doctor because his father is one, but really he is an artist. He suffers and even gets sick because he is not fulfilling his dharma."

"His life purpose."

"Right. It is rare to find someone who is living their dharma. Most times they do what they want, not what needs to be done. There are only two things people are interested in today: money and sex. That's it. People do not live up to nor do they even know their dharma. They make money so they can have new clothes, a car, a pad, but it is all for the sex program. Everything they do is for sex. 'Hello baby.' 'Come back to my place.' '*I have a nice car*,'" he lilts.

"How do we know our dharma?"

"First we look to the trikona houses, but this is for another day."

"Trikona?"

"The triangle houses: 1, 5, 9. The 1st is the house of Self, the body, where we are now. The 5th is the mind, or intelligence, where we are going.

The 9th is our spirit, or luck, what we inherited from the past."

"So someone's spirit is a reflection of what they did in a past life?"

"Of course. This is why it is the luck house. It is what we brought with us into this life. Someone who has no luck did not earn it in the past."

"Really?"

"Luck is everything, Poem. I know this one man, many years I am friends with him. He is a IDIOT! And yet, he became *millionaire* because of luck. He has no intelligence, no education, no ingenuity. He just bought a dollar store at the right time and now he is a wealthy man."

"Well I'm sure he worked hard."

"Many people work hard but not everyone becomes wealthy. He is a man of luck, selling plastic from China, things nobody needs, useless things, but because he made a fortune he goes around telling everyone, even me, how to live their life."

"So success made him a know it all."

"Oh yes. Very difficult to speak to this man. When people are successful in one thing, they think they know *everything* and they will not listen to you. They think they are geniuses but really, it is luck and nothing more."

Poem thinks a moment. "And so my luck?"

"Stop ruining it with your desires."

Poem looks at him thoughtfully. "And this is astrology."

"This is *all* astrology." Mantri stands and bows, "Namaste."

"Thank you, Sir. Namaste."

9 THE 8ᵀᴴ HOUSE

It is a sunny cold March morning. The last of winter's dirty white refuse trims the streets and buildings. Poem approaches the gate, lifts the icy deadbolt and inserts its key. The smooth sliding shackle slides out of its slot. He pulls the rolling gate open and wraps the chain back on its hinge. Blowing into his curled up fingers, he enters the inner lot of Malabar's Opera Department, a large self-contained triangular property that used to be a lumber yard. Located on Brock Street just north of the bridge, it is encased by white cinder block walls with baby blue trim, giving it the feel of a carnival castle without the turrets.

He unlocks the door to the main warehouse, enters the foyer and finds the light switch behind a row of 18th century soldier costumes. A large rolling rack with Austin's Rigoletto waits to be dragged over to shipping. He enters the short hallway to the punch clock, inserts his timecard and it stamps like a prison door shutting:

18 MAR 9:14 A.M.

The shift starts at nine but at Malabar if you get there before 9:30 you're considered on time. Poem is usually the first in. He walks back into the foyer, grabs the rolling rack and drags it laboriously outside to shipping/receiving across the court. He unlocks the grey security door and pulls the rack into the dark interior, finds the electrical box and snaps open the master switch. The room is suddenly awash in florescent light and cool jazz and the ceiling-mounted heaters rev into action.

He wriggles out of his knapsack, pulls out his swim stuff, hangs it under a heater, then organizes some notes, uses the washroom and hears Jay enter through his office door. He walks over to greet him. "Yes I!" he peeks in.

"Hey Poem, did you swim today?"

"Of course!"

"That's amazing. I don't know how you do it. I can barely make it here for 9:30."

Jay is a stout man in his mid-forties of Japanese heritage. He is slightly effeminate and loves to laugh. A painter, hipster, lover and beatnik philosopher, he has a gentle round face that could pass for Samoan. He unravels his scarf, unbuttons his coat and throws it all onto the chair. His desk is clean except for a tidy pile of magazines and a used-up desk blotter with dozens of elaborate doodles. He walks past Poem who steps out of the way to avoid his meaty frame. "Thanks for bringing in Rigoletto," he says.

"No problem."

Poem is the company driver here while Jay does shipping/receiving. A lot of their downtime is spent in Jay's office philosophizing on the arts, humanities, science and politics. He's the only one at Malabar who *doesn't* call Poem by his given name 'Greg.'

"Listen," Poem says. "I'm gonna make my first run. You need anything?"

"You going to McCaul?"

"Yeah. Jerry wants me to pick up Stan and bring him back here."

"Great. The rodent is coming home. All right, I gotta pack up these clothes. Say hello to the girls at McCaul!"

"I always do."

Poem pats himself to make sure he has everything he needs. He steps out through the office door to the badly encrusted cube van, unlocks the driver's side and pulls himself up into the musty cab. The familiar smell of motor oil and Belmont cigarettes sinks in. He cranks the motor and it bursts into life, rumbling frantically, releasing its customary puff of black smoke that drifts past him and around the corner like some evil apparition.

Feeling heat now coming out of the vents, he puts the truck into drive and heads out along Queen West. At McCaul he turns into the laneway bordering Malabar where he eases the truck into its well-worn groove then makes his way round the building into retail where Colin is pricing merchandise. "Hey Colin, you seen Stan?"

"Yeah, he's upstairs. Should be back in a minute."

He continues through the adjoining hall into rentals and sees Heather behind the counter talking on the phone. He nods hello as he rounds the corner and...!

There before him, a fit young woman with long, wavy, sandy blonde hair and a heart-shaped derriere, squatting to the floor, exposing a perfect backside from which a tight red thong groans out of her skin-tight jeans. He is transfixed.

"Hey Greg!" Heather's voice jars him and the spell is broken.

"Hey..." he looks at her and slides his eyes back to the thong. The woman turns, their eyes connect and a surge of bronze-coloured starlight pierces his heart and sinks to his knees. He barely maintains composure. *Oh my God. She's fucking gorgeous!* Their eyes remain locked as though recognizing one another. She nearly tips over, rising from the floor. Poem offers to help but she makes it up unaided, dusts her hands and says hi to which he responds, "Hey... uh... Is someone helping you?"

"I work here."

"Huh?"

"I work here. Who are you?" Her raspy voice is like liquid gold dripping off a nail file.

"Oh, I'm... Greg... the driver," he wants to say Poem.

"Oh yeah!" she recognizes the name. "Hey Greg, nice to meet you. I'm Maya." She is alert, petite, and a knockout! He sees right away she wears too much makeup.

Finding his centre, Poem says, "How long you been working here?"

"I started just before Valentine's Day, but just weekends and evenings."

"Oh. I guess that's why I haven't seen you."

"Yeah. I guess you just work days, huh?"

The sexual tension is overwhelming. They attempt small talk as Heather observes, amused.

"Yeah... So you working today?" he asks.

"Yup."

"Well, umm... Welcome aboard!"

"Thanks..." she smiles nervously, wanting to say more.

"Okay, well, I'm just waiting for Stan actually."

"Oh, he said he'd be back soon."

"'Kay... Thanks!"

He walks over to Stan's office, looks through the open door and stands next to it as if on guard. Maya is watching him. *Holy shit. She looks like Jennifer Lopez.* He smiles as she again squats but in the opposite direction and continues to pack the mannequin bags on the floor. His heart is racing. He needs a cigarette badly but doesn't want her to know he smokes. He is nervy and trying to be indifferent, watching this absolute angel pack the body parts of a disassembled mannequin. He would like to say something but what? After an uncomfortable silence he finally asks, "Is that a rental?"

"Yeah."

"Hmm... So... What d'ya do, Maya?"

"I'm a singer."

"No way!" his eyes light up. "Me too!"

"Really?" She stands. "I heard you're a musician."

"Yeah well, mostly I play guitar but I have a band and yeah, I'm the singer too."

She moves closer to him, "Cool, what kind of stuff do you do?"

"Oh it's pretty funky, pretty heavy, like Sly Stone smashing into a Led Zeppelin."

"That sounds amazing! Are you playing anywhere?"

"Uh yeah, we've played all over but... We're kinda looking for a drummer right now."

"Oh?" She wants to say more.

"Yeah, our last drummer quit, just like that."

"What happened?"

"Uh, he met this Christian girl."

Maya watches him, curious. "Oh well, sorry to hear that. I'm sure you'll find another drummer."

"Yeah. How 'bout you? You playing anywhere?"

She hesitates and Stan enters the room. "Ahah!" he says accusingly. "Jerry wants you to drive me to the warehouse, Greg. You ready?"

"Yeah, Stan. Ready anytime."

Stan is a runty guy in his mid-forties with a peach fuzz goatee and 70s style tinted bifocals. He is a diehard Trekkie and the de facto manager of Malabar's rental department. Armed with a short man's attitude, he is always trying to assert what little authority he has. "I'll be ready in a minute, Greg. Why don't you go wait by the truck?"

"It's cold out there, Stan. I'll just wait right here." He smiles at Maya who smiles back.

"You may as well go warm up the truck, Greg. I'll just be a minute. Maya, did you count those hats for me?"

"I'll have it done by the time you get back, Stan." She looks at Poem, "Well, I guess I'll be seeing you around."

"Oh yeah," he reassures her. "I'm here usually two or three times a day!"

"Okay. It was very nice to meet you uh... Greg."

Stan calls, "Maya, can you come in here a sec?" He disappears inside his office and Maya dutifully obeys.

Poem saunters over to the counter where Heather is grinning, "How ya doin', Greg?"

"Oh I'm cool. How 'bout you, Heather?"

"Same ol' same ol'... Hey I got another audition this week."

"Great," he is watching Stan's door.

"Oh it's just some play, doesn't pay well and there's nudity, but it looks interesting..." she wonders if he's listening, "Yeah, there's this huge *orgy* scene—"

"That's great," he is oblivious to her.

Stan and Maya emerge from the office, Stan in his winter coat and

55

tuque. "Try and get it done before I get back, okay? Thanks, Maya."

She nods obediently.

Stan approaches Poem, "Okay, dude, let's go. I got everything here," he pats his canvas bag. "Off to the warehouse, girls. Be back in two hours!"

Poem sneaks one last look at Maya before they exit.

McCaul is busier as they descend the steps and round the corner to the truck, Stan just keeping up with his shorter legs. Poem gets into the cab, starts the engine and pulls out enough for Stan to climb in. They head-out for Brock as Stan fumbles with his seatbelt. "Got any good music in here, Greg?"

"Uh, sure." Poem puts on a jazz station.

Stan listens for a moment. "Got anything more interesting?"

"They don't play Star Trek on the radio, Stan."

"Very funny, Greg. Try Q107."

"Awww no. I've already heard their entire play list. Twice. In one month."

"You don't like Classic Rock?"

"I do, but not when you play the same songs over and over again, Stan. I mean, Bob Dylan wrote more than one song, y'know?"

They drive along Queen West towards Parkdale, Stan checking out girls, and Poem thinking about Maya. "So what's the deal with—?"

"She has a boyfriend, Greg."

"Oh."

"Too bad, eh?" Stan smirks. "Oh well, ya can't win 'em all."

"I wasn't trying to win anything."

"Yeah right."

"So what does he do?"

"He's a drummer and a really nice guy. They live together. Yeah, I know her pretty good. She worked here last year too, before you came on."

They continue driving, not saying much, and eventually pull into Malabar's Opera department lot. Stan jumps out before the truck comes to a full stop and scuttles into the main building with his bag. Poem gets out of the cab and walks into shipping/receiving where he finds Jay in his office engrossed in a book. "All done?" he asks.

Jay looks up, "I love this job."

"Jay, I have to talk to you." Poem takes off his jacket and sits down.

"What's up?"

"Dude, I just met this woman who I think is gonna change my life."

Jay snaps his book shut. "What happened?"

Poem replays how he met Maya, the red thong, what he felt when their eyes first met, the ray of light penetrating his body, wounding his heart, the instantaneous connection.

"So you gonna ask her out?"

"Dude, I have a girlfriend."
"So?"
"And she has a boyfriend."
"So?"
"And I *live* with my girlfriend."
"So?"
"And she *lives* with her boyfriend!"
"So what's the problem?!"
"Dude, I'm not gonna ask her out."
"Look, you're an artist, she's a singer. What's wrong with a little extra-curricular activity? Especially between two creative and sexy people."

Poem looks at him doubtfully. "Ordinarily I would agree with you, Jay, and I know you're half joking but I can't shake this feeling, man. I'm serious." He turns to the window, "I really feel that this woman is gonna be meaningful to me. It doesn't have to be sexual. Maybe she's the singer that'll help propel my band! I don't know. It's fucked up what I felt for her."

"Well, you said you weren't exactly thrilled with your current relationship."

"It's just the sex, man, but I love Monique. She's like a sister to me."

"That is so sad."

"Oh man, don't go there."

"It's very important to have a muse, Poem, and to fall in love is the greatest gift an artist can get, even if it fucks up the rest of his life. Artists live for inspiration. You were in New Orleans, how'd it feel?"

"Alive!"

"Right. And American chicks?! Oh man, they're crazy down there!"

"Look, Jay. I have a good life with Monique. I like her family, her cats, our apartment, most of her friends, and I like her! I like her accent, that she sings, dances, that we can joke around, that we travel well together, that she likes opera! These are important things."

Jay gives a long bearish yawn, "It sounds like you're already married. You need some adventure, man! You're down on your band. You're looking for a drummer—"

"Hey! Her boyfriend's a drummer."

"Who?"

"Stan was saying Maya's boyfriend is a drummer."

"That's perfect! You can have an orgy in the band!" Jay grins and Poem looks at him to cut the crap. "You're looking for a drummer, Poem. Ask her. Maybe he'll be your next drummer and she'll be that 'magical' singer you dream about. Maybe that's what you're feeling. You heading back to McCaul?"

"Yeah."

"So bring her your CD. Either she likes it or she doesn't. Worth a shot."

"Yeah… Good idea, Jay. One step at a time, eh?" He walks out to his desk and fetches a CD from the top drawer. He comes back and slides it in front of Jay who looks at it and says,

"What would your teacher say?"

Poem reacts like someone just switched the channel in his head. "Mantriji?" He wonders. "He once told me that every time I leave my apartment I should ask myself whether it's increasing my 'being' or my 'prosperity.' He says if it does neither then it's probably a waste of time."

"Hmm, I'd agree with that," Jay strokes his chin. "And you need a drummer to prosper, right?"

"Right."

"And to prosper will help increase your 'being,' right?"

"Not necessarily."

"What d'ya mean?"

Two warehouse philosophers with time on their hands, Poem sits down and explains, "I once told him I bought a lottery ticket hoping to win big, that if I did, my life would be so much easier and I could commit to being a full-time student of astrology and philosophy. *He* said if I won the lottery I would be having a good time and all this philosophy and astrology would go out the window."

Jay laughs. "You think that's true?"

"I don't know. I just think it's interesting how misery and spirituality are linked. Like in astrology, the 8th house signifies both 'hardships' and the 'occult' so that the same thing that gives you a hard time also leads you to ask the really big questions, to wanna know the meaning behind it all."

"Makes sense."

"Like take the blacks in the South. They suffered the greatest persecution and yet, they are arguably the most inspired element in American culture. They created Jazz, Blues, Rock 'n' Hip Hop. Considered a blight, they are the light. It's like suffering gives you some special insight."

"The artist must suffer."

"The 8th also signifies 'legacies,' and it's interesting to see how the wars and catastrophes of humanity, the great waves of death that plague civilizations, always get memorialized. You'd think they'd wanna forget."

"Yeah."

"The 8th also signifies 'unearned wealth,' like inheritance or winning a lottery. Think about it, the Death house signifies unearned wealth! I guess a part of you dies when you get free money." Poem gets up and points out the directions as he speaks, "You know how I told you that the 1st house is east, the 7th house is west, the 10th is straight up, and the 4th is straight down?"

"Yup."

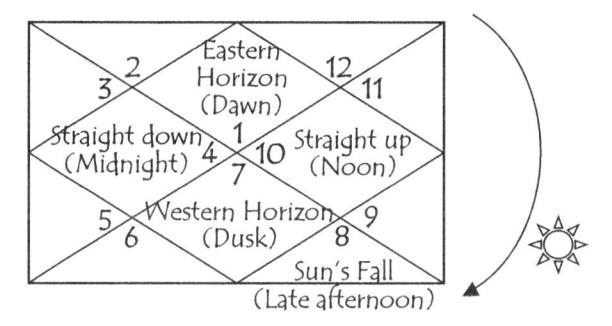

```
                Eastern
          2    Horizon   12
        3               11
              (Dawn)
    Straight down  1    Straight up
     (Midnight)  4   10   (Noon)
                   7
        5    Western Horizon  9
          6    (Dusk)      8
                    Sun's Fall
                  (Late afternoon)
```

"Well, the 8th house is that part of the sky where the Sun begins its fall in the late afternoon. It's where day begins to die and you already feel there's no coming back. The Sun just sinks like a stone from the 8th house. I have my Sun in the 8th with Rahu eclipsing, and because Sun signifies father, in my case my father died when I was really young."

"Wow."

"Yeah, so psychologically I try to make up the void with sex and metaphysics, both 8th house significations."

"Sex is the 8th house?"

"Yeah, sex—or at least the sex organs—in astrology is the 8th house, the Death house. Interesting, huh?"

"I remember reading in some magazine that it's after a war that people start fucking like crazy and the birth rate goes up by reflex to the number of people who have just died."

"Yeah, they're trying to soak up all the dead souls. So being the death house and signifying sex, it also signifies the occult because death and sex are supernatural things."

"Beautiful."

"And whenever you have sex, death, and the occult, you have…" he waits for Jay who has no idea, "Scandal!"

"Ahah!"

"It's the *house* of scandal, and disgrace, and sex appeal, and delusion, and so ultimately, suffering."

Jay contemplates this string of seemingly disparate things.

"Mantriji calls it the 'Cave house' because whatever happens in a cave is hidden from the rest of the world. Planets in the 8th become invisible. You know Marcus? He has both his Sun and Moon in the 8th. When Mantriji saw this he said, 'This man will sit in a room and use himself up.'"

"Wow."

"Yeah, and that's what he does: drink beer, watch TV, smoke a little thang. Man, as soon as the gig's done, he can't wait to get back to the crib."

"Hmm."

"So the 8th signifies things *hidden* from the world, like sex, genitals, secrets, and unforeseen tragedies. Marilyn Monroe had a prominent 8th house. The same thing that made her sexy also made her tragic."

"And you can see all this in her chart?"

"Oh yeah! It's why we immortalize her, like Jimi Hendrix, same thing. We like our heroes dead so we can deify them, make them bigger, make them into anything we want, like a big-ass legacy!"

"Yeah."

"The 8th is also hidden *knowledge*, like Tantra, astrology, the tarot, channelling spirits, or even just being aware that these things exist, like dark matter, or parallel universes, whatever metaphor you wanna use. And you need metaphor to explain what you can't fully understand. You need it sometimes just to digest. But when you do, people say you can't use metaphor and be factual, that somehow science means the death of metaphor and by extension the death of religion and morality."

"Interesting."

"The 8th also has to do with dreams and the paranormal, psychology, things that on the surface seem irrational. It's like the intellect of the emotional mind!"

"You're losing me."

"Just think of it as knowledge you can't *truly* verify until after you die."

"Greaaat."

"I'm just saying that it's people who are *suffering* who want to know these metaphysical things. *They* wanna understand the meaning of it all, why life is unfair, why someone with half their intelligence and talent makes it big while they struggle like us, working for 12 fucking bucks an hour," he ends on a depressive note.

"Yeah," Jay feels his pain.

"Mantriji said to me a few times that nearly all the people who come for readings or even lessons will have some big problem they need help with, usually just to identify it. If someone's life is going great, they have no interest in astrology. What for? Life is great! Only those who suffer *beyond their comprehension* will seek the advice of an astrologer. So I guess he figures if I had a lot of money, I wouldn't be so interested in astrology." He ponders this while Jay sorts out everything that has just been said. "I like it now because it explains a lot, but I'm not looking to become an astrologer, Jay, I just find it interesting. There's a lot to memorize though," he stares at the pile of magazines, "The thing I like about it, to tell you the truth, is studying with Mantriji."

"Yeah, you don't get that from books."

"It's amazing, Jay. He lives in just a simple one bedroom apartment, hardly owns anything, almost no furniture, sleeps on the floor, doesn't want any attention or favours from anyone. His whole apartment is just books.

That's all he does is study and teach. He says the only thing worth talking about is scripture, that everything else is just gossip. Man, I wish I could have such a simple life. I mean, you just sit next to him and you always feel better. He just radiates calmness, presence, and being."

"Yeah."

"Like, he'll stand there with the book in hand and teach what's not in it." Poem picks up a magazine, "This is just information, my man, but can you turn it into knowledge? What I'm getting from him is the oral tradition of India, knowledge that's been handed down from teacher to student since ancient times, that is the domain of *only* teacher and student. He's passing onto me the energy and insights from long ago through *his* teachers and so on; like the book is the corpse and the guru is the animus."

"Yeah," Jay has an epiphany. "It's a living transmission is what it is."

The two are silent as a distant cop car sounds its ambulatory ring. "I've had a few good teachers," Jay says, "over the years and yeah, you always get something more by just hanging out with 'em. You don't even have to talk about art, and I guess it's their 'being' that makes the difference."

"This is what a lot of people don't get, that there's a difference between knowledge and information."

"Right."

"How would you describe the difference?"

Jay thinks a moment. "I think that information is just that: information. If something is Greek and you don't understand it, it doesn't stop it from being information, but at the same time it can't become knowledge."

"It has the potential."

"Yes, it *can* become knowledge if you read Greek but it's just information if you can't. Or even if you *can* read it and get the information that's there, if you don't really understand it or if you understand it only superficially, then I don't think you can call it knowledge."

"Knowledge is something you understand and *know*. It can't be taken from you, like an education."

"Exactly."

"And you can always give information but you can't always pass along knowledge."

"Beautiful."

Poem sees through the window Stan approaching, "Oh oh, here comes the rodent. Let's ask him."

"He won't get it. He's a friggin moron!"

Stan opens the door and walks in.

"Hey Little Man," Jay greets him.

"Hey Shithouse," Stan retorts.

"You ready to go?" Poem asks.

"Yeah, in a couple minutes. Jerry just has to bring me something."

"Hey Stan…" Jay begins coyly. "Let me ask you something. Me and *Poem* here…" (Stan always sneers at this name) "We were just having a little discussion and we want to know what someone of your lofty intellect thinks."

Stan gives him a sideways glare.

"We want to know what you think is the difference between 'knowledge' and 'information.'"

Stan contemplates this and looks at Poem then Jay as if he's onto them, "No difference. No difference at all. Why do you ask?"

"You don't think there's a difference between knowledge and information?" Jay asks.

"No. They're just two different words for basically the same thing."

"Basically. Okay Stan, thanks."

Poem says, "Dude, I don't know where you got your education from, but I suggest you demand a refund."

Jay guffaws, but Stan, quite convinced he is right, takes it in stride. He sees Jerry place his bag on the rear step of the truck. "Great! Okay Greg, let's go."

Poem puts on his coat and grabs the CD.

"See ya, Poem," Jay winks good luck.

Stepping outside, Stan sneers, "Poem… Your mother didn't name you that."

"That's cuz she didn't know who I was yet."

Stan grabs the bag and they enter through opposite sides of the cab. Poem starts the motor while Stan looks at him and asks, "So, what's the difference between knowledge and information?"

"One is what you know, the other is just data. It doesn't become knowledge until you understand it."

"Yeah that's bullshit. They're both the same thing."

Poem looks away, shaking his head. He knows Stan likes to wear his ignorance like a badge. He puts the truck into drive and the two head for McCaul barely speaking a word, Stan checking out girls, Poem anticipating Maya. They drive into the lane next to Malabar and Poem lets Stan out before sidling the truck into its usual spot. He locks-up and walks to McCaul where he sees Stan talking to Maya on the entranceway platform. She is in her winter coat sitting on the bench, having a cigarette. He's relieved to see her smoke. "Hey, Maya!"

"Hey Greg," she is happy to see him.

"Mind if I join you?"

"You smoke?"

"*Just watch me*," he lilts and pulls out a pack. He is about to light up when Stan says,

"Watcha doing, Greg? Don't you have deliveries?"

"Yeah I'll get to it, Stan." He defiantly lights the cigarette.

Stan lingers till the silence is awkward. He opens the door and hesitates before saying, "See you inside, Maya."

"The list is on your desk, Stan!"

Poem pulls out the CD, "So listen, I brought you something." He hands it to her.

"Oh wow! This is you? Power of Eternal Music, eh...?"

"Yeah, it's me and my man, Marcus, demo quality, but it'll give you an idea of what we do."

Maya turns the case, "16 tracks!? Holy shit! You recorded all these tunes?!"

"A lot more than that, Maya. I've written over three hundred songs and we've demoed close to a hundred of them."

"No way!"

"Way. This is like a greatest hits."

"Wow! I can't even finish one song and you've got a greatest hits?!" She holds it to her ear, wondering what it sounds like.

"So... I hear your boyfriend's a drummer."

"Uh... I guess Stan told you."

"Stan has a pretty big mouth for such a little guy."

She laughs charmingly, a tinge of smoker's cough on her sexy voice.

"I hear he's pretty good."

"Yeah, he's definitely good," she wants to change the subject.

"Is he looking for a gig?"

"Umm... sure. I'll give it to him and see what he thinks and I'll let you know." She fans herself with the CD.

"Cool, thanks." Poem takes a drag off his smoke. "Sooo, how 'bout you? You looking for a gig?"

"Um, I don't know," Maya looks at her feet. "I was singing for a while, y'know, in clubs, but I don't know. I just don't like being in smoky bars."

"But you smoke."

"Yeah," she laughs. "But I'm giving this up." She holds out the stub of her spent cigarette, drops it to the ground and kills it with her boot. "I'm just coming out of a rough spell."

"Sorry to hear that."

"I love to sing but I just don't wanna play in smoky bars no more."

"I hear ya, Maya, I really do. But unfortunately smoky bars seem to be the only places bands *can* play."

"No...! There's theatres, concert halls, stadiums."

"Stadiums? That's big time. You have to do the baby-steps first."

"Well that's where I have a problem. I already did all the baby-steps and now I want something better."

"Yeah... Listen, how old are you?"

"26. How 'bout you?"

"Uh... older than that," he laughs.

She looks confused, "You don't look *that* old."

"How old?"

"Y'know, where you don't just give your age, you make some smart-alecky comment instead."

"You are very wise, Maya."

"You must be in your thirties then."

"Good enough! Well, give it a listen and let me know if—what's your boyfriend's name?"

"Tony."

"Let me know if Tony likes it and if he wants to jam some time. And if you like, maybe you can sing in the band as well."

"I thought *you* were the singer."

"I am but I can always use some help. I like having different voices, y'know, like in opera, they have different characters, different ranges."

"Well, I don't know much about opera but I think I know what you mean, like, in a musical."

"Right." He butts his cigarette into the antique floor ashtray. Maya rolls her eyes, picks up her squished filter and does the same. "So I'm just saying if you're interested."

She gets up and looks at him suspiciously.

"Maybe you can join us, okay?"

She's not sure what to say.

"Anyhow, think about it."

"Okay. Thanks for the CD," she holds it up.

"No problem," he looks at her fondly. "I gotta go now but you know where to reach me," he pats his jacket, indicating the company cell.

"*You're the driver,*" she lilts. "Okay. I'm working on Monday so I guess I'll just see you then."

"Cool, Maya. See you then."

They shake hands like it's a date. Poem walks down the steps, turns up the lane towards the truck with sunshine in his stomach and looks up to the clear blue sky. *This girl is gonna change my life.*

10 RIVER DJALLON

Poem, Marcus, Maya and her boyfriend, Tony, have been rehearsing for almost two months under the name 'River Djallon,' a mystical river in Africa that joins all rivers to their source. The vibe has been nothing short of a love fest. Tony is sweet, disciplined, a fantastic drummer, but Maya struggles with her parts and secretly feels stifled doing back-ups. Marcus has doubted her role from the start. They are using Tony's rental space, the upstairs suite of an electrical motor-parts shop just north of the tracks at Dundas and Keele. The room is dimly lit with no windows, just two standing floor lamps and a fluorescent ceiling light with red overlays. Equipment is piled everywhere.

It is late June and rehearsals have been going well. Nearing the end of a challenging reggae/funk tune, they refrain into their mics:

"In Babylon!"

Marcus yells, "Yes yes yes!" as the band riffs into a climactic cadence and BANG! Their collective chord fades nicely into the silence. They look at one another and erupt: 'Oh Man!' and 'That was great!' hurling mutual respect and praise. The boys have just completed their entire first set flawlessly.

Marcus is moved, "Man, that was deep, yes man, very deep."

"You guys are great!" Maya says, watching proudly as they excitedly congratulate each other.

Marcus lays down his ol' man wisdom, "Y'see? Ya see?! That hard work shit is payin' off, know what I'm sayin'?"

Poem looks back at Maya who approaches him, stepping around her mic stand. "So when are *you* coming in, Maya?"

"Ahhh..." she laughs, trying to be cute.

"Seriously, why don't you sing? All ya gotta do is *lean into the mic.*"

"I know, I know. I just forgot. I'm mostly just listening," she fumbles through her lyric sheets.

"You have a great voice, ya know, and we worked out some really nice harmonies. Did you forget?"

"No...!" she wants to change the subject.

"Do you really want to sing with us, Maya?"

She leans forward and slowly whispers, "I am having...problems...in my relationship."

"What d'ya mean?"

She whispers again, her eyes bulging with what she cannot say, "I can't...talk about it...right now."

Poem looks back at Tony who's smiling and chatting with Marcus. "But you're all right. You guys aren't breaking up or anything."

"We'll talk...later...okay?"

Poem turns to face the band, still not comprehending.

Tony says, "That was cool, Poem!"

"Uh... thanks, man. Good job on the bridge."

Marcus gets sentimental, like taking a knee at half-time, "Boys, we been rehearsing a lot and it's comin' along, it's comin' along." He searches his pockets for a lighter, "But we are there. We are *frickin* there!"

"Yo I'm headin' out," Poem says. "You comin'?"

Tony says no and Marcus says, "Yo, wait for me!"

Poem passes Maya, who slinks around him, and grabs his cigarettes and sunglasses and opens the door. An explosion of sunlight pierces the warm dingy room. He recoils, puts on his shades and presses through. Shuffling down the stairs, through the propped-open grey metal door, Marcus follows and the two emerge into the late afternoon heat of a gorgeous summer day. There in the bleak industrial street, standing next to Poem's Z28, they light up cigarettes as Marcus beams, "Man, it's goin' on, it's goin' on."

"It's sounding good," Poem agrees.

"Yeah, Tony is cool, man, very cool."

"I'm so lookin' forward to giggin' again, Marcus. I feel like it's been so long since we been out there. We really have to promote this one, man. People gotta know we exist!"

"I hear you." Marcus takes a drag. "Hey, why you always tryin' to get Maya in there, man? I don't think she really wanna sing."

"Ya think?"

"Uh uh, nooo."

"Funny. Mantriji said the same thing, that she won't allow herself to be heard because she's got Saturn in the 2nd house."

"So then why you tryin' to make her sing?"

"Man, she keeps saying she wants to sing and she comes to every rehearsal so why be fatalistic?"

"Man, are you still uptight about your singin'?"

Poem looks away.

"Man, every time you get a chance, you always tryin' to back yourself with someone else. I notice that about you."

"Dude, I'm a great guitar player but let's face it, I'm not a great singer. If we could have her doin' harmonies and eventually some lead, shit, that would be cool."

"Well if Master G says it ain't gonna happen then how you think it's gonna happen?"

Poem shakes his head while Marcus looks down at the road. "Hey Marcus, I'm not sure what to make of this but when I asked Maya just now why she wasn't coming in, she said—well, she whispered to me…"

Maya suddenly emerges through the doorway holding her purse, looking ready to leave. She spots the duo and nervously walks over. "I'm sorry, Poem, that I haven't been singing. It's just that, well, fuck… I'm having serious problems with Tony."

"What?!" Marcus reacts sharply.

"What's the problem?" Poem says.

"Ah, it's complicated. I don't know," she looks down. "I just told him right now, I want out."

"What?!" Marcus erupts.

"I don't wanna live with him no more. I feel like I'm suffocating!" she looks up.

"Wait a minute," Poem is beside himself. "Are you saying you and Tony are breaking up?"

"I know you didn't see it coming, Poem, but it's been building. He's giving me shit after rehearsals when you're not there. He says I should learn my parts better and not be so timid."

"Well you should."

"Hey, I dunno what's happening! All I know is I love you guys and I love your music and I just wanna be a part of it in some way," she is upset and beginning to shake.

Poem puts his hand on her shoulder, "But you have such an amazing voice, Maya. You just have to get over your shyness."

"I know but… I don't know," she looks down.

"What the rass is going on here?" Marcus says and Poem wants to hug her,

"So… what does this mean, Maya? Are you outta the band or what? How's Tony takin' it?"

"I don't think too well. He just told me he wants to quit music."

"WHAT?!" Marcus can't believe it.

"Yeah. He's packing up right now."

"Awww," Marcus groans and drops his weight onto the car like all the air has been let out of him.

"We just had another fight and we're done! He wants to quit music."

"I don't believe this!" Marcus is shocked. "We just put in, what, two months of rehearsin' with you guys?" He understands full well what this means. He and Poem have lost count of how many drummers they've auditioned and played with over the years. He flashes back to all the rehearsal spots, the endless back and forth, the disappointments, the wasted nights. He utters a meek Trinidadian, "Oh no."

"Fuck that. I'm gonna talk to him," Poem says.

"Me too," Marcus follows.

Poem flicks his cigarette into the street and looks at Maya and her purse, "Are you all right? What're you gonna do?"

She wonders what he's feeling inside, if he knows. "I'm heading home." She starts towards Junction Road and they watch her march away, not knowing what to do. They look at each other and suddenly come to: "Tony!" They rush through the doorway and up the stairs to find their wounded drummer packing his gear.

"What'cha doin', Tony?" Marcus says as they approach.

"I'm packin' up, man. I'm done."

"Dude, what's going on?" Poem says.

"Man, I fucking hate music!"

"What?!"

"I FUCKING HATE MUSIC!"

"Tony, what's up with you?!"

"What, she didn't tell you?!"

"She said you were breaking up."

"Yeah, that's right!"

"But Tony, we love you, man. You guys are really cool. What happened? Does this have anything to do with the band?"

"I'm not gonna talk about it, Poem!"

"So what's that…? You're done? Just like that?!"

"Yeah, just like that."

Poem looks at the floor as Marcus lets out a disapproving, "Mm Mm Mm!"

"Well at least you still have a singer, right?" Tony says awkwardly and Poem looks at him surprised,

"Dude, we don't need a singer, we need a drummer!"

"Sorry, man. I need to take a break. I really, really like you guys, I really do. I just need a break, okay?"

"So we'll call you?" Marcus says.

"Don't bother. Just pack up your gear. I'm done!" he sweeps his hands.

Poem and Marcus with great solemnity slowly pack up their stuff and walk out, wishing Tony well.

Down the stairs into the lot, in a trance, guitar cases in hand, it is one of those moments when everything you've worked for comes crashing down around you like a hail of broken egg shells. They robotically pack their stuff into Poem's car and close the hatchback, lean against it and light up cigarettes, both not knowing what to say. They silently smoke and gaze into the distance, like having just learned the death of a loved one. Two minutes into their contemplation, Tony races down the stairs and stops to look at them one last time, "See ya, guys." He heads towards Junction Road and they watch him disappear, wondering if he'll catch up to Maya.

"Can you fucking believe this, Marcus?"

"Man, I am shocked. I don't know what just happened."

Poem looks at the ground then up at the skyline, "Ya know, Marcus, it sure hasn't been easy with you and me."

"No it hasn't."

"I don't know why that is. We're good people, not hurting anyone, but every time things start looking good, something always happens and… I feel like I need a change."

Marcus tries to read his face. "So what're you sayin'?"

Poem takes a deep breath and looks east over the urban landscape, "After Burt left for that girl, man, I told myself I would put music down for a bit or change it up in some way. I like writing, Marcus, *you* know that, and now I'm studying Jyotish. I'm tired of all these drummers dragging another six months out of us and we get no further ahead because just as things start flowing, they up and leave because of some girl."

"Yeah."

"You know I can always go back to New Orleans."

"Yeah?"

"In fact, I'm beginning to think I *should* go. Monique's cousin is offering to cover my flight, pay me in cash, even lend me her mother's car, if I could just take care of her son for a couple months."

"What're you a babysitter now?"

"Well, at least I'll be a babysitter in *New Orleans*."

"You said he was a spoiled brat."

"Well that's why they need me. I'm the only one the kid respects. And I think I can help him, Marcus. Plus, Malabar's gonna lay me off till Halloween cuz it's the end of opera season. And now no band?!"

It sinks in that once again they are drummerless.

"I'm just gonna go and see what happens. Take some CDs. Maybe I'll get lucky."

"I don't know if I like that idea, my man. What's gonna happen to me?

You gonna just leave me here?"

"Listen, Marcus. How long we been at this?! How many drummers is this?! It ain't happening, man! I wanna be in New Orleans."

"Man, that's all you been talkin' 'bout this whole friggin year!"

"That's cuz it's the coolest city in the world, man! Listen, *we're* good, but who in Toronto, really, in *Toronto* is gonna sign us to a deal? It's all pop shit here!"

"I know."

"This could be an amazing opportunity."

Marcus reluctantly concedes, "Well... y'know, the States really is where the shit happens but I don't know about you takin' off like that. Is Monique cool with it?"

"Are you kidding? It was her idea!"

"Whatchoo talkin' 'bout?"

"We're still going through a bit of a rough spell, y'know?" he looks down. "She's pissed that I didn't attend her salsa competition—she's apparently very good now—but I don't know. Do I really wanna go watch her tear it up with someone else?"

"Yeah, he'll probably have his hands all over her."

"Thanks, man. In the meantime, she's bugging me to get married and buy the house but all I can think about is oh God…"

"Still no sex?"

"Aww man," Poem groans.

"Aww man," Marcus feels his pain.

The two are silent and cranky now. They discard their cigarettes and Marcus says, "Well you ain't exactly ugly, my man, so why you think that is?"

"I think she's holding out till we get married."

"So she's holding you hostage."

"Seems that way."

"You wanna have kids?"

"I dunno, Marcus. I want my children to inherit my wealth, not my struggle."

"That's a good policy, man."

"Yeah I know. But until *we* start making money, I just don't wanna make that commitment."

Marcus shrugs, "Makes sense to me."

"Yeah, but in the meantime I gotta live like a priest."

Marcus takes a deep breath and shakes his head, "Well, I don't know what to say, my man."

"Listen, I'll just go. The separation will do us good. We've been living together four years, y'know?"

"Yeah, well… Just be careful. She's a sweet thing. She may have plans of her own."

"I know. But if she needs to get something out of her system then let her. I don't wanna be around. I feel like I got some things I need to get outta *my* system, y'know?"

"Tell me about it."

"I'll just go and see what happens. Free rent, American money, a car."

"Sure. Check it out. Just remember to come back."

"Don't worry, Marcus. It'll be mostly business."

"Yeah… Business…"

"Yeah. And it won't cost me a thing."

11 PREDICTION

It is a beautiful summer day. Poem sits across from Mantri who smiles benevolently, flipping through a small book in Hindi, his head cleanly shaved. His skin resembles moulded copper with fine lines creased into his forehead like folds of silk. The balcony door is wide open and a warm breeze punctuates the room. Poem has firmly decided to go to New Orleans. He is anxious to hear what Mantri thinks but will wait till the end of the lesson to tell him.

Mantri finds his page and looks up over his reading glasses, "How are you, Poem?"

"Oh I'm good, Sir. And you?"

He laughs in his jovial way, "I am *good!*"

Poem looks out his balcony door to the lush green foliage overhanging the rail. A black squirrel explores the limb and there's the sound of pigeons cooing nearby. "Do you have pigeons on your balcony, Sir?"

"Yes, they made a home here last week," he glosses the page.

"And you just let them stay?"

Mantri looks up, "They are about to be parents, Poem. It would be wrong for me to chase them away."

"It doesn't bother you?"

"They have greater concerns than me. It is not easy raising young. It is God's gift."

"You know they're just rats with wings, right?"

Mantri laughs. "I am helping their karma."

Poem shakes his head, "How can you stand that constant cooing?"

"It is the sound of love, Poem. Everyone falls in love in the spring. This is the way it is. I cannot stand in the way of it."

"Well, you're a better man than me."

"Oh no," Mantri chuckles. "You are a good man. You just need to learn patience."

"Realistically, will that ever happen?"

"You *are* patient. Just allow it to be."

Mantri stands up with book in hand and approaches the blackboard. He draws a natal chart, fills in the natural zodiac and begins, "It is very important for anyone to understand their Svabhava, that is, their fundamental nature," he circles the 1st house. "Otherwise, he may walk blindly through life never fully understanding his purpose, his challenges and strengths. Some may find it and they shine. Others roam about never fully centred. In this mixed up world, no one knows their nature anymore. They have no way of finding it. They are in school early, learning the system, the system becomes second nature to them and they lose themselves to it. Even if he has a strong chart, we must look to *when* he will run the opportune time. You've read Vimshottari Dasa system?"

"Yes."

"Speak." Mantri leans next to the chalkboard.

"Well, this is a system of timing based on when certain planets become active in the chart. Otherwise they are latent."

"Very good."

"And according to the position of planets in the signs—"

"Not signs. Houses. The signs are the native. If he has watery planets in Taurus then he has phlegm throat, he is spitting all the time, because Taurus is the 2nd sign, the throat." He scribbles a rudimentary body next to the chart. "The 1st sign is Aries, the head," he cups his head. "The last is Pisces, the feet," he looks down then continues while touching each corresponding body part, "Taurus is the face, nose, mouth. Gemini is the twins, the two arms. Cancer is the chest, the feeling part, the mother. Leo is the upper stomach, or solar plexus. Virgo is the loins, the lean virgin. Libra is the hips, the balance of the native. It is the midway point between Aries and Pisces, between torso and legs."

"Cool. I like how you explain it."

"Scorpio is the 8th sign, the penis, or sexual organ of the native. Next is Sagittarius, the thighs," he rubs his outer thigh, "like a horse. Capricorn is the goat that depends on its knees. It signifies our ability to stand alone."

Poem scribbles away in his notebook.

"Aquarius is the calves; it is a human sign. The water bearer leans over to pour from the pot," he poses like a discus thrower, "and reveals the strength of his calf. Pisces we know. Where we find planets in these signs we would expect either good things, like big chest in Cancer, nice waist in Libra, or bad things, like weak knees if Capricorn is afflicted. Do you know this girl Lucy? She is Carmel's friend. Big breasts!" his eyes light up.

"Ho yeah," Poem remembers.

Mantri draws a quick chart on the board, "She is Cancer lagna with

Jupiter deposited and her Moon is strong—I think 5th or 7th house. Big breasts!"

"Yeah I remember."

"We know this other woman, Sue." He erases the chart and quickly draws another, "She is Leo lagna with Sun in her 10th. We would expect large shoulders, big breasts, but Sun is conjoined Saturn. This Saturn restricts that part of her, that most prominent upper body part of Leo. She should be a lion, *big* upper body, *strong* arms, like a king. Instead, she is meek on top, frail shoulders, small boobs."

"Hmm."

"In this case, Saturn is afflicting her ruler, the Sun, lord of Leo, and it is aspecting her Moon, the mother, in Cancer. The upper chest, shoulders, boobs, is all being suppressed by Saturn."

Poem nods. He is getting the idea.

"Saturn is in Taurus so maybe some kind of skin problem on the face or bad nose."

"She told me she had a nose job."

"Ahhh, you see? She must have been running Saturn."

"Hmm... Amazing."

"Mars will give him cuts and burns in that part of his body in which it sits or aspects. Look for moles. Saturn, depending on what sign it occupies, we could see weak knees, bad kidneys, im-potency, headaches. But do not predict disease or injury till the dasa comes."

"The planetary period."

"That's right."

"And this tells you which signs and houses become active and at what times."

"You got it!"

"And that part of the body *afflicted* by a planet will experience some kind of injury or illness when that planet runs its period."

"Right."

"And the *timing* of that planetary period is determined by the position of the Moon at the moment you were born."

"That's right. Time of birth should be *precise* for this system to work."

"So then from that time onward, from the moment of your birth, you fall into a fixed sequence of planetary periods that recur on smaller and smaller scales and every time you enter a new period, certain houses in the chart are activated to reap that part of your karma that can't unfold all at once."

"Very good!" Mantri beams.

"So if your 10th house, or career house, is activated by a strong planet, you could get a promotion."

"You *will* get a promotion!"

"And if the 10th house is afflicted, you lose your job or have to accept one you don't really want."

"Very good," Mantri looks at Poem with the pride a father feels for his maturing son. He knows the challenges Western minds face when learning something as ethereal as Jyotish. Every subtle breakthrough is important in building conceptual platforms and sometimes the simplest things you learn last.

"So can I ask you something, Sir? This system of prediction, as the author describes it, is predicated on humans living to a 120 years. Isn't that a little optimistic?"

"Humans lived longer in ancient times, Poem. 120 years was considered a normal life span when these rules were written."

"Really? Because I always thought we live longer now than ever before."

"This is European civilization and it is based on recent history, maybe just the past two thousand years."

"This is recent?"

"Oh yes. There are many stories, including in the Bible, of people living hundreds of years. Moses died at 120 years."

"But isn't that just an exaggeration?"

"These stories are far older than what most people think. They are passed on from a much earlier time. Noah's flood is the same flood of Gilgamesh, same story. Many cultures speak of a flood in ancient times. We don't know what happened, only that all cultures speak of this event and of people living much longer than we do now. In India today you will still find men in the mountains who are 150 years old."

"Really?!"

"Oh yes. We think we are advanced because we have fancy computers and pills, but a man who lives in harmony with nature, who lives a slow-paced life, no electricity, who eats the right foods in the right season, who understands how to breathe, what to talk, when to bathe, when to have sex, when not to; this man is living a natural life."

Poem bites on his upper lip, wondering whether or not to believe this. He recalls a story from the BBC. "You know, Mantriji, I saw this report on the news once about this yogi in India who was supposed to have lived without water or food for like, years. He was brought to this hospital where the doctors claimed he hadn't eaten or drank anything in three days! He didn't even produce urine."

Mantri's eyes light up.

"The yogi said he had been living this way for many years, no water or food, and there he was in this sterile room, a complete anachronism, locked up like some prisoner."

"Tsk tsk tsk," Mantri clicks his palette, shaking his head.

"The doctor said he was a living miracle! They couldn't explain it. *He* said he does it through some yogic discipline—I think it was goddess worship?"

"Right."

"And get this. They said they were 'monitoring' him to figure out how he does it so they can train their soldiers how to survive times of scarcity or imprisonment. You think they're gonna teach goddess worship to the military now?"

Mantri shakes his head.

"And the reporter goes on about how these men are the source of India's myths about great sages. In other words, he denigrated it to the myth file! And yet, there he was in the flesh, sitting right behind him, this old man living on nothing but the air he breathes and the reporter is talking myths?!"

"This is the way of the world, Poem."

"This should be friggin front page news! A man living without water or food?! Come on! Instead they say, 'We'll keep him under observation.' I bet he could live the next *year* without water or food and it still wouldn't make front page news because some senator will have had an affair with a male prostitute! In fact, we'll probably never hear about it again and if you tell someone, they'll say 'impossible,' but how many stories you think they run on UFOs in America? Amazing. A miracle sitting in a hospital bed and no one sees it," he shakes his head.

"No one wants to believe that which he cannot explain. It is very difficult for the ego to accept this."

"So they just turn their backs?"

"If the ego cannot accept it, there is nothing we can do."

"But then how do we trust anything we hear? It's all opinion, like Richard Dawkins."

"Who?"

"Oh some scientist—I think he's a scientist. He goes around telling people if they believe in God, they're delusional."

"Hmm."

"Yeah, he puts everything into what they call Neo-Darwinism. He's obviously never had a religious experience so he dismisses people who *have* as crazy. And he's considered to be a great man, a man of science—you know the type; he has tremendous faith in his point of view."

"Hah, good one," Mantri smiles.

"I once heard him in an interview when he was asked, 'What about all these inspired religious works like Bach's Mass in B minor'—which is a favourite of his. 'Could such profound works have been produced without believing in the supernatural?' You know what he said?" He puts on a stuffy voice, "'Oh these things could have been written without believing in

God.'"

Mantri laughs.

"Yeah, like they would have composed a sacred mass to Science," he rolls his eyes. "He totally misses the point!"

"Poem, these men are great in their field but they are in their egos and so they are limited. They have no understanding of the divine. They are just limited."

"But if you try to talk to one, they'll look down on you, say you're deluded. They'll get their colleagues to gang up on you, kick you out of the association, revoke your membership, discredit you for not being 'scientific.'"

"This is the way of the world, Poem. It is upbringing, conditioning, life experience, that makes people believe what they believe."

"Yeah, but it's *his* belief! Just like a Christian believes in the Jesus metaphor, *he* believes in a mechanical world devoid of meaning, of poetry, of wonder."

"Everyone believes in something, even if it is in nothing."

"Yeah but it's the intolerance I can't stand."

"But now you are being intolerant towards him," Mantri tilts his head.

"I like science, Mantriji, and yes, there is a lot to learn from Neo-Darwinists but there is a great deal to be learned from the mystics and sages too. So I'm not really being intolerant towards him so much as pointing out his intolerance towards others."

"It is all the same," Mantri says.

"Well, let me tell you one thing I saw on the internet."

"On the computer?"

"Yeah, on the computer."

Mantri leans against the wall.

"It was some kind of lecture he was giving to what looked like a roomful of scientists. This one guy, who looked like everyone else, gets up and asks, 'In all your years of investigating this question of God, have you ever come across *anything* that you couldn't explain, that would give you at least *some* pause?' Without blinking or thinking, Dawkins looks at the guy and says 'No!' in this smug English tone. No elaboration, no humility."

"Tsk tsk tsk," Mantri shakes his head.

"And the audience erupts into a *standing ovation*, like they had all just won a new car!"

Mantri can't believe it.

"Now think about it, Mantriji. Not only did he completely dismiss the guy, but all his cronies, this group of scientists, or engineers, or whatever they were, jumped up in adulation, not only to support what he said, but to belittle the one guy who had the nerve to ask! It was one of the most ignorant displays I'd ever seen, and from a roomful of scientists!"

"Science or no science, Poem. People are people and they will cut off the heads of others to make themselves feel taller."

"But what do you say to atheists who are convinced they are right?"

"Atheists are like rebellious children who don't fully understand or respect their parent's authority. They are better off being Buddhists."

"Why do you say that?"

"Because there is no God in Buddhism. There is only Nirvana. They could learn a great deal about the mind and themselves from Buddhists and they don't have to believe in God to do so."

"Well I find it frustrating. I'm not even religious but somehow this level of bigotry against religion? I understand why people think religion is responsible for so many of the world's ills, but it's not guns that kill, right? It's people who kill."

"It is bullets that kill, but let us complete our lesson."

"Sure, Mantriji. Sorry."

"No no. It is better to think too much than to think too little."

Mantri resumes writing as he speaks, "Now, the planetary periods, or dasas, last 6 to 20 years, and the sub-periods, or bhuktis, can be from a few months to three years. Still, smaller periods break down into months, weeks and sometimes days. If we were to continue to calculate downward, this same sequence, into smaller and smaller periods, we would see that ah hah, this moment is Venus, and in two minutes it will be Sun, and in less than a minute it will be Moon, then Mars, followed by Rahu, and Jupiter, and so on." He draws a crude pyramid scheme on the board.

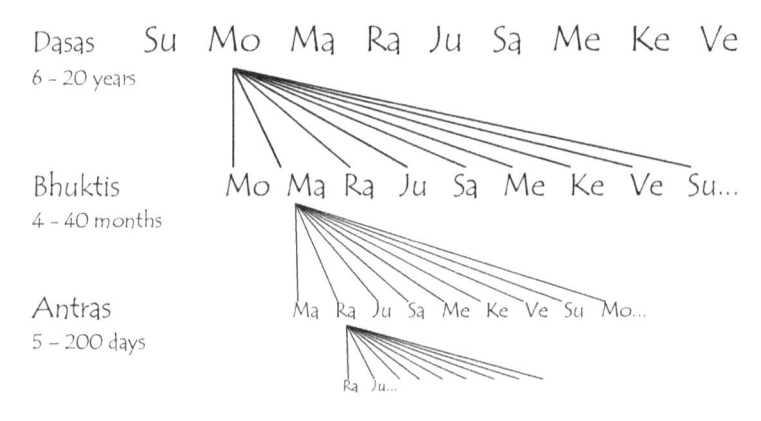

Dasas   Su Mo Ma Ra Ju Sa Me Ke Ve
6 – 20 years

Bhuktis   Mo Ma Ra Ju Sa Me Ke Ve Su...
4 – 40 months

Antras   Ma Ra Ju Sa Me Ke Ve Su Mo...
5 – 200 days
                Ra Ju...

"...Like this, so that our predictions could, if we have the *exact* time of birth, be good down to the minute, even to each breath."

"Wow. You can really predict down to each breath?"

"Day or week is good enough."

Poem looks at his notes as Mantri continues, "Each of these planetary periods, fixed in their order, is activated when its time comes. Then according to their significations, we make the prediction that *this* part of the karma will fructify for better or worse because it is *time*!"

"So a season for everything."

"That's right. It can't all happen at once, no. Karma takes time and this is the sequence in which it unfolds."

"But how do they know this? I mean, where does this system come from?"

"No one knows where it comes from, only that it was very old when it was first written. The oral tradition is very big in India. Astrology is much older than books. It is older than written knowledge. The ancients had no electricity for lights, no paper for writing, they watched the starry sky. This was the paper on which they wrote their lives. No television, only the sky, only their environment. They were *focused*!" he raises his forefinger.

"No distractions."

"No. Just them and nature. The Rishis were very learned, very insightful men. They had their Einsteins and Darwins. They were the academic priests of their time, before separation, before material science. They knew higher mathematics, how to infer and categorize, when to plant, when to predict famine, when to war, how to appease the Gods."

"The Indians came up with the idea of infinity and nothingness, right?"

"That's right. They had *big* numbers and very small numbers."

"So if anyone could come up with a method for cycles, it would be the ancients who were around long enough to observe it for thousands of years."

"The ancients were very smart men. They were patient and observed through *generations*. They had foresight. They handed down their knowledge knowing they themselves would inherit it. Sometimes the entire lineage of a family is in one pursuit, like medicine or scripture or astrology. They knew everything comes in cycles. They witnessed it over centuries. No one knows why some dasas are short and others are long, only that these calculations are old, that is, they have *stood up* against the test of time. They are the map and directions to your karma, what to expect and when."

"So this solves everything!" Poem rubs his chin, gazing out the window at a stream of white cloud. "Our lives are 'forecastable' down to the minute, down to each breath, based on a mathematical system formulated in ancient times by the savants of India using astronomy as their base."

"Everything we do, from the most mundane things, like striking a match, to the epic weddings and funerals of our lives, all these things become permissible, *probable*," he raises his finger, "at the appropriate time based on *this* system, the Vimshottari dasa system."

"Hmm."

"Our solar system is one big clock and the universe is unfolding as it should," he taps the board with his chalk. "The planets reveal a migration of souls, dying and resurrecting, landing here and there, born at the appropriate time for *their* karma, like migrations of, what you call, 'salmon,' swimming back to their source to spawn and die. Our solar system is swimming with individuated life forms, either embodied or disembodied, trying to elevate their consciousness to become a better fish, a plentiful crop, a more successful bird, an actual human being."

"Wow!"

"These life forms, whether individuated consciousness or part of a group soul, come from *somewhere*. Consciousness does not die merely because it is no longer in a physical body, no. Each one of these individuated forms has gone through hundreds of thousands of lives, starting as a plant and making its way up to mammal and now human. With all this inertia behind each individual, it gives everyone a time and place to be born, only when it is fit to be born, and is part of a generational migration of souls trying to get back to the Godhead."

Poem is in awe, absorbing this cosmology. He puts down his pen and listens.

"Humans have a central 'I' or sense of being or cognition, but their lives are bound to larger cycles, or recurrences. They find themselves born, living what has been offered, making the most of it according to their strengths and weaknesses and reaping what rewards come their way, sometimes wondering why and how it all happened. Some struggle, others do not, or in a different way, and this is how one reads karma. This man suffers because he is hungry; this man suffers because he is insatiable. Both experience suffering but for different reasons. Many make the same mistake over and over and will continue to do so until they develop self-awareness. You've read Nietzsche?"

"A little."

"Our karma is in the inertia, or cause and effect, of the solar system, and here we are playing it out like puppets who think we're the sock instead of the hand."

Poem feels like he has just been given the Rosetta Stone of astrology, "So this is how we predict our lives."

"Slowly, slowly," Mantri warns. "Now we must take into account the *transit* of the planets."

"Nooo," Poem groans. "It's just getting harder again."

Mantri laughs. "Astrology is not an easy subject, Poem. You must study many charts, not just one, two, no. You must study *hundreds* of charts to get a feel for it, to understand the subtleties. Ask your friends, whoever you know, even a little, ask them for their time of birth. *See* their chart.

Research. Why did it work? Why didn't it work? See why this man looks this way, why this man prospered or fell from grace or was fired or married during this time or that."

"But how do we know *what* to predict?"

"When the lord of a house is activated, it gives the results of the houses it rules. The results of these houses will be experienced through the house in which the lord sits."

Mantri erases the board and draws Poem's chart.

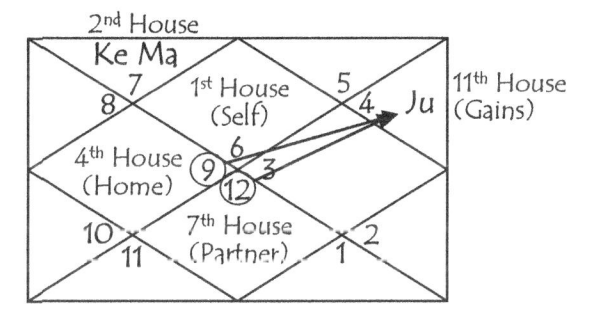

```
                 2nd House
                 Ke Ma
              7            5            11th House
             8     1st House   4  Ju    (Gains)
                   (Self)
                        6
             4th House  9
             (Home)     12    3
                 7th House         2
            10   (Partner)    1
             11
```

Pointing with the chalk, he says, "You are in Jupiter dasa and your Jupiter is exalted in the 11th house. Jupiter in this chart rules 4th and 7th houses. The 4th is home, the 7th is partner; the 11th is the house of gains. You have made a home and gained tremendous support from your girlfriends."

"That's true. And y'know, it reminds me of an old joke. What d'ya call a musician without a girlfriend?"

Mantri shrugs.

"Homeless."

Mantri laughs and the two men slap hands.

"This is good one," he says. "But you are now in Mars bhukti, a sub-period of Jupiter dasa. You feel impetuous, sexual, and you want to speak your mind, but my advice to you is don't say it. First write down on piece of paper five times what you want to say and ask yourself why? If you have no good reason, don't say it. It is probably nonsense. If you have to say it, wait a day and then say it. But it is better to just let this time pass."

"Really?"

"Uh," he nods.

"Why?"

"Mars is in your 2nd house: family, food, money. It is with Ketu. You want to smoke, drink alcohol, you will have a mystical experience. Just don't break your family."

"Really?!" This is not good news. Poem bites his lower lip before announcing, "Well, Sir, I've decided I'm going to New Orleans for two months."

"Oh?"

"Yeah. You know how I was down there for a week over New Year's Eve and again in April? Well, I really like it, Mantriji, and I'm sort of sick of Toronto. Our drummer just quit and I'm being laid off work… So now I have an opportunity to go!"

Mantri is caught off guard. He sits down. "To play music?"

"Well, I'm taking my guitar so I'll try and play somewhere."

"But how are you living down there?"

"I'm staying with Monique's cousin where we stayed before. She needs someone to look after her son. In fact, she's paying me American money and providing a car."

"How old is the boy?"

"Nine."

Mantri looks at him doubtfully, "Poem, what do you want taking care of this child?"

"I think I can help him, Mantriji. Plus, I figure when I'm down there, it'll be a good opportunity to meet people, you know, in the music biz."

Mantri takes a deep breath and reconsiders. "Well, then you must go."

"Yeah, I think it may be a good time to meet people."

"We'll see."

"What do *you* think, Mantriji?"

"I think you have better things to do than baby-sit a child. You are a philosopher, man! You are doing UofT Philosophy! Don't you have classes coming up?"

"I still wanna do that, Mantriji, but I'm just looking at this as an opportunity."

"What about your classes?"

"I'm postponing till January."

Mantri shakes his head.

"Look, if I can't accomplish something on this trip and I see that I'm still getting nowhere then I decided I'm gonna give music a rest for a while and just focus on writing, astrology, and going to school."

"Philosophy!"

"Yes. But right now I'm going to New Orleans."

"And blow off some steam."

Poem looks confused.

"You are running Mars, Poem. Mars always has to let off steam. Your Mars is in Libra, so you will release it through people. It is a fiery planet in the 2nd house of food. You will drink alcohol; you will exhaust this part of your karma. You lost your drummer and now your job. Is this good news?"

"Not really."

"And you are in Mars bhukti. What do you expect to find there?"

"I just wanna go, Mantriji. Can you tell me what will happen?"

Mantri lifts his hands into prayer position. "We will see what happens."

"What do *you* think will happen?"

"I think you will come back and resume your studies next year."

"I'll be back in October. Do you think I'll get a record deal?"

"We'll see what happens," he doesn't want to say more.

"Okay, Sir. Well, that's the plan. I'm leaving in August and I'll be back by Halloween."

Mantri pulls out an ephemeris and flips to the appropriate page. He pens a line next to October 31 and surveys the planetary positions for that month. Poem is waiting for some insight. "We will see you in October then," Mantri says.

"No prediction?"

"You will have a good time," he smiles, but Poem sees he is not pleased.

"I'll still be around till August."

"That's good. We will continue with dasa system. Namaste," he abruptly stands.

"Okay, Sir. Namaste."

Poem feels an awkward twinge of guilt as he pulls out his wallet and customarily slips a 20 dollar note under the coffee mug pen holder. This is neither the insight nor rosy prediction he was hoping for. He smiles insincerely, eases up out of his chair and heads for the door, knapsack in hand. Looking back at Mantri, he says, "See you next week, Sir."

"Namaste."

Act 2 – Passion

♂

New Orleans Loka
(Rajas)

1 ROUTINE NEW ORLEANS

Poem finds a parking spot next to Sacred Heart Elementary. He's 15 minutes early. Bebop music with saxophone soloing rings out of the 90.7FM frequency: Louisiana heritage music you don't hear anyplace else. As usual, pockets of after-school uniformed children mill about on the sidewalk, in the pickup zone, as cars come and go. There is gabbing, playacting, screeching and laughing, as teachers chat and make sure everyone gets off safely. Poem wonders whether to have a cigarette so he turns off the idling motor and steps out into the dense sunny heat. He locks the doors and heads down General Pershing Street, smoking a Marlboro that goes down like chocolate. Turning towards Napoleon, he flicks his spent cigarette and stops to wipe his sweaty brow. *Oh the humidity!*

Around the lush fenced-in field, he strolls up the side entrance walkway into the almost empty, air-conditioned school. Past the gymnasium and to the music room, he looks through the small rectangular window and sees Julien and Maggie at the piano. He opens the door quietly. Maggie looks up and smiles as Julien types away in mid-recital. He winks back and quietly slides into one of the chairs. Julien finishes and he claps bravo, startling him.

"Hey Poem!" Julien blushes and Maggie declares,

"Good job, Julien. You're really improving." She looks at the clock, "Okay, that's all for today but nice playing!"

"Yay!" he quickly gathers his books as Poem approaches the piano,

"Hello, Miss Harris."

"Hello, Mister Poem," she stands up to greet him.

"Sounds good, Julien," Poem ruffles his curly brown hair.

"Thanks. Can we go now?"

"That's why I'm here."

"Popeye's?"

"I have something better."

Julien groans.

Poem turns to Maggie, "So how you been, girl?"

"I'm a little wiped. Was out late with Sean and his cousins from Baton Rouge. Saw Carol Tate and the Black Suede's at Checkpoint Charlie's."

"Oh yeah?"

"They were awesome! I know the fiddle player, Danielle. We went to the same school."

Maggie is a freckly beauty with curly light-brown hair and a tall fleshy body. Originally from Denver she is earthy yet dreamy and likes the Grateful Dead, one thing Poem could never get. He met her his first week here, picking up Julien from his lesson. They've since become good friends.

"Can we go now?" Julien whines.

"Yes, we're going." Poem turns to Maggie, "So we still good for Friday?"

"Definitely. I think maybe just meet me at my place. I have some friends I wanna introduce you to. We can head out from there, aw right?" she winks.

"Aw right," he winks back.

"Okay Julien," she finishes. "Don't forget to practice your etudes."

"I know," he groans.

"See you, Miss Harris," Poem says and she gives them a double thumbs-up.

They leave and walk down the hall out into the swampy heat, Julien whining for air conditioning while Poem leads the way. He unlocks the doors and Julien contemptuously tosses his bulging knapsack into the back then climbs in front. Poem shuts the doors behind him and rounds the car to the driver's side.

"Can we listen to—?"

"No!" Poem knows he wants Q93 Rap.

"Why...?" he fidgets.

"I told you, Julien. You can listen to it on your own time but when you're with me it's *live* music, okay? No computer music, got it?"

"Yeah," Julien groans. "What's the difference?"

"The difference is one is performed, the other is manufactured."

"I know. Robot music," he does his spastic android routine.

"I'm not saying it's robot music. I just want you to understand how to play from beginning to end and not just program what someone else did. You're learning to be a musician and yo, you know you've improved. You heard Miss Harris. And pretty soon I'm gonna have you improvising too, ya hear?"

Julien isn't listening. He knows what's coming and looking ahead Poem anticipates it too. Seeing it first, that blessed red, blue and yellow sign, Julien erupts, "Can we have Popeye's tonight, Poem, please!?! We didn't eat there all week!!"

"Julien, it's Wednesday! Chill out! Plus you just had it on the weekend!"

"I know, but it's *sooo* good. Can we just eat there tonight, please?!"

"Look, it's not good to eat Popeye's everyday, okay?" Poem doesn't dare tell him he had it last night. "Don't worry. I have something good at home."

"What...?" Julien pouts, uninterested. He stares out the window, imagining a plump breaded drumstick in his hand. He raises the phantom chicken leg and simulates it crashing like a doomed airplane into a tub of red beans and rice with delicious gravy splashing everywhere.

This is the routine of Poem's daily life here. His duties begin when Julien's school day ends. He picks him up and they drive home either up Napoleon or around St Charles. Poem will ask him what he's learning and Julien will say nothing. He will beg Poem for Q93 Rap and Poem will say no. Poem will ask what do you mean nothing and Julien will plead for Popeye's and Poem will four out of five times say no. They'll arrive home and Julien will race to the house, forgetting his bag, to greet his always enthusiastic and salivating brown Lab. They will walk the dog together while Poem waxes on prepubescent psychological and sociological themes then Julien has an hour of play time for friends and basketball before supper and homework. Poem will help with assignments and piano until Lynette arrives and she will happily take it from there.

It's not a bad life although it's starting to feel routine and he's got a month to go. He's made a few friends, seen a lot of bands, played a couple open mics, and sat in on a jam. During the day he reads a lot, mostly philosophy and astrology, memorizing planets in the signs. He cleans the house once a week, keeps correspondence through email, runs errands for the family, visits with friends, walks the dog—especially lately because he has worms—and now he's beginning to write the verses to an idea he has for a musical. He likes being here but he misses Mantriji and Monique's childlike smile and laughter.

"Are you and Miss Harris in love?" Julien pokes his glasses back, scanning the couples in a bustling street-side patio.

Poem is amused, "Julien, I am not in love with Miss Harris. I like her. She is my friend, that's all."

"But you're a boy and she's a girl."

"It is possible for boys and girls to be just friends."

"Girls are stupidheads."

"Your mother is a girl."

"No she's not. She's my mom. I mean the girls at school."

"You just don't understand them. *We* think like boys and *they* think like girls. We're opposites and really, it's a wonder we get along. But somehow we do and if we didn't there would be no *you!*" he pokes him and Julien makes a squishy face.

Julien is a bright, hyperactive nine-year-old with a boyish frame, curly brown hair and a phlegmatic mouth. His defining feature is his full-rimmed Buddy Holley style prescription glasses. He seeks attention by being difficult, saying things like, "I just don't see why they even have to exist."

"Girls?"

"Yeah."

"You're crazy." Poem looks in his rear-view mirror and poses a grand philosophical question, "Ya ever notice how you need a cup to hold your drink?"

Julien twists his head.

"Y'see, a cup ain't a cup unless there's something to drink out of it, and a drink ain't a drink unless there's a cup to hold it. Get it?"

Julien has no idea what he's talking about.

"So the two need each other like a man needs a woman. They *full-fill* each other, thus finding their purpose and identity."

Julien has a rare quiet moment as he contemplates.

"Don't you like any girls at school?"

Julien takes a few seconds before answering no.

"Well, that will change, believe me."

They make it home and the routine unfolds. Lynette arrives an hour and a half later with equal fanfare from the dog. Having eaten at the office and Julien already fed, she relishes in just vegging on the couch with her son, caressing his back, listening to the events of his day and offering her take.

Lynette is tall and skinny, in her early thirties, with short brown hair, a pale complexion, thin lips and a cute accent. She *looks* French. She is shrewd, hardworking, exacting, resourceful, funny when drunk, but quick to judge and therefore single. Lawyering for a large firm is still new to her and she suffers from lack of sleep. Poem is the common-law husband to her favourite cousin and she likes having him around although they don't have the chemistry to be pals. She knows Julien really likes him, that he stabilizes the house, but she really wishes she could find a man.

Poem enters the living room to see mother and son crashed together on the couch, watching Samurai Jack. He collects his things when Lynette asks, "Hey Poem, you going out tonight?"

"Naw, I'm stayin' in," he fumbles with the laptop cord.

"This is the third night in a row you haven't gone out. Is everything all right?"

"Yeah I'm cool. Just really into studying right now."

"Astrology?" she looks back at the television.

"Yeah, it's really interesting. Do you know that George Bush became President because of his brother?"

"Everyone knows that," she rolls her eyes.

"No, it's here in his chart. Check it out." He puts down the laptop, finds the sheet of paper and squats next to her, displaying the handwritten chart.

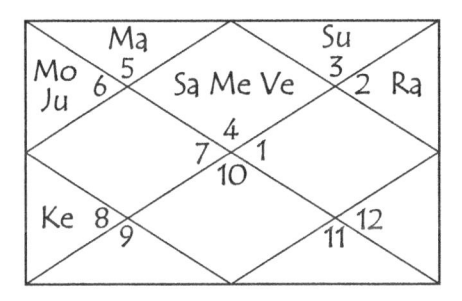

```
         Ma        Su
    Mo  5         3
        6  Sa Me Ve  2  Ra
    Ju        4
            7    1
             10
    Ke  8            12
         9         11
```

"Look. He was in Saturn dasa when he was elected. Saturn's in his 1st house with Mercury, lord of the 3rd. The 3rd signifies younger brother, plus Saturn aspects the 3rd *from* the 1st."

Lynette stares at him blankly as Julien fidgets.

"And look," Poem points, "He was running exalted Rahu-sub in the 11th house of Gain, and 11th lord Venus is with lord of the 3rd. So his rise comes through his younger brother being his benefactor, especially given that lord of the 3rd is strong, having gained directional strength."

Lynette gives him that look one gets when things aren't working out. She is about to say something but stops, then begins, then hesitates. Finally, "You know that I'm a lawyer, right?" She pauses and he nods, knowing how hard she's worked. "I'm actually really smart," she adds. "I have no idea what you're talking about."

"I know it sounds technical but it's here! I see it. It's amazing how the two correlate; *this* chart with *his* life."

"Poem, why aren't you out there playing somewhere?"

"Y'know, I did that and I'll do it again. It's just that you go to these places, looking to get on, and it's fun when you do, but the rest of the time you're just hanging out, smoking, trying to make conversation, order a beer, y'know? If it's open mic, you sit through guys trying to be Dylan or some half-wit poet who's better off telling it to his therapist."

"That's a little hard."

"You don't know what it's like out there. In the beginning it's okay, even fun, but lately I just feel like I'm wasting my time, like is it *really* increasing my being or prosperity?"

"How else are you gonna meet people?"

"I'm meeting people. But I've been here a month, Lynette, and I've seen a lot of bands. I think I'm ready for some downtime, ya know? Enrich the mind," he pokes his head.

"All right. You do what you want. I find this astrology thing interesting." She lowers her voice away from Julien, "Can you tell me when I'll meet a man?"

"I can look into it but y'know… I'm still learning too."

"How long does it take to become an astrologer?"

"About 20 years."

"What!?"

"Well, to be a good one. Don't worry, I'll look into it and let you know."

"Thanks." She resumes cuddling her son.

Poem collects his things and steps to the adjoining room when the phone in the kitchen rings. Hoping it's his dad, Julien leaps up, "I'll get it, I'll get it! Hello?

"Who?

"Sorry lady, you have the wrong number."

Lynette asks who it was and Julien says, "Some girl."

The phone rings again and Julien answer, "Hello?

"No, you have the wrong number.

"Yeah, that's our number but there's no 'Greg' here."

Poem hears this, "Julien, wait! It's for me!" He shuffles to the living room and grabs the phone. "Hello?

"Hey Maya! How are you?" He steps out of the room. "Uh huh.

"Yeah. No, they just know me as Poem."

Lynette and Julien eavesdrop.

"No…! What happened?

"Aw, sorry to hear that. Whatcha gonna do?" There is an extended pause. "That should be cool. I'll ask and get back to you. Where can I reach you? Let me write this down." He scribbles her new number. "So, when would you be arriving?" He stands in the doorway of the living room, looking at Lynette and Julien who are watching him. "Yeah, that was Julien. He's cute. Okay, see you, Maya." He hangs up the phone.

"Who was that?" Lynette asks.

"That's Maya, my band mate, or *former* band mate. She was the backup singer in my last band."

"Oh?"

"Yeah. She just got fired from her job. She's wondering if she can come here for a visit."

"You wanna bring a girl down here?" she raises a brow.

"She's my friend, Lynette. Her boyfriend was the drummer in my band until they broke up and he quit music. Anyway, we're just buds, nothing more. Is it all right if she comes and stays with us for a week?"

Lynette doesn't know what to say. She said Poem could have a guest while he was here but she didn't think it would be a girl. "Where's she gonna sleep?"

"She can sleep in my room and I'll bunk with Julien. Is that all right with you, Julien?"

Julien looks confused, "Your real name is Greg? That's weird."

Poem smiles. "My real name is Poem, but my mom didn't know that when I was born so she named me Gregory after her favourite actor. It took a while before I figured out who I *really* am."

Julien is still adjusting to this sudden paradigm shift.

"So is it all right if I bunk with you? I'll take the top bunk."

Julien nods an enthusiastic yes.

"Good, so is it all right with you, Lynette?"

She's still not sure about this. "Does Monique know her?"

"Oh yeah, they've met a couple times. It's not a problem. I have plenty of women friends."

"What's she like?"

"Oh, she's fun. You'll like her. Everybody loves Maya."

Lynette thinks and reluctantly agrees, "Well… okay. I guess a week won't hurt."

Julien can't stop grinning.

"When's she coming?"

"She said she was going to Barbados first and from there she wants to fly here, around October 10."

Lynette hopes she isn't going to regret this, "Well, if it's okay with Monique then I guess it shouldn't be a problem."

"Cool. Thanks, Lynette." Poem turns around with a skip in his step. "Maya's coming," he smiles. "This should be fun."

2 SHARED DREAM

"Maya. You up?" Poem calls from the top bunk in Julien's room.

"Yeah, hey…" her muffled voice answers from the guestroom. A thin closed door separates them.

It is morning, after 9 a.m. Lynette and Julien are gone for the day. Poem lies awake, craving water, recollecting last night, him and Maya, another night out, drinking, smoking, dancing, meeting new people, checking out bands, good food, having a really great time and—*Oh my God!* He remembers. *We made out last night. Oh my God! We were all over each other. I made out with Maya… Sexy Maya…* His sober shock slides into a devilish grin and he looks at the door, "That was cool last night, huh Maya."

"Yeah, I had a great time, Poem. That band was awesome." She is lying back under the covers, thinking of their first kiss in the gallery of Tipitina's, seeing the band and stage from above, the feathered costumes, splashing lights, Poem spinning her, hanging on tight, catching her just right and their lips coming together for the first time.

"I really like dancing with you, Maya."

"Me too, Poem, me too."

Maya's been here almost a week. She has endeared herself to Lynette and Julien, so much so that she was invited to stay an additional week. Lynette finds her fun, interesting, and easy to meet guys with. Of course, Julien has a crush on her.

"How do you feel?" Poem asks.

Maya lets out a long stretch, "Like I could use some company."

Poem throws the covers aside and leaps to the floor with a loud thump, just missing the Krusty Krab Lego set. He pauses at the door, takes a deep breath and opens it. There is Maya lying in bed, holding up the covers, her tanned, fit body in red bra and panties. He can't believe it. But like a dog with unguarded meat on the table, he cannot resist. He slides into bed next to her and they embrace, giving into an urge that has haunted them since the beginning.

They've been out every night, partying, dancing, playing pool. Everybody loves Maya. She is radiant and vivacious, a natural gabber with a beautiful face, always attracting, both men *and* women. They've been doing their 'just buds' routine for everyone and it was legit. Few suspected, not even them. She helps him with daily duties, errands, preparing food, laundry, watering plants. Now they lay, lips and limbs entwined, in their underwear, kissing, rubbing, savouring every caress, like warm sweetly-spiced tea. Their growling stomachs make them laugh so they decide to shower, dress and head out for breakfast.

At the local bakery they indulge in coffee, beignets and cigarettes. Leaning against a short fieldstone wall, they talk, sip coffee, and feel the air gradually get hotter. Poem's thinking about Monique. *Maybe she'll be cool with it. She said I could sleep with Lynette, but I think she was joking, and she knows I'm not interested anyway. She said I could sleep with Adele but how could I? Claude would kill me! Maybe she'll be cool with me sleeping with Maya.*

Monique is a magnanimous woman who in fits of universal love has on a few occasions declared to Poem that he could have sex with either of her cousins. This unusual stance was meant to relieve the pressure of their almost nonexistent sex life. Poem suggested women outside the family, but Monique insists that only a woman she knows and trusts can have sex with her boyfriend. She's very European that way. He wonders if *she's* sleeping with someone and this thought brings him strange comfort. But he makes it clear and Maya agrees that they must keep this from Lynette and everyone who knows Lynette and everyone who is associated with anyone who knows Lynette, which is pretty much everyone they know here.

"I can't believe this is happening," Poem says, squeezing Maya from behind, smelling her smoke-stained hair. "I didn't think when you came down that this would happen, but I gotta tell ya, Maya, I dug you from the first time I saw you."

"I know," she moans, feeling his wide hands against her.

"But you were with Tony and I saw how close you were, and honestly, I had no problem with it, really." He steps back, "In some ways I wish you were still together cuz at least we'd have a band," he laughs.

"Sorry."

"Hey, it's not your fault, Maya, seriously." He grabs her hand, "I'm just saying I was happy to be your friend."

"Me too, baby. I totally thought you were so cool when I met you, and when I heard your music I couldn't believe you worked for Malabar. You guys are awesome! And…" She takes a long drag of her cigarette. "Tony was really jealous of you, Poem."

"Really?! Why?"

"He knew I liked you."

"What?!"

"I told him I had feelings for you. You didn't know?"

"I'm oblivious at the best of times, Maya. I had no idea. I just knew you guys were together and I didn't think about it. Only that I always thought you had a really great ass."

"Thanks," she laughs.

He adores her rusty chuckles. "So what happens when we get back to Toronto?"

They start walking, pensively, thinking very different thoughts.

"I don't wanna go back to Toronto, Poem. Not right now."

"Really?"

"Yeah. After this I was gonna go visit my dad in Montreal. His wife is a reporter there. I might stay with them for a while."

Poem suddenly realizes this could be over just as it's beginning. "So you're taking it day by day, huh?"

She says yeah as if apologizing and Poem says, "No worries, Maya. Day by day, right?"

She smiles.

"Listen, I have to run a few errands then I wanna nap before Lynette gets home. You game?"

"Sure, baby."

"Julien's dad is pickin' him up from school so I'm free all day."

"That's great," she caresses him, "A nap would be nice. Weekend's coming up!"

They head back to Lynette's, pick up the car and head out to Magazine Street where they park in a residential area and come across a large wooden lawn sign that reads:

THE ANGELIC CENTER
CHILDREN IN THE EYES OF GOD FINDING THEIR WAY OUT OF THE DARK

They stop, Poem's arm around Maya's neck, her hand stuffed into his back pocket. They look up the ceramic gnome-littered lawn to a stark white modest yet regal looking bungalow trimmed baby blue with Christmas lights. A wonky neon sign blinks 'Come on in!' They look at each other and grinning from ear to ear, head up the picketed walkway to a blue doorframe adorned with figurines. They enter the incensed foyer and hear muffled reggae coming from the back. There's a display of booklets and brochures. One sign reads:

40% off Healings!
At these prices you can't not be healed!

A large room to the right looks like a bookstore with smaller rooms interconnecting throughout the house. There are colourful clothes, jewellery displays, postcards, scented candles, love potions and effigies, all having to do with angels. Poem steps into the main room to check out the books, while Maya continues up the hall. A rather plump, gentle-faced black man in his mid-fifties with long rattling braids, dressed in a blue African-style caftan, appears from the adjoining room. He says hello to Poem in a voice higher than you might expect, given his girth.

"Hi," Poem says, wondering if he's related to Aaron Neville. The man watches as Poem checks out a print of a blood-red devil with black horns, spaded tail, snow-white puffy wings and a yellow ring-halo. He looks back at the man who says in southerly fashion,

"The devil's not a bad guy. They just demonized him."

Poem grins. "He's a fallen angel, right?"

"Yes, and the closest to God."

"Why did they demonize him?"

"Because he is unabashedly smart in material things, or as we would say: cunning."

"Like Dick Cheney."

"Exactly."

"So is he worthy of our love?"

"We are *all* children in the eyes of God," he smiles.

Poem finds a book titled 'Angels and Astrology.' He picks it out and the man quotes as he reads, "The planets are like angels; they influence human affairs according to their nature."

Poem looks at him, "I guess you know all this."

"This and more."

"Like what?"

"You are a divine being. I get that from you. You've come a long way. Do you know what you're looking for?"

Poem reacts like waking up. He thinks about it and concedes, "I'm looking for love, just like everyone else. Is there anything else?"

"Love is the binding force of the universe."

"Beautiful. Do you run this place?" Poem puts the book back on its shelf.

"I live here with my partner and we do readings, have groups, educate the public on the nature of angels and how to know the angels that are already with us," he points out his invisible friends.

"Can you tell me, what exactly *are* angels?"

"They are messengers of God."

"Okay, I get that but what are they made of? What's their substance? Do they belong to the Earth or are they aliens from another world that primitive minds gave wings to because they came from the sky? Or are they just metaphors for our higher nature?"

The man is impressed with this level of inquiry. He explains slowly, "They are not of the Earth, they belong to the Sun. And being from another world, yes, you could call them alien. And yes, they are the *immaterial* beings we aspire to."

"How so?"

"Do you believe in Evolution?"

"Of course."

"So to what state will humans evolve?"

"Good question." Poem mulls it over. "I think we will probably continue to develop our intelligence at the expense of our physical bodies, like how they depict aliens in the movies, these sexless, frail-looking walking heads who express most of their energy mentally."

"And what about beyond the flesh?"

"You mean beyond death?"

"Well, beyond *our* world."

Poem feels the atmosphere change. "You're talking about living in another realm or in another dimension where most of the time we can't perceive what's around us but from time to time, due to some effort on *their* part, or a breakthrough on *our* part, they're able to cross into our dimension so that we experience them inter-dimensionally."

"You sound like an intelligent man. What do you do?"

"Well I'm a musician and a writer but I seem to make my living doing everything else," he laughs. "I'm studying astrology, Indian astrology, and it gets pretty deep when you begin to see what's there."

"Astrology is the chess of kings. So you're an astrologer."

"Uh… not yet. That is, *one* day, but I can't say I'm one right now," he feels the need to explain himself. "It's a 'big program' as my teacher would say, so I have a ways to go."

The man nods, watching Poem's mouth.

"I know a lot of people call themselves astrologers but to me an astrologer is something very high, someone who understands forces more subtle and profound than what everyday people concern themselves with. I've only ever met one astrologer in my life and that's my teacher, Mantriji, and I've seen him do incredible things. Compared to him most people just give astrology a bad name."

"Whatcha doin' in N'awlins?"

"Hanging out for a couple months, seeing if I can meet someone who's gonna sign me to a record deal," he hopes that doesn't sound naïve.

"So how's it going?"

"I think I'm in the wrong town."

"Why ya say that?"

"I'm hungry for knowledge and I have this teacher back in Toronto. But I'm here instead chasing what seems more and more like a dream."

"A record deal."

"Yeah."

"I've known a lot of musicians in my time who think a record deal will solve all their problems, but really that's when their problems begin."

Poem looks down at the floor, wondering about his life, all the music he's written, the people he's met, him and Maya kissing, the sense of wanting something more.

Maya walks into the room. "Hey Poem, you should see…" spotting the man, she stops. They exchange hellos and she puts her hand on Poem's back. "This place is cool. They do readings."

"Would you like a reading?" the man asks.

She looks at Poem who shrugs, "How much?"

"We are all children in the eyes of God, just trying to find our way outta the dark. We accept donations."

"Works for me," Maya says.

The man chuckles and motions for them to follow him. They are led through an adjoining room, down a hall, to a small cluttered kitchen that is the source of the reggae. A portly white woman in her fifties with long rust-brown hair and reading glasses, dressed like a fortune teller, is seated at a card table next to an open window, reading the newspaper. The man calls her Martha and lowers the volume on the stereo. They exchange greetings and his name is Jessie. Martha clears the table and ceremoniously drapes it with a dark blue velvet cloth. She lowers the blinds, lights a candle, and invites them to have a seat, her face already perspiring. Poem and Maya sit across from her as Jessie watches, standing, clasped hands on his protruding belly.

"May I see your right palm?" Martha asks in her Southern drawl.

Maya offers it and the woman looks, "You want more money, you want more respect, you are looking for true love."

"Wow, it's like you can see right through me."

Poem groans, "You could say that about anyone."

Martha looks at Jessie who tells her that Poem is an astrologer and no shrinking violet. Martha examines Poem and nods. She cups Maya's hands with her own, mumbles some words, and disappears into a trance, her pupils rolling under fluttering lids. She begins slowly in a lofty monotone voice:

"EVERY ONE OF US HAS CONTROL OVER OUR ACTIONS, BUT WE HAVE VERY LITTLE CONTROL OVER THE *OUTCOME* OF THESE ACTIONS. DO YOU UNDERSTAND?"

Both Maya and Poem nod, Maya frozen to her seat, Poem trying not to laugh but recognizing that something has indeed arrived.

"WE MAY AIM TO DO RIGHT, BUT IT MAY TURN OUT WRONG. ALWAYS REMEMBER, NO MATTER WHERE YOU GO, HE WHO PAYS THE PIPER CALLS THE TUNE. THINK CAREFULLY HOW YOU'VE SEEN THIS IN YOUR LIFE AND HOW IT CONTINUES EVEN NOW."

"Yeah," Maya gets it.

"LET YOUR HIGHEST ASPIRATION ORGANIZE YOUR LIFE. BUT FIRST YOU MUST BE CLEAR ON WHAT THIS IS. WHEN YOU KNOW WHAT YOU WANT, LIFE BECOMES SIMPLE, ALL THE RULES ARE ALREADY WRITTEN."

Poem murmurs and Maya looks at him.

"INVEST IN THE PROCESS, NOT THE OUTCOME," Martha's eyes flicker open and shut. "DON'T EXPECT MUCH AND YOU WILL GET A LOT," she grins.

"I don't want much," Maya says.

"YOU MAY NOT WANT MUCH BUT YOUR DESIRES DISRUPT THE LIVES OF OTHERS. YOU DASH EXPECTATIONS! YOU GO LOOKING FOR OPPORTUNITY BUT WHEN YOU RIDE A TIGER, YOU GO WHERE THE TIGER TAKES YOU," she smiles spastically, rocking back and forth like an exalted blind man. "YOU NEED TO SIMPLIFY YOUR LIFE, DECIDE WHAT YOU WANT. YOU DON'T KNOW YET, YOU ARE CONFUSED. JUST REMEMBER: YOU CAN NEVER GET ENOUGH OF THE THINGS THAT WON'T MAKE YOU HAPPY."

"Huh…" Poem looks at Jessie who nods.

"SIMPLICITY IS GOOD. THE MORE PRIMITIVE A THING IS, THE MORE RESILIENT. SIMPLE TENACITY, THAT'S WHAT YOU NEED. DEFINE WHAT YOU WANT AND REMEMBER, IN THE DARK A TICK IS WORSE THAN A TIGER. WHAT'S YOUR QUESTION?"

Maya looks at Poem before asking, "How long should I stay in New Orleans?"

The oracle digests her inquiry. "IT IS BETTER TO BELIEVE IN SOMETHING THAN NOTHING. WHEN PEOPLE BELIEVE IN SOMETHING, IT IS GOOD FOR EVERYONE. IT CREATES ORDER AND UNDERSTANDING, THE ABILITY TO RELATE. YOU ARE HERE TO TAKE CARE OF SOME BUSINESS FROM A PREVIOUS LIFE." She looks at Poem, "THIS MAN IS YOUR DOORWAY. HE IS A MAGICIAN, A HIEROPHANT, YOU KNOW HIM FROM BEFORE. HE WILL LEAD YOU TO THE NEXT DOOR. BUT ONCE YOU OPEN THAT DOOR AND GO INSIDE, KNOW

THAT YOU CANNOT GO BACK, THAT THINGS WILL NEVER BE THE SAME. YOU ARE HERE TO UNTIE THE KNOT. DO IT SKILFULLY AND YOU WILL BE FREE. RUIN IT AND YOU WILL BE BACK AGAIN AND AGAIN."

"So what, like a month?"

The oracle does not respond. Maya and Poem are silent. The voice concludes with, "I TELL PEOPLE ONLY THINGS THEY ALREADY KNOW. THAT WAY I'M NEVER WRONG."

The spirit seems to fall back into Martha and her head sways with eyelids flickering wildly. Suddenly she is calm and opens her eyes. "How'd it go?" her voice is normal again.

"Ask our friends," Jessie says.

Poem and Maya are unsure. "Uh… Well I guess it was mostly to Maya she was talkin' but I thought it was cool. 'Ya can't get enough of the things that won't make you happy?' That's profound. And sums up all of Western Capitalism if you ask me."

Maya is silent, still processing.

"Thank you, Martha," Poem says. "That was really interesting. Where do we leave our donation?"

"Just put it on the altar," she gestures.

Poem turns to see a bracketed wall-shelf holding a ceramic bust of the Virgin Mary, garlanded with colourful Mardi Gras beads. Maya and Poem get up and bow graciously. Poem places 20 dollars next to the sacred statue on top of some Powerball tickets. Jessie hands him a brochure and escorts them to the front door. Poem says, "Thank you, my man," as they leave. The door closes and Maya says,

"You called her 'man.'"

"Huh?"

"She's a woman. You didn't see that?"

He's dumbstruck. "I thought there was something weird about him."

"Yeah, they were totally lesbians. That was obvious."

"I called her 'man.'" He looks back at the house, "That was stupid."

"I'm sure she took it as a compliment."

"Maybe she thought I said 'ma'am.'"

"Thank you, my ma'am?!"

They laugh.

Reorienting themselves, they head for Magazine Street while discussing the reading, grab some lunch, stop at the Food Market, and head home to organize groceries. They hang out on the front porch, drink some beer, and feeling the Sun begin its afternoon fall, head upstairs, undress into their intimates and crawl into Maya's bed. They sleepily cuddle and grind for a while until the weight of their heat lulls them into a deep, otherworldly sleep.

Poem opens his eyes. He sees people in the room, people he doesn't recognize. But he isn't alarmed. Somehow he's one of them. He looks at Maya who is visibly upset, ordering them to leave. Poem blocks her out and enters the hall. There along the corridor he sees all kinds of people, different ages, races and manners of dress, some look 19th century. They smile as he walks by. Down the staircase he sees the entire house filled with people hanging out like a party of loners. They talk and make no sound yet there's the murmur of voices and cocktail music all around. He descends past a row of women on the stairs and suddenly feels an intense energy from above, like a rumbling thunderstorm. Looking up, he sees Maya flying down, trying to corral people out of the house, but they aren't listening. He wonders why she won't just chill out.

Poem is loving this yet he knows he's in a dream. He shuffles through the main floor, digging everyone, wondering where's Lynette. A few bohemians from the 1940s hang out by the piano so he joins them. A friendly looking middle-aged black man in a grey bowler hat tickles the ivories. Poem sits next to him and plays along, the man doing bass and Poem shucking chords. The music begins to flow. Maya appears, bobbing her head, "Hey I like that jam!" They play what now sounds like a clavinet, grooving along to the funkiest chords ever. Poem looks at the man who smiles back. They recognize each other but the scene suddenly changes from the house to onstage with coloured lights, a band and audience out front, all hopping to the ultra-funky beat. Maya finds a microphone and wails in that over the top way of hers. The audience goes wild but the band is all in the piano: what Poem plays on the keys is orchestrated into full ensemble, which he controls intuitively. "Man, I gotta remember these chords when I wake up!"

Everyone in the club spills out into the street, laughing, running along the river, swinging their way home. He wonders where Maya is and turns around. She is running towards him. "You were awesome, man!" she leaps through the air into his arms.

"Are you all right?" he asks. She wriggles free and bolts towards Lake Pontchartrain. Poem chases her, both of them flying like Valkyries on jet skis. They sweep over the houses and roads, land on the levee and look back over the parks and lots when they suddenly realize all that water thundering out in the lake is the salty tears of broken hearts. Maya feels an overwhelming sadness and Poem consoles her. She looks up at him like his daughter and the scene changes again. They are next to a campfire dancing with tribes-people of whom they are members. Poem is about to give her away to be wed when he looks up to see a huge dragon circling overhead. He grabs Maya and they run from the fire, away from the others, into a dense forest, through jungle terrain, back to the familiar and lush neighbourhood of Lynette's street.

Maya is unable to speak. Poem tells her it's time to go back in. They look back one last time to survey their epic journey before entering the house.

Poem opens his eyes. He sees the ceiling and realizes he has just come out of a dream, an incredibly *lucid* dream. He turns to Maya who opens her eyes and looks at him.

"I just had the most amazing dream," Poem says.

"Me too!"

"Were there people in the house?"

"Oh my God!" she freezes. "Yes! There were all kinds of people in the house!"

"And we had a jam!"

"Yeah! You were wailing!"

Poem's eyes bulge with amazement and Maya is speechless. It dawns on them. "We just had the same dream!!"

They spend the next five minutes freaking out over their collective dream-state odyssey. He recalls her getting angry and she recalls him calming her down. They both remember the same chords on the keyboard! She remembers jumping and he remembers catching her. They verify each other's moves, moods, perspectives and words. It feels surreal but there is no denying, they were lucid and together, even communicating, in one massive dream sequence or hallucination. It's like they tapped into the astral light of New Orleans. Even returning to the house was their agreed cue to come out of it. They knew they had to leave, but why? They hear the front door downstairs. "Shit! Lynette!" They burst out of their bubble. Poem grabs his clothes and bolts on his tiptoes into Julien's room where he hastily scales to the top bunk. Maya closes the door behind him and sneaks back into bed, the floor creaking like mad. They hear Lynette's pumps walk to the bottom of the stairs.

"Hey Poem! You around?!" she hollers up.

"Uh yeah, Lynette!" he sounds wired. "Just sleeping. I'm so tired—I dunno… I'm just so tired."

"Where's Maya?"

"Just resting!" she spasms from the other room.

Lynette says nothing and they hear her clatter to the kitchen.

Poem whispers, "Maya, we'll just tell her we wanted to nap cuz we're going out tonight. You go down and sweet-talk her. She loves you. Just say we were drinking. She's French, she'll understand. I'm gonna pretend to sleep for a little while."

"Where we going?" she whispers.

"Just say Tipitina's. Dr. John'r something."

After more goading and wanting desperately to avoid Lynette, Maya goes downstairs and tries to make casual conversation, saying they were up late and got especially drunk, but Poem was okay to drive. They were just napping to be rested for tonight. Lynette isn't suspicious by nature and at this point she doesn't care. She's in touch with Monique who's enjoying the place to herself. Plus, she likes having Maya around. She knows her and Poem will be gone by November.

Poem eventually makes his way downstairs. It turns out Lynette has plans tonight and is in a *great* mood, chatting and laughing with Maya. He breathes a sigh of relief for life's distractions. They all start drinking and eating before Lynette excuses herself to get ready. She asks Maya for makeup advice and calls Dee, her colleague, and they impulsively decide to join Poem and Maya at Tipitina's tonight. Being from San Antonio, she says, "This'll be fun. How often do you get to see Dr. John in New Orleans?"

Poem and Maya pretend like it's a great idea but they would rather just figure out this dream. They put on the veneer for Lynette and dress up, Maya in tight red jeans, push-up bra and jacket; Poem in black Mexx longs, motorcycle boots and pork pie hat. He insists they take separate cars 'just in case' and finally alone, he and Maya resume reviewing their dream, smooching at every stoplight, making sure the others don't see. Inside the club with Lynette and Dee they play up the 'just friends' routine to such an extent that it draws strange looks from the girls.

"Is everything all right with you and Poem?!" Lynette yells above the music.

"Uh yeah, we're just good friends!" Maya shouts. "And ya know, sometimes even good friends…! Uh… y'know?! But we're okay, we're good!"

It's a great show and following the final encore everyone disperses into little groups and lines to the bathroom. Lynette and Dee have been up since 6 a.m. so they bail. Poem looks for Maggie whom he saw earlier then makes his way back to the front doors, looking for Maya. He finds her talking with a greasy-looking guy in a white Rasta hat and STAFF t-shirt, sitting on the ticket counter, digging her. Not an unusual occurrence, he walks up and says, "Hey Maya, you ready?"

"Hey Poem," she smiles. "Meet my new friend Sammy!"

The guy jumps off the counter. "Heya Poet!" he shakes Poem's hand like it's a done deal.

"It's Poem," he corrects him.

"Riiight," the guy sizes him up.

"Sammy says we should check out this club close to Lynette's, what's it called?"

"Snake'n'Jake's," the clean-faced white Rasta says. "A lotta cool people hang out there after hours, y'know?"

Poem is interested so Sammy gives him directions. They say goodbye and maybe they'll see him later and Sammy blows Maya a kiss. They head out the door to the car, trying to recall their lucid dream now fading from memory. They have slightly different takes on what it means but they agree they must be more connected than even they suspected. And now that Lynette's gone, they wanna celebrate!

They drive to Oak and Hillary where they find the grassy lot Sammy was describing. Sure enough on the opposite side is a rickety glorified shed of a speakeasy with a large green wreath hanging over the door. They park nearly right in front and make-out for a while before entering.

It is a small, dim, quaint room with Christmas décor everywhere, even a Christmas tree; retro but not contrived. A few people hang out in pairs, around tables, at the bar. They seem friendly and make eye contact as Poem and Maya walk in. She recognizes a couple so she starts talking to them while Poem sidles up to the bar and chats with the keeper whom he recognizes as well. He finds out the club opens before midnight and it's mostly local staff and musicians working into the wee hours that end up here. They'll drink till sunrise, head out for breakfast, then go home and sleep into the afternoon.

Poem and Maya order drinks and the place gradually fills with smoke and people. The dartboard gets busy and the music more interesting. Sammy shows up with a few friends and they hang out by the main table near the front door. Poem skanks while Maya bounces between him and Sammy's gang and the place begins to feel like a 'wreck-room' with 40 of your closest friends all hanging out professionally, personally, sexually, and pharmaceutically.

The front door opens and a groovy West Indian funkstar with baby dreads stuffed into a green beret walks in. He has sharply defined facial features, slithering like some cartoon voodoo priest, wearing sunglasses at two o'clock in the morning. He spots Poem and the two come together like long lost brothers, shaking hands, a quick shoulder tap, perfect strangers recognizing each other like they went to the same school in another lifetime. "Hey, man, how ya been?" Poem says and the hipster speaks,

"Yo cool, man, good to see you. I gotta get to know you, man." He points to Poem's head, "I want that hat," he grins and continues to the back of the club.

Poem looks at Maya who makes her way over, "Who's the guy in the moonglasses?"

"I don't know. I've never seen him before."

"It looked like he recognized you."

"Yeah, I feel like I recognize him too. It's weird. I didn't even think about it. I just saw him and said hey, how are you, where you been?" Poem looks over at the guy at the far end of the bar talking with the keeper. "He reminds me of someone but I don't know who. He says he wants my hat."

"It's a great hat." Maya picks up the groove to the next tune and Poem joins her. They grind it up on the dance floor while Sammy watches and the funkstar approaches. Poem sees him check out Maya's ass.

"Don't stare so hard, you'll lose an eye."

The funkstar grins. "There's something about you, man," his voice is smooth and raspy.

"What's your name?" Poem asks.

"Duke. Yo, where you from?"

Poem gives his standard line: "Same place as you, man: Earth."

Duke loves it! He slaps him high five and sniggers like Flavour Flav, "It's the Man from Earth! Wooo I dig you, man. You's a gangsta! What's your name, brother, and who is your fine—I hope—sista?"

Poem gives a Cheshire grin and flourishes with his right hand, "This is my lady, Maya." She curtsies. "And *my* name is Poem."

"C'est what?" Duke tips his head.

"Poem."

Duke lowers his shades, revealing intense, sensitive eyes, "Yo man, that is the most beautiful thing I ever heard. Whatcha all doin' in N'awlins?"

"I'm here looking for a record deal and Maya here is looking for herself," he laughs.

The three start to chat when Duke says, "Listen, man. Gotta go. Be back. Will you be here?"

Poem nods.

Duke shakes his hand, heads to the door and stops. He looks back and frantically waves Poem over. Poem joins him and the two men step outside.

"Yo, are you fo'real, my man?" Duke says and Poem doesn't know what to say. "You is deep, brother. I know *you* know but I bet you *don't know* that you haven't even begun to scratch the surface of how hip in actual fact you really are, know what I'm sayin'?"

Poem wonders if he's gay by how thick he's laying it on. They start talking and Duke suggests they get a drink. Poem insists on buying and Duke does not resist. But first he has to make just one quick run. He'll be back in five minutes, if Poem could just order anything and meet him back at the bar. Twenty minutes later Duke shows up and they talk for a while about philosophy, astrology, jazz, opera, Sweden, and why Americans know hardly anything about Canada. Duke tells Poem that he knows the Neville Brothers. He even has Cyril Neville's Hammond organ in his living room just up the road where he lives with his folks.

Poem wants to check this out so he walks over to Maya who's in the middle of a conversation. "Maya, let's go with Duke. I wanna see his organ."

She gives him a look that says she would rather not.

"Maya, this guy grew up in New Orleans! He knows the Neville Brothers! Maybe he'll have some good connections."

Maya thinks about it and clearly compromising her better judgement, agrees to go along. They say goodbye to their newfound friends and head outside.

"Yo, just up the street," Duke says and they follow as he limps on like a jester.

The crickets get loud and Maya makes eyes at Poem, "Are you sure about this? I don't know about this guy. We don't even know who he is!"

Across the street and a few doors down they get to a beige house hidden behind two bushy crape myrtles. He leads them up the side entrance and they follow him in. Turning left through a door they find themselves in the front room of the house: a messy, dim, narrow room with a couch, kitchen chair, small amp, furniture, lamps, strewn clothes, patch cords, a red five-string bass, a pile of cassette tapes, boom box, music stand, and as Duke promised: a large wooden ol' school B3 Hammond organ sitting in the middle of everything with manuscripts, ashtray, coffee mug and a mickey of brandy on top. It is pocked with cigarette burns and welts from being on the road, a couple keys are snapped off, but it has the majesty of Mount Rushmore. Duke gets behind it and starts pumping along at low volume so you mostly hear his fingernails clicking the keys. "Gotta keep it low cuz Pops an' Trix is sleepin'."

The next couple hours are spent smoking, drinking, listening to a frenetic, eager to please Duke go on about himself and New Orleans. He is edgy and cultured, narcissistic and entertaining. He treats Poem reverently, calling him 'Ultra Cool' and the 'Cat in the Hat,' always followed by, "I want that hat." It blows their minds when he picks up the bass and starts slapping down a groove because other than Marcus, he's the only left-handed, string-backwards bass player they've ever seen. That both Duke and Marcus have the same West Indian features and complexion with baby dreads, sunglasses at night, wiry bodies and a hustler attitude, makes it a little eerie, like a continuation of their surreal dream and Duke is the hookah-smoking Caterpillar.

For Duke, 'gangsta' is a universal synonym for good. If the music is groovy, it's 'gangsta;' if the food is tasty, it's 'gangsta;' if the joke is funny, it's 'gangsta,' and so on. At one point he asks Poem for eight dollars and Poem hands him a ten. Duke calls him 'gangsta' and disappears for 15 minutes.

"What a guy," Maya says. "That's the second time he split like that."

They talk about bailing. It's past 5 a.m. It's been great but they're exhausted. Duke gets back all energized but Poem tells him they're starting to crash. They really need to go. Duke will not hear any of it but eventually relinquishes and sees them to the door. They exchange phone numbers and guarantees of a future jam. "I wanna hear you play your gi-tar," Duke says.

"I'll call you," Poem promises. "Thanks again for everything."

They head back to the car, tired and titillated by another full night of partying. In this town you can always find the next place to drink and if you have a willing partner, you may never stop. They drive to Lynette's where Maya will have to sleep alone and Poem will bunk in Julien's room. It's too bad they can't sleep together but they're in love, and obstacles only bring out the romance of it all. Finally arriving home they enter the house to the first rays of dawn.

3 PENISES & PROPERTY

"Hey baby."

"Hey doll."

Maggie and Poem greet one another just outside a little café on Magazine Street. She is smoking, dressed in earthy colours, long gypsy skirt, v-neck t-shirt and burgundy cowboy boots. They hug and she says, "I hear the chocolate cheese cake here is fabulous."

Poem admonishes her, "No one truly needs chocolate cheese cake, y'know."

"Hey, don't try to deny me one of life's great pleasures."

"Yeah, but then y'all complain about it afterwards cuz it goes *straight* to your hips!" he laughs. "Then *we* have to watch it while you jiggle it down the street; all that chocolate cheese cake," he squats and she punches him.

"You're bad!" She checks out her behind, "This is just water retention."

"Water retention?! More like chocolate retention."

She smacks him hard—"Ouch!"—and ditches her cigarette. Poem opens the door and follows her in. Taking in the sweet coffee aroma he says, "It's like standing under the armpit of a rich Columbian."

"Eww," she groans and they continue their banter, being served, settling in, facing south and soaking in the November sun. Poem lights a cigarette and sips his coffee while Maggie takes her first bite of dessert.

"Mmm... God, this is better than sex!" she moans, kneading the creamy cake with her tongue.

"Honey, if that's the case then you're just not doing it right."

She snorts, nearly shooting a piece through her nose. Knowing she is being indulgent she gathers back her dignity, reclines into the chair and groans while melting the exquisite dessert in her mouth.

"Y'know, you could make a very good living charging men to watch you eat cheesecake."

"Sorry, I get carried away, I know. It's been a while." Temporarily satiated, she comes to life, "How are you, Poem? I miss you. I miss our talks. What's going on? I thought you were going back to Toronto."

He loves her energy and misses their platonic, pressure-free friendship. "Yeah, I know it's been a while since we actually sat down and talked."

"I just see you at work and I have no time!"

"I know. It's okay, Maggie. I'm here now."

"So how's Maya? She still around?"

"Yeah, she's definitely around," he grins. "She's out with Lynette for the day gettin' some new clothes. Y'know, she came packed for a week and it's already been a month!"

"Wow, a month already? Yeah, you guys seem inseparable."

"I'm sorry if I neglected you, Maggie. It's just that she wanted to go out every night and I felt obliged and... I just lost track of time." He blows out a long stream of smoke and chews on a raw cuticle. "I have to tell you something," his tone is confidential and she draws in closer, looking concerned. "Me and Maya are in love."

"Duh...!" she responds like he just insulted her.

"What?"

"That's frickin obvious, dude, and it was from the beginning! Who did you think you were fooling?"

"Really?" He takes another drag. "Um, I guess we were mostly just trying to fool Lynette."

"Well maybe ya fooled her but ya didn't fool me." She resumes eating her cake to spite him.

"Well, we kept it secret for obvious reasons."

"Yeah, you have a girlfriend in Toronto," she points her fork at him.

"Yeah..."

"Who's Lynette's cousin!"

"Yeah."

"And you live with her!!"

"Yeah." Poem looks down, both dreading and relishing his predicament.

"So what now?"

"Well..." he hesitates, still figuring it out. "I told my boss in Toronto I wasn't sure when I'd be coming back, so... I got them to hire Marcus, my bass player, to replace me."

"Really?! How'd they take that?"

"Not so good. Now I have to pick up my car," he smiles crookedly. "I was storing it there while I'm here cuz I told them I'd be back. It's just a stupid driving job anyway."

"How's your girlfriend taking it?"

"Uh… well, this is where it's weird." He takes a deep breath. "She's cool with me staying."

"Really?"

"That's what she says." He sips his coffee. "She said she'll come down in December for a week then we can head back to Toronto together. I start a philosophy course in January so either she doesn't suspect or she's just cool with it. Monique is very French that way."

"What way?"

"I just find European girls are not that uptight when it comes to extra-curricular sex."

"Yeah, right," Maggie doesn't believe a word of it. "Poem, you can love only one woman at a time."

"That's bullshit! And I know because I'm living proof."

"So what? You think you can have this lil affair with Maya and get back with your girlfriend in Canada?"

"In Europe that could happen."

"This is not Europe!" She reaches for a cigarette and Poem hands her the lighter. "So what about Maya, what about now, what're you gonna do?"

"I don't know," he looks down.

"How old is she?"

"26."

"And you?"

"I'm older than 26."

"You're 10 years older, Poem!"

"Look, all I know is I'm having a blast and we've played a couple shows and we're meeting all kinds of people and I just wanna stick around and see what happens," he is eager and defensive and by Maggie's reckoning, confused. He senses her ambivalence. "Look, shit happens, okay?"

"I thought you were *'Mister Spiritual,'* with a guru and everything, *beyond* all this material stuff."

"Well I still am. I just like to make love."

Maggie shakes her head, wanting to oppose him but how can she? "Do you even have papers to work?"

"No, unfortunately." He bites his lower lip, "I mean, I know I can waiter or bartend or something if I really need to, under the table, but I hope not. I have to sort things out with Lynette and like I said, I can't stay indefinitely cuz all my stuff, my car, my apartment, my Strat, *everything's* still in Toronto."

"And your girlfriend."

"Right."

"And your family."

"Right."

"Don't you miss any of them, Poem?!"

"I do… But honestly, the one I miss most is Mantriji."

"Your astrology teacher," she sags.

"Yeah, he's the one I think about most, the things he taught me and the ideas it spawned." He pulls into the table, "Y'know this stuff, like cosmology and physics and philosophy; I've always been interested in these things but it was always a bunch of unconnected browsings. I just feel like astrology brings everything, all these disciplines, together under one mystical umbrella: the scientific with the spiritual, y'know? And that's what I miss. We had some very enlightened conversations," he gazes into the street. "He reveals the connections between things that on the surface seem to have no connection at all."

"Like what?"

Poem thinks a moment. "What do penises and property have in common?"

She gives him a wry smile and thinks to herself, "Mmm. You need a penis to protect your property?"

"Bravo!" Poem is impressed and she takes a diva's bow.

"How they're connected I have no idea."

"Well, they're both ruled by Mars. Mars is war and war is waged by penises, and it's all to acquire land, so you're right, you need a penis to protect your property."

"Ha!"

"In astrology Mars signifies sexual desire as well as land. Does he have land? Look at Mars in his chart."

"Okay. What else?"

"Well, the 4th house," he motions downward, "is below the earth. It rules 'home' and 'property,' where you put your stake. The *lord* of the 4th will show you the *soul* of this property and the 4th house shows you its content. You have to blend these factors and measure it against how much money he has, which you consult other houses to determine, then you make your best educated guess what kind of property he is likely to own, *if* he owns, how many, does it come from the father's side, mother's side, or does he just rent?"

"Sounds complicated."

"Yeah. And that's why you need a teacher. Astrology is not easy, man. There are so many things to consider when you look at a chart but when you know what to look for, it's awesome how insightful it can be. I've seen Mantriji do it and he's amazing." He stares at the road as a large truck rattles by, "I feel like he's giving me the glue to understanding not only astrology but the whole friggin universe."

Maggie looks at him doubtfully, "Do you really believe the planets control everything, Poem?"

"I'm starting to think more and more yes. I mean, freewill is more rare than you think. Like ya ever try and tell someone they're being an ass and *they* don't think so but you and everyone else sees it but somehow *they* don't? They think they can choose when *not* to be an ass but most of the time they don't even realize they're *being* an ass, so what does that say about their awareness, and how do you will *anything* without being aware?"

Maggie wonders if he's talking about her.

"You think you can make things happen but are *you* making it happen or does it just happen? Where's the first cause in it? *You* think you're willing it but in actual fact, it's all part of a web of cause and effect and you're the surfer who thinks he's the wave," he rocks his chair, "You can go left or right but you're pretty much limited to where the wave takes you and that's what karma is. That's *my* wave theory," he laughs. "Think of karma as the wave and freewill as the surfer. A good surfer can make things happen, even turn back because he has freewill, but a weak surfer will just ride it out. He may even look great doing it, but he's just lucky because really, he's just riding a wave," he slides one hand over the other.

"So... It's our *freewill* that stops astrology from being a science?"

"Yeah, but as Mantriji would say: 'There's no bad astrology, only bad astrologers.' And this is why it'll always be a pseudo-science because it depends on the will of the native and the skill of the astrologer. The more freewill you exert, the less the chart can be used to divine your future. That's what I learned."

"So it doesn't always work."

"That's right. But as Mantriji would say: '99 percent of the time, astrology works.'"

Maggie cracks a crooked smile, not sure what to think. "So what're you gonna do?"

"I wanna stay here a bit." He thinks. "I figure I got till January when my course begins. I dunno what's gonna happen with Maya. I feel like I'm walking a tight rope."

"Yeah...!"

"But I also feel like I been on a roll since she got here, y'know? Lynette likes havin' us around, Julien *loves* it, and I'm having a blast. I don't think I ever drank so much."

"Well, be careful with that."

"Oh, no problem, it's just... It's so *easy* here. And you don't have to worry 'bout gettin' stopped." He lifts his hat and scratches his head, "It's just money that's the problem. I'm not making much with Lynette and I'm still paying rent in Toronto, and I still got over six grand in debts." He takes a long deep breath and letting it out, shakes his head. "Maurice says I can always bartend under the table but I dunno, like do I wanna be a bartender now?"

"Yeah, I did that for a couple years and yeah, it can wear ya out."

"I just feel like I wanna do something different. I'm tired of working dead-end jobs just so I can be in a band."

Maggie nods, knowing all too well the musician's struggle. She teaches piano privately and in two separate schools and it seems like she's always working, always juggling, accommodating other people's schedules. And yet, there's never enough money. She sees other musicians, more talented than her, making even less.

Poem leans onto the wobbly table, "We've been gettin' in like, 4 a.m. every morning and by the time we get to sleep it's close to five," he sighs. "And I can't sleep past nine!"

"Oooh," she feels for him.

"So now I'm addicted to coffee," he holds up his cup.

"What about Maya?"

"Holy fuck that girl can sleep! She sleeps right till noon, sometimes till two. I can't believe it. By the time she gets up I've been up five hours, and come nighttime I'm startin' to feel tired and she can't wait to go."

"Well she *is* 10 years younger, Poem."

"That has nothing to do with it! I'm just not used to getting by on only a few hours sleep. Shit, if I slept as much as her."

Maggie looks at him sideways.

"I don't know. I feel like it's all just staving off an inevitable crash. That glorious day when I can finally... just... rest," he deflates into his chair.

"You make it sound like dying."

"God, maybe that's what I need, a good dying," he laughs and Maggie's not sure how to take him. "Y'know, I'm running lord of the 8th in my chart right now and I tell you, the 8th is the 'death house' but it's also the 'sex house.'"

"Do I want to hear this?"

"I mean, the sex has been amazing but sometimes I feel like it's dying, like every ejaculation takes me closer to God, literally and figuratively."

"I don't wanna hear about your ejaculations, Poem! You just better take care of yourself. You look like you lost weight." She scoops the last of her cake.

"Yeah, no I'm cool. I just have to nap, that's all."

She rolls her eyes. "So then, things are good—I mean—with you and Maya?"

"Well, for the most part I would say pretty awesome actually. I really dug her when we first met and felt even *then* that she would be significant to me. And now I see it happening, like I'm watching my destiny unfold." He retells the story of the thong, the flash of light, their immediate connection and recent shared dream.

Maggie listens, amazed, envious, impressed.

"I feel like we have karma here, like she's gonna be my wife."

Maggie can't believe it, how much his life has changed in the short time she's known him. It seems somehow not true.

"There's just one thing," he shakes his head. "The only thing about her. She's a guy magnet."

"Well, she is pretty sexy, Poem."

"There's this one guy in particular... Y'see, we were telling people we're 'just friends' to keep it from Lynette, so here he is coming onto her right in front of me and I'm having to play this game while wanting to clean his clock."

"Who's that?"

"Y'know the door guy at Tipitina's, the white dread?"

"Oh, Sammy?"

"You know him?"

"Everyone knows Sammy. What, Poem, Sammy got designs on your girl?"

"I just get this weird vibe from him. Maya says he's sweet and he knows his way around but I dunno. He's a slippery fellow."

"Oh he's definitely sly."

"Did you date him?"

"I wanted to when I first met him but then I saw how he rolls. He thinks he's a player cuz he's got his own band and can get you into Tipitina's free. I sort of lost it for him once I saw how he does it. Nice guy, but sly." She reaches for a cigarette.

"Well, there's him and now I notice even Duke gets jealous when he sees me and her gettin' into it. I'm giving her a little kiss and he's like, 'break it up, break it up!'" he waves his arms.

"Really?! Is Maya aware you feel this way?"

"I think so, but, I can't stop her from being herself."

He's in a riddle like a mouse in a maze. He got the cheese, gorged himself, now how to get out? "I don't always feel so easy about the situation, Maggie. I'm not a jealous guy, but sometimes..." he brandishes his spoon like a weapon, "I have to protect what's mine."

"The penis."

"Yes."

"That's not good."

"I know. It's barbaric and I don't like it. But that's what this situation brings out in me. And here's where it gets *really* weird." He takes a long sip of coffee. "Originally we were keeping it a secret because we didn't want Lynette to know but..."

Maggie leans in.

"When I agreed to stay beyond October, Lynette told her father back in France to stay there because I was still here and she didn't know how much longer I'd be. But now he can't wait so he's coming back. And not only that, her uncle is coming to visit too."

Maggie is suddenly loving this.

"So when they get here, where's everyone gonna sleep? I'm bunking with Julien, Maya's got the guestroom, Lynette sleeps with herself, there's a couch downstairs but there's two of them coming. So you know what Lynette said?"

"What?"

"'Why don't you and Maya just bunk together?'"

"Are you serious?!"

Poem nods.

"Wow, she *is* European."

"That's what I'm saying! I don't know what to say and at the same time I don't wanna fuck it up."

"Hmm…"

"So when her father arrives, I'm sleeping with Maya and it's Lynette's idea!"

"This is crazy."

"I know."

"You're her cousin's boyfriend!"

"I told her we were going through a bit of a rough spell and I'm not sure if it's gonna work out. She just listened and said nothing, just that she likes having me around and that I'm a good influence on Julien."

"Yeah, I still don't get that."

"What, that I'm a good influence?"

"Dude, you drive with a mickey under your seat."

"Well you can do that here!"

She gives him that look, "I know you're a good guy, Poem, really smart, into all this spiritual stuff. Does Julien know you like Maya?"

"In that nine-year-old heart of his, I'm sure he knows something's up. And I think he's a little jealous, but it's kind of cute actually."

"You don't think Lynette told your girlfriend."

"I don't know and honestly, I don't even wanna think about it—you feel like drinking?"

"Uh…" she looks at her watch, "Okay. Miss Mae's?"

"Of course." He takes his last long sip of coffee. "You know, I feel it's about time I be honest about Maya, but the thing is, when I said we should just be ourselves, you know what she said?"

Maggie shrugs.

"That we shouldn't have to advertise it either."

"Hmm," Maggie is beginning to smell something.

"Yeah. But in the meantime we could be in a place full of strangers, all over each other like crabs on a carcass, y'know? It's like keeping it a secret helps fuel it."

"But that's not a problem now. You can go public, right?"

"Okay, here's the thing." He levels with her, "When we get invited places, we come together as pals, but for instance, guess who gets us into Tipitina's every night?"

She thinks about it.

"Yeah. Sammy. And it ain't because of me. He's always doing *her* a favour. But why would he continue to do so if we're no longer 'just friends?'"

"Hmm…"

"So I'm the one who brought her here, introduced her around, and now she's got the shine and *I'm* beginning to feel like a tourist." He looks at the busy street, the familiar wooden facades and elegant trees. "I feel like she's usurped my life here."

"Not with me, honey."

"Thanks, babe. I needed that," he smiles and they touch hands, "I know you liked her too when you first met."

"Yeah I thought she was fun and really good-looking but you're Poem, man! You're awesome!" she picks up his hand and he feels the love. "Have you talked to her about this?"

"Y'know, it's mostly good. I'm just voicing my concerns, that's all."

"Are you committed to her, Poem?"

"That's hard to say. I mean, I don't want anyone else, and yet, I still love Monique. And I guess Maya's right; I have to deal with that first before I can truly commit to her."

"I thought you two were in love."

"We are! We're just being Libertarian about it. Plus keep in mind she's coming out of a 10-year relationship."

"That doesn't matter! When you're in love, you're in love!"

"So you think if I truly love her I should just drop everything?"

"I would! Poem, if she truly loves you," she looks deeply into him, her breasts on the table, "and she considers this more than a fling, then she will be ready to commit to you *now*!"

"God, you sound like Monique." He contemplates the paradox that is his girlfriend back home, whose morality actually liberates her. "If you love something, wouldn't you want it to be free? I mean, isn't love the all-pervading, binding force of the universe? Doesn't true love always come back to you?"

"I don't think that works in real life."

Poem lets out a heavy sigh. "I can hear in the distant north my life back in Toronto slowly ripping apart." He ponders his precarious circumstance, "Lynette wants me here because Julien's grades are improving. She wants Maya here because her confidence is improving. Look, I'm not gonna advertise that we're together but you go ahead, Maggie, tell all your friends. Gossip is fine with me."

"Protecting your property?"

"It's not mine, remember? Love is all-pervading."

"More like all-consuming."

He sighs. "I do feel like I'm being consumed."

Maggie cannot possibly add more. She feels the marked connection between them and it is good. Beneath the long fingers of dusk, they get up and Poem walks her to her bike. She gets on and he watches her ride away towards Miss Mae's. How cute she looks in her long skirt and boots, peddling, bumping along under lush green oaks. It makes him feel dirty for driving a fossil burner. He sighs, turns east towards his car, and strolls into the approaching night.

4 THE GUESTROOM

"Hello?

"Hey Monique! How are you?

"Yeah I'm good. How's work?

"Uh huh.

"Busy... *Really* busy. Sorry I didn't call. I was meaning to get a phone card—

"Right, you mentioned that—well, I prefer writing anyway. I just haven't been on the computer.

"Yeah, me 'n' Maya been playing around—I mean, gigging—and uh... played a few gigs. We're gonna sit in again with Sammy's band next week.

"No, money's not good. You have to be hooked up here to make money, same as Toronto.

"I dunno, I wonder. I like it here cuz it's a cool place to be but it may not be the place for me. We'll see. I'm still having fun."

"She's good. With Julien.

"Yeah, he's good. Doing much better in school.

"*Definitely* his attitude is improving.

"No, Maya's around. She's uh... somewhere 'round here. We're good.

"I don't know. We're meeting lots of people and there're some good opportunities. I just wanna see what pans out.

"Of course I miss you. How's salsa?

"And Adele?

"Oh that Claude...!

"Well, it's pretty packed. Her father's here, uncle too. Neither one speaks English. It's pretty funny sometimes.

"Uh well... y'know... We're making due.

"Well, Lynette's got her room, Jacques is bunking with Julien, and Stéphane, uh... he's got the couch downstairs.

"Me? Well, I'm in the guestroom.
"Maya? She's also in the guestroom.
"Yeah, we're both in the guestroom—
"Hello? Hello…?"

5 SIX FEET UNDER

Poem and Maya bump along the gnarly pavement road on Oak Street, listening to late night WWOZ. They stop in front of Snake and Jake's Christmas Club and see people standing out front with no obvious parking in sight. "It's busy," Poem says. The clock reads 1:11 a.m.

He looks to his right, to the weed-infested parking lot, then glancing back he reaches behind Maya's seat and reverses the car into the intersection. He turns and gingerly bumps up over the sidewalk into the lot and squeezes in between two other cars. They step out with vodka tonics in hand and Poem sees a couple making out in the car next to him, their arms wrapped around each other like a Chinese riddle. He locks up, slides past the spectacle to the rear of the car and whispers to Maya, "Someone's making out in there."

"What... alone?"

"No...! What d'ya mean alone? He's got a girl!"

She laughs. "Cute."

They collect themselves, check for smokes, wallet, keys. Poem puts his hand on the trunk.

"You leaving your guitar in there?"

"Yeah," he looks up. "Temperature's not too bad."

They turn their attention to the club and saunter through the parked cars and across the road through a small group of people. One guy is yelling into his phone, "I certainly *did not* want the condom to break! That's why I WORE ONE!!"

They enter the dimly lit Christmas room buzzing with familiar faces and a lot of new ones, all talking above the soulful southern funk coming out of the speakers. Some at tables, others at the bar; no matter how many people are here, it always seems full. But tonight it is absolutely packed. The dartboards are taken while girls bounce on the dance floor, undulating bumpers to people coming in and out of the front door. It's like everyone's treading water and their drinks are the lifeline.

They make it to the bar and the keeper says, "So whatcha having?"

Poem and Maya drink-up and he hands her their empty cups, bumping a sourly-perfumed woman who gives him an approving look. "Do you know how to make a Bloody Bobbitt?" he says and the bartender is stumped. "It's the same as a Bloody Mary but instead of celery, you use half a pickle."

She guffaws. "I'll see if I can find some pickles for ya, baby, and when I do," she makes a paring motion, "Off with their heads!"

"Thanks, baby."

The perfumed woman says, "So what's *your* name, hotshot?"

"Poem," he says but she doesn't hear him.

"Porn?"

"No. Po-em." He enunciates into her ear, "A di Poem."

The club is noisy and she hears 'a deep poem' and suddenly doesn't know what to make of this unusual man. He sees her confusion and turns to Maya who's talking with Maurice, a local sax player and regular here.

Maurice steps towards him and they hug. "There are some really interesting people here, Poem."

"Oh yeah?"

"Maurice says that guy down there," Maya points to the back corner booth, "is a for real astrologer."

"Really? I gotta talk to him. Is he busy?"

"He's just hanging out like you," Maurice says. "You should meet him. He's really interesting and very nice. From out of town."

Poem leans over to catch a sightline of the astrologer speaking to a couple women sitting opposite him. He has a full head of silvery hair and looks up to make eye contact. There is a flash of recognition and he returns to his conversation. The keeper returns with two blood-red Bloody Bobbitts which she places in front of Poem, each with a half pickle on ice, like dismembered appendages. He winces and pays her, hands Maya her drink, and they squeeze on down the bar to the where the astrologer is holding court. Maurice salutes and shuffles off to the dance floor.

The last booth is blocked off from the rest of the club by a large speaker adorned in plastic holly. They step past the invisible threshold into a bubble of relative tranquility where they hear the astrologer say, "But the thing is, you can't *prove* or *disprove* the existence of God."

He is a man of authority, warm and handsome, of north European descent, with bright blue eyes. Sitting opposite him are two women with a third standing, distracted by the party. A young man leans over him, listening intently, while a few others are hanging around.

Poem slides in with Maya in tow.

"Science is a method," the astrologer says. "It is *not* the truth. Science cannot deal with first causes," he looks at Maya.

"You mind if we listen?" she asks.

"Not at all. I was just explaining to these good people that science cannot discuss the spiritual world because it is built on a material philosophy." His air is commanding and worldly. "The best we can do is either dismiss it or label it 'inconclusive,'" he grins. "And being *limited* to the material world, science cannot answer everything because not everything in the world is material. Take this dark matter mystery. Do they know what it is? They know it exerts gravity, but is it material?"

"Well, it must have substance if it exerts gravity," Poem says.

"Ahh, but what *is* gravity?"

"Well... It's a field, right?"

"Precisely! And you cannot *see* a field, but it *does* influence everything within its range. I personally believe that mass of what they call dark matter and dark energy is mostly just the weight of parallel universes pressing into our own, that is, other *worlds* that interpenetrate our own and vibrate on a completely different frequency from what we perceive to be material. And we can detect these other worlds only en masse or..." he looks around, "psychically. There is no machine that can measure psychic phenomenon because machines are material and they can measure only materiality."

"What about heat?" the guy next to him says.

"Heat is material. It involves atoms. Even *light* is material because it's made of photons."

Poem says, "You don't think that unseen mass out in space—uh, dark matter—is just the accumulated debris of failed stars, planets, and so on?"

"Since when does the debris outweigh the edifice?"

"I guess only when it's destroyed."

"Do you think the universe is already dead?"

"That's a good question. Perhaps *we* are the ghosts of a spiritual world."

The astrologer chuckles. "Where ya from, young man?"

"Aw, same place as you, man: Earth!"

They laugh and the astrologer slides him a wiseacre smile, "Now that is being presumptuous, wouldn't you say?"

"We're from Toronto," Maya cuts in.

"I've been to Toronto. Nice city."

"It's all right," Poem says.

"Don't believe him. Toronto is fucking awesome!" Maya declares and the astrologer likes her sass.

"But it really is a mistake," he says, "to think we will ever find a *piece* of dark matter. It's not like dark chocolate," he chortles. "The universe is vast, my dear, not only *out there,*" he looks up, "but *in here,*" he points to his heart.

"People hear this idea of multi-dimensions and they always think that it's somehow *out there*, out in the ether, or another part of town, but what about the dimensions within? How much dark matter is in us?" The two women nod. "How many *dimensions* do we have? Is our body in one universe and our mind in another? Are we separate from one another or are we connected the way opposite hands are connected?"

"Some say we're all water," Maya says.

"We are! Nearly all water, with just enough *earth* to keep it together, enough air to *perceive* the whole thing, and of course the *fire* to make it go!" he makes a fist. "But as all rivers eventually lead to the sea, so do we all eventually merge into this vast ocean of consciousness."

"That just sounds like a poetic way of saying 'when you die, you die,'" the woman standing says. "That what makes you *you* is gone forever or '*merged* into the ocean of consciousness,' as you would say."

"Everyone is so afraid of annihilation. They want to be around to see what happens but believe me, I'm 62 years old, I have my moments when I am tired of living, tired of being." He looks at Poem, "Can you imagine never sleeping, never being able to rest or die, to take a break from life? This would drive you insane!"

"Well, that explains old people," Maya says and everyone laughs.

"So then," the woman standing says, "There's no life after life?"

The astrologer smiles. "I would rephrase that and say 'life *between* lives.' And yes, there is life between lives, just as death necessitates life, and the other way around. Or as Niels Bohr would say: 'It is the hallmark of any deep truth that its negation is also a deep truth.' Like how black holes exhaust their mass through the stars."

This suspends everyone and he explains, "They say all this mass collapses into a black hole that becomes infinitely dense, but really, that's a cop out. Where does it go? It's not just gonna disappear or clump together into something infinitely small. Like everything in the universe, it must have an outlet. And I believe that outlet is the stars."

Everyone is silent.

"We don't see the pipe connecting the black hole at the centre of our galaxy to all the stars of our galaxy because the exchange, 'the tube,' is inter-dimensional. But I assure you there *is* a connection and this is ultimately what fuels and connects all the stars within the electromagnetic field of our galaxy, the way you get wireless through the house. Stars burn because they are part of a larger system, connected to the source, the way these Christmas lights are connected through a wire," he points out the random LEDs rimming the ceiling like a band of constellations. "You don't see the tangled wire, you see only individuated lights, seemingly random and separate, some closer, some further, yet they are all part of the same line, invisibly connected and deriving their energy from the same source."

"I hear you're an astrologer," Maya says.

"I prefer Astrologist."

"Oh? Why?"

"Because Astrologers have a bad name," he winks at the ladies.

"Why is that?"

"Because too many of them don't know what they're talking about! They study for a year or take a weekend course and think they've mastered the subject. What's worse are these blasted zodiac columns in the newspaper. Most people think *this* is astrology!" He takes a sip of his drink.

"Isn't it true that science rejects astrology?" the woman standing says.

He gives her a long look, considering whether to indulge or dismiss the question. "As I was saying, astrology is a *metaphysical* subject, do you know what this means?"

"You mean, the spiritual world?"

He rolls his eyes, "Yes, we can call it 'spiritual' but that word is too vague, too overused, too Hollywoodized. The metaphysical is that part of the world we don't see and *can't* experience except indirectly, like dark matter. We infer its existence when we can't explain something but we recognize that it has order or an invisible source. Like why is lunacy more prevalent during a full moon?"

"But if you can see it or experience it even indirectly, why can't you prove it scientifically?"

"It *has* been proven."

"Really?"

"Yes, of course. There are many scientists who have experimented and found, like astrologists, varying degrees of success and correlation."

"Then why do people think science is against it?"

"Because most people are idiots! Look, you had Carl Sagan and a relatively small group of scientists in the 1970s denounce astrology in *The Humanist* magazine," he rolls his eyes, "because they could think of no feasible way for it to work. Did they spend even a year investigating it? Did they visit with astrologists all over the world to measure and compare results, to get more than one point of view? Did any one of them go out and get a reading?! They dismiss it for being unscientific, yet how unscientific are they in dismissing something they did not study?! You see, scientists are often in error but rarely in doubt. Do they know what good astrology can do? Do they understand its antiquity, its therapeutic value, its cosmological implications, or do they just sit there and arrogantly dismiss facts with theory?"

Poem likes this man. He is eloquent and forceful.

"Twenty years ago they didn't know about dark matter; now it is all they talk about, saying it makes up 96 percent of the known universe and they don't know what it is?! It seems that science over time has only *increased* our ignorance." Everyone laughs. "Besides, astrology never claimed to be scientific. How could it be when it relies on the ability of the reader? But a bad doctor does not make the whole of medicine bad."

"I once heard," Maya says, "that something like two thirds of all medical diagnoses are wrong?"

"That doesn't surprise me," the woman on the right says. "I don't know why people are so hung up on things being scientific anyway. Ya can't see God through a microscope."

"But you *can* see it through a telescope," Poem says.

The astrologist nods touché and adds, "I think there is something particularly special about astrology because at its core it *is* mathematical and so people expect it to be scientific."

"I think astrology is where art meets science," Poem says.

"That's good; the subjective and the objective. I like it. Yes, these so-called scientists in the seventies did a great disservice by denouncing astrology the way they did, however, astrology as it is practiced in the mainstream today, that is, the highly imbecilic business of Sun-sign astrology, *needs* to be reigned in—I acknowledge that—but they threw the baby out with the bathwater!"

"A homicide."

"Which is the habit of ignoramuses! And when you listen to their criticisms, it is clear they have only the most superficial understanding of the subject. Their words, their conceptual approach, all reveal their ignorance and disinterest, and yet, I have heard so many pontificate on this subject which they know almost nothing about. As Newton once told Halley in defence of astrology: 'I have studied these things which you have not!'"

Poem nods, having heard this quote before.

"Yes, it is the great fear of the Literalist that you may know something he doesn't. Oh he can't stand that and he would rather have you drown him in a teaspoon than admit it. That part of it is cultural. There are certain things that require an elevated consciousness in order for you to understand." He looks at Poem, "Are you familiar with the language of the stars?"

"Actually, I'm studying the Indian method with a teacher for about nine months now."

"Really? That's fantastic!"

"Well, he's in Toronto and I haven't seen him since August."

"Oh, I'm very sorry to hear that. You must miss him very much."

Poem reflects on how much in the midst of all this partying, how anaemic he feels, like missing an essential food group. He envisions the warm light of his teacher so far away, like looking at a star on a wintry night and imagining himself on this bright warm island in space. "Yeah…" he looks at Maya, "Yes I do."

"My name is Gabe, by the way. Gabriel Hawson," he reaches out to shake hands. Poem and Maya introduce themselves and everyone at the table does the same. Poem as usual has to clarify his name. "I hear it's very difficult to learn Indian astrology without a teacher."

"Yeah that's true because to learn it you have to have some access to Sanskrit. I don't think many Westerners have written on the subject or know it that well, not well enough to teach it through a book."

"Who's your teacher?"

"Mantriji."

"Beautiful."

"Yeah, he's from India. Been doing it a long time. He's close to 70 now, totally old school, y'know? The real deal."

"You're very lucky to have found him. You must have been very interested in the subject."

"Well, actually no. I didn't know anything about Jyotish, and I didn't find *him*, he kind of found *me*."

Gabe looks at him, puzzled.

"I was at a friend's place getting ready to leave when he showed up early for her lesson, something he never does because he lives only five minutes away. I was actually trying to avoid him," he laughs. "But I met him just as I was about to go and he invites me to sit in. Next thing I know, I'm the subject of their lesson, getting an impromptu reading that like, changed my life."

Gabe smiles.

"I mean, it wasn't what I expected at all. He was able to put dates to key events and that's what kind of blew me away, y'know, like what about freewill? So I went back and went back and went back and before I knew it, I was his student."

Gabe looks at him curiously, "So why are you here?"

"What d'ya mean?"

"Don't you know that this man came to you, to find you? When the student is ready, the teacher will appear. Do you not see how providential this meeting was, this story you tell? You were meant to meet this man. He would not accept you as a student unless he saw something in you. This man is your *teacher*!"

"Yeah… I mean… I'm gonna go back eventually. I just kind of…" he looks at Maya, "I'm just here playing for a bit."

"Playing?"

"Well, we did a lil gig tonight," he puts his arm around Maya.

"My son," Gabe implores him, "You are in the company of a great man, this—what's his name?"

"Mantriji."

"Yes. He can reveal to you the meaning of the world! Why are you here in this time warp, this swamp of broken dreams, where people drink just to keep from drowning?"

"But I'm a musician."

"Do you not know that astrology is the highest form of music? Pythagoras called it the 'music of the spheres.'"

"I hear you but I've already written so many songs. I'm just looking for a way to make some money off it."

"In New Orleans?"

"Why not?"

He appreciates Poem's idealism but he's going to set him straight, "In some ways this is the most beautiful city in the world, but it is a museum, a morgue for the suffering, for the desirous, for the prospering to feed off; a reckoning place for former slaves and a drunken carnival for tourists to lose themselves. It is a swamp of exploited souls broken by the founding of America and it will one day be purged, and believe me, when that day comes, you don't wanna be here. You are only a tourist here."

"But I love this city. I feel so connected here." He looks at Maya and hesitates before saying, "I'll tell you about a dream me and this lady had." He leans into the table and recounts the lucid, clearly supernatural shared dream and everyone listens amazed.

"You know," Gabe says, "that New Orleans is six feet below sea level."

"Yeah," Maya heard. "That's why all the graves are above ground."

"Do you understand that water signifies and in many ways *facilitates* our collective unconscious on this planet?"

Poem says, "I know that in astrology the water signs are the most spiritual."

"Yes, they are the most sensitive to the fluid depths of our unconscious because they themselves are fluid." He outlines on the table, "On the Earth, most people live above sea level, of course, but when people live below sea level, by whatever circumstance, they are living below the natural threshold between the conscious and unconscious of our planet, that is, between the atmosphere and the ocean. In other words, they tap into their psyches and are more prone to 'freak out!'"

Everyone is silent.

"You can easily lose yourself, or your mind, or even your life, living below sea level."

The guy standing next to him says, "I need a drink," and leaves.

Gabe says to Poem, "I know the Indian system is very sophisticated and apparently very old. They have the lunar mansions, what are they called?"

"Nakshatras."

"Yes. There are 27 lunar mansions that correlate to, I guess, the sidereal month of the Moon, and apparently they're very accurate. Did you study them?"

"We just barely touched on them. I have a conceptual understanding but it's like learning 27 new signs; not easy. I'm still trying to master the 12 signs."

"Well, you never fully master them, son. You have to let them master you."

"You mean like channelling?"

"Let me just say don't let your *brain* distract from your judgement."

"Hey!" Maya blurts. "Carol's here!"

Carol is at the front door, talking to Maurice and one other guy. She's an attractive redhead with a big aura and flirtatious smile. Maurice points to Maya and Carol waves.

Gabe says, "I'll be back," and he slides out of the booth, revealing a pot belly and burgundy cowboy boots.

The woman next to Poem says, "I don't know what to make of this stuff. People believe what they wanna believe, in whatever comforts them."

Poem shrugs. "Well, how can we agree on objective truths when everyone's having a subjective experience?"

"I just think ideas are spread not because they're true but because they're appealing."

"You sound disappointed."

"You try being raised Catholic."

"I was."

"So what happened?"

"I became an astrologer."

"Hah!"

"Y'know, I heard once that when you scratch a cynic you get a disappointed idealist."

She gives him a long look, raises an unlit cigarette, reconsiders it then walks away.

Carol shuffles in and gives Maya a hug before turning to Poem, "Hey baby, you takin' care of this beautiful young lady?"

"Every night," Poem grins and Maya smacks his stomach.

"So whatcha all doin'?"

"Just talkin' astrology."

"Astrology!? Don't you know that's the devil's work?"

"You mean like jazz?"

"I just know what my minister said."

"Did he say it was astrologers who first found Jesus?"

"Huh?"

"Yeah, the three wise men, the Magi, who followed the star of

Bethlehem."

"Oh yeah!"

"Well, what do you think a Magi is?"

"I dunno."

"A magician, astrologer, mystic, someone who understands prophecy and the supernatural. They predicted a king would be born in the west so they came from Persia bearing presents."

Carol tilts her head, confronting a paradigm shift. This is her favourite part of the gospel: three wise men following a magical star and finding baby Jesus in the manger. Gabe arrives back from the men's room in time to hear her say, "I just always took it on faith that astrology was nothin' but blind superstition and you shouldn't believe in none of it."

"Well, what do you believe in?" Gabe says, sliding back into the booth.

"I believe in Jesus Christ."

"Oh, so you believe in the virgin birth?"

"That's right."

"You don't think that's superstitious?"

"I don't know what you mean, Mister."

He introduces himself and she does the same. "Super-stition," he breaks it down, "speaks to the super-natural. A virgin birth is a supernatural event, wouldn't you agree?"

"I guess."

"And yet the church warns *against* the supernatural, correct?"

"Yeah."

"Do you know that Jesus was first discovered by astrologers?"

"Yeah, he was just sayin'—"

"Sammy!" Maya announces.

Poem turns to see Sammy by the door with his bass player, surveying the club. Maya starts towards him as Poem watches and she greets him with an affectionate hug—*What?! This is the sixth time they've hugged today! They hugged at rehearsal this morning when we arrived, they hugged when we took off, they hugged at our gig tonight, they hugged when we finished our set, they hugged when Sammy left, and here they are hugging again?! What the fuck is going on?!* He hones in on them, his internal heat rising. *They seem really happy to see each other, like it's been a long time, like they couldn't wait.* He feels his cheeks and collar flush. *What is going on here?* He wants to leap over there and punch Sammy in the face. It's been leading up to this. He should know they're together by now. *What do I gotta do? Stake my claim?!*

He squeezes through the crowd to where Maya and Sammy are talking and compels them apart with his body, "Sorry, I gotta talk to Maya for a sec." He grabs her wrist and coerces her to the door. She laughs nervously but obeys.

"What's wrong, Poem?"

He coaxes her through the entrance out into the cool night to where almost no one is around. She turns and shakes loose of his grip and stumbles back against the wall. "What's your problem, Poem?!"

"Why the fuck are you hugging Sammy so many times today?! You act like you haven't seen him in months the way you hugged him just now!"

She is stumped, realizing how obvious they've been. "Fuck, I'm sorry, Poem. I'm just happy to see him, that's all. He's been a really good friend."

"How?!"

"Well, you have Maggie… I have Sammy…" she looks down, searching for more. Maya's been here two months, long enough to have made a few of her own friends, but they're all Sammy's friends.

"That's not what I'm talking about, Maya! He knows we're together and he's doing this to diss me, and you're just letting him!"

"I am not! We're just friends, okay? This has nothing to do with you, Poem."

"I don't like the vibe with you two. I feel like a friggin pariah around you guys, like *I'm* the outsider."

"Well you keep saying stupid things, Poem. Like who cares about Wagner?! Really, who cares?! We're not all friggin philosophers like you. Sometimes I just wanna have a normal conversation."

Poem can't believe it. "Maya! It's me, Poem! Remember?!"

She shakes her head, not knowing how to say it. "Poem, look…" She takes a drag off her cigarette and finally levels with him, "I like Sammy, okay?"

Poem feels his heart sink and his cheeks flush red. He connects to when they first met, how hard it hit, how he knew even then that his life would change. He flashes to their first kiss, to their miraculous dream, to their secret lovemaking, to his quitting his job, to Lynette telling them to just share a room, to Monique finding out and moving all his stuff to his mother's house.

"Are you fucking kidding me?!" he stares her down and she looks away. "Are you FUCKING KIDDING ME?! I stayed here because of YOU!!" He is pissed. She approaches him and he blocks her almost violently from getting close. He wants to punch her and he can't believe it. She is not his love but a stranger, a stranger who's playing him. He looks up at the Moon. *Holy shit! It's a full moon!* It hangs fat in the southern sky, stark and beautiful, razor cold, like the eye of another universe looking down. What primordial force has drawn him to this rage, to this outburst, to this sudden jealousy and thirst for violence? His lips curl with betrayal as he looks deeply into the soul of this sick moon. *This is not me. This is not me!*

He promised Jerry he'd be back to work then changed his mind. He was to continue studies with Mantri but stayed here instead. He had a loving girlfriend but admitted him and Maya are sharing a bed. He had a great apartment in Toronto but said he wasn't coming back. He came here for music but he stayed for Maya. Now he doesn't want her. He has compromised everything to prolong a dream and now it's over. He's not here for music, he's here to feed the Moon, and it is sucking him like a whirlpool.

"No, no, NO! You are not going with Sammy, you are with me! I didn't give it all up to hand you off to someone else. I can't believe you just said that! Who are you?!"

Maya finds her centre and coming to, pleads, "I'm sorry, Poem. You're right. I dunno. I'm just so confused. I mean, we're staying with your girlfriend's family, y'know? That's pretty unusual, wouldn't you say?"

"Who the hell's been whispering in your ear, Maya?!"

"I don't know if you're gonna get back with Monique."

"Are you fucking kidding me?! All my stuff's moved out! I have nothing to go back to! I can't believe this!" He turns and walks out into the intersection. It's like a bomb just went off inside his head. He knows he messed up. He's beginning to see it from other angles and it doesn't look good. *What have I done?* He thinks of Mantri who predicted:

"You will drink and have a good time... Just don't break your family."

"Oh God! He knew! He knew this would happen! Why didn't he warn me?! I'm running lord of the 8th!"

"Poem!" Maya calls and he turns around. "I'm sorry, baby. I don't know what I was saying. I just drank too much, that's all."

Poem wants to believe her but he doesn't. He knows something just broke. Do you fight for a girl who has designs on someone else? He feels like a rung in a ladder. He retreats to the opposite side of the road when a pair of headlights suddenly dawn. Maya backs up onto the curb and waits for the vehicle to pass then runs across the road to embrace him in a long affectionate hug. He looks down and she licks his nose, "I love you, Poem. I really do. You changed my life. I was so unhappy with Tony and I thought that was it, this was my life and it would never change. And then you came and *everything* changed! You are my hierophant. It's because of you that I'm here singing in New Orleans. I sang in New Orleans, can you believe it?"

Poem feels validated for the first time.

"Sometimes I just forget," she looks down. "Sometimes I can't believe that I met you."

He lets her go. "What d'ya mean?"

"I guess I feel like you're my husband now and I can't believe this is happening. It's like I'm running from it."

Poem feels his heart do a 180 and it throws him like the outside row of a merry-go-round. He shakes his head, "It's too much, Maya. It's too much.

I can't stay here right now. Look at the Moon."

She looks up, "Wow."

"Let's go. I just want you to myself right now." His eyes are tired and she touches his chest. "Show me that you mean it."

She gives him that familiar look. They hug and he doesn't have the energy to second guess it. He just wants to lie naked with her, to feel the flesh of their love, which is never hindered by fear or doubt.

"I have to say goodbye," she says and he agrees to go back in. They kiss and gather themselves. "How do I look?"

"Beautiful."

They enter the bar to a different room. Sammy and gang are hanging around the big table, playing darts. Poem hears them ask if she's all right. He sees the crowd in back chatting, Gabe standing next to the bar. He smiles as Poem approaches, "Did you see the Moon?"

Poem sidles up next to him, "I think I'm losing my mind to that moon."

Gabe laughs. "It is not the Moon, young man, but the swamp of your desires. Remember, you are not in New Orleans; it is in you. Go to where your teacher is. You don't want to be six feet under," he gestures to the people in the club, dancing, chatting, losing themselves.

"Don't worry. I got a levee." Poem asks for his email and Gabe hands him a business card. He looks at it and says, "I nearly lost it just now." He motions to Maya, "And now I have to go prove my love." He sighs wearily. "Any parting words of wisdom?"

Gabe thinks and says, "Yeah. Don't end up six feet under."

Poem gives him a long thoughtful look, shakes his hand, and acknowledges the divine in him. He turns and sees Maya saying goodbye, avoiding Sammy who's looking for another hug. He walks over to the big table and says, "Yeah, me and Maya got some love to make," he glares at Sammy who looks away.

Maya smiles and the two exposed lovebirds head for the door. It feels like they're good again. So he kisses her cheek and she giggles like a bride as they walk out into the moonlit night.

6 JESUITS & ROCK STARS

Poem opens his eyes to darkness. He looks at the window and sees slivers of sunlight squeezing through the blinds. It is morning.

Maya's still asleep, breathing like a smoker. He watches over her, admiring her beautiful young face, red spotted cheeks, full lips and mascara-flaked eyelashes. How at peace she looks. He admires her ability to sleep. He's always up early. He can't sleep. He hears people talking and moving in the kitchen below and it reminds him today is Sunday; most likely everyone's home. He heaves a sigh and thinks of last night. Maya shifts a bit. He looks at her and recalls the Moon so ripe, how he was itching to fight till he looked up and felt himself falling into that moon. *I can't believe she said that to me. She's into that ragamuffin?!* He thinks of Monique, of their apartment, their drives to Texas, her laughter, sweetness, and beautiful long legs. He wonders if it's truly over, if any true love can be truly over.

He lifts Maya's arm, squeezes himself out of the sheets and sits upright on the side of the bed. Maya groans, shifts around and nods off again. He marvels at her oblivion. *Is it because she's young or because she hasn't fucked up her entire life that she can sleep so soundly?* He gets up, gets dressed, drinks bottled water, closes the door behind him and heads for the washroom.

"Shit!" He has another hickey. He washes up, brushes his teeth and steps quietly downstairs to gather his books.

Lynette shouts, "Mornin'!" from the kitchen but he is slow to respond. He quickly collects his stuff and steps out to the front porch where he pulls on his boots and makes for the street, his heart racing.

Walking towards Carrollton he stops, lights a cigarette and takes a long deep medicinal haul. He continues walking, birds are chirping, the sky is blue. He scratches the back of his head, agitated, "I don't know why but I feel like she's playing me." He is sad and angry. *This is not me. I was never jealous of Monique and she was doing salsa! What's up with this?!*

He makes it to the Camellia Grill where he picks up a large and sits on the bench next door. He takes out the ephemeris and opens his pad. Sitting there out front of the Cold Stone with his coffee on the ground, he looks up the planets and eyeballs the ascendant for New Orleans, latitude 30° north, around 2 a.m., when all this went down. He draws a chart with Sun in the 3rd house.

Wow! Virgo lagna. My lagna.

Where was the Moon?

Taurus! That's my Moon! And Mars in the 7th? The desire to conquer others.

He learned from Mantri that *when* something happens will tell you a lot about *what* happens.

"Just read the significance of an event the way you read the character of a person."

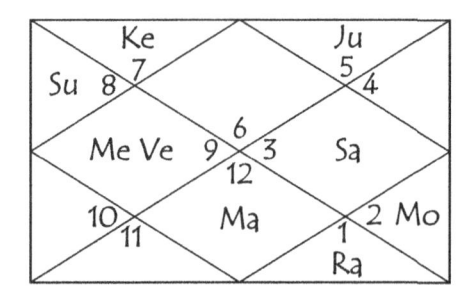

```
          Ke           Ju
       Su 8  7       5    4
              6
         Me Ve 9    3   Sa
                12
         10         1   2 Mo
            11    Ma
                       Ra
```

Okay, so Mars the fighter is transiting my 7th house of relationships and Saturn aspects Mars and I'm running Mars! Man, I wanted to punch that girl. He examines it closely. *Saturn is friggin killing me! Aspecting my home and partner and Jupiter, my main dasa lord!* He looks at it in the 12th house. *Fuck! I'm losing everything.*

Some tourists pass by looking for the grill. He takes a sip of coffee and toggles his neck. "So what's good about this chart?" He sees Rahu in the 8th, which explains the hickey, but the only good thing here is exalted Moon in the 9th house of guru. He thinks of Mantri. "What am I doing here?" He stares across the street then quickly packs up his books and begins walking. He is impatient to be somewhere but has nowhere to go. Lynette's is full. Maya won't be up for another three hours. He's got no place to go.

He sips on his coffee, walking towards Tulane University. He read about their philosophy department. They have a whole program on metaphysics. He remembers Mantri saying,

"Those who suffer in life look for answers, those who are successful, no. They will look only after they realize their dissatisfaction with material wealth. At that time they will turn to those who began the search sooner."

He thinks of his ridiculous state here in New Orleans, like in some bad movie. *Why am I here? Is it for me or for her? I thought I'd be back in October. Now it's December?! How'd that happen?!* He is spinning in the whirlpool of New Orleans. "Fuck, I can't go home."

He thinks of Monique and their beautiful Taurean apartment: a three-bedroom ground-floor hideaway low-budget urban castle, nestled behind old pines, master bedroom on the second floor, his own space, two cats that roam about. It *feels* like home and now it's gone. Monique loves pillows and scarves and books and candles and jazz and skirts and stained glass windows and opera and art movies and painting with oils and writing poetry and burning the edges of the paper. *I had a cozy Taurus and I went for a crazy Gemini! What kind of astrologer am I?!*

He was blind, distracted, self-absorbed. Monique spent two nights packing all his clothes, books, papers, equipment, and just heaped it onto his mother's porch. He remembers his mom on the phone:

"You get back here NOW and fix your life! So help me God, I have no room for all this stuff!! You are KILLING ME!!!"

He held the phone from his ear, even Maya could hear; this woman could draw blood. He thinks about his music, his manuscripts, his tapes. It's the only thing that matters to him, his life's work, and now his mother's threatening to get rid of it?!

His heart is pounding like it's gonna burst as he zigzags the grid of streets through East Carrollton. He makes it back to Lynette's where he reluctantly enters the house and finds her and her father in the kitchen. They can see he's distressed.

"Are you all right, Poem?"

He leans back against the sink and they watch him sympathetically. He wonders how they could forgive his infidelity. "My heart… is breaking," he holds it with his right hand. "I don't know what to make of her," he looks up at the ceiling.

Lynette bites her lower lip and Poem gets it. He grabs the phone and walks out to the front porch where he makes a call, "Yo Duke, you up?"

"Yeah, I need someone to talk to right now. Yeah, right now, man. I'm dying.

"Thanks. Be right over."

It's been a week since he saw Duke. Maggie's visiting Colorado and his friends back in Toronto seem remote to him now. Duke loves to talk and it's sometimes exhausting but you always learn something, about him, about New Orleans, about music, about racism. His father's a well-known musician with cancer who rarely leaves his room upstairs and his mom is a strong compassionate woman whom he calls Trix.

Duke grew up playing bass and piano and studied music in university. He toured with a couple different acts and lived in Sweden for a while. He seems to know everyone in New Orleans and can get you in anywhere free by the sheer guile of his tongue. A difficult character to forget, there's brilliance to everything he does and says, like he's the gatekeeper here so you'd better listen. Eccentric and adorable in a scary way he embodies the voodoo gangster vibe of this ancient city.

Poem stops at the Rite Aid where Earl the ol' security guard greets him with, "It's the man from Earth. Yawee!" and the staff all smile good-heartedly. He gets to Duke's who opens the door and heads back in, still in his pyjama bottoms.

"Hey Duke, I hope you weren't sleeping."

"Naw man, was just gettin' up." The blinds are shut and the room is a mess; the couch is strewn with bedsheets and a pillow. Duke is unshaven and grey with a honking cold sore on his upper lip. He tosses the sheets aside, offers Poem the couch, and says he'll be back with clean glasses. Poem settles in and starts a cigarette when Duke returns and organizes everything on the top board, "What's happenin', my brother? Why this crazy hour?" He opens the brandy and pours him and Poem a glass.

"It's noon, man."

"I know, but in China it's midnight!"

"Yo Duke, I just need someone to talk to, someone who'll listen. A lot of shit's been going on with me and Maya."

"Yeah, well I told you she was trouble."

"Dude, you said that only because *you're* interested, okay?"

"She's a sweet thing," he licks his chops. "So what, you havin' woman problems now?"

"Sorta."

"Man, I bet you could have any woman you want. You is Ultra Cool, man! The Cat in the Hat! You could have any woman, guaranteed." It sounds like he's about to ask for eight dollars.

"Y'know, Duke, I find that a lot of these really good-looking women—I mean, the *really* good-looking women—they all have these fucked up psychologies, like they expect the guy to do everything."

Duke nods, not disagreeing.

"And you get these guys who'll play that game, but it *becomes* a game, y'know, because it starts with a game."

"Yeah."

"But the girl goes for it. She goes for the big feathers, the big talker, the 'great opportunity.'"

"Yeah. You think that's Maya?"

"I hope not, Duke, but I think… there's a *little* of that in her."

"There's a little of that in every woman."

"I dunno, man. I thought I knew her but I'm watching her and I see how she attracts men and every one of them wants to do her a favour. But when they see I'm part of the picture, they're not so eager to wanna help no more. She probably thinks I'm a liability."

"Poem, you got your own thing goin' on. She's *your* singer, man. You ain't hers."

"I stayed here because of her, Duke. I didn't have to. I could've gone back to work and been here for Christmas." He looks down, shaking his head, "I stayed because I dunno... We had this dream and... I just felt like it was meant to be. I believed in it but, lately..." He takes a sip of brandy. "I feel like her friends are pulling her away and she's resisting less and less."

Duke doesn't know what to say.

"When she first came down here and we, y'know, got into it, we got a reading from this channeler who said I was Maya's hierophant, that my purpose was to show her the door, but that once she stepped through, there would be no turning back."

"So?"

"So I feel like maybe last night she opened that door."

"Man, just get yourself another girl."

"Dude, it's not that easy! I had a good woman and... I just don't know if I should stay or go."

"Bro, you're askin' the wrong person. You know how I feel about dis town."

"Yeah, but I also know you've been around. You lived in Europe, man! You know there's more to this world than New Orleans."

"Uh uh, not according to me."

"Duke, you know what I'm sayin'."

"Man, I don't even know you no more! What's with all this pity-pat self-pity bullshit?!"

Poem is taken aback.

"All I hear from you so far is complainin'!" He lights a cigarette, agitated. Poem wonders if this is not the best time to see him, before he's had his drugs, drinking on an empty stomach. "I heard you play, man. You's a gangsta! What d'ya mean you don't know what to do?!"

"Listen Duke, I've known you a couple months now. It's been fun. I know you already think I'm a legend, that I haven't even begun to scratch the surface of how hip in actual fact I really am but look, man, I know you're fighting your own demons too."

Duke looks away, not wanting to get into it.

"I don't know what karma it is that keeps me here but I feel like it's beginning to tear me apart."

"So fall apart, man! Let that be your inspiration. Do whatever it takes to be here, man! Here! C'mon! You is Ultra Cool Poem! You don't wanna be anyplace else."

There's an extended pause when they hear the radio upstairs playing Sunday morning gospel music, Trix singing and the floor creaking above. Poem settles into the couch, "You know, when I was in high school, if you'd asked me what I wanted to be in life, I would've told you one of two things: a Jesuit or a Rock Star."

Duke looks genuinely surprised.

"I went for rock star though because they get more chicks."

Duke sniggers and takes a drag, "You too much, Poem. I wouldn't a taken you for no Jesuit. I know you a spiritual brother, but priest, uh uh," he shakes his head.

"Well you see what I've become."

"What, a hybrid?"

"I was always just really curious to know where we came from, man, and why we're here, y'know? I guess cuz my father died when I was young." He stares at the wooden organ, "I remember looking into his coffin and wondering what happened?" He recalls the funeral music during the service. "I think I took to music because it's the most sublime language there is."

"Yeah…"

"So I started playing, reading, writing music. That's all I did in high school, man. I thought everyone else was an idiot. I just wanted to make my own music and really, I had absolutely no interest in doing covers."

"Ya gotta pay your dues, Holmes. It can't always be about you."

"I just figured there's gotta be a million guitarists who can already do Jimmy Page, so why would I want to?"

"Imitation is the highest form of flattery, my man. First you imitate, *then* you originate."

"Ya, I don't get that because then everything becomes derivative, like one big daisy chain, you know?"

Duke looks at him strangely.

"When I was in school, I took this interdisciplinary course in Montreal where one of the workshops was by this French dude, a famous choreographer—I forget his name—but he had this assignment for everyone in class. Now imagine this: 50 people, all artists, and the assignment was to go up in groups of three and he had this painting he did. He wanted us to study it, 'surrender ourselves' to it, then dance openly while everyone else watches."

"Whew," Duke imagines the scene.

"Of course the dancers were the first to volunteer, practically stepping over each other to get on, but when the dancers started to run out, the non-dancers started to sweat because we knew everyone would get their turn. So we just sat there terrified at the prospect of having to improvise a three-minute dance solo, induced solely by an impressionist painting!"

Duke laughs.

"And y'know, it hurts longer the more you wait so I said fuck it, I'm going on. The painting was horrible. I felt nothing—more like I'm trying to feel something and it's like waiting for a bowel movement." He gets up off the couch. "I got up there and closed my eyes and did this hybrid movement between like, tai chi and sneaking my girlfriend up the stairs of my mom's house at three o'clock in the morning," he does a silent creep. "It was an excruciating three minutes."

"I heard dat."

"So we broke for lunch then reconvened and it turned out this famous French dude had over the break composed an entirely new dance piece based on *my* movements! And not only that, he made me the lead!"

Duke can't believe it.

"So there I was, the principle dancer in this composition, largely of my own invention, supported by an ensemble of *real* dancers, and he said to the class—now get this—that he ends up getting more original ideas from non-dancers because dancers are so full of repertoire, it's hard to get anything new out of them. But a non-dancer doesn't know what he's doing, so he's liable to come up with something new."

"Hmm."

"I guess that's how I see myself, Duke: a poet trying to be a musician and a musician trying to be a poet."

"I just hear a whole lotta tryin'. Forget the tryin', man. Just do it!"

"I'm doing it, Duke! My whole life and *identity* is in doing it, man! I mean 'Adi Poem?!' Do you know how much shit I take for Adi Poem?!"

They are silent before Duke asks, "How'd you get that name anyway?"

Poem sighs. "It means:

A di-sciple of the **P**ower of **E**ternal **M**usic."

"I remember. But where's it come from?"

"So I read this book about an American doctor who went out to the wilds of Australia where she hung out with this aboriginal tribe and one of the things she learned is that they're named not after their lineage but by their individual genius. So if a guy likes to cut stone, you call him 'Stonecutter' cuz that's what he does. If you're the healer, they call you 'Healer.' In other words, your name is who you *are* and not what you inherited.

"So I asked myself, if I was named after my greatest attribute, what would my name be? Then it came to me: 'Poem!' I'm a poet, always have been, I can*not* be, and I always felt that music is an extension of that which I can't put into words."

"Ya you right. Music is somethin' else."

"So around that time, I just finished some recordings and the singer asked me how I want the credit on the CD. I said 'guitar by Poem' and she loved it and it became my stage name. I added Adi later, a Sanskrit word. It means the original vibration of Creation, which I call the Power of Eternal Music."

"Deep, man."

"That's where I couldn't separate the Jesuit from the Rock Star. But honestly, Duke, I think it's too deep for people. Even the astrology thing, I don't know what I got myself into."

"Why you say that?"

"Man, I went from listening to rock to listening to opera and dude, I lost some friends along the way. It just took me to another plane, like it was a *step-up* in my evolution as an artist. And you may think I'm crazy, Duke, but I'm beginning to see that astrology is the next step up from here."

"That's crazy, man."

"Look, I just know that when I first started getting into the 'art' of it, I saw that what I strived for and what I thought all artists strived for was Truth, to speak a universal language, to be eternal."

"Sounds to me like you aim to live forever, my man."

Poem is dumbstruck by this sudden revelation uttered nonchalantly by a half-drunk savant. "Y'know, Duke, mythology speaks through universal archetypes like astrology, whether Shakespeare, Wagner, or Dark Side of the Moon. There's something universal and transcendent about it and this is what I aim to do: to be an artist and to therefore be a seeker of Truth."

"Ya, you's a Jesuit all right."

"Or am I being pretentious?"

"I think you would of made a good teacher, Poem. I remember the Brothers who taught me. They were good, y'know? Thoughtful. It wasn't about programming so much as getting you to think. I know some of them went on to be priests."

"Man, I couldn't take being a priest and yet, I haven't given my music career the Full Monty either. So I guess you're right. I'm a hybrid."

Duke is learning so much about Poem.

"I think it has to do with the 12th house, y'know? Jesuits and rock stars, cuz the 12th has to do with loss and to be a priest means losing yourself, giving up your friends, society and personal ambitions. A rock star loses himself to his fans and ends up losing his privacy, dignity, and a lot of semen along the way. One is locked up in a monastery, the other in a hotel room, and they're both prisoners."

"They're just opposites of the same thing."

"Y'know I got my lord of the 12th in my 8th and right now I'm *running* lord of the 8th."

"Which means?"

The lord of loss in the house of sex? "I don't know, Duke."

"So you really *is* a priest, huh?"

"No man, I'm a rock star! I just have priest-leanings."

They laugh and light up fresh cigarettes.

"The thing is," Poem says, "Do you know how many talented people I know who are in some form of a soup line, and people with half their talent are sitting on top because of some connection or good luck?"

Duke nods, having seen his own fortunes wax and wane. He rose up early with his father's name, scored gigs, got to be pretty good, toured the U.S. and Europe, made money, met interesting people, developed a serious drug habit, moved abroad, married a Scandinavian blonde; all the vicissitudes of a legitimate jazz musician. Of course it became an all consuming addiction that resulted in a nasty divorce and Duke ending up back in New Orleans on his parent's couch. "Yeah, that's the way it is if you let it. What're you gonna do about it?"

"Duke, I'm fucking broke, man. I need to make some money."

"Is that all you worried about? If that's all it is, man, then don't worry. It's done."

"What d'ya mean 'it's done?'"

"I'll just get Trix to hire us to play the Christmas party at work. We'll get Maya to sing and you and I'll accompany."

"Ya mean Christmas carols?"

"Yeah, Silent Night, Jingle Bells, that sorta thing. We'll just swing it. Gotta be good for a few hundred bucks."

"Just the three of us?"

"Yeah."

He thinks about it. "All right. When do we start rehearsing?"

"Rehearsing?! Man, you don't know how to play Jingle Bells?"

"I can play it, Duke. I just never done it before." He looks over at some sheet music, "I just gotta find the tunes and learn 'em, that's all."

"Well you learn what ya gotta learn and talk to Maya. I could use some money too. I'll talk to Trixy later."

Poem sort of likes the idea but isn't fully sold on its legitimacy. If it's so easy to make money here, why is Duke always broke?

"So we good then? No goin' back to Ontario?"

"Look, I have to go back sooner or later, Duke. All my stuff's there: my equipment, my car, all my clothes and tapes are now at my mom's place. And she's threatening to throw shit out! But I'll stay till the end of the year and listen, man, I'll be back. We'll do the Christmas gig and I'll be back!"

"Now you talkin', bro. Now you makin' sense. This is the place to be, my man. N'awlins!" The two men toast. They have once again found camaraderie in a bottle. A figure passes the window and a few seconds later there's knocking on the door. "What time's it?"

Poem looks at the alarm clock next to him, "Just after one."

"Aw that's Josh—hey man, gotta wrap up. I got a lesson thing, almost forgot."

"Sure, Duke. No problem."

Duke steps out and Poem thinks about going back to Lynette's. Maybe Maya will be up. He wonders about this gig. *Oh well, it's something.* He hears Duke welcoming Josh, "Yo Ultra Cool, come on in."

"Ultra Cool...?"

Duke returns, followed by young pimply Josh, dragging his upright bass. He introduces him to Poem then says, "I know you don't like to see me drink, so I got drunk before you came." He sniggers spastically and Josh forces a smile. "Poem here is gonna be livin' in New Orleans *permanently*!"

"Oh yeah?"

"Yeah I'll be back, probably February or March. Just gotta take care of some business up north. But I'll be back."

"Duke was saying you're a pretty hot guitarist."

"Yeah I'm pretty good."

"What sort of stuff you do?"

"Oh I like to think of it as 'music of the spheres.'"

Josh looks confused.

"Well, I know you guys have work to do so I'm gonna go pass out or something. Duke, I'll talk to Maya and call you 'bout rehearsing for the Christmas gig. We should have at least one rehearsal, right?"

"I thought *we* were playing Christmas?" Josh says.

"Yeah, no worries, Holmes. There's 12 days of Christmas ain't there?"

At least he's consistent.

Poem gives them props and heads outside. It is midday and he's already high. The sky is blue and the breeze is cool as he strolls lazily to the car. *Guess I'll go find some Christmas tunes*—he stops and groans, "Christmas tunes...?"

7 INSIDE JOKE

It is a shadowy late afternoon a week before Christmas. Poem steps out onto the lit back porch to get some privacy. Julien is watching TV, Maya just got out of the shower, they have rehearsal with Duke in half an hour, and Lynette will be home soon. He keys in the phone card PIN followed by the 416 phone number.

"Hey Romona, it's Poem, how are you?"

She's happy to hear from him.

"Yeah, still Stateside.

"Yeah I know, I meant to get back to you. What's up?!" He leans back on the wooden stairs as she expounds on the other end.

"That's good.

"That's not good.

"Actually, I wanted to ask you about that. I'm in a weird situation right now and I have to come back to Toronto for a bit but I'm not sure for how long. I just don't wanna have to sign a lease. So I was hoping, y'know, if that apartment is still available.

"I'd really, *really* appreciate that, Romona, if you could keep it for me just a little longer, I would be so grateful.

"I'll pay you whatever I can. I'm just broke right now—worse than broke—I owe money.

"Definitely I can help you out with things around the house.

"I *love* shovelling snow.

"I really appreciate that, Romona. It'll be nice to see you too.

"I think around New Year's. Just need to book a flight.

"Well, you remember that singer I been playin' with, well, the house is feeling kind of small right now so she's gonna be moving into the band's house in January...

"Yeah, Sammy's band. Apparently he's moving out so they wanna rent his room.

"I dunno, Romona. I think it's over. There's no way she's gonna resist him forever and when I go… I think that's it. They played last night at Tipitina's, probably their biggest show yet, but Sammy said they wouldn't need me; he didn't have the extra amp. But *she* went on no problem and sang three songs!" he looks up at the light in the guestroom window.

"I got this lil gig coming up over Christmas, sort of a lounge thing, we're rehearsing tonight actually, Christmas tunes, but y'know, *our* way. I dunno. We haven't played yet and Maya is so undisciplined. I try to get her to rehearse but we always end up partying instead.

"Yeah I know, Christmas songs are not my style. It's just for the money.

"There *are* opportunities but honestly…" he sighs. "I feel burnt out. I'm really not into this loungy, carolly vibe—we're supposed to get everyone in the office singing," he rolls his eyes. "I don't even know why I'm here anymore. This is where musicians come to die. I convinced myself I was here for music, but really it was for love, and now I'm not even sure if that love is real. I don't even know who my friends are here."

Romona gives her take as Poem lights a cigarette and listens.

"Well, I can just stay here and be a complete outlaw or come back to Toronto and do philosophy.

"To tell you the truth, the outlaw thing is burning me right now. There's no juice, or maybe it's all juice, I don't know. I'm starved for spiritual food. I miss Mantriji. It seems all there is for me here is more partying.

"No, he's no good on the phone. Too ol' school, like it's a telegraph, talkin' all monosyllables. It's not pleasant. I need to see him, sit next to him. He's got a certain energy.

"Sure, if I wanna play Bourbon Street to tourists, covers, that sort of thing, but to tell you the truth, if I hear Sweet Home Alabama one more time, I'm gonna pop!"

She laughs.

"Seriously, I feel like I'm in a time warp here. I can see myself *dying* here."

She is sympathetic and concerned.

"Thanks, Romona. I appreciate that. Hey, thanks for listening. I'll see you in January, hey?

"Okay. You too. Bye."

Poem hangs up the phone and sits there relieved. He looks down the row of houses and majestic oaks and hears live music coming from somewhere. He thinks he may never be back.

The door opens and Maya peeks out, "Hey baby, Lynette's here and I'm ready. You wanna head out?"

"Yeah babe. I'm ready." He gets up and Maya holds the door for him. He says hello to Lynette and they pass Julien comatose in front of the TV. He picks up his guitar case, Maya has their bag; they exit through the front door and into the car.

"So is everything good?" she asks.

"Yeah, I got a place."

"With that girl?"

"She's not a girl, she's my friend." Poem turns the ignition.

"But you dated her, right?"

"That was a long time ago, Maya. Look, it's short notice, I had to find something. Besides, I've known Romona for years and we don't have sex. That part of our relationship is dead." He eases into the road.

"What about your mom's?"

"I thought about that but she's really pissed at me right now. Plus my sister works from home and uses the attic for her office."

Maya is silent. She doesn't like this little plan of Poem's to rent a flat in his ex ex-girlfriend's house. It sounds like she has money.

"It's snowing in Toronto," Poem says.

"You said she was a bra model, right?"

"She used to be, okay? She's retired now. She's way older than me, Maya. It was a long time ago."

They stop in front of the neon-lit Rite Aid and Maya sits there with arms crossed, looking ahead. "You coming?" he asks and she shakes her head. He gets out and walks to the entrance. The automatic doors open and Maya hears 'The man from Earth!' being announced from inside. She lights a cigarette and Poem returns a few minutes later holding a paper bag.

"I don't like you staying with this bra model. Didn't you say she was also a stripper?"

"Used to be, Maya, used to be. And high class, not cheap, okay?" He starts the car. "She's actually a very spiritual person." They merge onto Carrollton. "I never really met anyone like her."

"So why don't you marry her?!" she is peeved.

"Look, I just need a quiet place to stay where I can centre myself and focus."

"Yeah, I think you'll be focusing on her breasts."

"Maya, don't make excuses! I'm not getting involved, so you don't get any ideas about Sammy."

"Oh, so you're staying with your stripper-slash-bra model ex-girlfriend and you're *so* worried about me and Sammy?" she feels betrayed already.

Poem doesn't know what to say. The optics aren't good. "Look, I've been friends with Romona for years, it's different. You just met Sammy what, two months ago? And he's wanted you the whole time! And now all of a sudden his band needs a roommate?! Gimme a break! He's gonna be all over you!"

"That's not true."

"It *is* true. You're moving in with his band!"

Maya has to admit the optics aren't good.

"Why don't you just stay with Lynette till I get back?"

"I don't know, Poem, I need to move on. I've been there over two months now. She's nice, but she's your girlfriend's—"

"Ex-girlfriend."

"Your ex-girlfriend's cousin," she gives him an awkward look. "And it's not like I did Monique any favours."

"Look, I just want you to wait for me, okay, Maya? I'll be back. But I won't come back if you go with Sammy. I can't come back to that. Promise me you'll wait."

She recalls how they first met, how she nearly flipped, how her and Tony loved his music, their early rehearsals, his guitar playing, lyrics, the way he talked, the first time she saw his swimmer's abs. She remembers them grinding in that club in the French Quarter when they couldn't keep their hands off each other. He protected her from the dragon in their dream! She knew he would change her life and he did and now it's time to show her loyalty to him. "I'll wait for you, Poem. I promise!" They stop in front of Duke's and she hones in on him, "You are my husband, Poem, and my God, I am so in love with you!" She stares into his mouth, "I can't believe I found you. Promise me you'll come back. Promise me you won't dump me for Romona."

Poem is startled by the sudden shift, "Of course I'll be back. Don't worry about Romona. We're just friends. Just promise me you'll wait, okay? Promise me!"

She lunges at him and they kiss passionately, struggling to hold one another over the parking console.

"I love you, Maya."

"I love *you*, Poem."

They lick each other's faces and he wipes away her tears. All uncertainty fades into a warm, giggly security and they both take a deep breath, get out of the car, collect their stuff and walk up to the side door of the house. It is a beautiful starry night. Duke opens the door and heads back in and they customarily follow him.

The dim living room is its usual mess. Duke is nervy and eager for what's in the paper bag. Poem pulls out 26 ounces of brandy and Duke can't wait to try some. He goes to the kitchen for glasses while Poem tunes his guitar. Maya sifts through lyric sheets and lights a cigarette. She comes over and puts her hand on Poem's shoulder. He looks up and they start smooching when Duke walks in.

"Hold on, break it up, break it up!"

They're used to his jealous objections and smile at each other like on an inside joke.

Duke forces his way through, "I don't wanna see none of that, ya hear?" He places three freshly rinsed glasses on the top board of the organ and Maya pulls out a joint.

"*Look what I have*," she lilts.

"Well shit, don't just wave it around, girl. Put some fire on it," Duke sniggers and she lights up.

Poem watches them. How reluctant she was to come that night they first met. Now look at them, practically best friends. She's been coming here lately for 'music lessons' but Poem knows they're mostly just smoking and listening to old school. She says she found a lot of common ground with Duke because they both suffered emotional problems as children. Poem respects their growing camaraderie. He knows it's platonic. Better Duke than Sammy he figures. And Duke lives close by so it's a good place for her to go when Poem is working. Besides, Duke doesn't like Sammy and Poem likes that.

They each grab a glass of brandy, Maya's got the joint, Duke says by way of a toast, "To hip people making hip music."

They all agree and down goes the brandy.

Maya hands Duke the joint, "Hey Duke, I played Tipitina's last night."

"Oh yeah? How'd it go?"

"Pretty awesome."

He looks at Poem, "Did you play?"

"No, I wasn't invited."

"You talkin' Sammy's band, right? What're they, the Turkey Orchestra or somethin'?"

"The *Thunderbird* Orchestra," Maya says.

"Right. They all right." Duke hands Poem the joint, "You do better stuff, man. They should be playing for you!"

"Yeah, Duke."

"They're not bad," Maya says.

"They all right," Duke is unimpressed.

Poem hands Maya the joint and begins riffing on his guitar when Duke says to her, "Hey I got that thing you wanted—" She hushes him. He looks at Poem and changes the subject, "All right, so where we at?" He picks the papers out of Maya's hand, "Did you bring me charts?"

"Yeah, Duke." She shows him the list of songs with lyrics and chord changes. He fumbles through, pulls one out and places it on the top board. Poem is still warming up when Duke starts a loungy, vaguely familiar chord progression. Maya stands next to him, craning her neck towards the lyrics. Poem stops to see where this is going. Duke nods and Maya begins, "*Deck the halls with balls of holly—*" she said 'balls' instead of "boughs" and breaks out laughing, already stoned. Duke keeps up the vamp and she comes in late with, *"Don we now our gay apparel—"* She snickers, "Gay!"

Duke grunts and they split into laughter. It's a ridiculous scene. They are clearly high and having a good time.

Poem finds it funny but he knows this is their only rehearsal. "Hey guys, can we try to get it together?"

"Hey, no worries, Holmes. Let's do that again. One two three four…" Duke breaks into a more aggressive up tempo vamp of the same tune and Maya watches him to cue. He nods and she comes in with a bluesy take on the melody but fumbles the lyrics as her and Duke read off the same page. Poem and Duke take alternate leads and cadence the song nicely.

Maya's impressed, "Cool, let's try that again!"

Duke says, "No, man. You can make perfect only once," he sniggers and takes another sip.

"You didn't memorize the lyrics, Maya?" Poem asks.

"Uh…" she has a déjà vu.

"What? Is there a problem?" Duke defends her.

"I'm just saying that she had a week to go over the lyrics. I wonder, did she?"

There's a pause. "I looked at them," she knows she's unprepared.

"No worries, Holmes. Let's move on," Duke sorts through the papers and pulls out another song. He goes into the same loungy vamp as the last one, same key, different chord progression.

Poem tries to make out the song, "That's the same groove as the last one."

Duke flashes a sardonic grin then changes the rhythm to a 3/4 syncopation that sounds like O Christmas Tree. Maya comes in with a swinging version of the melody to her own lyric: *"Oh Jingle bells, oh jingles bells. I know you find me tasty. Oh jingle bells, sweet jingle bells. I'm feeling oh so wasted."* Everyone breaks into stoned laughter. Poem finds it funny and frustrating at the same time. He reaches for more brandy.

"Man, you too much, Maya. That's too funny," Duke laughs. "Okay, let's try that again. Hold on. You got the lyrics here," he flips the page for her to see.

"Ohhh…" she laughs, realizing she had the wrong song.

Poem says, "Duke, I'm playing that in another key. Can I see the chords again?"

"Uh yeah, you is right, brother. It's in a different key here. I just know it from before. Just play it in, uh…" he plays a couple bars, "F major, cool?"

"Uh… okay. You can't do it in G? That's the key we rehearsed in, right Maya?"

"Uh that's cool the way Duke's playing it," she shrugs like it doesn't matter.

"Okay," Poem sighs. "Let me figure this out."

"Hey you do that." Duke leaps up off the sofa, "I gotta go do somethin'. Be back in five minutes." He steps out to the kitchen and closes the door behind him.

Poem looks at Maya who says, "I dunno."

"All right." Poem starts fingering some chords and noodles for a bit when Maya says,

"Uh, I'm gonna go see something, Poem. You wait here. I'll be right back."

She leaves and Poem keeps transcribing. He lights a cigarette and leaves it burning in the tray. "Man, we got only three days." He moves over to the organ where he smokes and improvises, fiddles with some chords, does a little solo and—Duke and Maya enter the room, chatting like they just came out of conference. They are upbeat and ready to go!

"Let's do this!" Duke steps over Poem to get to the keyboard. Poem shifts back to guitar and Maya stands next to Duke who counts off, "One two three four!" He comes in with a funky groove to O Christmas Tree and it swings! Poem rides along and Maya comes in nicely. They get through the song on mostly spirit, some nice moments, a few mistakes, and a really nice ending. Duke is super-hyped, "Aw man, that was gangsta, man! Gangsta!! I gotta play you one thing before I forget," he starts rifling through his pile of cassettes. Poem looks at Maya who's having a great time just bobbing her head.

"Duke, it's cool," Poem says. "We should just run through these songs, okay? We can listen to your stuff later."

"No worries, man, I got it here somewhere," Duke sifts noisily through the tapes as Maya continues to groove silently. "Got it, man!" He rushes it into the cassette player, "Yo, check dis out."

Poem looks at him, wondering what's up. The music comes on. It's a low-budget 80s demo, derivative of early Prince but with more Louisiana.

"Is that you, Duke?" Maya coos. "Is that you singing? Really?!"

He grins and she is thrilled. They start bobbing together and Duke says, "This woulda been a hit if it weren't for my stupid manager."

Poem listens. *It's okay. They seem to be digging it way more than it merits.* He looks at Maya who's bobbing and weaving. He gets up and walks over, "You all right?"

She slips him the widest grin ever, "Ya baby, you?"

"Yeah I'm good. Just wonderin' when we gonna get back to rehearsing."

"Maya, check dis out!" Duke goes into falsetto on the recording.

"Woo wee!" Maya creams.

This goes on for another two songs and Poem is getting impatient. He has another sip, another smoke. He waits till the third song ends, "Hey Duke, c'mon, man. Let's get back to work, all right?"

Duke turns on him, "Yo whatchoo worried about, man?! Always worried! It's cool. We'll get it together. Quit being so uptight!"

Poem stares at him blankly. *Why is he being such an ass? Oh great, we have to hear the entire story behind this song too?*

Duke retreats into his head while Poem turns to Maya who smiles coquettishly. He gives her a long squeeze and she whispers, "I wanna fuck you," into his ear.

"All right, hand me the bottle!" Poem says and the three of them spend the next two hours drinking, dancing, mostly talking, doing the occasional Christmas tune, checking out Duke's tapes, hearing his stories, smoking Marlboros. Duke assures Poem they'll rehearse again before the gig, which is at City Hall on Christmas Eve day. They'll have a rental keyboard and a vocal amp. Poem can plug in through either one and they'll just have to make do with levels.

It gets way past 10 p.m. when they remember they have a show they're catching at 11. They agree to wrap up but when it comes time to leave, Maya says, trying to be cavalier, "Hey Poem, how 'bout I just meet you there, I'm gonna go with Duke."

"Uh… what'dya mean, Maya? Why don't we just go together now?"

"I'll just meet you there, okay? I wanna talk to Duke about something."

"How you getting there?"

"I'll drive Trixy's car."

"What?"

"Yeah, she let me drive it a couple times to take Duke to the doctor and stuff when you were working so I've been able to borrow it ever since. You know Duke is not allowed, right?"

"I don't understand why you don't just come with *me*."

Duke steps in, "Yo, what's with all this pity-pat bullshit, man! We'll see you there! Everything's cool. She just needs to tell me something, that's all."

Poem has no idea what to make of this. "If you're planning my surprise birthday party!" he blares. "It's not till APRIL!"

They look at him then each other. Duke grins wilily and Poem concedes, "All right, what time you be there?"

"Show's at 11, right?"

"Right."

"Be there at 11."

Poem stares straight ahead, not liking this one bit.

Maya half-apologizes, "Look, I need a life outside our relationship, okay? Now that you're going back to Toronto."

"I'm coming back, Maya!"

"I know, but I just wanna do this one thing, 'kaaay?" She puckers for him.

"You're sleeping with me tonight!"

"Of course, baby, it's not about that, really. I'll see you later, 'kay?"

Poem is really curious to know what's going on but he packs up his guitar, leaves and drives to Lynette's to freshen up. It's Sunday night so everyone's asleep as usual so he has to creep in the dark as usual. He leaves quietly and parks just off Oak Street. Locking the car he spots Mars in the western sky. *My lord of the 8th.*

Under the Maple Leaf marquee, the opening band slides out their equipment through the stage door. Poem pays the cover and strolls inside, recognizing staff and a few other faces. He enters the main room and stands in the middle of the vacant dance floor. Josh approaches him.

"Hey Poem, have you seen Duke?" he seems perturbed.

"Uh yeah, I just saw him. He'll be here soon."

"Yeah, I don't know about that guy."

"What d'ya mean?"

"I dunno," he sounds disappointed. "He says he's gonna meet me then he doesn't show up. I was supposed to give him a ride the other day and he wasn't home. I just feel like he's borrowing money all the time, we never get anything done. I mean, I really like the guy—he's an amazing musician—but… I dunno, I think he's on drugs."

Poem sighs. He knows Duke has a problem. "I don't know, man. You could be right."

Josh erupts, "Well I hate it! And I'm not gonna put up with this shit!" He storms off.

Poem watches him leave and wonders what's taking Maya and Duke. He walks over to the barroom and sees a shiny young woman with some money clothespinned to the rim of her low-cut blouse. She doesn't look like a hooker and is clearly having a good time, surrounded by what looks like family. He nods and she flashes him a smile. He gets his drink and heads to the back room where people play pool and converse loudly over the music. He remembers his first night here on New Year's Eve with Papa Grows Funk. *We had such a good time.* He misses Monique.

The music cuts off and the MC announces, "Tonight, Ladies and Gentleman, the Mighty Maple Leaf welcomes to the Crescent City, legends of the South. Give it up for Elmo Jackson and the Mississippi Flood!!!"

The crowd cheers and makes its way to the main room where the band rocks into a great southern blues, harmonica-laced, triple-threat funk explosion that just rocks and makes all the pain go away. Poem squeezes in, digging them, grooving to the people, wishing Maya were here. The dance floor is packed. Following the third song, he steps out to meander round the club, out back, through the side barroom and out the front door. He turns to go back in when he sees Maya and Duke emerge from the crowd in front of Jacque Imo's. They saunter towards him, Maya grinning from ear to ear.

"Hey Maya, where you been?"

"Uh… hey man, I'm just having a good time," she looks really stoned.

"What's up with your shit?" Duke grills him. "You go ahead, girl. I'll meet you inside." He winks at the bouncer who lets her in and Poem is beside himself. "Listen, man," Duke is hustling again, "Whatever went on tonight, I don't care and I don't wanna hear about it. Just promise me, man, that you will never let a woman get in the way of you and me!"

"I don't know what you're talking about, Duke."

"That's good, man. Just keep it that way. No woman is worth it, y'hear? You is my *man*!" he talks like he's creating a diversion, waving his arms, stepping up and down the curb. He says to the bouncer, "Yo man, what's goin' on?" They lock and fly. Duke introduces him to Poem who's preoccupied.

"Who's the sweet thing?" the bouncer asks.

"Ah, just a young thang I'm bringin' up through the ranks." They laugh, slapping each other like on an inside joke.

Poem sees this and says, "Nice to meet y'all," and goes inside to look for Maya. The band is rocking and the dance floor is packed. He pushes his way through and eventually makes it out back where he sees Maya near the patio doors, talking to Maggie—*Cool! Maggie's here!* He approaches them and Maggie says, "Hey…!"

They hug.

"Where you been, Poem?" she asks.

"Wherever this lady's been. Except for tonight."

Maya rolls her eyes.

"How 'bout you, Maggie, what're you up to?"

"Maya's just telling me about this guy Duke you're working with. You're doing Christmas Carols?! That's so cute."

Maya laughs and Poem rolls his eyes, "Yeah, it's fun but we still have a lot of work to do," he looks at Maya who gives him a sour expression.

"She was telling me he's a genius," Maggie says.

"Genius?" He looks at Maya, "You think Duke is a genius?"

"You don't think so?"

"Why, because he's weird? Eccentric doesn't make you a genius, Maya. *Beethoven* was a genius. You think Duke is in the same league as Beethoven?"

Maggie is beginning to feel uncomfortable, "I'm just gonna go freshen up. I'll see you all in a minute."

"Me too," Maya starts but Poem grabs her arm,

"Can I just talk to you?"

Maggie smiles nervously and heads for the ladies room. Poem watches her walk away then focuses on Maya who shrinks under his glare.

"Hey Poem, nice to see you," she says meekly.

"Why are you saying that?!"

"I don't know," she sounds worried. "I just feel like you're slipping away," she can't look him in the eyes.

"Maya, are you smoking crack?"

"Oh God!" she is startled. "I just wanted to try some."

"Are you fucking serious?! You're smoking crack now?!"

"I just wanted to try it, Poem. Just once. I won't do it again, I promise. Don't tell Duke you know, okay? Promise me!" she embraces him frantically and he steps back.

"I don't know what the fuck is going on here but you need to chill out, Maya. Just calm down, okay?" He puts his arms around her and she hugs him desperately. "I won't say anything. Just promise me you won't do it again."

"Oh God, I love you, Poem." She hugs him with all fours and the two make out passionately, squeezing their faces together. "I wanna marry you so bad, baby. Please come back. Don't leave me here!"

"Okay, okay, Maya. Don't worry. I'll be back, but just don't let yourself get caught up in this shit, okay?"

She gives him a sobbing assurance and they hug and sway along to the ballad now being played. Holding his shoulders, she wipes her eyes on his shirt as he rubs her back and kisses the top of her head. It is a loving sight when Maggie returns, "This is an improvement."

They break and Maggie offers a joint so they head out back and Poem agrees to fetch three Vodka tonics. He heads to the side bar, thinking there's no sign of Duke. He's curious so he walks out front to see the bouncer who says,

"Aw ya, Duke left 'bout 10 minutes ago. He went to get some medicine."

Poem thanks him and goes back in. He passes the young woman with the clothespinned money to her chest and smiles. She says hi and they sidle up together against the bar. Poem can't help but look at her impressive chest. By his reckoning, there must be 80 dollars there! "Can I ask you something?" he says.

"It's my birthday."

"Oh. Happy birthday uh—"

"Tracy."

"Tracy. Happy Birthday, Tracy!"

"Thanks," she smiles like she wants him now.

He orders three vodka tonics and asks if she would like one. She holds up her glass of wine.

"I guess people have been buying you drinks all night."

"I can buy my own drinks," she says. "Round here it's a tradition that ladies wear a clothespin on their birthday so that wonderful men like yourself can pin money to my chest."

"Really?"

"You didn't know?"

"I didn't know it was a birthday thing."

"Yeah, so instead of buying me a drink, why don't you show me how generous you can be?" she is seducing him with an obvious ploy.

"All right," he gives in and takes out his wallet, "Keep in mind, I'm a struggling musician."

"Even a five will do," she smiles.

He knows he's being hustled but she's really cute and it is her birthday and when in Rome… He looks at his cash. "Uh, ya got change for a 10?"

She beams, clearly amused. "Just clip the 10 and pull out a five," she projects her left breast forward. He looks at them, her round 36 inch Ds, nestled firmly into a tight red low-cut blouse, the cleavage just begging him in. He carefully places his hands over her chest and gingerly opens the pin, slides in a 10 dollar note and pulls out a five. She heaves, aroused.

"Happy Birthday!" he says and the bartender interrupts. Tracy wants more of his attention but seeing the drinks, figures he's got somewhere else to be. He pays and squeezes the three cups together, "Nice to meet you, Tracy."

"What's your name?"

"Poem."

She looks at him curiously, "Where you from, Poem?"

"Same place as you." He clicks goodbye and leaves her flustered.

Entering the back patio, he sees the girls laughing in the corner table. He places their drinks down and Maya asks if he saw Duke. She seems better now and says, "Hey it's sounding good, I think, the Christmas tunes?"

"Yeah it's cool, Maya. I just found it a little frustrating tonight."

"I know."

"We can't be preparing for shows and getting all fucked up before we even know our set. We need to be more focused."

"I know, Poem. You're right."

"It could be cool what we're doing and I don't mean to be a downer but…" he reconsiders and says it anyway, "I didn't get into music to be doing Christmas carols, y'know?"

She looks at him, disappointed, "Duke is right. You *are* uptight."

"Why am I uptight, Maya? Because I don't go along with everything he says?"

"Because you're not being fun! Everything with you is so serious."

"Oh God, I've been partying every night since you got here! That's three months straight! I'm burned out, man! You know I love to party but work is work and party is party. I'm not in my twenties like you!" he catches himself as Maggie watches. "I'm just tired of this life. I want something more profound!"

Maya looks at Maggie then excuses herself and leaves. Poem watches her and Maggie says, "Are you all right? You seem on edge."

"Aw God," he groans like it's been a long day. "I wanna go back to Toronto and yet, I wanna stay. I wanna study philosophy and yet, I wanna keep playing. I wanna have profound conversations and yet, I wanna have fun. I wanna write my musical and I wanna learn astrology and I wanna stop drinking! I want Maya to come with me to Toronto but she wants to stay!"

"She says you're coming back in a month."

"I hope a month, or two. Honestly, I think it'll be longer. I have a small problem with a big debt."

"Oh."

"I'm just afraid that when I do get back, everything here will be different."

Maggie shakes her head, having lived here almost five years. She places her hand on his, "Don't worry, Poem. Nothing ever changes in New Orleans."

This is more comforting than she knows. He looks back at the bar, this rickety ol' club from before Noah's flood. "You're right," he says.

"So you'll be back in the spring?"

"I hope."

"Well, I for one am going to miss you." She reaches over the table and kisses him right on the lips.

"Thanks, Maggie. I'm gonna miss you too."

She sings, *"You don't know what it's like to miss New Orleans."*

"C'mon. Let's go check out the band."

They go inside and find Maya next to the bar talking to the birthday girl. Maya grabs Maggie's hand and they head into the main room. Duke appears in the front door and approaches Poem,

"Yo, I'm lookin for Maya. I need a ride home."

Poem leads him to her on the dance floor where Duke shouts over the music that he has to go. Maya is willing to drive him but Poem objects. She is staying with him he says. Duke insists that Trix needs the car but Poem yells above the music, "It's just down the street, man! Why don't *you* drive?! You afraid of the cops?!"

Duke considers this but Maya is uncomfortable with the idea. She feels responsible for the car. Poem has put himself out so many times for these two that he expects just this one night, they can return a favour. Duke senses this and feeling his masculinity threatened, he looks at Maya who says, "I wanna stay with Poem. I'll call you tomorrow." She rubs Poem's arm and Duke gets the message. They leave the crowded dance floor and walk Duke outside and down the street. He unlocks the car and climbs in uncomfortably behind the wheel.

"It's a straight line from here, Duke!" Maya waves.

It takes a few cranks but he manages to start the motor. Poem knocks on the window for him to lower it. Crouching down he says, "Drive safe, my man," and kisses him squarely on the lips. Duke is surprised but doesn't react.

Poem and Maya step back as he jerks the car out of its spot. He peels into the road then jolts to a stop, then hobbles the car forward.

"Thank God it's an automatic," Maya says.

They watch him drive away with the brake lights popping on and off and suddenly realize, "Shit! It's a one-way at Carrollton!"

He stops at the traffic lights three blocks up, turns right, then left, then right again. They hold their breaths until he disappears from view, then head inside where they see Tracy by the bar, dancing solo with the money corsage. She asks Poem to join her and he politely accepts and Maya goes looking for Maggie. They start moving together when Tracy gets touchy, grinding his leg, and Poem has to pry himself away. "Listen, I should go find my girlfriend."

"Oh, is that your girlfriend?"

"Yeeeah," he thought it was obvious.

"Well I don't see you running to her," she drops a finger seductively onto his chest. He thanks her, leaves, and looking around, makes his way through the gyrating crowd. He finally finds Maya in the backroom with Maggie.

She sees him and abruptly stands, "Did you pin money to that girl's chest?"

"Uh... yeah."

"Really?!"

"It was only five bucks."

"That's not the point!"

"Maya, it's her birthday! It's a tradition here."

She can't believe it. What a fool she's been. She rushes out through the crowd towards the front entrance and Poem looks at Maggie, who says,

"It's a tradition for single men."

It dawns on him. He turns and rushes after Maya, bumping people along the way. He gets out front, looks around, and spots her down the street, crouched against the ceramics store, crying hysterically.

"Maya, Maya! What's wrong?!"

She is sobbing and shaking so intensely that he recoils before crouching to comfort her.

"GET AWAY!" she screams and he backs off.

"Maya, what the fuck just happened?! What's wrong?"

She is rolled up into a ball, having a fit, moaning, trembling. He wonders about her mind. "Is this the crack?" he says and she sobs louder.

"Maya, I love you. Please tell me what's wrong. I didn't mean anything with that girl."

"GET AWAY!" she screams and he retreats.

My God. She's broken. What have I done? He looks up. A nicely dressed middle-aged black man in a grey bowler hat approaches them. He looks friendly and concerned and says to Maya, "Are you all right, Miss? Is this man hurting you?"

She continues to shake and cry, her face buried in her crossed arms, rocking fetally.

"I'm a friend of hers," Poem says and she again bursts into tears. "I mean, we're together."

"Get away!!" she screams, her face strained with popping veins and mascara lines.

"It looks to me like she wants to be left alone," the man places a hand on her shoulder.

"We live together," Poem says. "We have to go home."

The man looks at Maya who's a complete wreck. "Young man, I think you'd better go."

Poem looks at him sideways then down at Maya. *This makes no sense.* He steps back and watches from a few cars down as the stranger and Maya talk it out. *What the hell just happened?* He scans the people in the dimly lit street, the old colourful wooden buildings, uneven sidewalks, and unapologetic parking. *I'm gonna miss this town.* He looks up at the moonless sky and spots Saturn in the 10th house in Gemini. *My karma here has ended.*

He hears Maya and the man laughing and turns to see him help her up off the street. Then like a guardian angel he delivers her to Poem who approaches them gratefully. She is a sniffling mess, badly in need of a tissue.

"Thanks, huh?" she says to the man.

"Will you be all right?"

She nods yes.

He gives her a blessing, taps his chest, and holds up his crucifix to remind her of the Christ within. She understands. He says to Poem, "Take care of this one. She has a lot of love to give."

Poem nods and the gentleman squeezes Maya's hand, "Have a good night, Miss."

"Good night."

The man walks towards Joliet Street, past the throbbing Maple Leaf. They watch him disappear and Maya says, "Can we just go home now?"

"Sure, Maya." But then he remembers Maggie.

"Forget about her. Let's just go."

Poem agrees. He knows he won't be seeing a lot of people for a while. He picks up Maya's hand and they walk slowly to the car. "You okay, baby?" he squeezes her finger.

"Yeah," she's a little embarrassed. "Sorry. I'm better. I just… It's not something I can talk about. Please understand. But I'm better now."

Poem respects this and doesn't pry. He's happy to have her back on side. He wonders, "So what was so funny just now with that man?"

"Oh nothing," she looks down. "Just an inside joke."

Act 3 – Illumination

⊙

Jyoti Lokā
(Sattva)

1 DIAMONDS ON THE BOTTOM OF THE SEA

Poem steps out of the elevator to Mantri's door held ajar by the same old brick. He can already smell the incense inside. He pauses and smiles. It's been a long time. He enters the hot stuffy apartment like walking straight into New Delhi, closes the door behind him and looks through the kitchen to see Mantri standing at the table, radiating his supernal light.

"Mantriji, Namaste. So nice to see you again."

"Namaste, Poem. How are you?" Mantri is happy to see him and they shake hands across the table. Poem would like a hug but feels toxic next to this shiny Master. He removes his scarf and coat, hangs it on the back of his chair, takes a seat and looks around. *There's a whiteboard now!* It modernizes the apartment. Everything else is the same: stray books and oddly placed furniture, clothes folded over chairs, mattress on the floor, windows sealed shut, the kitchen table cluttered with books, papers and binders. He spots 'The World's Dirtiest Joke Book' and looks curiously at Mantri who says, "It's to wake up people in Gita class. They are too full of, how you say, 'precon-ceeeved' notions."

"So ya zing 'em with a one-liner?"

"Oh yes. Very important for people to wake up."

Poem has not heard his accent in a while and it takes some getting used to.

"Sometimes people get offended by jokes and they never come back. What is this man talking, what do blondes and manure have in common?"

"What?"

"The older they get, the easier they are to pick up."

Poem laughs. Mantri is a celibate so there's something especially absurd about him telling this joke.

"If anyone is offended by this," he looks soberly at Poem. "They are not ready for Gita. They will, how you say, 'wilt' under its weight."

"I never would have thought that a dumb blonde joke could be the gatekeeper to higher knowledge."

"Oh yes. Sometimes what seems like the most innocent thing can be life's true test."

Poem nods, looks around and soaks it in. He can't believe he's here. The smell of Mantri's apartment, his food-stained shirt, sundown outside his window. He feels relieved, like he made it.

"So…" Mantri assesses his gaunt appearance, "How did it go?"

Poem looks at him wearily, "A lot happened, Mantriji."

"Oh?"

"Yeeeah," Poem searches internally where to begin. "I think you said I would be back at the end of the year and I said October and… You were right. I see how my Mars bhukti ends this month and I stayed almost right to the end. Like I just had to gorge myself!"

Mantri listens curiously.

"But I can tell you now, based on *personal* experience, that Mars with Ketu in the 2nd house truly sucks!" he shakes his head, hoping Mantri will elaborate.

"Where are you staying?"

"Funny you should ask. I ended up at my mom's place."

"With family?"

"Yeah. 2nd house, family."

"What happened to your apartment?"

"Me and Monique broke up."

"Tsk tsk tsk," Mantri shakes his head. He looks down like calculating something, "How did you get here?"

"Public transit."

"Tsk tsk tsk."

"My car's still at work. I couldn't start it but I have to sell it anyway cuz I need the money."

Mantri is uneasy with this new situation. Poem tells him how he was supposed to stay with Romona but after a couple nights it became obvious she had ulterior motives. "I just saw trouble coming and she's practically in the burbs and all my business is downtown, so I'd stop by my mom's, have some dinner, she'd invite me to sleep over, get an early start. I did that a couple nights and my sister was cool and I don't know, I just felt more grounded there."

"Ahh," Mantri is happy to hear this. "4th lord is exalted in your 11th house. Your mother understands hardship and it brings out her character to help you."

"Yeah well, she's really pissed at me now and yet she's putting food on the table."

"She's your mother, Poem. She made that promise long ago."

"Well, I just ended up staying there more and more and Romona got mad and… We had a falling out. She wanted to start something up again and I just didn't want that. Plus, her and Monique hate each other."

Mantri shakes his head. It's like a soap opera.

"So I'm staying in the attic of my mom's house, which used to be my room when I lived there, so it's not too bad. I just can't use it during business hours because it's my sister's office now."

"Are you working?"

"I gave my job to Marcus when I didn't come back in October."

"Are you doing UofT?"

Poem sighs, anticipating his disappointment. "I was signed-up to take an intro course but I really need the money, so I got a refund."

"No, Poem…"

"I'll start in the summer, Mantriji."

"You have delayed it almost a year now."

"I know."

"You lost weight."

"15 pounds."

"Tsk tsk tsk. Did they not feed you there?"

"They did, but I smoked and partied a lot, Sir, and I didn't sleep much. I could've stayed but I seriously needed a breather. Plus, everything of mine is here and honestly… I really missed you, Mantriji, and our lessons. I really thought a lot about what you taught me. It helped make sense of a lot of things. I like astrology and I like everything else you teach. I want to get back to that, to understand things for what they are and why people are the way they are, y'know?"

Mantri smiles compassionately, like he is about to impart some great wisdom. Poem hopes he will tell him it's all been a cosmic joke. Instead, Mantri leans back and says, "So what happened?"

Poem wonders whether he really has to explain. "What *happened*, Mantriji, is I ran Mars bhukti, lord of the 8th!"

Mantri smiles dubiously. "Speak."

"You told me not to break my family and I went ahead and broke it."

"Did you play music when you were there?"

"Yeah I played. We had some gigs—well… by 'we' I mean… Okay, here's what happened. You remember that singer in my band, Maya, remember we looked at her chart and you said she would never sing?"

"Saturn in the 2nd."

"Yes."

"Saturn in water sign in 2nd house of speech and she will drink alcohol to overcome her shyness to sing."

"Well did she ever!"

Mantri looks confused.

"She came to New Orleans in October to visit for a week and… she never left."

Mantri nods, not fully comprehending.

"We ended up having an affair, Mantriji, and Monique found out and so… No more Monique, no more apartment, no more job."

"Tsk tsk tsk," Mantri shakes his head. Poem has lost everything. This is lord of the 8th. "Where is this new girl?"

"Maya?" he says her name like some discredited god. "She's still down there."

"You left her there?"

"No, I wanted her to come with me but she wanted to stay. She feels like she can sing down there cuz… I guess cuz it's a good place to drink. She got to be very popular, especially with one group and they offered her a place to stay."

"And not you?"

"Well, I could stay with Lynette."

"But if you're together…?" he gives him that same puzzled look Maggie did.

"I know," Poem feels once again out-manoeuvred.

"Tsk tsk tsk," Mantri is beginning to get the picture.

"I just fell in love, Sir. Things were not working out with Monique."

"You have Venus and Moon in Taurus. You are the most romantic man on this Earth!"

Poem smiles at this. "Do you think it's possible to love more than one woman?"

"Of course! You can love a *hundred* women, but nowadays people all want to be number one, the *only* one. This is foolish thinking. What's wrong with having sex? Why do some women think they are so precious that no man is good enough to touch them? They are too good even for love."

"I think the problem is people confuse sex for love and the other way around."

"That's right. You are right. But you are dealing with convention and you can never destroy convention. Many times, it is not people but the convention they adopt without thinking. People are automatic beings. Love is free and they are not ready to be free, so they stick with convention."

"Well, not me!"

"What is this girl's chart?" Mantri takes out a pen, remembering Gemini lagna and Saturn in the 2nd. Poem recites the rest of her planetary placements as Mantri scribbles it onto a sheet of paper and holds it up, "Poem, what do you want with such a little girl? She has no money and no education."

"But I love her, Mantriji."

"You love sex. And this girl," he shows him the chart, "is a sexy puppy."

"Thaaat's true, but it was much more than that, Sir. We had this incredible mystical experience." He recounts the lucid shared dream, suggesting they somehow punctured a parallel dimension where all memories and residual lives remain.

"You are connected, this is right. It is funny that her name is Maya, but this is just a vasana."

"A what-now?"

"Something left over from a previous life. Some 'unfinished business.' It is better that you leave it now that it has played out."

"But I want to go back."

"To play music?"

"Yeah… I think. I dunno…! All I can think about right now is Maya, whether she's gonna go with this guy down there who's been hitting on her. I told her I'd be back in a month, or two, possibly the spring, but I *will* be back!" He looks at her chart and scratches his head, "She said she would wait for me but, I dunno. Will she wait for me, Mantriji? You think she'll be faithful?"

He looks at her chart, "No. Not for more than one month."

Poem can't believe it. He wonders how he's gonna get out of this one and suddenly feels embarrassed by it all.

"She is young and having a good time. She would be good if *you* were more stable, but you need stability yourself. You don't need this woman. She will ruin you."

"I feel like she already has."

"Oh yay! And you want more?" he raises a brow.

Poem sighs and looks down, "I really felt the energy of Mars, Mantriji. It was *searing* me. I felt jealousy and anger and betrayal. I didn't know these things lived in me. I never felt this way towards Monique and she was doing salsa!"

"Mars in your case is lord of the 8th. Not good."

"Why didn't you warn me? I thought I was gonna do well. I mean it's in Libra for God's sake!"

"But still, lord of the 8th. If I had told you not to go, would you have listened?"

"Probably not."

"Mars does his own thing. And now you are rubbing your face in it."

"Well, if she's not gonna wait for me then I have no reason to go back."

"What about music?"

Poem knows it is no longer about music. "I love music, Mantriji, and I'm really good at it and I always felt I would do well but y'know…" he gazes off outside the window, "I found the music biz is full of some pretty messed-up people. I just feel like I'm floating on another plane."

"America is a nation of egos. Unless you have one, you will be swallowed by her. Amazing this concept." He looks at the sheet of paper, "Some people know everything but they don't have the courage to speak, others know nothing but they *have* courage and *they speak*." He draws a generic chart and circles the 3rd, "Courage comes from the 3rd house; this is lower mind. You don't need intelligence to have courage, but it doesn't matter how educated or talented you are, without courage you can do nothing. Even the dumbest, laziest, most untalented people on this Earth become successful because they have one thing: courage!" he taps with his pen. "Look at George Bush. He has nothing but a family name. He is a dullard with no insight, eyes too close together, and yet because he has courage, he became President! Six billion people on this Earth hate his guts and he still walks up the Whitehouse lawn like a cowboy," Mantri does a broad-shouldered Texan strut. "That's courage!"

"Some would call it folly."

"Folly or no folly, America is the greatest nation on Earth because of courage. It is the land of opportunity. People do *anything* there. You want to see a man have sex with a crocodile, go to America. If you have money, you will see it there. Americans put people into space. You will never see an Indian man willingly go into space, no. This takes a cowboy. Americans are very courageous people. All you have is useless unless you have courage, unless you have, how you say, 'courage of conviction,' the courage to stand up, the courage to fight your opponent. Your friends will know, yes, your family may know, oh yes, but the world will never know without courage."

"Why is courage opposite the 9th house of sympathy?"

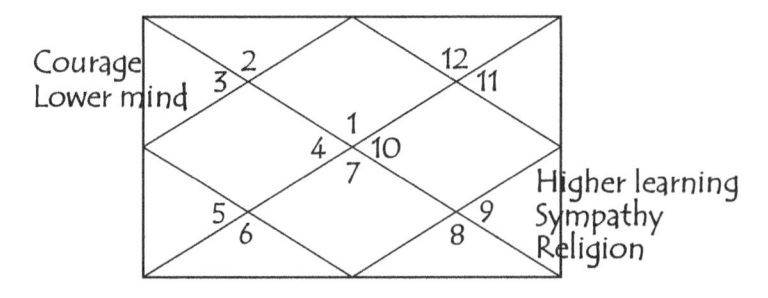

"9th house is the house of higher learning and so those with some kind of higher thought will have sympathy. They have broadened their mind and can walk in the shoes of others. The 9th is the house of religion, and so, the 3rd being opposite to it shows that courage is the spouse to faith. To be strong, to have conviction, requires faith, not always in God but in some cause, something you perceive to be noble. Intelligence has nothing to do with it. Courage is everything."

"So you think I ran from there because I don't have courage?"

"You are a Brahmin, Adi Poem. This life is not for you. You are creating universes, not doing, what you call, 'dog & pony show.' This is why Saturn won't let you have what you want because you are austere, man, a writer! Very difficult to spend time alone writing. You do enjoy pleasure but you want truth. Pleasure for you is a drug that keeps you from living up to what you know is true. If you had stayed in Orleans, you would be playing music, having a good time, but instead you are here."

Poem runs his fingers through his hair, feeling the fire of contradiction in his head, "I felt like that life was killing me, Mantriji. I mean, I had fun, but night after night after night, oh God! It was too much. It wore me out and I started prioritizing the wrong things."

"You were losing yourself."

"I never felt jealousy like I did for this woman, this 'little girl' as you call her. I felt like it was tearing me to pieces, that my heart was gonna jump out of my chest and beat the shit outta someone."

Mantri laughs and looks at her chart, "Why did you desire this girl so much?"

"I just felt really attracted to her, Mantriji. She's fun and beautiful and we had this dream and… I dunno. I felt like I was seeing my destiny in her."

"Are you sure you weren't just seeing yourself *through* her?"

"What d'ya mean?"

"You are gifted, Poem, a great man, but you don't know. You don't see yourself. Your ruler is debilitated. It doesn't matter how much you have to offer, how much smarter or talented you may be, you will feel less than others and call it humility. You don't see your greatness because you are blind to yourself. People get strength from you, they take your strength, but what do you get from them? You are left, how you say, 'holding the bag.' You empowered this woman. Without you she would not have come to this town, Orleans, to this life. She would not have met all the people she did. She would not be where she is! This all happened to her because of you."

"She didn't even come to the airport to see me off."

"Oyo…!" Mantri can't believe it. "And you left her there to be eaten by others," he shakes his head and Poem is horrified. "They will eat her because she no longer has you to protect her. They will tell her you abandoned her and she is already hurt by this."

"I had to come back, Mantriji, and I told her I would return. She didn't want to come back to Toronto."

"Gemini lagna is very opportunistic," he points to the chart. "With Moon aspecting from the 7th, she will meet people and things will happen. She is what you call 'party girl.' She needs to be around people in order to shine. She reflects them and this is why they like her. People like looking into a mirror, especially a good looking one. My advice is to let it go."

Poem leans onto the table, holding his weary head, his eyes downcast. He already knew it was over. He looks at her chart scribbled crudely onto a sheet of paper. *That's her karma, all those planets in the 5th, the fun house.* "I actually considered right near the end, when she started calling me 'husband,' I actually considered marrying her, Mantriji, but mostly out of fear, fear of losing her. I wanted to marry her to make sure no one else could. Is that stupid or what?"

"You lost your father when you were a child and this is why you are afraid of losing. But the key to not losing is to not want in the first place. Just as opportunity can be lost through inaction, so suffering can be reduced by right expectation. In this case, you are running Mars. Mars signifies passion and desire. Venus is wanting, but Mars is conquering. You just lost your head thinking you wanted something, that you had to fight for it, but instead of punching, you alienate with your words, in your case, by being sharp. This is Mars." He searches his pile for a sheet of paper. "Ahh..." he hands it to Poem. It is the printout of an email with the following line:

When you find yourself in a hole, the first thing to do is stop digging.
Will Rogers

Poem grunts like he just hit bottom. He realizes Mars is a spade and he's been using it to dig his own grave. "Wow," he stares at the page, like finding the antidote. "Do you think Monique will take me back, Mantriji?"

"What makes you think you will want her more this time? She will be less trusting now."

"Well, she *is* distant, but I just feel like she's my home."

"Poem, you broke her. It will never be the same. She has Sun in Taurus. Very hard for the bull to move backwards."

Poem feels like his entire life is melting and the only things standing are a couple shards of family. How negligent he's been, not just in New Orleans, but in everything. "I can't believe it. I can't believe what I've done to my life. What the fuck was I thinking? I'm a frickin idiot!"

"You are in shock realizing how you've lived up till now. Understand, this is Saturn who matures at 36. You are now 36. Saturn is in your 7th house. You lost Monique because of sy-co-phants," he sounds it out. "English is very tricky language," he winces. "You just haven't met the right people yet, Poem. You need *good* people, *lucky* people, people who make *you* lucky, not just take yours away. I will tell you a little story.

"A man once went to India to look for a famous Master who was known to see into the future. When he got there he looked everywhere for this Master, in the plains, in the jungle, in the foothills. Finally one day ah hah! He finds him and approaches the sage with all due respect and praise. Bowing before him, he asks, 'Oh Master, can you tell me my future?' The sage looks at him and says, 'Yes, I can tell you your future, but first you must tell me who your friends are.'"

Poem is suddenly suspended in space and the universe seems to rotate around him. *My God…!* He thinks of all the struggling, dope-smoking, under achieving musicians that are his peers, his best friends! How he always felt like he was bowing to their limitations, thinking he needed them to achieve his vision, but instead he picked up habits, became complacent, falling always to the closest centre of gravity. What happened to his artistic ambitions? He shakes his head, illuminated and profoundly disappointed, "I think I been hanging out with the wrong people."

"Saturn in the 7th and people use you to transform themselves. They are reborn *through* you, but I tell you, if you only knew how to *use* people, you would be very successful in life."

"I know what you're saying, Sir, I really do, but I struggle with that. I don't know. It feels so self-serving."

"If you allow the world to eat you, Poem, it will."

"But isn't it good karma to help others?"

"How can you help others if you cannot help yourself? You can show them how to walk but do not walk for them or they will come to treat you as their servant. Jesus Christ was a king!" he clenches his fists, "King of kings! But he was treated like a bloody slave because he helped people and they crucified him for it."

"I have to learn to be more of an asshole I guess."

Mantri looks at him the way a father does in conveying a harsh unspoken truth, "Poem, sometimes it takes, as you say, 'asshole,' to be successful in this world. People are not nice to each other. They eat each other like dogs and for what? Money? Sex? Status? All temporary fleeting things. People today do not understand *permanent* things and so they are not moral. They think they live today, die tomorrow, with no consequence. They will sacrifice their future, their family, their entire lineage, to feel good now! But it is temporary. Even someone who jumps off the CN Tower can believe he is flying for a while."

"I notice when you're being decent, people accuse you of being weak. There was this one guy, Sammy," he rolls his eyes, "who was after Maya. Man, even when he *knew* we were together and he *pretended* to be my friend, he would *still* hit on her right in front of me!"

"Tsk tsk tsk."

"And I'm like, turning the other cheek, letting him know but not being a jerk about it but he keeps doing it like it's a game. One time I nearly slapped him and Maya ends up calling *me* a brute!" he looks hurt. "He's just this weasely guy and his friends started turning on me and pretty soon even

Maya begins telling me I'm being uptight because I don't wanna shoot darts in some pub at three o'clock in the morning!" he falls back into his chair and Mantri smiles.

"You had no reason being there, Poem. It was fun but now what? It is better that you ground yourself in your mother's home than lose yourself to jealousy and alcohol. These people, Maya and Sammy, they are not for you. They are everyday people. You are a mystic. They will drive you crazy with their mundane talk. Stay with your mother, forget everything else. It is just pride, identity, ego. Forget this girl. You need to rest."

"I need to find a job, Mantriji."

"No! The most important thing for you right now is food and sleep. For one month. Everything else is unimportant. Get your weight and strength back. It is good that you are with your mother. She will feed you the right, how you say, 'soul food.'"

Poem sighs. He looks at the scribbled chart, the piles of books and papers on Mantri's table. It is good to be back in the field of his Master, where what is unknown can be known and everything makes sense. It is a world of scholastic spirituality this Jyotish. It makes him feel at home but he wonders about his career. "Mantriji, do you think I should stick with music?"

"In India we have a saying: Do something for five years. If it works, good, but if you are not prospering after five years, try something else."

"Hmm."

"Is it working for you, Poem?"

"Clearly not."

"Maybe it's time to try something else."

Poem rocks in his chair, contemplating this salient point, feeling liberated from what has become his identity. He thinks about all the songs he's written, too many to have recorded or seen the light of day. "Do you think I'll ever be successful, Mantriji, that my music will ever be recognized?"

Mantri looks to the ceiling like summoning spirits then smiling benevolently he says, "There are many diamonds on the bottom of the sea, and every now and then one of those diamonds is discovered and brought to the surface for the whole world to see. And everyone marvels at its brilliance, value and beauty. But the rest of the diamonds remain on the bottom of the sea."

It is another Zen moment as Poem contemplates this undeniable truth. It's not exactly good news but it makes him feel better. "Well, this diamond is back and feeling a little rough." They laugh. "I want to continue our studies, Mantriji. I want to know what you know."

"It is a very big program," Mantri warns.

"I know, and I have all the time in the world right now. It's just…" he bites his lower lip, "I'm a little short on donations."

Mantri gives him a long look of consideration before breaking into a smile, like he never doubted it. He picks up two books from the table and holds one up in each hand, "Do you wish to continue with the 12 signs or will we begin Nakshatras?"

Poem recognizes the one book as Krishnamurti and therefore extremely hard. He points to the other hand, "I like the 12 classic signs."

Mantri puts the Krishnamurti down and raises the other book with both hands. "Thank you, God," he says, like having just received a divine blessing. He hands the old hardcover edition to Poem, "Find this on the computer, where to buy this book, Volumes one *and* two."

Poem examines it. 'How to Judge a Horoscope' by B.V. Raman. He flips through the yellowy pages. It is a detailed book of analysis with over a hundred charts in the South Indian style. It looks serious. "Okay," he smiles.

"Come Sunday at five o'clock and we will continue with Braha."

Poem thanks him profusely and pulls out his wallet.

"No no!" Mantri protests. "We are just talking, two friends, that's all."

"I really appreciate this, Mantriji. I really thank you for listening to me and I am so grateful to be back in Toronto with you. I will order these books and I will see you Sunday. Namaste," he puts his hands into prayer and bows to his teacher.

"Namaste. Now go home and eat."

Poem is elated. He puts on his coat and scarf, shakes Mantri's hand, picks up his unopened knapsack and heads for the door.

"See you Sunday, Sir."

"Namaste, Poem."

2 PAXIL

Poem leaps into the sky blue pool. It is warm, a little too warm as usual. He crouches in the shallow end, adjusts his goggles, waits for the gap, then pushes off into a smooth reaching front crawl, pulling the water beneath him in long powerful strokes. Watching the lane line below, he takes an extra breath, readies for the flip turn and… nicely done. He pushes off, glides across, picks up his stroke and completes his first 24 laps.

This is Poem's early morning respite from the world. He has no money coming in, he has to find a job, his mother's in agony over him, he knows Maya is gone, Monique returns his calls but there's no intimacy in her voice, Marcus doesn't call unless he calls him first, Romona claims he owes her a month's rent, his employment counsellor said he looks depressed, he has to vacate his room during office hours, and his sister complains how stuffy it is every morning.

But this blue community pool with its wrinkled senior citizens, worker's compensation cases, tattooed morning hipsters, social workers and triathlon wannabes is Poem's everyday salvation from anxiety. He used to win swim competitions in high school but abandoned it for music as they seemed incompatible lifestyles. He returned to it after a back injury and it's become a religion to him, a place to bash out his demons. He is about to push off again when ol' Joe, swimming towards him, yells, "Oh oh oh!!"

He stops. "Hey Joe, what's up?"

"My friend, you are a young man. I need your help."

"Sure Joe, what's wrong?"

"I lost my ear piece." He demonstrates with his thumb and forefinger, "It's just little but very expensive, custom made. It fell out." He surveys the deep end, "Can you help me find it?"

"I'll do my best, Joe, but I'm nearsighted so I'm sort of useless in the pool. But I'll look," he assures him.

"Thank you."

Joe stands back as Poem pushes off to resume his laps. The water is chlorine blue with surface light bouncing off the bottom like dancing spirits. He makes it to the end, flips and glides, finds his core, scans the line, wondering what the earpiece looks like. His third lap in, he sees a blurry pimple on the blue line. He stops, treads water and peeks under the surface. "Hmm." He takes a deep breath and dives for the bottom. The blur is a flesh-coloured diaphragm-shaped stone with a polished metal hole, like a diamond in the rough. He grabs it, resurfaces and wades over to Joe standing on the deep end ledge who looks at it, elated,

"Thank you, thank you, thank you! You are my very good friend. You saved me a lot of trouble."

"No problem, Joe. I'm glad I could help. My eyes are not so good."

"They did just fine. I owe you one," he awkwardly shakes Poem's arm.

"You don't owe me anything, Joe."

Poem resumes his laps, completes his workout and heads for the change room, waving to Joe on the way out. He showers, gets dressed and heads out into the icy cold. Malabar's warehouse is just down the street. He recalls his cushy driving job, walking to work, swimming in the mornings, two hours downtime every day. It's why he enrolled at UofT. He figured he could earn another degree with the amount of downtime he had. He wonders how Marcus is doing.

Through Little Portugal, under the bridge, Poem walks through the East Roncesvalles village of his youth. It is a gloomy grey morning and he muses as he walks: *Saturn signifies the elderly, Mercury signifies short journeys. Mine are both in watery Pisces and here I am, swimming laps in a pool with senior citizens.* He looks at the snow and frozen water lining the lawns. Saturn is cold, he is winter, and always has a lesson to teach. Poem went from Jupiter to Saturn when he left New Orleans. Mantri calls Toronto 'Saturn Town' because of the many outcasts who come to this cold city from all over the world.

He arrives home to the warm house of his youth. His mom is in the kitchen. He removes his shoes. "Hey Mom."

"How was your swim?" She is seated at the table, sifting through bills.

"Good. I found this one guy's earpiece—"

"Good, maybe now you can find a job."

Poem's mom is a petite woman with an attractive face and short greying hair. A lifelong student of the School of Hard Knocks, she is stern and dutiful with a serious mouth, chiselled cheeks, and eyes that could shoot laser beams. She grew up orphaned in post war Poland then immigrated to Canada when she was 19. Her husband died when she was 36, leaving her with three kids, a mortgage and no life insurance. This was *her* Saturn in the 7th house. A factory job provided all the income she would ever know and she was often squeezed to the point of nervous breakdown.

Forty years of seniority and she is recently retired with a good pension but still raw from a lifetime of nerves. She warned Poem against going to New Orleans, having a premonition it would turn out bad. Now she makes sure he knows this misadventure of his exacerbates every ailment she's ever had. He is about to open the fridge when she says, "There's breakfast on the stove."

He lifts the lid to an unappetizing mix of eggs, sausage, cheese and cherry tomatoes, thrown together into a hardened heap of yellow manure. "I was hoping to make something different."

"Yeah, I remember when I was young and we couldn't get food."

"Okay, Mom, I'll eat it but I don't know why you have to just throw everything—"

"I know," she pooches. "Life is hard when you don't get what you want."

He nods obediently and scrapes the concoction onto his plate.

"Finish everything. I don't want it to go to waste."

"Sure, Mom." He sits at the table and forces it down with copious amounts of ketchup.

"What is your plan for today? Are you going looking for a job?"

"I have a doctor's appointment this morning, acupuncture in the afternoon, and I'm seeing Mantriji this evening."

"Again with this teacher?"

"Yes…!"

"Are you making any money with him?"

"You don't make money—Listen, it's not about that, Mom. I'm learning something I'm really interested in."

"Astrology," she is dumfounded.

"Yeah, *and* philosophy, *and* cosmology, *and* mathematics, *and* symbolism."

"I think you're better off learning computers."

"Mom, anyone can learn computers. Millions of people know computers. I'm doing something different."

She looks at him sternly above her reading glasses, "I don't mind feeding you, Greg, but as long as you stay in my house, you have to look for a job. I don't care if it's minimum wage so long as you are working, then you can stay. And I don't want to hear anymore talk about astrology."

"It's not just astrology…" he lets up, knowing he'll just make it worse.

"If you want to live by your rules, you can go back to that prostitute, Romona."

"She's not a prostitute, Mom! She's a high class stripper, okay? There's a difference."

"Greg! You had a good woman and I don't know why you didn't listen to me, why you had to go."

This is Poem's cue to leave. "Okay, Mom. I'll get out of your hair." He stuffs the rest of the food into his bulging cheeks, thanks her for the meal and heads for the attic. His sister is on the phone, waving her hand, shushing him. He nods defensively and gathers his books and clothes. His guitar case is in the corner. He hasn't touched it in weeks. He opens a drawer to get his health card and finds a strip of paper that looks like a large fortune cookie note. It reads:

> The tragedy of life is what dies inside a man while he lives.
> Albert Schwiezer

He looks at his sister working, stressed out on the phone, trying to ignore him; his guitar case next to the exercise bike. He made a deal with his mother: no more music till he finds a job. *She's such a friggin Capricorn.* He moves down to the second floor where he puts on some quiet music and begins organizing papers. He has two job postings: Admissions Clerk at UofT and Administrative Assistant with the City. It all looks hopelessly boring and he starts preparing cover letters.

It gets to be late morning when he takes note of the time, gets dressed and heads for the doctor's office just down the street. Entering the ground floor of the corner lot house, he sees his always tanned doctor talking to the always cantankerous receptionist. He nods hello and sits in the always packed waiting room. Bartok's Concerto for Orchestra plays louder than it should. He looks through the magazines for a bit, wondering how many sick people have handled them. One article grabs his attention and he is knee deep into it when he hears his name. He looks up and his doctor is smiling with folder in hand, motioning for him to come on in. He follows and they enter a small examination room where Poem gets up on the table.

"Well, well, it's been a while," the doctor says. "We nearly threw your file out. I can't make a living off healthy people."

Poem marvels at his leathery face, wondering if he's hooked on vacations or tanning parlours. "I was just reading this article—"

"Good. Now what can I do for ya?"

"Well, actually, my employment counsellor suggested I talk to you because… Well, she just looked at me and said," he pooches his mouth, "'You look so sad. No one's gonna hire you if you look so sad.'"

"Are you depressed?"

"Uh, yeah, I guess I am. I mean, I was just in the States for about five months and a lot of things happened. I had what you might call a scandalous love affair that I really regret now. It cost me most of my life here in Toronto. I lost my apartment, I'm unemployed, livin' at my mom's—she friggin hates me—I'm six thousand dollars in debt, I have to sell my car, I'm considering giving up music entirely and I have no idea what to do with the rest of my life. Maybe I need someone to talk to, like a therapist or something."

"How did you let all this happen?"

"You might say opportunity coincided with a breach in my ethics, fuelled by American-sized doses of alcohol."

"Are you still drinking?"

"No. I stopped three weeks ago."

The doctor looks in his file. "Do you still smoke?"

Poem nods reluctantly and the doc says, "Wait here." He returns ten seconds later with a clipboard. "I want you to take this survey. Just answer the questions as truthfully as you can and I'll be back in five minutes. Just press hard."

Poem looks at the questionnaire. It is a five choice sliding scale from 'Most of the time' to 'Almost never' printed on white, yellow and pink carbon papers. He likes doing surveys and gets to work.

'Do you feel sad?' the survey asks. *Well, most of the time.* He checks the appropriate box.

'I feel agitated or restless,' the survey says. "Yeah. Most of the time," he checks the box.

'I feel worn out.' "You know that's right." He checks the box.

'I feel so guilty I can barely take it.' "God, it's like they can see right through me." He checks the appropriate box, enjoying himself, and this goes on for 50 questions. He completes the survey early so he looks at the pink carbon copy that has the grading scheme. He adds it up and voila! He's one point into 'Marked Depression.'

The doctor enters, "All done?"

"Not only that, but I added it up for ya."

The doc takes the clipboard and does his own addition. "Well, according to this you have marked depression. Let me ask you something. Do you pray?"

"Why, is it that bad?"

"No, I mean you're Roman Catholic, right?"

"Not really, at least I don't think so, not anymore. I like philosophy. Why, you think prayer would help?"

"Not if you don't believe, I'm afraid," he scribbles something out in his file.

"Look, I think I just need someone to talk to, doc. I've been through a lot and I'm obviously in a huge upheaval right now. Maybe an objective ear would help."

The doctor gives him that look that only doctors give when you self-diagnose in front of them. "I'm afraid psychoanalysis has gone the way of the dodo bird. They found it about as useful as astrology."

"What d'ya mean?!"

"It's obsolete, son, that's all. Probably screwed up more people than it helped."

Poem bites his lip.

"The withdrawal from alcohol may be at the root of your depression, but just to be safe, I want to prescribe something I think will help."

"Prescribe?"

"Well, it's a medicine that helps lift your mood when you're feeling blue. Y'see, sometimes the brain runs out of certain chemicals or gets out of whack and we have to bring it back into stasis with chemical supplements."

Poem watches him gesticulate like a salesman.

"What I'm recommending is that you start a treatment to help lift you out of these doldrums and after a month or so you can go out and find that dream job."

He sounds Pollyannaish and Poem is confused, "Are you talking about an antidepressant?"

"Yes, that is the clinical term. I think you should try it, Greg. I recommend Paxil." He gets out his prescription pad and starts writing.

"Paxil?" he's never heard of it. "I really am not that into pills, doc. I don't know if I want to take an antidepressant."

"Oh it's perfectly safe. You won't feel anything for at least a month. Then gradually, very slowly, you'll notice that colours will start looking brighter, the sky will seem more blue. You'll feel like there's something good about your life."

Poem can't believe it. It's like he's channelling the guy who sold it to him. "You know I'm not working, right? How am I gonna pay for this?"

"Are you kidding? I got a whole closet full!" he thumb-points back into the hall.

Poem scratches his head, "Okay. I guess I'll try it."

The doc skips out of the room and returns with a week's sample pack which he tosses at Poem. He assures him he won't feel a difference for at least a month but that he will thank him when the time comes. They walk out to reception where he says, "Come back in a week for your next pack." The receptionist books a time, writes it on a business card and slides it in front of Poem, never once looking up.

Poem leaves the office and heads for home. Thankfully his mother is out so he has the main floor to himself. He slides open the sample pack, pops open a bubble, and out comes a tiny orange pill. He examines it before swallowing, then makes a sandwich and eats it while listening to the radio. An hour passes when he showers, gets ready and heads for the streetcar. It takes him to the subway where he waits for the train. It arrives and he enters.

He's surprised to see it so busy inside. It's like the aftermath of a war. People look depressed, the air is stale, the mood is grey, you can taste the grey. Missing ads glare ugly white light while the floor is crude with the soot of countless boots. All the seats are taken, people stand reluctantly, everyone looks ashen and tired. A woman with a big nose naps, swaying to the bumping car; a young man next to her sits with trance on his iPod; an old man looking flush and scaly, his wife ignoring him, reads the advertisements; teenagers attending the same catholic school look past one another, too shy to speak; there's an afro with a pick in, different tuques and hats, one with ear flaps, one guy looks like he just killed someone; bags on the floor, heads bobbing unconsciously. *What a mess of humanity.* They're like walking toothaches, swaying to the click-clacking train, victims of an industrial revolution, stone gargoyles locked in time, like everyone's got a cold or some disease or they just got bad news.

Poem's not sure why he's thinking this way. Wasn't he just diagnosed with marked depression? He should be more understanding. He feels an unusual lightness develop in his stomach, like a plant growing in fast motion. He looks around. *Everyone's so friggin miserable. What's wrong with them?! Don't they know how beautiful life is?!* He feels his neck loosen and here comes a chill. It's like he's bewitched all of a sudden. He looks at all these tortured faces and can't help but grin. His stomach feels like he's on the universal love-vibe yet he can taste the isolation around him, the fear and anxiety of everyone in the car. *Wretches on their way to the ovens, human fuel for the advancement of commerce. All hail the mighty dollar!* He wants to yell, 'What's wrong with you people?!' and barely refrains then leans back, suddenly on a wave. Holding the pole, he feels in his chest a silver roll of energy penetrate him and he looks around: blue veins drip down worried faces, racing through the colon of this city like so many turds to the sewer house. *Man, this is just weird.* He can't stop smiling and he loves it. He is so blessed to be alive. His stomach is full of sunshine! He surveys the anguished prisoners, spotting one shiny face in this nightmarish crowd. She is looking at him, an older Jamaican lady dressed for an office job. It's like she can see through him, to the source of his joy and hope, like they're both on the same tightrope, and he gets it! This is Paxil!

Oh wow! This is good. This is really good. He feels the drug in his heart, feeding his veins. He wants to tell everyone that God loves them, that they are all synapses in the mind of God, incomplete souls swimming upstream to the light. *It's Yonge and Bloor already?!* He feels compelled to say goodbye but refrains, winking only to the lady on the Paxil frequency.

He flows through the subway door, through the undulating humanity at Bloor Station to the Yonge line where he finds another glob of depressed passengers who don't know the meaning of life. He gets off at St. Clair and practically skips his way to the clinic, feeling chipper for such a grey day. He leaps up the stairs to the red brick house, enters and approaches Sally sitting alone at reception. She knows he's suffering from depression and greets him solemnly, wondering what he's smiling about.

"Hey Sally!" he is happy to see her. "How are you?"

She looks at him, concerned, "I'm okay. Are you okay?"

"I'm great!" he beams.

She wonders if he's drunk. She looks in her appointment book and whispers, "You're here for depression, right?"

"Yup," he grins.

"Well, did you win the lottery on the way over?"

He laughs uproariously, "Good one!" He looks around then leans in, "I took an antidepressant."

"Oh no, Greg," she sounds disappointed.

"No no, it's really good. I'm digging it."

Nadia emerges from her office. She sees Poem and greets him softly, "Hi Greg."

"Hey Nadia!" he goes for the hug.

She's confused and whispers, "You're here for depression, right?"

"Yes siree!" he lets her go.

"Okay, well..." she looks at Sally who shrugs. "Just follow me."

Poem trails her into the office where they settle into their chairs and she levels with him, "You don't seem depressed, Greg."

"I guess it's mild depression," he laughs.

"Do you need a treatment?"

"Well I'm here. May as well. If you're offering."

She doesn't know what to make of this behaviour. He sees her confusion and admits to the Paxil.

"Today?"

"Yup!"

"You're not supposed to feel anything for weeks."

"Well I must be really sensitive because honestly, I feel like I'm on a party drug right now."

She shakes her head and jots a note of this anomaly as he sings, "*My stomach's in love with the Moon.*"

"You really are one of a kind, Greg." She gets him into position to commence acupuncture and he tells her about New Orleans and the resulting tragedy of his life. It is a spirited conversation and Nadia wonders why she's treating this man. She would like to be this happy.

The treatment goes about 20 minutes. Poem thanks her and she wishes him good luck. He sees Sally on his way out.

"Greg, please don't take an antidepressant. It's just not you, okay?"

"I dunno," he grins. "I like this new me." He winks goodbye and heads out into the twilight. The colours are definitely brighter. The stores are all shiny and new. The tail-lights of cars look like demonic stars and he feels cozy in his skin as he struts down the dark residential street with rush hour piling up at the intersection. It's hard to see with all the headlight pollution illuminating random patches of snow like so many fallen ghosts. He passes Spadina Road and walks down the incline, feeling self-illuminated and whole.

Across Bathurst and through the back, he makes it to Mantri's building, calls up and skips out of the elevator and into his warm apartment.

"Hey Mantriji, how's it going?" he reaches to shake his hand.

"Namaste, Poem. How are you?" Mantri looks at him strangely.

Poem removes his coat and sits down. "I saw the doctor today."

"Oh?"

"Yeah, he said I'm depressed, y'know, cuz all the shit I went through in the States. He mentioned withdrawal from alcohol, which I never thought of…" he rubs his chin and Mantri picks up something unusual in him. "Anyway, he prescribed me this antidepressant—"

"Don't take it!" Mantri warns and Poem freezes.

"I already did."

Mantri looks surprised, "How do you feel?"

"I feel GREAT!" he exclaims and the two burst out laughing, like it's contagious.

"Poem, I can't believe such a great man like you needs this little pill."

"I'm just checking it out, Mantriji, and y'know, so far so good," he gives a double thumbs-up.

"How are you paying for this?"

"Honestly, I think he has too much so he's just looking to unload it."

"Into your head?! Oh yay! You do not have a problem, Poem. This is just wrong thinking. You have food in your stomach and roof over your head. Already you are above half of humanity. You feel depressed," he frowns, "because you did not get the object of your desire. But this is just desire, nothing more. If you were to acquire this object then what? Would the desire cease? No. You would possess the object and *still* be in desire, but now for something else! A man is satisfied not by the quantity of food but by the absence of greed."

"Wow. That's true."

"You are full of desire and desire creates doubt, doubt in one's Self, a feeling of not being whole or complete. Desire takes us towards something and away from our Self," he puts his hand on his solar plexus. "You cannot be whole if you have desire, no. Only if there is no desire can you feel complete."

Poem listens attentively, buzzing on the Paxil. Mantri's words feel like skilful fingers massaging his soul.

"Desire is in the intellect. You are Virgo lagna, very intellectual man. The intellect belongs to the senses, to duality. There can be no oneness in the intellect because it is always comparing, weighing, measuring." He pauses to see if Poem is following. "But we cannot stop desire or we will cease to exist because we must have at least the desire for self-preservation in order to live! Desire is everything and everything is desire, but desire in itself is not bad, although it may lead to bad things. If we *misuse* our desire, it will create more desire and *this* will lead to doubt, fear, jealousy, frustration, and finally anger. It is only the higher-self that does not suffer these things because it does not desire. It is *beyond* the senses."

"How can it be beyond the senses?"

"If you take away all sense perception, like this, how you say, 'Helen Keller' lady. She had almost no senses and yet she existed. She eventually did learn to communicate, but without the senses, the being is still there, the cognition remains. It is that part of us that witnesses all the rest. It *watches* desire but is not affected by it."

"So, if we can't live without desire then the trick is to desire the right things."

"Ahh, this is good one. You have said it beautiful. Once you are in karma, you can't get out of karma, so it is best to chase liberation instead of material gain."

"Y'know, I get it, Mantriji, I really do. But at the same time, we do need *something*, y'know? Like right now I have *nothing*! I have less than nothing. I *owe* money."

"This is your karma." Mantri grabs a pen and doodles as he speaks, "Saturn aspects all the most significant indicators in your chart: your lagna, lagnesh, lord of the 10th, Moon, 9th lord and 9th house of luck, 7th house of partner, 4th house of property—oh God! Everything positive in your life is held back by Saturn. What does this mean? Saturn is an old man, and so you procrastinate like an old man that doesn't want to go. Me, I have Saturn aspecting my lagna. See this box here?" he points to the ever-present wooden box next to the water cooler. "Four years I've been meaning to take this box down to my storage unit. Four years! But because Saturn is here, aspecting my lagna, I am just procrastinating. I will do it tomorrow." He looks at Poem sternly, "You miss opportunities by staying back and then you get depressed. Why didn't I act you say. But Saturn is austere. It does not care for material things, so you say you don't want it but you regret afterwards that you did not get it. Very hard to change regrets," he shakes his head. "There is nothing wrong with you, Poem. You are an intelligent man with a good heart. You must overcome Saturn's negative influence on your life, that is all."

"How do I do that?"

"By giving expression to the best qualities of Saturn: discipline, perseverance, objectivity, applying your experience, not giving up, being ruthless like death, becoming king—not by entitlement—but through merit. But *do not* procrastinate. It is death for you to do so. Your life will pass while you are waiting for it to happen. Your time will come, you will see. Right now it is not so easy." He looks down at the page, "Saturn is transiting your career house and Jupiter is in your 12th, tsk tsk tsk. What do you expect?"

"I have no idea, Sir,"

"You just need to calm down. Mars for you is no good for family or for money or for education. Once your Mars bhukti ends this month, you will be able to find a job. But don't screw it up," Mantri wags his finger. "This is good time for you to be in school. Rahu bhukti is coming. Yours is in 8th position, 'secret knowledge,' in 12th position from the Moon, 'large institutions.' It is *hidden* from the world. This is good time to study by yourself." He eyes Poem for a moment, feeling his condition. "Anxiety is good because it forces us to do something, but if we have nothing to do, then it will kill us. My advice is to just relax and rest and let the next week pass. Do you smoke marijuana?"

"You think marijuana would help? I'm trying to get over drinking."

"Alcohol is no good; maybe to talk or lose judgment, or how you say, 'inhibitions.' But for spiritual work, no; to memorize, no. Alcohol should not touch the lips of those engaged in spiritual work."

"And marijuana is okay?"

"There are many wise men in India who smoke, how you say, 'ganja,' but they will not touch alcohol. Marijuana is from the river Ganges, the spiritual artery of India. It's amazing," he shakes his head. "India is the only country in the world with 500 million people on a spiritual program."

"Interesting. Here it's the opposite. They use wine to eulogize Christ and you have all these red-nosed priests."

"Europe is very different place. It is cold there. They spend their days thinking of ways to shield themselves. When you are so concerned with preserving the body, you become materialistic. Alcohol is for the body. It heats and relaxes, but too much fire; side effect is agitation and violence. Alcohol is good for courage, to lose your judgement, to conquer, to how you say, 'get what's mine!'" he clenches his fist. "But for spiritual work, for knowing oneself, for inner peace, alcohol is no good."

"But courage can be found in compassion. I mean, look at Ghandi."

"You are right. Many feel that compassion is weakness, to turn the other cheek is a sign of surrender, but no. Compassion is a *high* thing that puts a man above his animal nature, closer to his divine Self, closer to God. Tell me how different the world would be if all this money being spent on wars was spent on development. But governments are not operating on this frequency. They are Kshatriyas, warriors, like in the Vedas. The Brahmin caste—that is, the educated class—should sit on top and have sway over the Kshatriyas. But in this castless system we live in, the warriors have kicked out the Brahmins, using them only when useful to themselves. The

Brahmins are no longer on top. They are below the Kshatriyas. They are lucky to even get their funding! This is why wisdom is gone from government. This is why violence rules the day. Because the warriors are in charge."

"What can we do about it?"

"Nothing can be done. You must continue to wake up in the morning and brush your teeth."

"Y'know, it seems to me that so many of the qualities you need to be successful in the world are directly counter to the qualities you need to be spiritual. Like what you say about marijuana; it's a peaceful vibe when people get high, but alcohol?" he shakes his head. "You can lose everything to alcohol," he looks down. "You know, one of the reasons why musicians got labelled outlaws is because of marijuana."

"That's right. But in India we have a saying: You will never find a musician in jail."

"Really? Why?"

"Because to play music requires a good heart, and a man with a good heart does not belong in jail."

"Interesting. Here they make it like musicians are so bad."

"This is the fashion here, but this is not music. Music is a language of the heart, and true musicians are babes, innocent people. They are not criminals, even if they are troubled. Why would you put a sensitive, creative being in jail? Musicians are revered in India. They are considered to be the voice of God."

"Interesting, the difference."

"Here, people are hobbyists. They play music for fun, what you call, 'three chords,' and some become very successful, but they are not really musicians. In India, musicians spend the whole of their days studying music, practicing ragas, trying to find the voice of God. They are not doing, what you call, 'Heartbreak Hotel.'"

Poem laughs. "That's funny but yeah, a lot of these young musicians are more impressive with a blow dryer than they are with a musical instrument."

"Right. Here it is fashion, not so much music."

"So you're saying that even if a musician in India is found with drugs, they won't throw him in jail?"

"What good is it to put a musician in jail? He is the voice of God. What place does God have in jail? No. Musicians are *good* people, not criminals. They have *good* hearts. They should help him with his problem, not throw him in jail."

"Yeah… It's definitely different here, but ya can't confuse being a rock star with being a musician. When I was growing up, to be a rock star meant to *look* the part, then maybe some music lessons, maybe not. But ya had to have the look, the image, the attitude. I heard very little music sometimes."

"Do you know this Madonna lady?"

"The singer?"

"Right. She sings and dances but does she know how to play music?" he twiddles his fingers, like on a harmonium, "To write music, like you?"

"I doubt it, Mantriji. She's more of an entertainer, like a celebrity."

"Oh yay!" he bobbles. "She is world famous!"

"Well, she is a great dancer."

"Amazing this concept. She shakes her ass and for this the Prime Minister of Israel greets her at the airport. I saw it on TV. The leader of a country goes out of his way to greet this woman like she is some head of state, and yet what does she do? Just shakes her ass on stage, and here is the Prime Minister bringing her flowers. This is the world we live in."

Poem laughs. "Do you like her music, Mantriji?"

"No. This is bullshit music. I like this, how you say, 'Sarah Brightman,'" his face lights up.

"I've heard that name."

"Oh she is very nice lady. She is married to this man, Andrew Lloyd Weber."

"Oh yeah," Poem is unimpressed.

"She has beautiful voice, and so, how you say, 'graceful,'" he holds his fingers up like savouring a truffle. "I saw her at this Roy Thompson Hall, my friend took me. I wrote her very beautiful letter telling her that she is the voice of God. I don't know," he recalls fondly. "I said to my friend I must give her this note so he took me in the back after the show. People were waiting and she came out, very nice lady. She said hello to everyone and I gave her my note and she thanked me," he smiles at the memory.

"I never would have guessed." Poem struggles to picture his teacher in the glitzy environs of Roy Thompson Hall, standing in line backstage to get a peek at Sarah Brightman. He wonders if when she accepted his note, if she felt the spiritual power of this humble admirer. He suddenly feels like he knows nothing of Mantri's life, this man who is his light. "Sir, how come you never married?"

"I had many opportunities, Poem, but do I want to live with a talking machine? No. I will marry only a woman with a PhD, otherwise what will she say? 'Hello?' 'How are you?' 'Pass the remote?' Nonsense! I need peace, not gap-shap."

"That's a little hard."

"That is life, Poem. To be married is not easy. You must first find the right partner, not just someone who is good in bed. I had many women who wanted to live with me, take care of me, have my baby, but I just couldn't. It is not my karma. I have found that when it comes to married people, in most cases, 'happy is he who sees not his unhappiness.'"

Poem understands this sentiment. He's seen several of his friends marry only to complain years later that life is longer than they expected. "You never met a woman you wanted to marry?"

"The ones I would marry are smart enough to not marry me," Mantri laughs.

"Did you ever have girlfriends, like when you were younger?"

"Oh yes, I had women interested, some even offering a dowry, but somehow it never worked out. Either she was ugly, or bad teeth, or uneducated, or one arm, and I just said oh God, do I want to torture myself with this woman? Karma is very tricky thing."

"You really did not want to get married. What were you like back in India?"

"I grew up in Delhi. I was what you call 'troublemaker,' bodybuilder," he does a curl and Poem is surprised. "I would work out all day pumping weights. My father never encouraged me the way a father should. I wanted to be a doctor but he would not give me the money. There were days when I was so angry with my life that I cursed him to his face. 'Why did you make me?!' I said. 'You couldn't keep your penis out and now here I am suffering!' Oh we had big fights."

"Sounds like it. So what did you do?"

"I went into government service and became a lawyer. BIG program, lots of exams, memorization. It was too much," he shakes his head. "I worked in government for many years while my brother's fame grew."

"What was your brother?"

"Oh yay! He was very big astrologer! BIG astrologer! People would come from everywhere, including America."

"Really? How about you?"

"I was into making trouble and having a good time. I left the astrology to my brother. He predicted I would become spiritual and go to America, that I would live there, but I did not believe him. I was too young. It didn't seem, how you say, 'probable.'"

"So how did you get into it?"

"He died."

"Oh. Sorry."

"It is all right. People die. He predicted it would happen. He drowned during a religious ceremony. That's it."

What a strange story. "I guess certain things happen only in India."

"Two thousand people showed up to his funeral. This is how great a man he was. He helped *many* people. I was his younger brother so I inherited his books, scriptures, notes, everything. I read a little and became fascinated, and so I studied with whomever I could, Raman, Krishnamurti, Sivananda. I had many teachers and many experiences and I even opened up my own institute for astrology. I nailed the sign right on the front door of my house. Many people came and I improved, and one day this American woman was so impressed with my reading that the next day her friend came and after said I should come to Toronto. I could make big money there she said; many Indian people, many jobs. This was 1968. I came and went back, came and went back, and eventually got a job here working parking lots."

"Are you serious?!"

"Oh yes. My English was no good so you take bullshit jobs within the community. I was supposed to be working and sending money home to my family but once I got here, I just wanted to learn English. So I went to classes, tried to make friends with professors—I was not interested in money. I just wanted to learn to speak with people and at the same time, I was having more and more people come to me for astrology. All my nights were taken up by endless study and people stopping by. After not too long, I had a few students who wanted to learn Jyotish, Ayurveda. I knew some Sanskrit but I went to the university to learn more and became friends with the professors there."

"Were these professors into astrology?"

"Oh yes, very interested."

"You said before that you were with the Jehovah's Witnesses."

"Right. 11 years I studied with them. Very good people. I wanted to learn the Bible, and they teach it free. You will meet some dedicated and educated people in Jehovah's Witness. They are not stupid people, no. They let me come and study with them but I was too much trouble. I asked too many questions. 'How can the physical body ascend into Heaven?' 'What does this mean, virgin birth?' But they always try to make you see it *their* way. I did not interpret the way they did and they put down Hindu religion in front of me. They told me to abandon my gods and accept *their* god. Only their god could save me. I said, 'Jesus Christ could not save himself, how is he gonna save me?' They did not like when I said these things so I had to go. But I learned and memorized so much from the Bible, especially what you call John. This is my book, the gospel. They are good people, Jehovah's Witness, and I still have some friends. I just could not accept a narrow view of the world. They did not like my astrology. I say three astrologers predicted the birth of Jesus Christ and you tell me you don't believe in astrology? I remember he said, 'I'm not saying it doesn't work, just that I don't believe in it,'" Mantri laughs. "It is this narrowness I could not take."

"Right."

"During this time I had no phone for 10 years."

"Really?"

"No. I did not want to speak to anyone. I felt the karma of this time was for me to focus on my studies, to learn more, improve my English, focus on spiritual practice. People were looking for me, they want me to read their chart, to give advice, but the problem is you can be right a hundred times but when you are wrong once, they will never let you forget it. This is why I have so many offers to stay with people but I never go. They say they will put me up, they will take care of me, but I know as soon as I get there, they will ask me everything, how to do this, when to do that, they will bloody *eat my head* with their constant talking. Better to be here, alone."

"So how did you come out of it?"

"One day, you know this Edith lady? Very nice lady. I was teaching Sanskrit at a yoga studio on College near Yonge Street and this woman knew who I was, that I was Robert Svoboda's teacher. She wanted to learn Jyotish but I was not teaching it then. She would ask me *every* time, and one day I told her to meet me in the coffee shop at 11 a.m. I had no intention to meet her so I did not go," he shrugs. "In the afternoon I went to teach and when I passed this coffee shop, I saw her. It was four o'clock in the afternoon and she was still waiting for me. I could not believe this. My heart broke for her. I walked inside and we talked. I decided I would teach her. She showed commitment and I could not refuse."

"Wow. She was determined."

"Oh yes. Very good lady, Edith. She told friends, they told friends, it was time for me to get a telephone and now I have many students again. Amazing," he looks up.

"So I guess I have her to thank."

Mantri smiles. He looks tired. Poem still feels the Paxil beaming like a lighthouse from his stomach and he imagines Mantri as a young man, getting into fights, dating women. "Well Sir, this was really interesting. Thank you so much for opening up to me."

"You are just like a son," Mantri says tenderly. "How do you feel?"

"I feel good. Calmer. Less trippy."

"This is a funny pill you brought here. It is good for talking."

"Yeah, I know. I feel like you and I finally partied together."

"Huh, that is right. I will see you Sunday, Poem." He stands.

"Sure, Mantriji. Already looking forward to it." Poem gathers his stuff, puts on his coat and bows to his most wonderful and complex teacher, "Namaste, Sir."

"Namaste."

He leaves the apartment and decides to walk home. It'll take him an hour he figures but it's not too cold. He doesn't want to lose this euphoria on the subway. Besides, what's the rush? He'll only be moving away from the light.

3 EGO IS IDENTITY

"So?"
"So...?"
"How do you feel?"
"Oh, you mean the Paxil."
"Yeah."
"I gave it up."
"Why?!"
"Because it felt like I was on some drug."

The doctor looks over his file, pen in hand; he does not approve. "What happened?"

"Well, the first day was great! I mean, I partied that day."

The doc looks at him sternly.

"I mean, what happened..." Poem describes in vivid detail his experience on the subway when the medicine first kicked in, how the riders turned into stone-faced gargoyles while he rode a pulsating wave of silver ecstasy.

"First day?"
"Within like, two hours."

The doctor scribbles something in his file. "It's impossible that an antidepressant produced this reaction. Are you sure you didn't mix it with anything?"

"What, like snorted some Advil?"

The doctor rubs his chin.

"I didn't take anything except vitamins that day. It's the Paxil."

"What happened next?"

"When I took it the second day, it was still pretty good but I noticed that by the end of the day, that initial sunshiny feeling turned into this gnawing sensation in my stomach. The third day was even worse. I had this corroding in my guts that was just begging me to get off the stuff."

The doctor listens, taking notes.

"The fourth day was Superbowl Sunday. I watched the game with my sister and by halftime I wanted to jump outta my skin. It felt like my stomach was eating me from the inside, that whatever light there was before was now just this sickly metallic saccharine feeling."

The doctor is not used to such explicit descriptions and tries to capture their psychedelic flair in his notes.

"I decided even before the second half started to throw the rest of the pack out. I just could not take it. It was like puppies brushing up against me from the inside."

"Wow."

"I called my friend who's a naturopath and he suggested I take this Bach Flower Remedy whenever I get anxious, just a few drops under the tongue," he demonstrates. "So I picked some up and y'know, it worked!"

The doctor is skeptical.

"Honestly, I think the combination of *stopping* the antidepressant, mixed with taking this flower remedy, is what ultimately got me out of it—like empowering myself—and I just feel better now," he gives a toothy grin.

"Well, that *is* good news," he is unimpressed. "Whatever works, right? One thing for certain, son, you sure have a powerful imagination."

"Thanks, doc. And hey, thanks for trying." He jumps off the examination table, shakes the doctor's hand, and sees by the clock it is 5 p.m. He leaves the office and makes his way home where he finds his mother in the kitchen preparing leftovers.

"Hi Greg. So... no job yet? Nothing, nothing?"

"Y'know, it'd be great if you didn't remind me every time I walk in."

"You have to work, Greg. You need money to live. No money, no funny."

"I know, Mom. I took economics. I'm just saying there are other things to talk about."

"I don't want to hear about 'the stars,' Greg. Call Marion."

He walks to the stairs and hollers up to his sister.

"Do you have to yell?"

"Well how else she gonna hear me?!"

"Greg, go upstairs and call her! There is proper way of doing things!"

He hears his sister shuffling down so he sits at the table. His mother puts a plate in front of him, "Sad how some people have to work for food but for you, poof, like magic, here it is. What would you do without me?"

"Well, obviously I would be either dead or rotting away in some gutter."

"Hi Greg," his sister walks in. "How's it going?" She sits down and starts helping herself.

"I just got back from the doctor's." He recaps the appointment for them.

"It's all money," his mom says.

"I'm sure he thinks he's helping," his sister reassures.

"But ya know," Poem says, "I've talked to a few people in the past week and I can't *believe* how many people I know who've either *been on* or who *are on* antidepressants."

"It's a quarter of the population," his sister read.

"Wow! Can you imagine, one in four people walking around on this stuff? It's like invasion of the body snatchers!"

His mom and sister give their takes on why society is the way it is. "It's all money," his mother reassures and Marion tells them what Oprah thinks.

"Well, what does that say about us?" Poem says. "That we have everything we need, yet we're all depressed."

"We have it too good," his Mom points. "Make sure to finish the salad."

Poem looks, "Mom, why did you slice up the steak into the salad?"

"Hey, that's good steak! Just eat. It all goes in the same hole anyway."

They resume dinner when Poem says to Marion, "By the way, I'm seeing Monique tonight."

"Good!" his mother interrupts. "Maybe she'll take you back."

"I'm just stopping by to pick up more stuff."

His mother sighs wearily.

"Well, tell her I say hi," Marion says.

"I will."

Poem washes the dishes and everyone settles in for their separate evenings before he gets ready to leave.

"Say hello from me," his mother says. "She's a good woman, Greg."

"I know."

It is dark out as Poem walks towards Sorauren Ave, feeling the lake chill on his neck. He rounds the corner and sees that homeless guy, Jack, or Steve, or Rick, or something, walking towards him with his ever-present art supplies in hand. "Oh no…"

"Hey hey hey!" the bum scrounges and Poem stops.

"Hey uh… Strack," he awkwardly tries to fit a bunch of names into one. "How'd you like that chicken the other night?" He's referring to a tub of warm leftovers he gave him on his way home from a dinner party.

"A little tangy," the bum complains.

"You're welcome."

"Oh, so I guess I owe you a *big* thank you?! Because *you* helped me live *one more day!* Yeah, one more day of pain, one more day of corruption!"

"It was just an act of kindness, man."

"Oh you're *so kind!* I don't need kindness, man! I need justice! Do you know what compassion means, man? It means justice! Do you know what justice is? It's the *opposite* of poverty. Do you know what that means, man?!"

"Dude, are you so self-centred because you're homeless or are you homeless because you're so self-centred?"

"Hey man! The more laws you create, the more criminals you make! Quit judging me and start judging the Man! Do you know that money is nothing but an illusion? It's a broken promise, man. And '*use*-ury' is the original sin of the whole Western world!!"

"I did not know that."

"Look at them, hiding in their cozy homes, slaves to their comforts," he gestures to the lit windows. "They don't wanna be like me! They wanna be in a coma in front of the TV! They're too *tired* to do anything, to even *think*, because of their job, because of their wife, because they don't wanna wake up, they don't wanna see! People don't understand they spend most of their lives asleep!"

"Yeah I get it! Just don't take it out on me."

"Fuck you, man! You try living on coffee and cigarettes. You think anyone really gives a shit? Go ahead, mock my cynicism. Just cuz I ain't rich like you!"

"Yeah I wouldn't…"

"God is dead, man! He died of cancer! And we're just walking around like shadows of a spirit world, flaunting the death of our father." He tugs at his beard, "Man, the whole world is sick but they hate to see warts like me. They'd rather cut off a wart then clean their own feet! I'm telling you, man, everyone's asleep—you got a cigarette?"

"Uh yeah." Poem digs out his pack and extends one.

"I'll take two, thanks," he helps himself. "Good to see you, Paul."

"It's Poem." But the bum's already rushing ahead, having hustled two cigarettes. "Oh well, I guess you can't train a snake who not to bite."

Poem turns onto Garden and walks to the front of his old apartment. He looks up the narrow lot, through the bushes and pine trees that obscure the inset house from the street. "Wow." He walks the cracked icy sidewalk with its border of snow leading to the side of the house and a surge of nostalgia floods his heart. He trips the motion detector and is awash in light. Five seconds later, Monique is at the side door, greeting him,

"Hi!" she smiles, radiant and gracious, seemingly happy to see him.

"Hi Monique!" he is thrilled to see her. It's been six months. They embrace in a heartfelt hug, lingering for a moment till Monique breaks it up. She steps back and welcomes him in. He follows her into the kitchen where a cute blonde is standing in her coat, looking ready to leave.

"Poem, this is Kasha, my new roommate. She's from Poland."

Kasha smiles uncomfortably, knowing this used to be his home. She sort of curtsies, "Nice to meet you."

He greets her affably and they stand there looking at one another. "Well, I was just going," she smiles and makes her way to the front door with Monique following. Poem looks around the kitchen. *Wow. It's home, and yet, it's different. No more whiteboard.* He looks down and sees Patzy, his favourite cat, looking up at him confused. He calls her and she is coy but recognizes his voice. He squats to pet her as Monique walks in.

"Kasha thinks you're devilishly handsome."

He stands up. "Oh yeah? Well, tell her I'm available," he laughs.

"Sure, she knows how faithful you can be."

"Look, I told you. I just have an irrational fear of marriage."

"So you disgrace yourself in front of my family?"

"It didn't feel like disgrace at the time!"

Monique raises her hand to stop the surge. The other cat walks in.

"Tigger!" Poem calls, but he scoots off. "Boy, he's grown."

"He was just a baby when you left. He doesn't know you anymore."

"But Patzy does."

"That's cuz you nearly fed her to death," she is suddenly amused by the memory of his often over-zealous love.

"I know. Sorry 'bout that," he smiles. It's an inside joke how he nearly killed her with Fancy Feasts that turned into fatty liver, how that cat had him around her paw, and they burst out laughing, feeling their mostly good history together. It's a relief and they look at one another fondly. Poem walks into the living room and wow, it is her beautifully Taurean womb-vibe that he loves so much: colourful puffy pillows and cozy furniture, dried up flowers and esoteric books. He soaks it in and his heart feels the loss. Monique enters as he shakes his head, about to cry.

"Are you okay?"

"I can't believe I'm here, Monique. It feels so familiar and strange at the same time."

She is sympathetic but keeps it to herself and Poem is still getting used to this new distance between them. "How's your mother?" she asks.

"Oh she's always trying to get me to feel her pain."

"That's all mothers, Poem."

"Yeah, but this one's got a real good case. She says hi, by the way. My sister too. I think they miss you."

"Tell them hi back. You know she's just worried about you, right?"

"Yeah I know. She'll be happy when I find a job. She believes that work is the reward you get for being alive."

"So is it okay then, being at home?"

"Well, I get what I need but not what I want."

"Good. Think of it as a cleanse."

"Oh it's a douche all right. Look, I love my mom, you know that, but we're too much alike and we have opposite agendas. Try and reconcile that!

I mean, the woman feeds my stomach and starves my soul."

"She just wants you to start making money, Poem."

"I know, but you don't do that by crippling someone with your fears."

"You just have to try and see it from her point of view. Didn't you once say the biggest obstacle to truth is thinking you already know it?"

"Yeeah."

"Well then shut up and try to see her point of view for a change. She loves you, Poem, or she wouldn't put up with you. You're a special guy and your family's concerned because it's like you're not even thinking about your life. You're always up there in the stars—ya have to come back to Earth sometimes!"

"I know, Monique, you're right and that's why I decided I'm gonna give music a rest for a while. I need to get practical for a change so I'm just gonna go through with it and do philosophy at UofT."

She wonders how practical this is.

"I know," he misunderstands her concern. "I just got tired a playin' the same ol' licks, y'know? It may sound fresh to others but it got cliché to me."

"You're such a good player, Poem. I don't know why you don't just play."

He visualizes Saturn. "Look, I just need to take a break for a while. I'm learning a different kind of music now." He spots a Scientific American on the couch. "Besides, I wanna keep my mind fresh for new ideas. That lifestyle was killing me."

"You just have to know how to pace yourself."

"Mantriji thinks I should study philosophy cuz I have a strong sense of form and metaphor."

"How is Mantriji?"

"He's good. I'm seeing him two/three times a week now."

"Really?"

"Yeah, I'm really into it, Monique—of course still looking for work but… I gotta do something in the meantime."

"So are you gonna become an astrologer?"

"I just like learning it, more like theory. I get enough practical with Mantriji. He's amazing what I've seen him do. Mostly I just wanna understand what it means to be a bundle of intersecting fields occurring in time."

"Can you tell me if I'm gonna be rich?"

They laugh. "Look, I'm doing all the talking here. How are you? How are your parents? I'll bet they're really pissed at me."

"You're right about that, but they're good. I'm good. Lynette's good. Julien really misses you."

"I know. I miss him too. He cried when I told him I was leaving."

Monique smiles. "Everyone's good, Poem. I'm just a little worried about *you*."

"Don't worry, Monique. I'm still here," he puts his hands on his chest. "Besides, with Venus and Moon in Taurus in the 9th house, Mantriji predicts I will never go hungry."

At this, Patzy strolls into the room. Poem sits on the footstool and waits for her to come. The cat looks at him, unsure, so Poem lets out a long baritone Om chant to which Patzy tilts her head and steps up, finally recognizing him. "Ommm," he resounds, one long note after another like he used to and Patzy crawls into his lap and purrs like she just found home. He stops with the contented feline and looks about the room, feeling the warm love of family here, the love he took for granted. Now he feels like a ghost. He looks down at the cat with tears in his eyes and slowly breaks down and cries.

Monique watches him sadly and Patzy wonders what's wrong. Tigger approaches as he sobs, "I am so sorry, Monique. I am so sorry it came to this."

"It's okay, Poem," she is becoming emotional herself. "Sometimes things happen."

He looks up, feeling unworthy, and gathers himself. "Sorry. I didn't mean to pull a heavy."

"That's okay. Take your time," she puts her hand on his shoulder. "I'll get your stuff." She walks out while he sits there on the floor with the two cats, mourning the life he once had. Gradually the black cloud lifts and he hears Monique in the kitchen. He gives Patzy one last look of recognition before getting up. Walking in, he sees a medium sized cardboard box on the table filled with familiar odds and ends, mostly stuff he doesn't need. Monique looks at him uncomfortably and he reluctantly concedes,

"Okay, I'm gonna get going. Thanks for letting me stop by."

"Of course."

"It was nice to see the cats."

"Yeah. They were happy to see you too."

"And you too, babe. It's funny, yours is the love I fear the least."

She gives him a strange look and they hug. He picks up the box and she sees him out. The cats follow and one bolts for the door. "Tigger!" she shouts, but it's too late. He's escaped.

"Sorry. I only seem to make your life harder."

"Take care of yourself, Poem."

He walks out the front path into the lit street and looks back before continuing on, wondering about his life, Monique, New Orleans, Maya, Mantriji, his mother, his debt, his itchy head, his need for renewal. The lamplights make the houses and poles look metallic blue. It seems so unreal, walking down his childhood streets, round the corner where he got his first

French kiss. He recalls the houses he's been in, the people that have come and gone, front lawn football, street hockey, collecting chestnuts, building snow forts, the sapling that's now a red oak.

He makes it to his childhood home where the hallway light is always on. He passes his mother in the living room, saying, "Fine!" to whatever she said. He climbs to the attic, to his old bedroom where he wrote and recorded so many songs. He puts the box in the corner, sits on the bed and thinks for a while. *How can I break from the past?* He gets up and walks to the dresser mirror and kneeling down, looks at himself, at his dry wiry hair, his tired, no longer youthful face. *My God. I'm a man.* He rubs his eyebrows and scratches the sides of his head, feeling agitated and frustrated with long rows of tension running through his dry scalp. He's thought about it for a while but it always seemed extreme, but now he's no longer the boy he used to be. Maybe this is the night. Maybe this is when it ends.

He gets up, knowing where to find it, in the closet, in the bottom drawer. He spreads a towel out on the floor. He takes off his shirt and with the device in hand, readies himself in front of the mirror like he may never see it again.

"Goodbye."

Zrzrzrzrzrz... Leaning forward, pulling his hair up from his neck, he applies the buzzing clippers and feels them snipping his hair. He has to do it slowly or the blades seize and it frickin hurts. He's never done this before and tries different angles, like yoga postures, cropping his thick brown hair, from the front, from the sides, making sure it falls on the towel. He goes through degenerating stages of scraggliness, from a serial killer, then Larry Fine, to a threadbare chemo patient, a Hare Krishna on acid, and finally— *Oh my God!* His scalp is covered with raw blotches of eczema and he looks bedraggled like a junkyard dog. Where you can see his skin he is ghostly white.

"Shit, I'm gonna have to shave this." He checks the awful, uneven job, with patches of hair everywhere like desert brush. His head is a disaster and the eczema radiates heat, making him feel cold and vulnerable. He ties a bandana round his head and cleans up the hairy mess, rolling it up into a spongy ball, then quietly makes his way to the second floor bathroom. He spends the next hour learning how to shave his head, contorting and cutting himself, holding a second mirror, using his foamy fingers for eyes. He finally gets it clean, rinsing himself three times. He can't believe how white he is, how sensitive his scalp is to the cold. His skull feels like it's been dipped in menthol. He looks at himself. "Wow... Is this me?" It seems so incomplete, like a primordial version of him. He is baffled and discerns a family resemblance: without the hair, he has his sister's eyes. He showers and feels for the first time warm soothing water against his dry itchy scalp. It feels soft, clean, slippery and good. He shivers with delight in his buoyant new head, bobbing under the shower spray, liberated.

He dries off, gets dressed, and introduces the new look to his sister who laughs and his mother who cries. He looks like his cancer-ridden father before he died. His mom begs him to grow it back but he won't commit. He retires to his room where he puts on a tuque and sitting in bed, wonders about his father's agonizing death. He was too young to really know his dad and was not allowed to see him in his hospital bed. "Rahu ate your father," Mantri once said. He learned later it was in the beginning of his Rahu dasa that his father passed.

He looks for the printout of his own natal chart and examines the dasa sequence.

"Oh shit! I just started Rahu bhukti this week!" His Rahu is in Aries, the head, with Sun: heat in the head. And it lasts two and a half years! 8th House.

"Hmm… Maybe this is *my* death, *my* transformation."

He gets up, removes the hat and looks into the mirror. He sees it now. He sees his dad. He has no pictures but he remembers. *I am my father's son.* His whole life he's been a dead man's son.

"When you have no father," Mantri said, "You have no direction. The father is the Sun, the stone, the prime mover, the source of light. When a boy does not have this he will be like a stray planet, a comet, falling to the nearest star. Without a father you are always looking for a home."

He changed his name to Poem, looking somehow to belong. He could do this, to what others seemed inconceivable: ignore his heritage, abandon his lineage, forget he ever had a family name. "You're practically an orphan," his own mother once said. He never gave much thought to his father, how he died. Some say identity comes from the father's side. All pictures, all remembrances, disappeared the day after his funeral. It was his mother's way of coping with a horrible situation. It's been a void ever since, like a condemned house you pass everyday on your way to school and you just accept that it doesn't exist. Perhaps this is why he pursues universal truths, trying to make sense of the cosmos when the answer is in his father's heart.

All suffering is desire and desire comes from ego. Sun is ego. Father is Sun. Hair is identity. Ego is identity. Shave my head, lose my identity, start again, be reborn.

"Hmm…"

He recalls something Mantri once said:

> *"Like a diamond, you can only chip away at yourself and hope someone notices your light. Then you will change the world, slowly, indirectly, unevenly, because you exist."*

4 KARMA, 9/11 & HITLER

"Namaste, Sir."

"Namaste, Poem. How are you?"

"I'm good." He removes his jacket and slides off his tuque, revealing his pale bald head which Mantri is still getting used to.

"You look just like Sivananda!" he says proudly.

Poem rubs his exposed crown, still feeling weird about it. It's been two weeks and the eczema is gone, although his scalp gets itchy after only a few days growth so he just shaves everything and keeps the goatee. It's his new Mr. Clean look and tautology that suffering comes from desire comes from ego comes from identity comes from hair. Ergo, it's all in the hair. But when people ask him why he shaves his head he says it's because he wants to look 'super-intelligent.' But he was not so intelligent to have waited till spring so he is in February learning the enormous utility of bandanas and hats. Mantri explained that Sun in Aries aspected by fiery Mars creates too much heat in the head, and because Rahu eclipses his Sun he has during Rahu bhukti taken to wearing hats.

These are the metaphorical insights that bond Poem to Mantriji; to understand the poetic language of karma and watch it play out through the mathematics of astronomy. "I got those books from India," Poem says. "How to Judge a Horoscope," he digs them out onto the table.

"Ahh, good." Mantri examines them.

"I started reading the first book but I don't know half the time what he's talking about!"

"Oh?"

"Yeah. It's not written very well. Like, the intro is good and the mechanics are clear, but when it gets to the analysis, I just find it very difficult to follow, like how did he get from there to here?"

"Poem, there are no good writers of English in India. They write from a Hindi way of thinking. It is 'Hinglish,'" he laughs. "This is why it is good that you, a beautiful writer, is studying this subject so that one day you will write about it but from an English way of thinking," he twists his hand.

"I thought these educated Indians studied in England?"

"Some of them do but they *think* in Hindi. Every language has its own psychology. You think in English; this is why you can write clearly. But these Indians are bullshit when it comes to English. I can explain in English but I am thinking in Hindi."

"Well you're very good."

"Oh no, my English is no good."

"You know what, Mantriji? You may have an accent and your grammar may be succinct, but you have a more sophisticated vocabulary and understanding of this language than *most* English speakers."

Mantri laughs. "I need to enun-ciate better. Like here," he grabs a notebook out of the pile and shows Poem an underlined word, "How do you say this? Spa-lend-or-iferous, spen-difrus…"

Poem looks at the word. "Splendiferous," he says easily.

"Right. How you say spi, spa, ssspa?"

"Go like this: Pa."

"Pa."

"Now 'pla,' like 'place.'"

"Pla. Place."

"Now go, 'Spa.'"

"Spa."

"Ple."

"Pla."

"Spla."

"Spa."

"No. 'Sspla.'"

"Sspla."

"Good. Now 'Splen.'"

"Splend!"

"Right. Now 'splendifff.'"

"Spendifff."

"Don't forget the 'spla.' Now say 'diferous.'"

"Difruss."

"Okay, now splenn-dif-ferrus."

"Spendufras."

"Close. Say splenn-diferous."

"Spendiferous."

"Don't forget the 'l' part. 'Sple.'"

"Sple."

"Splendiferous."

"Splendiferous."

"That's it! You got it!"

"That's good?" Mantri continues mumbling the syllables to himself.

"Don't forget the 'l' part."

"English is very tricky language."

"It's a bastard tongue." Poem looks at the table, "Y'know, these books were pretty cheap, huh? Only six bucks each."

"From India? That's expensive. How much did you pay for shipping?"

"Twenty dollars."

"That's good!"

"Books are that cheap in India?"

"Oh yes. For six dollars you should buy three books."

"How do people live there?"

"It is not like here, Poem."

"But six dollars is nothing."

"Here? No. But there, it is worth something."

Poem looks at the picture on the back cover, "Why do you say he was such a great man?"

"Oh yay! Raman wrote many books and taught many classes and knew many important people. He was a sage on this Earth."

"He corresponded with Carl Jung?"

"Oh yes. Raman is BIG astrologer. His family puts out this magazine," he shuffles through the pile, pulls out The Astrological Magazine and hands it to Poem who gleams the cover.

"Was he a doctor?"

"Oh yes."

"Of medicine?"

"Of literature."

"So he's a writer."

"And scientist."

"Sounds like an interesting man. Why is his book so difficult to read?"

"Because you haven't learned to read it yet. You must understand how to *infer*. In India it is assumed you will study with a guru and the guru will teach you how to read the book. You come to me because I am teaching you Jyotish. Without me you could not learn it."

"Aren't there any Western writers that write about Jyotish besides this Braha guy?"

"There are writers in English but they mostly write, how you say, 'cook books.' But what good is a cookbook if you will never see the same chart twice?"

"How do *you* do it, Mantriji? You're usually right, even without a chart."

"I've been doing it a long time."

"But how do you know without a chart?"

Mantri smiles like he's about to reveal his secret. "I do prashna."

"Prashna?"

"Prashna is 'horary astrology,' or the chart of the moment. Every event has its own time of birth and when you meet someone for the first time, or say, someone asks you a question, you can learn something about them or find the answer to their question in that very moment you meet them or when the question is asked."

"How?"

"First thing every morning, I calculate what time each sign will rise for that day. Right now, I know that Cancer with Moon is rising and Mars with Rahu is aspecting from the 10th house. People are worried over their careers and public image. They are fighting because of it. At 6:09 p.m., Leo will rise with Jupiter deposited and exalted Venus in the 8th. There will be, how you say, 'make-up sex,'" he smiles. "This just gives an idea. It is not hard to do but it requires time, time to memorize. But once you get into the habit, you will know a great deal about the person you meet, what his issues are, what will be his question. A good astrologer knows the question before it is asked."

Poem tries to grasp all this, not sure how to write it down. "Do you believe in chance?"

"No. There is no chance. There is a reason why the leaves fall as they do. Everything is a knowable quantity and if these are understood and measured against each other, predictions can be made. This is the role of science, to predict perfectly the outcome of certain knowable forces. Where the forces are not understood, we have the illusion of chance, but there is no chance. Everything unfolds, how you say, 'mechanically,' and it is the aim of astrology to understand this mechanism so as to predict the pro-bability of the future. The only true unknown is consciousness. It is a man's consciousness and freewill that reduces certainty to mere proba-bility. A man has the inertia of his life acting upon him but he can always make a choice. This is why we study astrology, to understand what not to do."

"And a man's karma is part of that inertia, right?"

"Karma is everything. Astrology is based on karma, and karma is Newton's third law of motion: 'For every action there is an opposite and equal *reaction*.' We see this cause and effect occurring within the context of space and time, but space and time has its *own* cause and effect, its *own* karma, and *this* karma is discernable through astrology."

Poem listens carefully.

"Every individual has his own personal space and time, that is, beginning and perspective, which we see in the natal chart. The time vector is determined by time of birth, the space vector is the location. Time is continually flowing, like a river, and the space, or *context*, is always subtly changing. This is why you cannot step into the same river twice. Remember," he points up, "Karma has two sides: time and space. To know the chart at any given moment is to know *what time* it is in the karmic sense, what is being given birth to, to know when is best to make hay," he scribbles onto a piece of paper. "It is the same with humans. Were you born at a good time or is it a difficult life? Is this a life for hay or to work out bad karma?"

"But karma necessitates reincarnation, correct?"

"Right."

"What proof is there for reincarnation?"

"Ha! Do you want to be here all day?"

"I mean, is there scientific proof?"

"There is some proof in the scientific sense, but there are *many* cases where people recall past lives through some, how you say, 'epiphany,' or through meditation. Sometimes they experience it through hypnosis or what they call 'regression.' There are many cases where very young children, three or four years old, talk of other places or families and know all the names or they will speak another language they've never heard. There is a very famous book you should read by this man Ian Stevenson: '20 Cases for Reincarnation,' or something like this."

Poem writes it down.

"In this book he writes of many instances of young children who recount details of past lives, and he investigated it. He is a doctor. Very good book. Most people forget their past lives at birth but these children remembered up to four or five years of age. There are also prodigies in music or math, like Mozart, people who come out of the womb 'readymade' to play piano or do calculations or memorize things. Many people for thousands of years in every culture have talked about reincarnation. The early Christians knew about reincarnation. Their prophecies from the Old Testament talked about the return of certain prophets at a later time. But it is difficult for Western minds today to accept this. They try to have a simple answer for a complicated thing."

"But if reincarnation is true, why are there more and more people? I should think it would always have more or less the same number of souls, no?"

"There are several answers to this. The first is that not all who are born are reincarnated from the Earth. They are coming from other worlds. It could also be that earlier epochs did have large populations but they were destroyed because of a meteor impact or something like this. It used to be that souls would reincarnate every thousand years but now it is more frequent and so they may all be coming at once. There is also this idea that as the animals of the Earth are reduced in numbers, their souls, or essence, is being used up by human beings, which explains 'energetically' the animalistic behaviour of some people on this planet. We don't really know. These are just ideas."

"And karma is behind it all."

"Right. Just remember, the *space* context of karma is in *what* will occur, the *time* context is *when* will it occur. Depending on when and in what space a thing begins, the result will be accordingly. A good space and the result is happiness, getting along; a bad space and there will be suffering, isolation, how you say, 'acrimony.'"

"So, where there's hardship, a transformation has to occur."

"Right. A life of suffering is a life of redemption and transformation. It forces the person to wake up to the reality of the situation, to open up to a higher order, whether to praise or curse it, doesn't matter. People always turn to the supernatural in their time of crisis."

"Or injustice."

"That's right. Injustice often makes no sense in a small way, but in a larger picture everything has its place and certain things require a past life in order to make sense."

"Like an undue amount of suffering or success."

"Right. When there is no merit behind someone's suffering or success it is because of karma."

"So like George Bush, not the brightest guy and yet he became President."

"Right. This is good example. But Bush has one thing many do not."

"What?"

"Courage."

"Yeah, you said that before but I don't know. I mean, this man had the whole world by his side after September 11 and all he did was make enemies of everyone. Do you remember September 12? The entire country yearned for understanding and the world was with him and what did he do? Just took 'em to war. Two wars. Like, *literally* a no-brainer. And they're calling him a great leader?! Seems to me that a man of *real* courage would have said, 'No, we will not continue this spiral downward. We will change course!' This to me would have been an act of courage."

"You do not understand the eagle," Mantri wags his finger. "For an American to turn the other cheek is a sign of defeat. Americans want to be number one! They put everything they had to be first on the Moon. They had to set an example by going to war, to say this will happen to you too. But no one could stop the war. Wars are not the whims of individuals; they are the fate of nations and are tied to the planets. Look here." He stands up next to the board and draws a chart with Virgo lagna. "Remember September 11?" He writes in the planets while muttering to himself and Poem watches like he is about to get the goods on what *really* happened.

```
         Su
    7    5
  8   Me   4  Ve
          6
  Ma Ke 9   3 Ju Ra Mo
         12
    10        2 Sa
      11    1
```

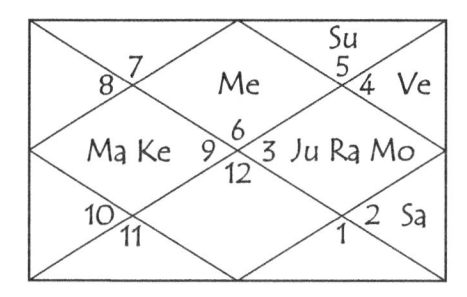

"This is the moment the first plane hit, what you call, the 'Twin Towers.' See here," he taps the ascendant, "Virgo lagna. This crash is the result of a plan. Virgo organizes and plans things. With exalted Mercury deposited, this is a brilliant plan! Now, just see how the Sun is lost in the 12th. This indicates the authorities were asleep."

"The Sun is father."

"Right. It signifies government, leadership, kingship. It is in another world in the 12th."

"The 12th house signifies loss."

"That's right. The authorities were lost in this moment."

"But the Sun is in its own sign."

"Right. The Sun sits well in Leo. It is at home here. But when the lion is at home what does he do? Sleep, gets lazy," he feigns a yawn, "goes for a nap. He feels safe in his own house and here it is in the house of dreams."

"So all that comfort and sense of well-being and they let down their guard."

"Oh yay...! Just see what happened. America the Great is now the most paranoid nation on Earth because of just a few men. Now see here, Mars is very strong."

"The God of War."

"And it is with Ketu, the headless demon. Together these planets make ghosts, shamans, visions, and terrorists."

"Riiight."

"In this case, Ketu takes Mars to a headless extreme. Fanaticism! It is occurring in the 4th, the house of home and comforts, the community, the homeland. In Sagittarius it now signifies finance, banks, the Treasury!" his eyes widen. "These men hatched a plot to bankrupt the United States of America. And here, Mars is lord of the 8th."

"Downfall," Poem knows all too well. "But what about the Moon and Jupiter aspecting from the 10th?"

"Doesn't matter," Mantri waves his hand. "They are with Rahu. Everything in this combination is taken to an extreme by the nodes. The Moon is nearly eclipsed, signifying some transformative potential, and

Jupiter is strong, so the native—in this case the U.S.A.—*will* prevail, but only after they lose what is dearest to them."

"You mean Freedom?"

Mantri nods.

"But that means the terrorists win."

"The terrorists can never win. They can only make their enemy miserable, more cruel, more low, like themselves."

"Well it seems the plan is working because the U.S. government is bankrupting itself with two wars and a policy of rendition."

"See here," Mantri points. "This is Sagittarius and Gemini, 4th and 10th houses, dual signs. They attacked the Twin Towers with dual signs on the cusp."

"Riiight."

"They are now in two wars."

Poem is amazed.

"They are more divided than ever."

"Okay. So would a good astrologer have been able to see this coming?"

"No. This is not something that is easily predictable. But these terrorists—oh yay! Either they had an astrologer or they were very, very lucky."

"How so?"

"These are religious men who planned these things. They will consult with spiritual savants of all kinds to make sure everything goes according to plan. I would not be surprised if they planned for this specific time."

"And 911 is the number for crisis."

"See these two planets, Mars and Ketu," Mantri circles them. "They are troublemakers. They are in Mula Nakshatra."

"The Lunar Mansion."

"Right. There are 27 Lunar Mansions."

"One for each day of the cycling Moon."

"Right. In this case both Mars and Ketu are in Mula Nakshatra, here in early degrees of Sagittarius. Mula is the left side, the demon side," he rubs his loin. "It is the root, getting to the root of something. It is ruled by Nriti, the goddess of chaos and destruction."

"Wow!"

"Oh yes. This combination situated in Mula Nakshatra brings destruction to the homeland and in particular to the Treasury."

"This is amazing, Mantriji! Do you really think they had the foresight to bankrupt the Treasury?"

"If this was not their plan, this is what they did."

"So they're winning."

"That is another matter. We'll see how it goes."

"So Jupiter and Moon have no positive effect on this Mars/Ketu conjunction?"

"In this case the terrorists are signified by the lagna, which puts Jupiter, Moon and Rahu in the 10th. This is *their* mission and it was violent and successful. But for the victim, signified by the 7th house, *their* 10th house is the terrorist's 4th house," he flips his hand, "The opposite. Do you see?"

"Uh yeah… You flip the chart."

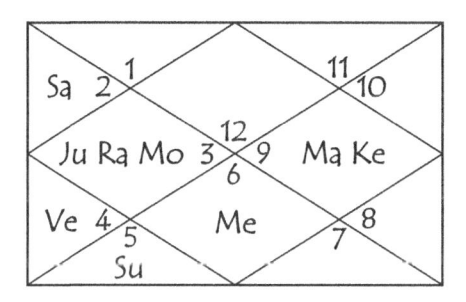

```
         1            11
   Sa  2            10
              12
   Ju Ra Mo 3    9  Ma Ke
              6
   Ve  4         Me      8
        5                7
       Su
```

"Right. And see this combination in the victim's 10th house?"

"Mars and Ketu?"

"Right. Now *America* is going around the world terrorizing everyone who won't go along with her. What did Bush say?"

"'If you're not with us, you're with the terrorists.'"

"Right. As you sow, so shall you reap. They do now what the terrorists did to them."

"So in the eyes of the terrorists, America is the terrorist."

"America to them is what they are to America. The two cannot exist without one another, like opposites attracting. America is not fighting Sweden, it is fighting Iraq. And so *their* two destinies are entwined," he twists his fingers.

"Sir, what do you think of these conspiracy theories that say the American government did this to itself to justify going to war?"

"Ridiculous. America is an eagle! An eagle does not eat its own."

"But don't you think there are vultures in eagle's feathers?"

"It is possible but my guess is no. People who say America or CIA did this say this because they don't want to believe that, how you say, 'towel heads' could pull this off. But Arabs are very smart, very cunning people. It would be best not to do business with an Arab."

"Why do you say that?"

"You can go ahead. But come back and tell me how it went."

"I'm sure most Arabs are good people."

"Oh ho. Most people, Poem, *most* people, whether Arab or no, are good people, but the culture of some is to exploit others. This is cultural, not racial. The Arabs gave us math, astronomy, Aristotle! We should not lose sight of this."

"They used to say the same about Jews. 'Never do business with a Jew,'" he wags his finger.

"The Jewish culture is a great culture because they question everything. They are intellectuals but they also stick together. People don't like this and next thing, they are persecuted for sticking together. But they stick together because they are persecuted," he twists his hands into a Catch 22. "Nothing is without its cause, and karma makes sure all is just."

"But what if someone is being victimized or abused. Is it because of their karma?"

Mantri gives him an amused look, "Tell me, if you saw a child being abused and it made you feel pity and you found out this child was Hitler reincarnated, how would you feel then? How would you treat this child?"

Poem contemplates the conundrum, "Well, like I'd wanna somehow redeem him or exorcise the demon from him so that no one would suffer from it again."

"Good," Mantri is impressed with this answer. "Man is the effluence of forces greater than himself. So long as evil forces can find a home in man, then they will continue to manifest in evil actions. Let us take this Hitler for example." He erases the board. "This is what you call 'Mars gone wild.'" He draws Hitler's chart with a red marker.

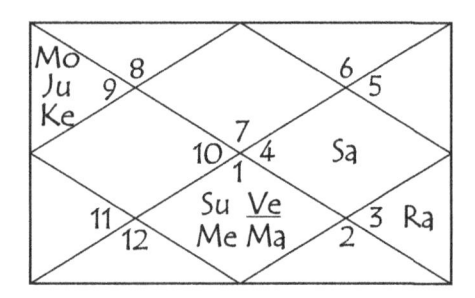

"Mars has too much shakti, too much strength here," he points to the four planets in the 7th house. "He was in Rahu dasa when he came to power. Very insatiable man. Strong drive for justice. All these powerful planets aspect Libra lagna from the 7th house, signifying foreign roads. This is the chart of a conqueror! Venus is strong but in enemy's sign. It does not sit well with the others. Add to this it is between Sun and Mars and this native has a sense of heat to him. Lots going on. He cannot be still. These two fiery planets give him strength. And see here, Sun is exalted and Mars is in his own sign in the same degree as Venus. This man became ruler of the world!"

"Temporarily."

"Everything is temporary, yes."

"Okay, but I'm sure there was more than one person born at this time with this same chart, so why was there only one Hitler?"

"We don't know about the others but they must have had some exalted position in some way, even if it is head of dog catchers. We always have to ask what is the age, sex, status and position."

"Okay, so *his* status?"

"He was Austrian born, one quarter Jewish, hoping to become a great artist."

"And his position?"

"He was in the right place to let off steam and his planets ripened at the exact times they needed to in order for him to lead. Timing is everything. If his Rahu dasa started even a week later, he may not have captured the right people at the right time."

"That's really interesting." Poem is dazzled once again with Mantri's ability to read the chart like a biography.

"The Moon moves quickly and so do our lives. Two of the same chart will not have identical timings. Something will always be a little different. Like they say in show biz: timing, timing, timing." He wonders if that's right.

"So what made him crazy?"

"Poem, we are all a little crazy, but his craziness came at the most opportune time to become insanity!" he clenches his fist. "He was in Rahu, and everything, his luck, his fortune, everything went his way, like riding a serpent. Rahu is exalted in his 9th, very strong in Gemini, powerful planets in the 7th. This man was Genghis Khan!"

"You mean, a reincarnation?"

"Oh yay! Rahu exalted in the 9th speaks of very powerful dharma, very powerful past life. The 7th house is 'others,' what is outside you. It is the opposite *to* you. In the Gita it is the battlefield where your life takes place. When prominent planets like lord of lagna are powerful in the 7th, this person will travel and live abroad opposite to his place of birth, you see?"

"Right."

"In this case he lives for the purpose of dominating others. This is not a married, content man, no. Saturn aspecting from the 10th makes sure of this. This is a very powerful man. Look at his 3rd house: three planets, not only in the Archer but in Purva Ashadha, the Undefeated. His Moon and Jupiter are both very powerful here but Ketu is making this combination of mind and benevolence into a dark force of paranoia. In this case the lower mind is not reasoning correctly and so it creates a fiction. And we see how this man hypnotised the masses with his fiction of a thousand year Reich."

"He was an amazing orator."

"Right. This combination of Moon and Jupiter in 3rd house of communications made him speak in a way that would hypnotize people.

This man was also a mystic."

"I heard that about him."

"Anyone could learn courage from this man."

"Mantriji! This is Hitler we're talking!"

"But we cannot take away what strengths he had. It took courage to get to where he got, good or bad. He instilled discipline in a broken people, just look at the films. His soldiers march with such precision! The power corrupted him and he went mad but in the beginning he was fighting the rest of Europe who defeated Germany in the First World War. He was good for the Germans for a short time because he could rally them, but there were too many things, including mysticism, that brought him to insanity. He was the last of the Nordic Gods, the head of the serpent. You've seen the swastika?"

"Yeah, it's an ancient Hindu symbol he stole to give meaning to the Nazis."

"This man," Mantri shakes his head, "took a positive and beautiful symbol, still used in India today; this man took it and made it into an evil thing in the minds of most people."

"That must have been freaky for you to see."

"It shows how everything is relative and there are no absolutes, that the world occurs in the mind and it is the mind that makes the world," he sits down.

"I thought everything is karma?"

"The mind is predictable because it too is governed by karma." Mantri looks tired, like he has just poured all his life force into Poem.

"Wow. I feel like we covered a lot today, Mantriji. I am so grateful to be here with you. It's really helping me to understand myself and... a lot of things. It's an awesome poetic device."

Mantri smiles at the suggestion. "The goal of astrology is to know your karma, in what areas of life you will suffer, so you can consciously apply an equal and opposite force to offset this suffering towards a more peaceful, balanced life."

His cadence is defined and Poem knows there's nothing more to ask or say. He doesn't want to leave but he has to give him space. He withdraws a 10 dollar bill and with sublime gratitude, slides it under the penholder cup. He wishes he could give more, that he had a job.

Mantri smiles. "I have good food for you." He points to a white plastic bag on the kitchen counter with Styrofoam containers inside, "Take this and eat."

Poem gets up and examines it. It's Masala Dosa with sauce on the side. "Thank you, Mantriji!" He gathers his books and puts on his coat. "Namaste, Sir," he bows.

"Namaste, Poem. See you Sunday."

5 KINDNESS IS NOT WEAKNESS

It is a ripe blue August morning. Poem, coffee in hand, unlocks the door to the tiny Constituency Office on Queen Street West. He turns on the lights and computers, opens the back door and hangs up his bathing suit and towel. The office is crammed until he slides into place the disability ramp and drags out front the community garden bench. He transcribes a dozen voicemails before stepping out to savour his coffee and first cigarette.

"This is the life."

He sits on the bench, looking south over Dollarama at the beautiful blue morning sky. People walk by in shorts and skirts, following dogs, heading for the library, renegade seniors on Rascal scooters, kids heading to the community centre, mothers and strollers, artists and drunks, immigrants late for English class. You can see every demographic in the span of 10 minutes here on Queen West.

Poem asked Mantri in February if he could somehow help him find a job. Mantri prescribed a mantra to be repeated 432 times every morning. A reluctant Poem asked, "How many for just a part-time job?" But he tried it—however imperfectly—and coincidentally met the assistant to the local City Councillor who said they were looking for someone. He interviewed for the position and when asked if he could speak Polish, given his last name, he said in the little Polish he knows:

"*Lady, my Polish is very horrible, however, you have a wonderful butt.*"

Not understanding a word, they were impressed and he got the job.

Perhaps because he recited the mantra imperfectly, it turned out to be only a part time job that doesn't pay great but he is happy to have it and as Mantri says, following even a trail of pennies will *eventually* make you rich.

He had no prior experience in community or government work but he's in a Rahu sub-period now, which is conjoined his natal Sun. It means he is destined to work for some form of the Crown. It has been a gradual and rewarding transition into his new position. Being bald is not at all a problem. Judging by the men at City Hall, it probably helps him fit in. No more rocker, he's practically comrades with security guards and attracts a different kind of woman: more serious, more intelligent, more black.

"Hey boss," Ricky smiles as she passes by.

"Hey, Ricky." He squishes his cigarette and heads inside.

The office is already hot from the climbing summer Sun. Poem sits at the main desk, logs in and downloads his work. Doug the ol' hippie enters in his haggard blue jean ensemble. "Hellooo, young man!" he bellows creakily.

"Hey Doug."

"Anne not in?"

"I'm expecting her after ten."

"Okay, I will see you then." He turns and exits, leaving just the sourly smell of cigarettes and body odour.

Poem gets through a few emails and a couple phone calls before Anne arrives with her coffee. She is a hot-blooded, proud to be Irish, retired provincial worker who volunteers twice a week looking for some justice. Poem knows she likes to sit at the main desk so he slides his stuff over to the auxiliary. "Hey Greg," she says in her usual semi-annoyed way, "Did you see that new development at the foot of Windermere?"

"No."

"I can't believe they're building another condo! What is it with this city and condos?! Councillor Saundercook is a total sell-out! He just ruined the view for another two thousand people!"

"Y'know, I don't get the whole condo thing. You buy it and then you have to pay a monthly fee? What the hell is that?! I'd like to find the first guy who agreed to this and kick him in the balls."

Anne laughs, "Ha! Kick him once for me, Greg. How'd it go yesterday? Did you make it to City Hall?"

"The meeting was fine, I have some notes for you, but I must tell you one thing—I couldn't believe it."

Anne leans back and sips on her coffee.

"You know how the Mayor's been asking everyone to turn down their air conditioners to conserve energy? So I walk into City Hall and the place is freezing! I'm like, why is it so cold in here? Didn't we just get a decree? I see the receptionist in a cardigan and it's sweltering outside! So I asked, 'Why do they keep it so cool in here?' You know what she said?"

"What?"

"So people in business suits can feel comfortable. It's frickin August outside and idiots are still showing up to City Hall in a wool suit and tie! What kind of stupid world do we live in?"

"Some of the most powerful people are also the dumbest, Greg."

"I say lose the friggin tie, asshole, and wear a short-sleeved shirt for God's sake. It's summer!"

Anne hoots her Celtic laugh. "You should run for office, Greg. Most people don't think like you. They think it's normal that—oh God," she ducks behind her desk and Poem looks to see Fred walk in. "You deal with this, Greg. I can't stand this brontosaurus." She scoots into the back.

"Hey Fred," Poem greets him.

"I noticed they tagged that manhole on King and O'Hara, eh? 'Bout a month ago now but no one yets been by ta do the work."

Fred is an old union man with a Cape Breton twang. Long retired but ever vigilant when it comes to public works, he likes to walk around and point things out with his cane. He has a slight stutter, a vestige of his last stroke, and is used to telling people what to do, which is why Anne can't stand him and it took Poem some getting used to.

"I'll look into it, Fred. Are they gas cuts?"

"I reckon so, eh?" He lifts his ball cap to wipe his sweaty grey bangs. "By the way, someone's gonna kill themselves on the curb at Brock and Queen, eh? You should walk down there right now and take a look. It's liftin' up right in front of the Indian store. I nearly broke my neck, eh?"

"Okay, Fred. I'll check it out. How are *you* doing?"

"Oh, still mobile," he smiles then pivots round on his cane and leaves.

"He's gone, oh good," Anne tiptoes back into the office. "Did he give you another list?"

"Does two make a list?"

She shudders and Poem says, "Hey, remember that Somalian woman I was trying to get transferred and Martha said she didn't want to do it?"

"Yeah, I heard you on the phone."

"Well, she stopped by yesterday to thank me. She got the transfer."

"Good going!" Anne is impressed. "I thought you made a very good case."

"Thanks, Anne."

"Oh look, Greg. It's your girlfriend."

Louise walks in. She is a petite 70 year old flirt in shiny lipstick, pencilled eye-brows, clown rouge and chestnut-brown hair. They think she used to be a prostitute. *She* thinks she can still have any man. "Heya handsome, did ya miss me?" she says to Poem. "You know my neighbour Debbie heard shots again last night, didja hear anything?"

Poem looks at Anne and they both shrug no.

"Too many guns out there, that's the problem. Young people got nothin' to do. I say invest in schools now and not prisons later." She looks out at the street, "Some say good fences make good neighbours. I always thought the world needed less fences, less politics, less strangers, and more family—whatya say, Sugar?" she sidles up to Poem.

"I heard it said that enlightenment is not in what you get but what you leave behind."

"Ooh I like that, Sugar, you're a wise one ain'tcha? What time d'ya get off work?"

"Can't today, Louise. I have class tonight."

"I'll bet you have class every night. I like your head. You look like a young Eisenhower."

"Hey," Anne interrupts. "Did you get your motorcycle license yet?"

"No, fudge! I just don't have the funds, Sweetheart." She looks at Poem, "How'd you like to sponsor me?"

"Sorry, Louise. I'm still climbing outta my own debt."

She looks at Anne who pretends to take a call. "Shoot. Well, once my modelling career takes off I'll have plenty, but right now I gotta find me a rich boyfriend, know anyone?" she looks at Poem, "Someone like you, maybe a little older."

"I'll ask around. Hey, where was the shooting?" he looks to Anne to write it down.

"Where else? King and Dufferin. That's where it all goes down."

"Again huh…?" Anne takes note.

"Okay, Sweety, gotta go." She picks up her red shopping bag and heads out the door.

"That's the third shooting this month," Anne says.

"Amazing. They thought they cleaned up one intersection only to find everything just moved to another."

"Well if ya treat only the symptom!"

And so the day goes: discussions, files, phone calls, emails, the occasional walk-in and the usual regulars. A real cast of characters and a high profile job. Poem is seeing politics from the inside, how it really is community service. It feels at times like redemption for his years of navel gazing. It's a job that requires heart and he's discovering how good he is at winning over difficult personalities, a skill he developed among musicians.

"Are you leaving early?" Anne says.

"Yeah. Got a tutorial at five. You'll lock up?"

"Uh huh."

Poem is finally taking part-time philosophy courses at the University of Toronto, much to Mantri's delight and his mother's consternation. 'What can you do with philosophy?' is her nagging question. He almost didn't get into the program and considered taking Hindu Studies instead but his mom nearly had a nervous breakdown when she heard so he rescinded.

After 4 p.m. Poem gets on the Queen streetcar and heads downtown.

Looking outside he wonders about tonight, after class. *This should be interesting.* Tonight he's meeting Maya for a drink.

They haven't seen each other in eight months. She called a week ago, to his surprise, to tell him she was coming home to stay with her mom. He stares out the streetcar window at the people and cars passing by, storefronts and signs, remembering the morning he left New Orleans on New Year's Day, landing in Buffalo, guitar and luggage in hand, airport bus to the downtown terminal, another bus through the border and through nearly every damn town on his way to Toronto. He knew Maya wouldn't wait for him but wasn't going to admit it out loud. He remembers how they tried to keep it going, how they talked on the phone almost daily. He even wrote her letters and a poem. Then one day her voice changed. It wasn't even February but he knew, he could hear, he felt in her voice that she had slept with Sammy. The seal was broken, she was gone, and he would never touch her again.

After that she called him only when she needed free advice, and he indulged her mostly out of love, but it hurt sometimes and he found it easy to distance himself with less frequent calls. He gave up everything for the love he thought he had for this girl only to realize he had fallen for a façade. It was the time and circumstance, what Mantri called a vasana. Whatever it was it hurt. Saturn is Shiva and Shiva is transformation. Poem died and was transformed in his 36th year by a woman two thirds his age who brought ruin that would lead to his rebirth. And all of it discernible through his astrological chart.

He transfers to the Spadina car and heads north for UofT, reminiscing on Maya's naked body. "*What do you want with such a little girl?*" he remembers Mantri asking.

He climbs the steps to Sidney Smith Hall and arrives early with a few others already in the lab. They are in the midst of an animated discussion with the TA.

"But truth really depends on your point of view," one student says.

"A *point* of view is subjective," the TA responds. "Philosophy is the art of objectivity."

"But Berkeley says there's no reality outside our individual minds; that if we really break it down, we cannot experience anything outside ourselves, and therefore the only thing that truly exists is me."

"God, that sounds so Bono," someone says.

"It's called Solipsism," the TA points. "And it's true that your point of view is the only thing you can truly prove."

"So I guess anything outside of me is a leap of faith."

"Everything is a leap of faith."

"So then we *are* alone," one girl says.

"Only if you believe Berkeley."

"There's no 'belief' in philosophy," the TA says.

"Wanna bet?" Poem mumbles.

"What does philosophy matter anyway?" a girl in the back says. "You don't have to understand a car in order to drive one."

"But ya do in order to make one."

"The point is," the TA says. "What makes us human is we *can* understand, so therefore we *ought* to. Like a cheetah runs fast because it can, like rams butt heads because they're rams."

"Y'know, it's interesting," another girl says, "that football was invented right after the great buffalo massacres in the 1880s."

"Why, because football players look like a bunch of stupid buffalo?"

"Well yeah, and when you think about it, what happened when all those buffalos were killed? What happened to all that buffalo energy? You can destroy the form but ya can't destroy the force. Is it any wonder that football became the doofus religion it is now?"

The class looks at her and the TA rubs his chin, "Interesting…"

A few other students arrive.

"I have a question," says a girl in the back. "Do you think it's foolish to search for certainties in an infinite universe?"

"Hmm…"

"Thcience is thuppothed to be thertain," the lispy guy says, "but it'th alwayth changing—well, when it comth to cothmology anyway," he seems to lose his point.

"So why would you ground yourself in something that is always changing?"

"When you think about it," the TA says, "The only *real* certainty is faith."

"But doesn't that imply morality?"

"There is no morality," one guy says. "We're just machines. We have no purpose."

"Gimme a break!" another says. "Where's there a machine that has no purpose?"

Poem comes in, "I say if order equals intelligence and we see that the universe is ordered, then we have to conclude it is intelligent and therefore there is an organizing principle, vis-à-vis God."

They look at Poem and someone says, "I think you just solved everything."

A few of them laugh and the TA smirks, "I doubt that."

Professor Jones shuffles into the room like a hospital patient, clutching his No Frills shopping bag of books. He is a dinosaur emeritus with a touch of Parkinson's and a hearing problem. He seems to affirm existence through his own voice. Essentially a Solipsist, he is bearded to the glasses, loveable but lost, an absent-minded master-slave to Rationalism where even numbers have no meaning. Poem asked him once what he thought of astrology and he just stared at him incredulously before simply moving onto the next question. He knows nothing of eastern philosophy; he just recommends other schools. Oblivious to his TA, he finds the wooden lectern and unpacks his stuff. His belt is twisted in back with a shirt tail hanging out.

"Okay, where to begin," he grumbles. There's mustard in his beard. "Le's see…" he flips through his binder. "Okay. Now. There is no God, you got that?"

And so it goes: Professor Jones soliloquies on the epistemological arguments of Descartes and George Berkeley. Poem finds it dry but interesting. He's learning there is only one state of consciousness in Western Philosophy; that you're either awake or asleep. There are no levels or in-between. There's no real distinction between the soul, the mind, and the intellect like in Indian thought. Instead of meditation, there's contemplation. Instead of oneness, there's duality, conflict, the dynamics of morality. And it seems to have peaked into a post-modern deconstructionist existentialism that somehow misses the point. He finds it insightful but overly intellectual and wondered why Mantri pushed philosophy so much until one day a subtle and profound shift occurred in his thinking. It was like sobering up after years of intoxication. The art of Philosophy is to successfully argue a point and is therefore the process of sharpening the intellect. It appeals to the skeptic in him. But like with everything academic, there is orthodoxy, and here it is Materialism.

The class ends on a high note with some lively questions and ideas about nihilism after which Professor Jones announces what's on TV tonight. Looking like he's not sure which way is out, he begins to pack his stuff while students make for the exit and the TA is flooded with requests. Poem scoots past them, down the stairs and out. He is on his way to meet Maya.

He crosses Spadina and Harbord to Borden Street, towards Bloor, wondering if she's already there, what she looks like, what happened the last few months. He makes it to Kilgour's side patio, looks around, and settles into one of the picnic tables. The waitress comes, he orders a beer, plays with his phone, looks at people across the road. The waitress returns and he looks up towards Bloor. *There she is!* Sexy Maya. His heart drops. She struts towards him, smiling, in tight red jeans and a translucent blouse, like she's on a mission. He stands and she hugs him like nothing happened. "How ya doin', baby?" her voice is happy and raspy. She's lost weight and has a sourly smell, like she's nervous or disturbed. He steps back. Her face is gaunt with new lines but she still looks great, even sexier than before, like she's been through a war.

"Oh my God!" she goes for his hat. He ducks and removes it himself.

She is shocked to see his shaved head. He smiles while she stands back and checks it out.

"What d'ya think?"

"You look intimidating," she smiles. "But way more handsome, like Air Force One. You look strong."

"Thanks, babe."

They sit across from one another, beaming with what used to be, marvelling that they're here together again. She is bright-eyed but looking spent and he wouldn't be surprised to find a tire tread across her back. Whatever little girl she had left in her is gone.

"So how was claaass?"

"Good. I'm doing philosophy like I intended and I really like it. And it's perfect because I'm also working for a politician now."

"Aw I love politics! I wish I could get into politics. Can you get me a job, Poem, please?"

He is taken aback. "Look, I've been there only a few months, Maya, but I can ask around. PLED-C is usually hiring but you have to be on EI. Do you have a Record of Employment?"

"I'd have to get one, baby. I'll look into it, okay?"

"I didn't say I'd get you a job, Maya, just that I would ask around."

"I know, I know," she seems anxious and takes a deep breath to slow herself down. "How are you, Poem? What's going on?"

He doesn't like her patronizing tone. "What d'ya mean what's going on? The last time I saw you we were promising to be 'loyal' to one another and in less than a month you were with Sammy."

"I couldn't help it, Poem. You said you would be back in a month but I didn't know what was going on. You said you were looking for a job, like how long was that gonna take? And then Sammy's new place didn't work out so he had to move back with the band. And since I was staying in his room, it just sorta... happened."

"How convenient."

"Hey, you didn't have to leave, y'know! You could've stayed at Lynette's, y'know!"

"How am I gonna stay with Lynette when I broke up with Monique and the rest of the family thinks I'm a demon? Meanwhile, you're living with Sammy's band and he's hitting on you since day one and you even *admitted* you liked him! No. I wasn't gonna stick around for that. And he couldn't even look me in the eye!"

"Yeah, he felt really bad about that."

"I knew! And really? What could I do, Maya? Kidnap you? Beat Sammy up? Gimme a friggin break! You were just being opportunistic and you proved me right, friggin Gemini."

He is bitter and Maya looks like she's about to erupt when the waitress arrives and they retreat momentarily. She orders a drink and the waitress leaves. "Sometimes I think you want to fail," she says.

"Why, cuz I didn't fight for you? I took care of you, I put myself out for you, I drove you everywhere, introduced you around, I even gave you half of what Lynette paid me to clean the house!"

She looks down.

"If you can't after all *that* know that I'm the man you want, then fuck you! I don't want you anymore! I told you many times, don't mistake my kindness for weakness."

Maya was hoping it would go better. The waitress puts a beer in front of her and she takes a long sip as Poem lights a cigarette and offers a truce, "Hey, let's just forget it, all right?" He raises his glass, "To love and forgiveness."

"Yeah…" she smiles awkwardly.

They toast and drink but she is silent.

"So what happened?" Poem says. "Why are you here?"

"Toronto's my home too, y'know!" she stops herself then levels with him, "Sammy turned out to be an arrogant ass."

Poem smiles.

"I know," she looks down. "I just saw how he rolled, Poem, like once everyone knew we were together, he acted like my boss. He talked me into getting a used car because once *you* left, my father got concerned for my safety and offered to buy me one. But Sammy ended up driving it most of the time."

"So he used you."

"A little." She takes another long sip. "He's really a sweet guy, Poem, but he's just like you, man, a friggin Aries."

"What's that supposed to mean?!"

"You guys like to be in charge. His band started doing really well and his whole attitude changed. He just became an ass."

"Like me?!"

"No, no, you're sweet, but you like to lead too. That's why you kept butting heads with him. But you are *miles* above him, Poem. Seriously, he was jealous because you're a better guitarist, you write better songs. He plays good classic rock, but man, you's a gangsta!"

It's like a piece of Duke just walked in. "You became his trophy, that's the problem. When I left he got you and felt unstoppable. I knew it was gonna happen. You gave him the shine to rise, but what did *you* get?"

"I was confused, Poem."

"You wanted his connections, Maya. Admit it. You liked that he knew so many people and places, that he could get you in free."

"No!"

"Yes!

"He's not that well connected, Poem. It's mostly just bluster."

"What did you ever see in the guy? You think he really appreciated you for who you are? Did you have a supernatural experience with him? Did you talk philosophy and astrology like we did?"

"No…! No, Poem. Listen, what you and I had was magical, it really was. I never experienced anything like that and it scared me, seriously. I remember the fortune-teller saying that you were the one to show me the door, that once I stepped through, I couldn't turn back." She looks up at the dusky sky. "My relationship with Sammy was earthy; with you it was all in the stars. I loved it but I needed grounding."

"And that ragamuffin grounded you?"

"For a while. Then he turned out to be a jerk."

"What about Duke?"

She hesitates. "That's why I'm here."

"Why?"

"It got out of hand, Poem," she is sweating and wipes her brow. "I understand why you left. I didn't get it before but now I understand. New Orleans is a friggin black hole, man. I couldn't believe the people, how catty some of them got. I wanted to leave so many times, Poem. I really missed you and I thought about coming back home but Sammy bad-mouthed you, man. He said you ran from there, that you couldn't handle the pressure."

"Yeah, the pressure of listenin' to a bunch of dropouts and their fucking lame conversations, talkin' *sitcoms* at three o'clock in the morning?! How much of that do you really think I can take, Maya?!"

"That's what they didn't like about you, Poem. They thought you were a snob."

"Why, because I'm not *fascinated* by their road stories?"

"Yeah."

"Well then I'm a fucking snob!"

"Duke used to defend you; he even got into a fight with Sammy over you. Man that guy loves you, Poem. I know I didn't want to pursue it when you first met him but he became like a brother to me and yeah, he once chased Sammy off with a baseball bat, I couldn't believe it. Pretty funny though."

"Unbelievable egos."

"Yeah well, I sorta became Duke's chauffeur once I got the car, which Sammy didn't like. One time…" she looks around to see if anyone's listening. "See, I felt really alone down there sometimes because I found myself living totally in Sammy's world. So I used to go by Duke's and…" her voice is weirdly loose.

"Maya, are you still smoking crack?"

She freezes and he instantly knows.

"Are you addicted to crack?!"

"I haven't had any in over two weeks, Poem, I swear. I don't even know where to get it here, do you?"

He gives her a stern look.

"How 'bout Marcus?"

"Fuck you! You're off it!"

"I know. Okay, I'm okay. I had to get out of there, Poem," she is nervy and practically eating her cigarette. "One day Duke tells me he needs a ride across town. I pick him up and we drive all the way to Jefferson. He says stop at this Rite Aid and tells me to just wait there, he'll be right out, leave the car running he says. So I'm waiting, looking 'round, having a smoke, and he comes rushing out telling me to go go go!! I'm like, is everything all right and he's yelling GO!! So I go and he's yelling FASTER and we're still in the parking lot—turn here, turn here, turn here he says! I'm like what's going on, why you so hyper? I can't believe it, Poem. He robbed the place!"

"What?!"

"He robbed the friggin Rite Aid and didn't even tell me, and here he is screaming at me to step on it!"

"Oh man."

"Yeah. I got so pissed at him, Poem. I don't care how much fun he is. Once he did that to me, put me in harm's way like that, and I don't even have papers to be down there?! I had to get out. I sold my car as quickly as possible—well, to Sammy who got it for a steal—but I called my mom and told her to *move over* because I'm coming home. I had to get out."

Poem is alarmed but not surprised. He was once Duke's ride deep into the 9th Ward to score some crack in between sets at the Spotted Cat. Of course, he didn't know that till they got there and had to wait outside, next to a stripped-down car, looking at the ghetto from the inside, wondering what's taking him so long.

"How *is* Duke?"

"He's in jail."

"What?!"

"He got arrested for possession and they linked him to the robbery. I had to leave. I didn't really get a chance to say goodbye to everyone."

"Wow. You're a fugitive."

"Not quite," she would rather not think about it. "But I couldn't believe it, that he did that to me."

"Maya, he's one of the biggest narcissists I've ever met! What did you expect? Especially when you start smoking his shit."

"Poem, I need to make some money. That's why I'm here. I didn't have papers to work in the States and I need my own place. I can't live with my mom. It's been only three nights and we're already at each other's throats. Can you help me out?"

"Look, Maya, I'll ask around, okay?"
"Did you get back together with Monique?"
"No."
"I'm surprised. Why not?"
"Cuz you can't un-ring the bell."
She looks away before asking, "Where you staying?"
"I'm house-sitting for a friend till the end of the year."
"You looking for a roommate?" she beams a toothy grin.
"Yeah, right. You went with that ragamuffin so as far as I'm concerned, you're diseased, honey."

"We should do something, Poem! Let's put an act together, like in New Orleans. Come on…!" She sings, "*We're like two feet that need each other to get ahead.*"

And so it goes: Maya trying to charm her way back in; Poem grumbling, doubting and wanting nothing to do with it. "I've had it with smoky bars," he says but she pursues him coquettishly, stroking his ego, hoping for a piece of *something*. He is open but feels no genuine warmth, only hollow tin words, like her accomplice is in the bushes. He wonders whether she is just hedging her bets. *Where's Sammy in all this?* She is either hurt or insincere, shuckin' and jivin', a contradiction of emotions but determined not to admit any error. She works herself into such a pitch, talking past him, hustling it seems, until he interrupts, "Look, Maya, what do you want from me? I mean really! What do you want from me?"

She is struck by his stance and doesn't want him to perceive a threat. "Nothing, Poem. I don't want anything from you. I swear."

"Nothing…!" he is dumfounded.

"Yeah."

Not even love. Not even friendship. She wants nothing from me. "Okay," he says. "You got it." He gathers his stuff.

"What's wrong?"

"You want nothing. That's what you get. Either you don't know what you want or you know *exactly* what you want and just won't say it. But if you don't say it then I'm outta here." He waits but she is silent. "All right then." He gets up and she is stunned. He steps back, picks up his knapsack and walks out into the street. He looks back and she is staring straight ahead, so he continues to Bloor, wondering if she'll follow him. He rounds the corner and waits but she does not come. He is disappointed but will not go back. *Kindness is not weakness.*

And so it goes: Maya leans onto the table and cries.

6 PERSPECTIVE

Poem stops in front of Mantri's building and puts the idling car into park. "Thanks, Ria." He kisses her on the lips. She smiles happily and shifts over to the driver's seat while he gets out and retrieves his knapsack from the back.

"Are you gonna be all right?" she asks.

"I'll be okay. I just need some perspective."

She flashes him a cutesy smile, blows a kiss, and drives off into the grey afternoon. He watches her disappear then enters Mantri's building. Waiting for the elevator, he heaves a heavy sigh. What a year it's been.

The Councillor he worked for was courted by one of the provincial parties to run in a by-election so she resigned her municipal post, confident she would win, but instead lost. It gave Poem a greasy close-up look at local politics and the divergence between what happens and what gets reported, the chasm between the private and public perception, and the absolute ignorance most people have for how hard politicians work. His contract with the City just expired after two and a half years and only four months into a full-time salaried position. Needless to say, he is feeling cut off at the knees.

He steps out of the elevator onto Mantri's floor and enters his apartment. "Namaste, Sir, how are you?"

"Namaste, Poem. You looking good, man!" Mantri bobbles his head. "Your shoulders are nice, strong, good chest." He's been noticing Poem's upper body development since nearing the end of his Jupiter dasa. Jupiter in Cancer, a water sign, signifies expansion of chest, and Poem has achieved this through diligent swimming.

"Thanks, Mantriji. How are you?"

"Not so good," he makes a sour expression. "I am having trouble sleeping."

"Why?"

"I have this buzzing in my ear," he rubs it with his finger. "It is very difficult. Oh God, it is karma, I know, and I must find how to fix it."

"Can't you see in your own chart what to do?"

"I see clearly what to do but I am acting against this move."

"Why?"

"Because to go that path would mean a great many changes. I cannot think only of myself. Don't worry, Poem, it will take care of itself. It is God's will."

"Yeah…" Poem lowers his head, feeling sad for the whole world.

"What is wrong, Poem? You have, how you say, 'long face.'"

"You know how we lost the election?" he sounds heartbroken. "Well, Friday was my last day of work. I don't know, Mantriji, it seems everything I do, nothing works out. Sometimes I feel like I just wanna die," he leans onto his hands and Mantri smiles.

"Don't worry, Poem. Death will come. You still have a ways to go."

"I just feel so uncertain, Mantriji. It's not exactly the best time to be looking for work, y'know?"

"Work will come, you will see. You are in Saturn now. For 16 years you were going to others, but now people will come to you."

"Yeah but when?"

Mantri takes a pen and pulls out a sheet of paper. "I will show you one good method. You write this in your book. This is a good way to answer 'when?' When will I find job? When will my package arrive? When will I meet someone? But use this method only when expecting results within four months."

Poem nods, scribbling along.

"When the question is asked, tell the client to pick a number from 1 to 12. This ensures *they* determine the result. Very important. The number they pick becomes the lagna and we note the time the question is asked and the exact longitudinal degree of the ascendant for that time. We add this degree to the degree of the house to which the question pertains. The sign it adds up to will be the element for this prediction—let us say… a fire sign," he draws a triangle. "So when the Sun next enters a fire sign, mark the date. Following that, when the Moon enters a fire sign, mark the exact time it transits the given degree. This is when the predicted result will occur."

"Wow. Does it work?"

"Oh yay…!" Mantri bobbles. "But only if the question is sincere."

"Interesting. Well, I've had a burning question since I got here. When will I find work is *my* sincere question?"

"Pick a number from 1 to 12."

"6."

"What time is it?"

Poem looks at his phone, "1 p.m."

"Good. You take this home," he points to Poem's notes, "and you answer your own question using ephemeris. You know how," he grins.

"Okay, I'll try."

"You have time now so no fooling around. You must start writing what I am teaching you because you are a beautiful writer who understands philosophy and you can convey in clear A-B-C language what people want to understand about this Jyotish program. I read that article you wrote for this lady in Vitality Magazine. You have a gift, man, to inspire! This is rare and valuable. You will make *billions* in Saturn."

Poem knows he's exaggerating but the prognosis looks good.

"Do you meditate?" Mantri asks.

"Sometimes. I like to meditate with a little music on."

"This is not meditation. This is called 'listening to music.' You must try to go without external impressions and focus on one thing. It is very difficult. I don't know how some people go ten days sometimes, just sitting there, breathing," he demonstrates with closed eyes, hands in lotus. "Amazing this concept. But come on. Let us begin our lesson."

Poem opens his notebook to a fresh page, feeling lifted and ready to write.

"Astrology was Mankind's first attempt at science," Mantri begins. "Have you heard of these Chaldeans?"

"You mean in Iraq?"

"Right. This is, how you say, 'Euphrates.' Many people in the West believe astrology came from this region during Babylon. It is said they recorded the natal charts of everyone born in their community for a *thousand* years."

"Really?"

"Oh yes. Just check with British museum. This is where so much of what we today call astrology comes from; the Kal-deans. How the ancients came to this system we don't know, but it shows us that they understood this universe in a sophisticated way. They understood our place and nature and they used parable to convey their mathematics. They understood that people are people and they are very similar but their lives are different, not so much by character as by placement. Do you follow?"

"You mean that people are not that different from one another but it's their individual circumstances that define them?"

"Very good. You could be the exact same as someone over there or in another time or country but you will develop and experience life very differently than they do, even though you are very much the same. One circumstance requires you develop your creative side, another requires you develop your executive side. Both are in you but what will you do in this lifetime?"

"Is that why we need many lifetimes, to develop every side?"

"Ahh…" Mantri sighs. "What truly separates us from one another is *time*," he points his forefingers. "Our perspective is governed largely by time. Space yes, where, but time also." He points to his seat, "I am sitting here in this chair but you are also sitting here, just not at the same *time*." He waits to see if Poem gets it. "I want you to understand the concept, not just the words." Poem puts down his pen. "Astrology is the *science* of time. Think of our solar system as a giant clock, but instead of two or three hands, it has ten hands! The seven planets, the nodes, and the ascendant. In Jyotish we don't use Uranus or Neptune because they take too long to orbit the Sun. Their influence on human affairs is very slow; for historians but not for us. We may view them as already forming up their own worlds, separate from ours, and they will one day ignite and feed their moons—as the Sun feeds its planets—so that 'being' and 'consciousness' can develop there as well."

"Wow. I heard that Neptune and Uranus were mentioned in the Vedas thousands of years ago. How did they know about them and why didn't astronomers know about them till just in the last two hundred years?"

"How they knew is a matter of speculation. That they are referred to in the Vedas is not. When you speak of astronomers, you mean European astronomers, the European tradition. All people here think with Western minds, through Western history. Not till Schopenhauer and Max Muller did Europe know of Indian knowledge and yet, Indian knowledge is the oldest surviving knowledge in the world! Still, these, how you say, 'Indologists' would examine India's history and come up with their own dates, their own explanations for this civilization so foreign to their own. They doubt the dates of Indian scholars just like they doubted the existence of Troy. These men are materialists! They examine culture the way a mortician examines a corpse, oblivious to the life that once was."

Poem is spellbound by Mantri's commentary.

"Indian astronomers knew of the precession of the equinoxes. Many ancient cultures knew it and they built their temples and monuments to reflect it. They were establishing harmony with the cosmos in all its detail and symmetry. This modern time we live in has lost touch with this connection. They simplify things for convenience sake, how you say, 'dumb down.' They simplified astrology a hundred years ago into 12, what you call, 'Sun-signs,' not for accuracy but for convenience. The tradition before was to look at the Moon sign but there are at least 144 Moon placements in a year, and who is going to write 144 horoscopes?"

"Why 144?"

"Because the Moon in Aries will act differently in May than it will in December. You cannot generalize. The Moon transits all 12 signs in one month; the Sun does so in a year. 12 times 12 and you have roughly 144 unique Moon placements in a year. Add to this the ascendant and you would multiply by 12 again. Add to this the importance of Saturn in the chart and you would have to multiply by 12 again. We must also look at Mars and Venus, and Jupiter is very important, you get the picture. There are too many variables for there to be only 12 Sun-signs of people. This was done to simplify and grow interest in astrology and to make money."

"Like everything in the West."

"But astrology is becoming very big now. It is growing but people still do not understand it. It works for them now and then, at key times, so they see there must be something to it but their understanding of it is childish, like children listening to this, what you call, 'Barney,' thinking this is music, not knowing there is Beethoven."

"Right."

"This is Sun-sign astrology. Just a little fun to remind you there is some higher order. People come to astrologers because they know there is something more than money and death, but the priest won't tell him," he laughs. "So they seek someone who is knowledgeable, who can divine these things for them. This is the role of the astrologer. He is not a psychic, no. He is an astronomer who understands that everything is connected and we each have a part in a larger whole, that if you did not exist, the world would somehow be different.

"Western minds are *capital-listic!*" he clenches his fists. "They want to make money! They write 12 horoscopes for astrology when no two charts are the same. This is to make money and at the same time it discredits astrology. You ask anyone who says astrology is bullshit if they have been to an astrologer and guarantee he will say no. He will know nothing about the ascendant, the Moon, Saturn, and yet he will speak as though he is an expert in all things scientific, putting down astrology and those who follow it because how could there be only 12 people in the world? He will call it a silly superstition on his way to church," Mantri laughs. "Before, astrology was only for rich people, for royalty, kings! For everyday people there is no need for astrology. They are not effecting change; they cannot do anything. Only powerful, educated people consulted with astrologers to help them with big decisions, wars, when to build, when to sign a contract. But this Sun-sign business, this 'what sign are you' nonsense, this is only for children playing with a toy. Astrology is a noble pursuit, the chess of kings. It is worthy of religious praise and yet, for money it was reduced to 12 signs and a fool's understanding of a sophisticated subject. It is no wonder thinking people dismiss astrology when it is presented this way."

"So are Sun-sign horoscopes useless?"

"They are very general and so… more wrong than right. But the astrologer who writes these articles is doing his best to interpret the transit of planets from the various Sun-sign perspectives. He is assuming people are in atma, living their soul purpose, which the Sun indicates, but it is like a loose net: it will catch only lazy fish. Humans are too complex, life is not simple. You throw a loose net and catch lazy fish. But for someone who wants to know their chart and not just some Sun-sign, they must go to a good astrologer and they will get ten thousand dollar's worth on a psychiatrist's couch.

"But never underestimate people's ignorance of cultures outside their own. They may speak knowledgeable but they know almost nothing. They are not wired to understand. Some insights are cultural and require a certain psychology. How does a layman understand music? Certainly not in the way a musician does, though they are both moved by it. They have, how you say, 'cultural' differences. But culture is just perspective. It is like group psychology."

"Is astrology common to all cultures?"

"Oh yes. Wherever you have civilization, you will find astronomy and astrology. The two are the same thing, but in the West the telescope divided astronomy from astrology. Astrono-*mee* is for measuring things, comparing. Astrolo-*gee* is understanding the *meaning*, the language of the planets and stars. Much of the history of ancient astronomy is stored in mythology and these myths are at the base of human development and understanding."

"So how should we take these mythological tales that on the surface seem fanciful, like children's stories?"

"These are just written for the children of humanity."

"How do you mean?"

"Most people who live everyday lives are not able to comprehend the vast cosmology of the Vedas. To do so requires *tapas*, that is, great austerities, sacrifice. Here in the West, where will you find people who willingly give up comfort? They are too attached, to their friends, family, to their partner, children, identity, and so on. The more they cling to material attachment, to their sense of 'I' in the world, the harder it is for them to comprehend profound thought."

"Why?"

"Because profound thought requires time, discipline, and self-denial. If one is so attached to their name, how is it possible for him to understand in a deep way that we are all one, that Atma is Brahma, that he is here today, gone tomorrow, that he is individuated and part of a whole, that when he stabs his neighbour, he is stabbing himself. He may say 'I understand' but he goes back to same job, same home, same habits as before, and in less than a week he is back-biting, criticizing, arguing. He does not get it because he is in the swamp of Prakriti."

"The material world."

"Right. For him, stories—children's stories as you said—are the only way for him to begin to understand, to have a window into a greater cosmology, one that would make him feel insignificant if he does not understand the true vastness of his mind. Most times he is busy making his own cosmology or he doesn't even speak this word. To him there is no cosmology, or he may think these stories are ridiculous, or he may believe. Doesn't matter."

"But it's better to know these stories than not."

"Oh yes. These stories, like Greek mythology, are based on a vast series of events that took place in the heavens from the time of Creation until now. The scale of the heavens is immense, *billions* of years old. We don't know how old; some say this, some say that. If we were to shrink the events, the astronomical events, on the scale of the universe down to a few generations, how you say, 'per-son—'"

"Personify?"

"That's it. We per-sonify it into something like what we read in the Vedas."

"So..." Poem surmises, "The stories of the Vedas and similar cosmologies are just the shrinking or condensing the scale of Creation down into a few human generations personified by gods and the various stories of Vishnu and so on."

"That's right."

"So the stars and planets are like gods and kings, comets are demons, and they all interact over vast scales of time, billions of years, and we reduce it through our personifications into a single life span."

"That's right. The comet that struck the Earth last time almost destroyed us. It wiped out nearly all life forms at that time."

"Like the dinosaurs."

"That's right. But how many times did it circle the Sun or the Earth, how many interactions did it make with the fields of other planets before it struck us? Did its orbit decay over millions of years and on the final one strike our planet? Could this vast scale of interactions be reduced and personified into a story of this increasingly perilous relationship between a demon, in this case a comet, and the Earth?"

"So a monster circles its prey before striking the Goddess and a civilization is doomed."

"Very good."

"Wow. I see what you're saying and I've heard this idea before but I have to wonder, how could a sage living five thousand years ago know the astronomical events of the universe since the beginning of time?"

"You know this idea of universal forms, of Plato?"

"Yes."

"You know this man Carl Jung?"

"Yes."

"He spoke about, how you say, 'arch—'"

"Archetypes?"

"Right. These are ideas, abstractions, that manifest through human thoughts and language."

"But are they real?"

"Slowly, slowly. The universe is on a vast scale. 20 billion years! Below that we have galaxies. They are on vast scales but not as vast as the universe itself."

"Right."

"These galaxies live and die within the context of the universe and they themselves give rise to smaller worlds on smaller scales. These smaller worlds live, breathe and die within the context of the galaxy. Further down we have *our* world, that is, our solar system, which itself is born, breathes, has life, and so on, and will in time die and be reborn."

"Wow."

"This world of ours, the Sun, the planets, has been around for billions of years, and to us it seems long, vast, slow, but it is experiencing life just as we do in the span of 60, 70, 100 years, only its life may be ten *billion* years!"

"So..." Poem sums up as Mantri nods, "If we condense ten billion years into a single human lifespan by personifying it, then naturally we see the solar system is born, is young, matures, has relationships, progeny, reaches its apex, then gradually winds down into retirement, decay and death."

"Right."

"And these myths are the cosmological tales of its various developments, interactions and traumatic events, like comets striking planets and planets giving birth to moons and so on."

"That's right. And when the sages are channelling these ancient events, like a tiny faucet underneath a billion gallon drum, they are seeing in their own minds, in their own consciousness, a *transposition* of these events into their own psyche and into their own timescale and metaphors. A planet may move achingly slow to us on our scale of perception but on the scale of planets, if we are to reduce ten billion years to a single human lifespan, say 100 years, we would see that a hundred million years to *us* is like one *year* to the perception of the Sun. Of course, we think in terms of *our* perception, but time changes just like space changes. It is varying and not always the same. Look here," he hands Poem a calculator, gets up and stands next to the board. "Type 100,000,000 divided by 365.25 days a year."

Poem does so and gets, "273,785."

Mantri writes, "So rounding off, what seems like 300 thousand years to us is only one day in the life of the Sun."

"Huh..." Poem is getting it. "Wow!"

"Divide by 24."

"11,408."

"So what seems like ten thousand years to us is but one *hour* in the life of the Sun." He draws an inverted hierarchy. "Divide by 60."

"190."

"So what seems to us 200 years in length, that is, more than two *very* healthy human lifetimes, is to the Sun but one minute. Divide by 60."

"3."

"Three years to us is but one second in the life span and perception of the Sun. These are just approximations of course."

Human perception		The Sun's perception
100,000,000 years	=	1 year
300,000 years	=	1 day
10,000 years	=	1 hour
200 years	=	1 minute
3 years	=	1 second

"Wow." Poem likes this. "You say the perception of the Sun. Is the Sun a living organism?"

"Oh yes. The Sun is alive like everything else, and the planets are his children. Some say the planets are the organs of the Sun, just like our heart, brain, liver, and so on. It's the same but a different metaphor. Our organs process different substances and energies and these planets also process different substances and energies. The Sun, like the planets, is a living organism operating on a level of consciousness that we cannot even fathom. Remember, the more refined a being, the simpler its chemical makeup, and we see that the Sun has the simplest chemistry in our system: hydrogen and helium, that's it. Just as a wise man shows his wisdom through the simplicity of his life, the more complicated our lives become the further we are removed from the wisdom of the Sun. Now just for fun, how many times does the *Moon* circle the Earth in one second of the Sun's perception?"

"Well... The Moon orbits the Earth almost 13 times a year so we multiply by 3 and we get 39."

"Very good. So you understand that consciousness operating on the scale of our solar system, that is, our Sun looking at the Earth would see the Moon orbiting it 40 times a second."

"Wow. Yeah I do see that. And at 40 Hertz it would make a sound."

"Ahh! And how many times does Earth orbit the Sun in just one minute of the solar system?"

Poem looks at the board, "Well... 200, right?"

"Right," Mantri smiles. "That would be three orbits a second! This is how fast our Earth is moving on the scale of the solar system. But on our scale it seems long, slow. Think now of how dynamic the interactions and evolution of our solar system is from this perspective and how many demons have attacked the Earth in its lifetime."

"Huh… yeah."

"So the ancients wrote according to their limited understanding and perception of the world. They had to personify it through their own minds into a form they and others could perceive and digest."

"That's amazing. But how?"

"Yoga."

"What d'ya mean?"

"There are certain things that can be done only with the mind, certain insights that can come only through an elevated consciousness."

"But then how do you verify this to see if it's true? I mean, what's more subjective than one man's consciousness?"

"This is where you are mistaken. An aware man is a wise man, and a wise man does not speak his own opinion; he conveys universal truths, ideas, themes, information, and so on. A wise man is never wrong just as a sunflower always follows the Sun. They have no say in the matter. It is their nature to be one with the Sun. A truly wise man is incapable of speaking lies."

"But they still have to use metaphors and this makes it subjective."

"A metaphor can never be wrong. But you are right; it is subjective, cultural. A metaphor is not scientific, no. But this does not make it wrong. There are facts and there is truth. They are not the same thing."

"What's the difference?"

"Facts are what you can see and measure; truth is what it means. This is why it is so difficult to agree on the truth because people think you need facts to determine the truth. This man has his truth, another man his own truth, but there is only one 'Truth.' There are no opinions when it comes to Truth. Opinions are only a symptom of the fragmentation of society. It is better that all believe in one thing than many things or there will be fighting and no cohesion."

"But what if they're wrong?"

"Doesn't matter. Even a god that has been made up has more power than no god at all. People can get strength from believing. There is no strength in not believing. We humans are limited in our understanding of the vastness of this world and our place in it. We think we know, but we know very little and it helps. We now have computers and cell phones but what do we do with it?" He cups his ear, "'Hi honey, be home in five minutes,'" he laughs. "We go through life with our heads down. We don't look up. In the city today you can't even see the stars. How are people supposed to wonder where they came from if they can't see the stars? You must work hard on the mind, you must sacrifice your pleasures and comforts; you must overcome identification with the body, with the ego, if you are to comprehend the vast cosmological truths of the universe. Only then will you resonate at a frequency which makes comprehension possible. Only then will you not be too distracted to hold profound thought. But until then, no. You will believe in the teller but not the tale. Or you will believe in nothing because it all seems ridiculous, like a newspaper horoscope."

"So these stories of gods and demons?"

"They are there for regular people to shed some light. And better to know these stories than not because your mind will at least open to cosmology, to the dynamics of a higher order. There is nothing wrong with these stories. They are quite detailed and in many cases correct. But mostly what gets handed down is a shortened version, a simplification, or generalization, or translation, so that by the time it reaches the listener, it sounds ridiculous. But there is nothing wrong with the story itself. Metaphors give meaning to phenomena and are a matter of taste and interpretation. People usually stick to the metaphors of their culture because metaphors are fundamental to how we understand the world."

Mantri sits and Poem feels like the sunroof in his brain just opened. He looks perplexed. "Mantriji, how could the ancient Rishis have divined these truths without the use of equipment like telescopes?"

"Do you know what this hologram is?"

"Yes."

"Speak."

"Well… My understanding is that what makes a hologram is that every part of a hologram contains a replica of the whole, like a magnetic field. It is always pointing in the same direction no matter how you slice it. I guess genetics are similar because you can take a gene from any part of the body and it'll have the code for the entire organism."

"That's right. Do you know this expression, 'As above, so below?'"

"Yeah. It means that everything has its correlation on larger and smaller scales, like fractals, the two extremes being a planet orbiting a star akin to an electron orbiting a nucleus."

"That's right."

"So are you saying that one can divine the expansive history of the cosmos by observing something small and short-lived?"

"Ahah!" Mantri is impressed. "Just as Jupiter, the largest planet, has the most moons, it finds it's equivalence in human affairs in wealth and expansive activities like charity, faith and children. It's equivalence in food would be ghee and sweets; its equivalent in the body would be fat, the abdomen; its equivalent in nature would be pumpkin, or sugar cane; its equivalent gem would be topaz, and so on. In the king's court, Jupiter is 'advisor' because he has a broad understanding, you see?"

"So all these things are various manifestations of Jupiter on different scales in different contexts so that when one moves, the others move as well."

"Slowly, slowly. They will all be influenced according to their nature as tuning forks resonate to only their pitch. I just want you to understand that what happens in small is a correlation of what happens in big. If one could somehow open up an atom of the Earth the way you read a book and see the life of that atom from beginning to end, one could infer the entire life of our solar system from it. But this is a big subject. We may one day come to this and try to understand it in a real way, not just theoretical."

"Well, its friggin fascinating."

Mantri looks tired. "There are many things that are difficult to understand without proper thinking, without the proper set up. The same mind that gets you into a mess is not the mind to get you out. If we are to understand our place in the universe, we must try to understand in a big way, to see beyond ourselves, to not feel threatened by the scale of things, to not get too caught up in our own petty desires and ambitions. We must think in terms of lifetimes. We must understand that consciousness is always here and *our* consciousness is a matter of perspective and this is because of space and time, space being our manifestation, and time, where we are on the wheel. Astrology is not causative, it is *indicative*, like a clock. The clock *says* the time, it does not *make* the time. There is no cause, only correlation."

Poem looks at him in awe. Several paradigms have shifted and he has certainly gained perspective. "Thank you, Mantriji," he bows with heartfelt gratitude. "What you taught me today is amazing and I will always carry it with me. I see how conditioned I am to accept a certain way of thinking, a linear way of understanding the world. I guess the enemy really is certainty." He pulls out his donation and customarily slides it under a book.

Mantri smiles. "I have good food for you," he points to the white plastic bag on the counter. It is prasad from the temple, brought by one of Mantri's students, which he customarily passes onto Poem. "Don't forget the prashna method I showed you."

"Of course. I'll get on it right away." Poem stuffs the bag into his knapsack. "Thank you, Sir."

"Okay, Poem. Namaste."

7 MEET MARKET ADVENTURES

"Ouch!"
"Are you okay?"
"Yeah. I guess that spot is sensitive."
"Let me know if you see anything."
"Okay."

Sonia is kneeling next to Poem, triggering pressure points in his abdomen. He is on the floor, eyes closed and alert to her fingers gently kneading his guts, looking for knots. "Ow!" She found another one. "Do you have to press so hard?"

"I'm hardly pressing at all," she varies the pressure to demonstrate. He looks up at her looking down at him, her luscious brown curls cascading. She motions for him to close his eyes. "Breeeathe."

He takes in a long deep breath, expanding his chest as her fingertips sink in. "Oww!!" She is on his heart meridian. He wriggles on the floor when a vision of Maya appears: *They are out front of Snake and Jake's. She tells him she likes Sammy.* "Oww!!" Sonia's fingers feel like a blunt spear against his chest. "Stop!" he howls and she lets up.

He opens his eyes. "I saw Maya, right when you touched me here," he puts his chin to his chest. "We were fighting and she tells me she likes someone else, and I realize in that moment, I fucked up my whole life chasing this... little girl."

"It's your heart chakra," Sonia presses softly on his meridian. To Poem it feels like a bruise, like his heart is one big wound. He struggles to take the pulsating pain and it sinks him into a suffocating void: *Him and Maya driving around New Orleans; she's making plans, sounding optimistic, while he's getting ready to leave.* "Ow!! Why is it so sore?!"

"Because you're heart is broken. You've been through a lot, Munchie. Two break-ups, losing everything, now a job you really love. Your heart is like a door trying to shut everyone out, but it's rickety cuz you don't really mean it, Poem." She looks at him tenderly, "You want to be open but the world shut you down."

He looks up past her to the ceiling, hearing her words, marvelling at her technique. They first met four months ago on the campaign trail where she volunteered for his colleague's ill-fated bid for City Counsel. They were teamed up because they both have Polish last names but once they got talking on esoteric subjects, it turns out that what Poem knows, Sonia wants to learn, and what she knows, Poem wants to learn it too.

Sonia is a tall shapely woman, thickly built with huge breasts. She has a bright generous face and loving countenance. Born in Poland, she is a practicing Buddhist with a wealth of knowledge in healing modalities and esoteric schools. Her status is 'healer;' her position is 'unemployed.' She's been in and out of retreats since the campaign and is always eager to share new information. Today she is showing Poem how abdominal massage and pressure point therapy can unlock traumatic memories stored in the organs and tissues of the body. It is having its desired effect.

"How do I open up?" Poem says. "How do I stop myself from being so critical?"

"By allowing yourself to fail! You've convinced yourself that if it's not perfect, you don't want it at all."

It hurts to admit but with every knot there's one more layer needing to be shed: unrealized hopes, regrets, missed opportunities, misunderstandings, a childhood beating that never really healed and the loss of a father that was never really filled. "I know that perfect should not be the enemy of good," he says, "but it would be nice if at least one thing could work out in my life."

"You have a lot going for you, Poem. How can you say it's not working?"

"I mean my ventures, my jobs, my career, my band, even my relationships. Nothing works out. It's all so temporary."

"Yeah, like life wouldn't you say?" She leans back, "Can you tell me one thing that isn't temporary?"

Poem is silent.

"It doesn't mean we shouldn't try."

"Yeah... I can't believe it. I'm friggin jaded."

"You have to clear up what's here, Munchie, because new love won't come if your heart is closed." She gets up and steps over him, fixing into a martial arts stance, feet on either side, squatting, using her weight to knead his pectorals as he groans into relaxation. "We stimulate pressure points to release dormant memories locked in our cells that over time constrict the flow of energy and cripple the body." Her warm strong hands remind him of his mother's when he was a child. "When there's no movement, we become a swamp, rotting in our own recurring memories." She stretches his arms out from shoulder to wrist. "The most important thing to be healthy is to have a good exhaust system and it starts here," she touches his head and runs a clinical stroke to his heart then quickly gooses his rear end. He squirms and laughs, crosses his legs, and they settle down again, her knuckles against his pecs. "A healthy mind can fix an ailing body but a healthy body cannot fix an ailing mind. By the way, I love your shoulders…"

There's a knock on the door.

"Yeah?"

Nick walks in, surprised to see Poem on the floor and Sonia squatting over him with their clothes on. "I hope I'm not interrupting."

"It's all right," Poem says. "Whassup?"

"I got an opportunity for ya." Nick is a weasely middle-aged IT guy with an alcoholic face and a two hundred dollar toupee. He supers the co-op apartments where Poem now lives and is extremely jealous of any women he has over. Sonia feels the vibe and steps back so the two can talk. "Ya know that place I been pitchin' to, Meet Market Adventures?"

"Oh, the Beer & Bongos Night?"

"Yeah." Nick looks at Sonia, "Hey I already trademarked that so don't get any ideas."

She looks at him strangely and Poem says, "Don't worry, Nick. Only you could pull that off."

"Well you know, they're a singles agency always looking for some new event and I just found out they have a Psychic Night."

"Oh yeah?" Sonia says.

"Oh yeah," Nick gloats. "They're into that spiritual shit." He squats next to Poem, "Their astrologer cancelled on them and Denise was asking me for a favour so I told her I'd help her out, y'know, cuz I'm a nice guy. I told her I know an *amazing* astrologer."

"Oh yeah? Who?"

"You!"

Poem is surprised, "I'm not an astrologer, man."

"What're you talking about, Poem? You study it all the time."

"Yeah I study it but I don't do readings. I've never done a reading. I just like learning and studying with Mantriji."

"Well that's more than me. And one of us is gonna do it cuz I already told her yes."

"What're you talking about?"

"Yeah, I told her you do the Indian astrology and she loves it. She wants you to do the event."

Poem is shocked. He looks at Sonia who looks happy for him, like it's a good thing. He sits up, suddenly in need of a paradigm shift. He's never done readings before and never really aimed to be an astrologer. He likes the subject, the theory, the cosmology of it, but what does he know about giving readings? Three stress lines crease into his forehead and Nick says, "Listen, how hard could it be? You been seeing this Maitra d guy—"

"Mantriji?"

"Yeah, for what, four years you said, right? Well shit, that's gotta be worth something."

Poem looks at Sonia whose familiar eyes give him courage. "How much does it pay?"

"A hundred and twenty bucks for two hours."

"That's not bad. When is it?"

"Tonight."

Poem jerks his head, reacting like he couldn't possibly have said tonight. Tonight is simply not reasonable. He would have to prepare for this. He's never done readings before. He needs to do the Virgo thing and bone up, study charts, get ready in a methodical way. Tonight is not right. Nick looks at him, waiting for a response, "It's tonight, Poem. Seven o'clock. She says be there for 6:30."

Poem is frozen. *How could this be? This simply is not.* Sonia on the other hand is thrilled for him.

Nick says, "You'll be doing me a huge personal favour, bro."

"You always say that."

"Yeah, but this time it's true."

Poem suddenly feels the weight of obligation on him like being thrown to his fate. At the same time he *is* intrigued and certainly eager to make the money. "Okay, okay, I'll do it, fuck. Where is it?"

"You know the Cock'n'Balls Pub on King West?"

"Cock and Balls?"

"I think it means something different in Gaelic." He hands Poem a yellow posted note with the name, address and Denise's cell number written jaggedly in red. Poem takes a deep breath, not sure what he's getting himself into. Nick says, "Great!" and scoots out, closes the door, and they hear him hop down the stairs.

Poem sits motionless with Sonia watching him. He's confused, like having just received impossible news. He slides over to the table and looks at his phone, "Holy shit! It's already three o'clock!"

"Are you okay?"

"Holy shit!" Poem jumps up, suddenly energized. "I'm gonna be reading charts tonight! I can't believe it! What the fuck did I just agree to?" He begins pacing the room. "Okay... How am I gonna do this?"

Sonia stops him, "Breeeathe."

"Astrology is not easy, Sonia. I don't wanna make a fool of myself and I don't want people to think astrology is bullshit. Oh God, what did I do?"

He starts pacing again.

"You'll be fine, Poem."

"I don't know…" he is suddenly filled with doubt. The whole world is material. There is no magic, only matter and science and even math is just an invention by hairless monkeys wearing suits and neckties, reporting the news, telling it like it is, this mistake, this random fluke of cosmic debris. There is no God, no meaning, no reason for anything; only molecules and electricity and infinite time for something, anything, to spontaneously occur. There is no intelligence, there is no consciousness, there is no prime mover or originating field! There is only matter, gravity, electromagnetism, mathematical constants and nothing more. Just listen to the news, just watch TV, the media, the culture, the cult of expertise. Astrology is ridiculous because they don't know how it works so how could it be? Only fools believe in astrology, only simple-minded, superstitious, highly suggestible, artistic, idealistic people accept astrology. It's all wishful thinking. He doesn't know how Mantri does it but there's some trick, it's something else, some luck or coincidence, some autosuggestion he is reading in the client, the way they moved their arm or foot reacting to a question. This gives it away that he is an architect father of two with a sharp tongue who lost his brother in a car accident when he was 24. What else could it be? What could thousands of years of astrology possibly prove? What difference does it make that all great civilizations have astrology at their root? They were primitive fools who thought in symbols, who believed the world was alive, that we are part of something greater than ourselves; the way an anthill functions, the way symbiosis functions, the way a nation functions. These fools of holism that believe in the bigger picture, that facts have meaning, that the planet is alive, that our actions have consequences, that being is 'a priori,' that mind is the matrix of matter!

Sonia stops him, "You can do it, Adi Poem! You already have the blessing of Mantriji. Nick believes in you, I believe in you, Ria believes in you. I love when you talk astrology because you know what you're talking about! You studied with an actual Master! That's profound, Poem, that you didn't just get it from a book. Mantriji opened this in you the way it was opened in him and now you have to open it in others."

Poem agrees it is a beautiful idea but he's never done this before. They'll be short readings. How can he understand the chart so quickly? Should he take books? Is the Moon really the most important factor? Saturn signifies hardships. What should he emphasize more? What if they don't know their exact time of birth? Most of them will want to hear their Sun-sign and he's doing Jyotish! It'll be singles so he should study afflicted 7th houses. What if they're cynical? What if they realize he's not really an astrologer? What if they think astrology is bullshit! *Oh God!*

Poem fetches a couple books and starts looking up random scenarios, not sure what to prepare. Sonia stands back, feeling his nervous energy. His phone rings. "It's Ria! Hey babe, you'll never guess what I got myself into." He explains the situation and Ria is excited for him but can hear he's clearly freaked so she offers to pick him up and be his assistant for the night. He thanks her profusely and they make plans. He hangs up and says, "I am so blessed."

"Listen, you're gonna do just great." Sonia looks at her wrist, "I've never done this before, Poem, but I believe in you and I want you to have this just for tonight. It'll help." She rolls the mala off her wrist, a string of 27 beautifully carved wooden beads that have been imbued with thousands of prayers and chants in Buddhist monasteries. He can't believe it. He knows how precious this is to her. She hands it to him and he finds himself almost involuntarily chanting,

"*Om gam gana pataye namaha…*"

It is a Ganesh mantra given to him by Mantri to help remove obstacles. He thanks her with breathless gratitude and they bow reverently to one another. She gathers her stuff, wishes him well, they hug, and she leaves. Poem proceeds to shave, shower and hit the books, all the while reciting, "*Om gam gana pataye namaha…*"

It gets to be six o'clock in no time and he has to decide what to wear. Ria calls and he heads downstairs. Nick's waiting for him at the front door, "Make a good impression, Poem. You'll be representing me."

"Sure, Nick," he rolls his eyes.

Poem leaves the house and gets into Ria's car, relieved to see her. They drive up King Street towards Spadina, Poem fidgeting nervously. Ria tries some light-hearted conversation but he is in another world.

"Sorry," he appreciates her effort.

"It's okay, darling. I understand. It's amazing you agreed to do this."

"*Om gam gana pataye namaha…*"

They find the place and a great parking spot nearly in front and Poem thanks the mala on his wrist. They climb the stairs to the second floor pub where the Cock'n'Balls marquee is a red rooster surrounded by bouncing billiard balls. The sandwich sign reads:

Welcome Singles to Meet Market Adventures' Psychic Night!!!

"That's me," he says nervously.

Inside it's a fairly typical bar with pool tables and booths. A group of people are mingling in back. A familiar looking blonde girl approaches them, "Are you Poem?"

"Hi. Are you Denise?"

"Yeah. Nice to meet you, Poem." They shake hands and he introduces Ria. Denise says they're in the winterized patio out back. They make their way through the crowd and find the two other readers setting up in the enclosed deck with outdoor heating lamps. The older woman is reading tarot cards and the man is reading palms. They both look like ordinary people. Poem was expecting gypsies. He sets up where he can plug in his laptop, a nice corner table with some privacy. Ria returns with sparkling water and Poem expresses his appreciation. His head is swimming with all sorts of jargon, significations and last-minute memorizations, going over ascendants like cramming for an exam. He checks his phone. *It's 6:55 p.m.!* He takes a long deep breath as Ria holds his hand.

"Om gam gana pataye namaha..."

Denise steps onto the patio and announces they'll be sending people in groups of three, one for each reader. "Everyone gets 10 minutes. I'll come round and give you a two-minute warning, okay?"

They nod and Poem sits there, trying to collect his thoughts.

"Good luck, darling." Ria shifts over to the next table and the first group of people walk in.

"Hi," Poem greets his first client. She is a red-headed woman, average looking, in her mid-forties. She sits down with a glass of wine, smiling, like she is really looking forward to this. "What's your name?" he asks.

"Wanda."

"And your time and place of birth, Wanda?"

She gives him everything but the year. When he asks for it, she says, "I didn't know we were supposed to provide you with the *year*!"

"Oh yes," he says like Mantri. "Year of birth is very important."

She looks around and whispers, "1963, but don't tell anyone."

"Don't worry. I'm an astrologer." He types in the numbers, "So what d'ya do for a living?"

"Aren't you supposed to tell me?"

His face flushes red. "Well, I can tell you what you already know or I can tell you what you don't know but need to hear."

"I'm a researcher."

"Ahh. We should see a good 8th house then." The chart comes on the screen: Cancer lagna with not such a great 8th but a powerful 7th. The ascendant is only 2 degrees. He wonders, "How sure are you of this time of birth?"

"Well, my mom said around nine but I think she was pretty busy at the time."

"Yes, well it's rare that anyone is born right on the hour so let's back this up a bit, maybe 15 minutes... ah hah!" The 8th looks strong now with

Saturn in its own sign. Good 6th house too. "Are you in medical research?"

"I work for a pharmaceutical."

"I bet a big one."

"Yeah, that's right."

She must be Gemini lagna, and with Rahu deposited? "Do you love to talk and you're like, super hungry for success?"

"I like people and yes, I'm ambitious."

"Okay…" Poem's getting the hang of this. "For future reference, I think you were born closer to 8:45."

She looks impressed while Poem searches the chart for obvious significations. He doesn't know where to start. *Which is stronger, her 8th or 6th or 10th house? Check out Jupiter.* He shakes his head. "So what would you like to know?"

"Um… I don't know. What do you see?"

"Uh… Well, maybe you've been having some health issues the last couple years, uh… Are you worried about losing your home?"

"No. Should I be?"

"No. Just curious." He doesn't know what to latch onto. "I presume you're single."

"Wow, you're good."

He smiles uncomfortably and examines the dasa sequence for her chart, "Well, I can see that right now may not be the best time for you to meet someone. It probably hasn't been since…" he looks closer at the column of dates, "July last year. But come May *this* year, your 7th house will activate and I predict you will meet someone."

"Uh huh."

"Do you go out with foreigners?"

"Almost exclusively."

"Ahah! Ketu in the 7th. I bet your parents don't approve."

"Actually, more his parents—yeah! It's always an issue with the parents—you're right. No matter what guy I date."

"Huh…" Poem just learned something. This goes on and he doesn't really give her a reading so much as figure out what's already happening in her life astrologically, but she is impressed. It comes out that her real struggle is with rival researchers at work. Poem convinces her she will eventually get the upper hand if she stays with a big institution. "You're 6th house is strong. Just try to be more… indispensable."

She thanks him and says she enjoyed it. He smiles, relieved, and Ria quietly congratulates him.

"Hey hey hey," a square-jawed Italian guy in a leather coat, belt hanging, gold crucifix on his chest, sits down with a beer and introduces himself as Tony. Poem gets his birth info and plugs in the numbers. "Hey Poet, you think I'm gonna be rich?"

"Let's have a look." Poem sees Mars in the 2nd house, "You work with your hands, right?"

"Yeah that's right. Somethin' wrong with that?"

"No, I just mean that you work hard for your money. You're busting rocks, sorta speak."

"Yeah, construction. How much you think I make?"

He has a difficult 12th house. "I say you're doing all right but you spend too much. You're too generous."

"Fuckin' eh. I just told this broad the same thing. So how can I make more money, doc? What's it say? Hey you doing all right here? They payin' you all right?"

"Not bad."

"You know how much money I made last year?" Tony looks at Ria who smiles awkwardly.

"Million bucks?" Poem shrugs, still trying to figure out his chart.

"Jesus, is that what it says?!" Tony glares at the screen and Poem calms him down, saying it was just a joke. "Ya had me going, doc," he laughs. "Hey what's it say there 'bout the babes? Any serious relationships or just fun?" he winks.

"I can't imagine you having any problems with the ladies," Poem indulges him.

"Yeah that's true, but I'm looking for something a little more, y'know, stable."

"You mean marriage?"

"Yeah. I keep meeting these stripper types, you know, and hey, don't get me wrong, I like that shit, but I want something better, y'know? Some nice classy broad who knows how to cook, y'know? You see anything there? Nothing too skinny. I don't wanna sleep with a cheese grater."

Poem laughs. "The solution is in the opposite house, Tony, so if you can't find the woman you want, you have to change something about yourself."

"What, like a… new cologne?"

"Probably *no* cologne would be a good start."

Tony looks at Ria who agrees. "Hey doc, she with you?"

"Sorry, dude. This one's taken."

"That's okay. I like this one chick," he thumbs back and lowers his voice, "The blond in the pink sweater. Nice rack! Tell her she's gonna meet someone in construction," he winks.

"Look, if you wanna meet the right woman, just remember, when *you* change, everything changes."

"Whatever you say, doc." He lays down a five dollar bill and shushes him like they have an arrangement. He winks at Ria, calls her sweetheart, and heads back to the bar.

A perspiring, obese woman, looking dressed for church, walks in with a drink and a half-eaten basket of yam fries, which she offers to Poem and Ria who respectfully decline.

"Ain't you just the cutest thing," she says to Poem then looks at Ria, "Why is it almost all women here tonight? I was hoping for some action!" she laughs like a heavy smoker and introduces herself as Kate.

Poem gets her birth coordinates. "So what'ya do, Kate, and what can I do for you?"

"I'm in marketing, honey, and my problem is 'unlucky in love.' Can you save me?"

"Hmm…" he analyses her chart, "Cancer rising…"

"That's impossible. I know my rising sign. I'm a Leo."

"Uh, this is not Western astrology."

"I don't care. I'm a lion. I know it, always felt it. Put me down as a Leo."

"Okay. Let's say… minus 8 degrees Leo."

Ria laughs.

"So…" he assesses her 7th house, "Unlucky in love are we?"

"Yeah, in the last year especially, I don't get it. It's like people don't want me around," she sniffs her arm pit.

Poem sees she went into Sun dasa last year and it's in her 7th house, aspected by Mars in the ascendant. *Oh God, she's on fire!* "I think I see the problem. You're in Sun dasa."

"Is that like a vacation?"

"No, it's just a span of time ruled by a particular planet."

"But the Sun is a star."

"I know, but for our purposes we say planet."

"That's stupid."

"And you're complaint is that you're not getting along with people?"

"Okay. So I'm a Leo. The Sun should be good for Leo, right? I know some astrology."

"Well, not really. I mean…" he wonders how to say it. "To me it explains more your recent, shall we say, in-com-patibility with people."

She stares at him blankly.

"The Sun is fire, and fire is heat. If it's in the 7th and aspected by Mars, it could mean anger and impatience towards others, like always criticizing or wanting the last word."

"That's just great! I thought the Sun was the giver of life!"

"Yes, but it can also kill." He points to the screen, "Aspected by Mars and you're probably quarrelling with people."

"Well someone has to be right!"

"Yeah, but then no one wants you around. You say you're unlucky in love?"

"Well it hasn't always been this way, honey. How long is it gonna last?"

"Um..." Poem isn't sure how to break it to her. "Just give it another five years."

"Oh you're joking, right?" her face turns beet red.

"It's not all bad, Kate. You just have to make the most of it, like a bad weather report."

"So what can I do? Is there something I can take, buy, what?"

He tries to be diplomatic, "You have a lot of masculine energy, Kate, and that's good! But especially during this time, I would suggest uh... try to be uh... softer, more feminine."

"Don't give me that shit. I'm a goddamn flower!"

"Yeah, a Venus Flytrap," Ria mumbles.

"I'm just saying, try to be more uh... mild, more..." he recalls Mantri's words, "Just *do* what you *don't do* and *don't do* what you *do*."

She looks at him, confused. "Sounds like a whole lotta doo-doo. You really believe in this stuff?" she looks at the screen. "You think it's all in the stars?"

"I don't know if it's *all* in the stars but I certainly think you can *use* the stars to help understand it."

She sits quietly, contemplating this as music from the pub spills into the pause. "So you think it's all in the stars," she sounds bummed.

Poem is learning his power here. "We do have freewill, Kate, so just think of it as a karmic weather report and just pack an umbrella."

She smiles like somehow she already knew. "So you don't see anyone in my future?"

"Well, there's this very nice Italian guy out there named Tony. He's looking for a more... full-figured woman."

"Oh you mean the guido. Yeah, he's all right. Okay, thanks for the advice." She pushes herself up out of the chair, nearly taking it with her, and Poem thinks he heard her fart. Ria gets up to help and they send Kate off with her drink and fries.

A nice looking woman in her twenties sits down and states her name and time of birth, like she was coached on the way in. She is an aspiring actress who recently met a producer from Spain who is here working for half a year. They had an incredible love affair that lasted a month before she learned he has a girlfriend back home. "I can't believe it. We dated only a month and already he's been cheating on me for three years."

This one's obvious. "You are Aries rising, what can I say? You're charming, you're beautiful, you're talented, but you are a child. Try to be less self-absorbed. He's here on a temporary contract and you're faulting him for having a life back home?"

"He didn't mention the girlfriend part."

"Did you ask?"

"No."

"Aries…! You didn't ask because you didn't want to know. The ram likes to climb, to scale the rocky heights, but once you get to the top and look down, you go baa!" he bleats like a sheep. "Cuz ya don't know how to get back down."

She's amused and has an epiphany.

"The thing about some women is the more they treat you like a king, the more they resent you for being treated like a king. One of the most important lessons I ever learned is that no one can actually *make* you do anything."

She chuckles, nodding, taking her lumps, while Poem riffs on truisms inherited from Mantri. He doesn't have to explain the planets or get technical. It doesn't matter that he's using astrology. He is counselling her based on female Aries rising with Mars deposited and Moon in the 5th and she wonders where he came from, how it is that he knows her heart, her sense of morality, anger and impatience. She is like so many souls raging against the system, not knowing the solution, losing herself to someone else's ambition, only to realize it one day from some astrologer in a downtown pub.

"I always believed," she says, "that we hate most in others what we don't like about ourselves."

"That's true."

"So what do you think I should do?"

He looks at her chart and rattles off, "Be patient, learn empathy, be good to your lover, and respect your parents."

This is unexpectedly cogent advice. She asks for his card. Ria writes down his info and she thanks them both and leaves.

"How are you holding up, Poem?"

"I feel energized. Like there's no ego in helping others."

"Good."

A well-dressed man sits down, Indian born, 1974, with a degree in computer programming and an MBA. He is surprised to see Poem using Jyotish and is fascinated with the software. His problem is he dates very good women but no one will have sex with him until after they're married.

"Are these virgins?"

"I don't think so, Poemji. I think it is just with me that they will not have sex."

"I see you make good money, from a very good family."

"My father's side."

"Uh huh." *His face is average, expensive watch; lord of the 7th is in his 6th.* "These women want you for your money, that's what you think. They delight in your expenditures while luring you with promises of sex."

He bobbles his head. Poem has nailed it.

"Do you want to get married?"

"Yes of course, but…" he leans in so Ria doesn't hear, "How can I buy the cow if I haven't tasted the milk?"

"I understand, but I'm the opposite: I like milk but I don't wanna own a cow." The two men laugh uproariously while Ria wonders what they're talking about. "Saturn in your 7th, man; you are prone to sycophants. Have you thought about dating older, more established women who have their own wealth and don't need yours? At least you will know they want you for you."

"My mother would not accept me marrying a widow but I do like older women, Poemji." He looks around and confides, "I had an affair once with a much older woman."

"So what happened?"

"I could not marry her. When I am 45, she will be 60. That's too much."

"Worked for Mohammed."

The man stares at Poem, wondering who he is, this white man with an unusual name, who practices Indian astrology and knows Islam. "Perhaps this is the answer," he says, thinking to himself. "It's funny, the lady who is doing the tarot cards, you know, she said I was a woman in my previous life."

"It takes a big man to admit that. Look, if what you've been doing ain't working then why do you think doing more of it will make you happy? You're in Saturn dasa. Karma time for you, my friend. Either go for an older respectable woman, divorcee, maybe someone you already know, or date someone at least seven years younger. Don't date your own age, that's what I say, because she will feel like your peer and that's why she will try to play you."

The man nods, impressed with Poem's rugged wisdom. "One more question, please. I bought a cancer fundraiser lottery ticket and the draw is this Saturday. First prize is a beautiful red Porsche. What are my chances?"

"My friend, I predict you *will not* win the lottery this weekend."

He likes Poem's candour. "You are an excellent astrologer!" He gets up, vigorously shakes Poem's hand and heads back into the party.

A nervy short-haired woman with pronounced marionette lines shows up, smiling, scratching her forehead, anticipating her turn. Poem sighs and looks at Ria like he could use a break now. She looks around for Denise and shrugs. The woman sits down.

"Hi. Your name is?" They go through the process again. This 30 year old geography major has Saturn up the wazoo while currently running Rahu. He examines her tense face and says, "Do you find that no matter what you do, it is never good enough, you are never satisfied, ya wanna sometimes jump out of your own skin?"

She nods affirmative.

"And yet, you probably hold yourself back because you worry, you think too much. Even when things are fine, you will find something to worry about, am I right?"

She nods.

"Well, I say most of what you worry about is a phantom. It doesn't exist. And this sense of never being satisfied, my prediction is that it will end..." he looks closely at the screen, "starting in September this year."

She smiles like it's the first good thing she's heard in a while, "How do you know that? I'm starting my masters program in September."

"See these symbols and this lil chart? This is a three dimensional representation of your karma, and according to this system certain things are destined to happen at certain times. Would you say this sense of anxiety started about two years ago?"

She calculates internally and nods, "You're right. That's when I left my job because I wanted to travel but it started a whole chain of really stupid things in my life, mostly that I somehow wouldn't let myself get what I want, even though I did everything I could to get it! Does that sound stupid?"

"You mean irrational?"

"Yeah, like I became hyper-aware of certain things. I don't know how to explain it. Not paranoid..."

"I think your problem is this," he points to her chart, "Rahu is revving you up while Saturn is shutting you down. It's like an astrological speedball. Do you procrastinate?"

"Oh God! How do you know that?"

"One in five chance. Look, I know the sting of Saturn, believe me, and I know it's an irrational thing. You want badly to do something but you don't do it. You won't allow yourself, am I right?"

He is preaching to the choir.

"You feel the urge and it's like some parent inside, some stick in the mud that manifests as some excuse, some alternate solution to what you really want. It'll give you a good reason, oh you will have reasons, but the reasons are always why you *can't* have what you want. It's hard to explain, I know, but I assure you, you are not alone."

She looks like she just found a friend. "I had no way of explaining it but you did just fine."

"You repel things, right? You push it away or take it personally. You don't wanna be around people and yet, you're afraid to be alone."

"I don't feel like a woman," she begins to tear up. "I feel like a failure. I feel like I know what's the right thing to do and yet, I can't bring myself to do it. I hesitate or try to get out of it and then I get mad at myself because I didn't get it. Weird, huh?"

"It's not weird, it's Saturn! I know a few people who have this, including me, and it's not easy. But I tell you, Saturn delays but it does not deny. Your big payoff will come when you hit 36. But who knows? It could be sooner."

"No, you're right. I always thought I was a late bloomer. That's why I'm going for my masters. Nothing else was working anyway."

"Hey, ya don't appreciate the value of an education till you get one."

She looks at him like he's much more than she expected but they have to wrap up just as it gets deep. She expresses her appreciation and reluctantly leaves. Poem takes a quick drink of water as the next client sits down. She is a snub-nosed fake blonde with a freewheelin' attitude who describes herself as a 'serial monogamist.'

"Oh yeah? Who's your latest victim?"

They laugh and this goes on. There is absolutely no break for the first ten clients. As soon as one is done, another sits down. Poem finally gets up and tells Denise he needs a break.

She says of course and apologizes for the overbooking. She's trying to give everyone a chance.

Poem and Ria stand up, stretch out, walk around, smoke. Ria says, "You're doing great, darling."

"Thanks, babe."

"Are you tired?"

"I was feeling energized but I can't believe how much mental energy it takes to read charts, one after another, but I think I'm getting the hang of it. I think I know way more than I gave myself credit."

"I think you're doing great! That one girl cried!"

"Two women cried."

"See?!"

She has a point. They finish their cigarettes, refill their glasses and Poem heads back in. Some readings are good, a few are great, a few not so good, a couple really hard. Three people don't know their exact time of birth so he reads from the Moon chart. It gets to be way past nine o'clock. People are getting antsy. Denise asks the readers if they can shorten it to seven minutes, then five. Everyone wants their turn, even though the event ends at nine. It gets to be 10 o'clock when Poem and the other readers are about to pass out. Denise feels bad but she is being a sweetheart, offering additional money. It is exhausting work. They greet their last clients, slouched in their chairs. Poem has a kind, vaguely familiar looking woman, 67 years old, who waited to the very end because of one burning question.

"I know you are an astrologer. My mother was a vegetarian, a communist, and a Theosophist, and believed strongly in astrology. She called it the religion of the future," she chuckles. "I have not had an easy life, young man, but I am beginning to enjoy it now that I am retired. I have only one question, please, tell me how much longer I have to live."

Ho boy. Poem puts his face to the screen. *Her lagna is okay; 8th house of longevity, hmm, hard to say; 3rd house of vitality, hmm, not bad. 2nd and 7th are death houses...* The wheels are turning but he is tired, trying to come up with an honest answer. He sees her looking on hopefully. She waited the whole evening.

"By my reckoning, ma'am," he looks her in the eye, "You have at least another... million or two million years to go."

It takes a couple seconds but she cracks a wide grateful smile, "I think you are very wise, young man."

"Of course, you won't be able to squeeze all that into one lifetime."

"Of course," she smiles and gets up. "You take care, Gregory. Get some rest."

Poem is stunned. *How does she know my given name?* He watches her disappear into the crowd. He looks at the mala on his wrist and falls back into his chair, exhausted.

Ria slides over next to him, "Are you okay?"

"I think that was one of the hardest things I've ever done in my life," he sounds worn and satisfied, smiling feebly with bliss in his stomach.

Denise comes around with cheques and thanks everyone. The other readers are grumbling but Poem is grateful for his very first gig.

Denise thanks him, "You did great, Poem. We're having another event in March. You interested?"

"Count me in."

She beams, gives two thumbs-up and leaves. Poem looks at the cheque and says to Ria, "I can't believe I did this. Holy Shit, astrology works! I can't wait to tell Mantriji!"

The palm reader comes over and they chat for a minute. It turns out he knows Western astrology but never studied with a teacher and doesn't feel qualified to do it professionally. "You're very lucky," he says. "Good astrologers, never mind teachers, are hard to find. You must have good karma."

Poem looks at Ria and says, "Yes. Yes I do. For some things."

"Well, isn't that always the way?"

"Yeah."

He leaves.

Poem and Ria pack up their stuff and head out as well. The pub is nearly empty but the street is busy. There's a group of patrons gabbing and smoking out front. They exchange friendly hellos and Poem gets into the car when he hears a woman say, "He's an astrologer."

He looks at the crowd. The energy is similar to a gig. He's the performer and they liked his show but they know he's from somewhere else. He rolls down the window and says, "Goodnight all," and they respond cheerily.

Relieved, he waves as Ria pulls out onto King Street.

8 ASTROLOGY 101

A motley crowd is gathering, Poem doesn't know why. Grey storm clouds drop from the sky. People are moving, grinding up against one another, while he struggles to stay on his feet. There's some commotion developing. Poem feels himself pulled in so he jumps onto the back of the minion in front of him. He looks over the headline to a huge swirling froth of humanity, like the churning of a galaxy, orbiting a mysterious hole. People are falling and calling to and from the centre out to the rest of the group—it's an emergency! A crime has occurred. Several multicoloured demons suddenly fly out of the centre and overhead with a Zeus-like character chasing them, hurling thunderbolts. They disappear into the outer void. Poem bears down to escape the glowing shrapnel and moves in closer to the source. Voices grow louder, there is scuffling in the crowd. Through a gap he sees a blue-skinned woman at the centre, lying on the ground, clothes torn, convulsing in pain. She is reaching for something. A man is holding her, freaking out. Tears stream from his face. He cries, "Is there an astrologer in the house?!"

"Huh?!" Poem wakes up, startled, his mouth dry. *What time is it?* The light at the window says morning. He looks at Ria who is watching him.

"Are you okay, darling?"

"Yeah... Yeah, I just had this really weird dream." He describes it to her and she says,

"Maybe the man was calling for an astrologer cuz she needed help with her karma?"

He gives her an odd look, surprised by the insight. He rarely remembers his dreams. "It's like I was at the creation of our galaxy with all of humanity pushing to be free, trying to attain immortality. And whatever those demons did or stole, it had to do with that woman on the ground. She was *sky blue*." He thinks a moment. "Maybe she's the fallen Earth and they need an astrologer to understand her rebirth."

"That's beautiful, darling." she puts her arms around him and he leans into her embrace.

"Have you ever seriously just sat back and really thought, I mean deeply, that we live on a spherical rock racing through outer space, orbiting a huge burning ball of gas and our only companions are the other planets, each of which has *its own* ecology and frequency and magnetic field?"

"All the time," she sighs.

"And just as these planets are kept together in a self-contained, organized system, so do stars cluster to form groups, and these groups cluster around our galaxy so you have all these fields within fields, scales within scales, worlds within worlds, like fractals. How much you belong to something is how deeply invested you are." He takes a long deep breath. "We belong to the Earth because it's very hard to escape its field but we're also within the fields of other planets and other stars, y'know? I wonder if intersecting fields have an accumulative or exponential effect."

Ria shakes her head, wondering how Wi-Fi works.

Poem turns on his side, facing her, "They say the influence of the planets is subtle, but then what's more subtle than the human mind?"

She smiles, liking his conjecture.

"We're not just part of a solar system, we're part of a star cluster and galaxy and we're even part of a cluster of galaxies. Our whole sense of identity is where in space and time all these fields intersect."

They lay there silently, arms around one another, watching the emerging light at the window. "We are electricity and therefore a field. And this Sun out there is our source and we're all just little wireless suns in all shapes and voltages emitting electromagnetic fields. And at the same time we're travelling through space at an incredible rate through *all kinds* of electromagnetic fields," he rubs his goatee. "Our solar system is orbiting the galaxy through new regions and frontiers, new plasmas, new influences. Who knows how they influence human affairs. Maybe electricity was discovered because we entered some new field of consciousness that allowed us to see it, think it, manipulate it, like general relativity or human rights. Just think of all these intersecting fields influencing our own field and the differential between it and us is unique to everyone and we call this astrology!"

Ria sleepily kisses his neck, aroused by his early morning philosophizing.

"And I guess that's the role of an astrologer, to apply the cosmos *wholesale* to each individual."

Ria yawns and rubs her eyes, "It's a huge responsibility, Poem. I heard what people were asking and some of them really took to heart what you said."

"I know. And there were a few times when I was so wrong, I felt like a complete idiot, like they must think I'm a total fraud."

"How can you be a fraud if you studied with a master for four years?"

He is grateful for her encouragement and licks her ear, "Thanks, babe."

Poem met Ria about two years ago and they've been dating ever since. It is a weekend relationship of physical attraction and emotional convenience. They're both at crossroads in their lives and non-committal in their determination to get what they want. He is an artist and freelance writer recently turned astrologer with what was a burgeoning career in community politics. She is a corporate communications coordinator who spends all her extra time on travel, talking about travel, and planning her next trip. They don't have a lot in common but none of that matters when you like to cuddle. They roll around for a while before they get out of bed and head out for their Sunday morning coffee and walk. Poem has his lesson at five.

They arrive back at the co-op to see Nick in his front window stretching his shirtless, wiry 50 year old body. Poem says, "He does that on purpose, you know."

"God, he looks like a turtle without its shell."

They enter the foyer hoping to avoid Nick and quickly make their way up the stairs. Ria hears Christy in her apartment so she visits her while Poem showers, gets dressed, and sorts through his books and notes. He pulls out a prashna method Mantri taught him in December. 'When will I find work?' is the question followed by the calculations. "I remember this." He calculated:

January 18, 6:30pm

He recalls how he thought it unlikely he would start a job at that time. "Great," he says, disappointed. It's January 21 and he's still unemployed. *Wait a second. Thursday was January 18 and that was the Psychic Night. Wait a second! They told me to be there for 6:30 p.m! Wait a second!!* "Holy Shit! Holy Shit!! HOLY SHIT!!!" He can't believe it. He nailed it! "Holy shit!!"

Ria and Christy come rushing in, "What's wrong?! Are you okay?!"

"I can't believe this!" Poem shows Ria the paper and explains it to her.

She's impressed but Christy says, "Well, it's not exactly like you got a full-time job."

"That wasn't the question." He shows her the page, "I asked when will I find *work*? Not when will I find a full-time job."

"That's amazing, darling. Can I ask you something?"

"Me too," Christy says.

"Okay, hold on," Poem puts up his hands. "Can I just bask in this moment for a minute without one of you trying to get a piece?"

They apologize and Poem gets back to organizing his notes while Ria and Christy continue their chat, now on astrology.

It gets to be 4:30 p.m. Poem kisses Ria and drives off to Mantri's. The lobby is wide open so he doesn't call up. He just walks in and Mantri answers his door surprised, "How did you get in?"

"I flew onto the roof and climbed down from there."

Mantri laughs. The two men exchange greetings and settle into their usual spots.

"You'll never guess what happened to me, Sir." Poem recounts the string of events that led him to reading the charts of nearly 30 people in three hours for a singles event. He relives his most significant moments, his failures, the tears, the challenges, and the mysterious last client who asked for her longevity and somehow knew his given name.

Mantri shakes his head, amazed, "This… this Psychic Night, this opportunity came to *you*. You did not seek it. You would never have done it or looked for it. This is why it came to you. Ganesh is saying you are ready," he bobbles his head.

"Not only that," Poem is eager to tell him. He pulls out the sheet of paper with the prashna method from December and shows it to Mantri, explaining how he got it exactly right. His first gig as an astrologer he predicted to the half-hour a month in advance. "How poetic is that?"

Mantri beams with pride, "Look how this works. You did not look for me. I came to Carmel's and there you were. Similarly, this opportunity came to you, you did not ask for it. Amazing this concept. You are definitely running Saturn now and Saturn is with Mercury, the astrologer, aspected by transiting Mars, lord of the 8th. Karma is funny thing." He looks at Poem with deep affection, "You are just like a son."

Poem can't believe how much his approval means to him.

"With this lady," Mantri raises his finger. "Never predict longevity or health for anyone. Even if you see clearly they have short life span, do not say it."

"Why?"

"Because no man is God and yet, people will treat the doctor, the psychic, the astrologer, like he knows what only God knows. If you say it, they may live with it the rest of their days. Even to a young man, he will recall his whole life that some astrologer told him he would die young and may even live his life with this attitude. It is a heavy burden for anyone to know their mortality and for the astrologer who tells it. Better don't do it at all. Just say, I do not predict longevity, thank you."

Poem reflects as Mantri continues, "It is always best to emphasize only one or two things in the chart. If you say too much, they will get nothing out of it. One thing, two things, they will remember and they will thank you. Too many things and they will forget everything in a couple days."

"I see how some want you to razzle-dazzle them."

"Razzle dazzle, as you say, may impress but it offers no help. Best you make one prediction about something in their lives, some incident or year of marriage or promotion, so that when you are right you will gain their trust. They will think how did he know this? He must know what he is talking."

"You mean, pull the rabbit out of the hat."

"Right. When you pull the rabbit from the hat, they will believe everything you say. If you don't know or not sure, best don't say anything. Better they think you know and won't tell them," he smiles.

"There were a few people, Sir, who didn't know their time of birth and I tried to read it from the Moon but it was not so good."

"We must always assume every chart is wrong until we verify it. We use the Moon mostly for prediction, not personality, but every chart is different. You will get better with experience, how to handle different situations. Sometimes we predict from lagna, sometimes from Moon. Many times you will be wrong in your prediction but as long as you know why you were wrong, then you can learn from it and be better in the future. Astrology is not absolute. Books are absolute but life is not. We must blend the many factors that make up a whole." He pulls out a pen and paper to illustrate his point. "Look here, you have three different colours and you have to combine them in unequal parts. Do you know exactly what the new colour will be or do you have to blend it first to see? If you know in advance what the colour is, you have mastered prediction. It is easy to blend the colours *and then* see what happens, but this is hindsight. The time has come and gone. A true Jyotishi knows what these separate colours will become *before* they are combined."

"Right."

"Just stick with the basics for now. You need to chew it. Really chew the fundamentals and study charts and you will get it."

"Do you really think I could be an astrologer, Mantriji?"

"Oh yay. You are a very smart man, knowledgeable of science and philosophy, interested in religion, in people, in symbols, in psychology. You have done many things and seen many people. Some take to the spiritual program too early and that's all they know. They cannot relate to everyday people, but you, you have lived. You will make a very good astrologer because you can relate to people. But it takes study, practice, devotion, and the desire to understand what goes on beneath the skin of this universe. A good astrologer can recognize a trend but a *great* astrologer can tell you what *will happen*."

"Y'know, one thing I did notice, it sort of came out here and there. I found that when I was talking to people… I would hear *your* voice inside me, like I'm channelling *you*. It's like I'm not telling them what *I* think, I'm telling them what *you* would say, like I'm giving them an experience with *you*, and I even move my hands the way *you* do. It was really interesting.

Does this mean I'm hooked up to the lineage?"

Mantri chuckles, "You have it, Poem. You just have to believe in yourself. I still hear my teacher when I speak and I am a 70 year old man. He was younger than I am now and I still see him as my father. I hear his voice in mine and I am sure he heard his guru's voice and it goes all the way back to the seed of all these teachers, all these voices, coming down to you, a seed that passes through time from the original teacher who got it directly from God."

"So in everything we can say there is a touch of God."

"That's right."

"Amazing this concept," Poem says like Mantri. "Y'know, I'm actually impressed with the quality of people who were at this event. I mean, it wasn't any one type but I would say most of them have post-secondary education."

"It is not difficult to find educated people interested in astrology, but sometimes difficult to find one who *admits* his interest in astrology. But you must be careful always how you speak to people because if they do not know astrology, some will take you for a fool that you are an astrologer. Remember, people who are expert in one thing think they know everything and it is easy to have an opinion on something you know little about. But you must let this go. Don't expect too much from people. I will tell you one story.

"One time, Pundit Nehru, the first Prime Minister of India, was walking with one of his ministers when this lowly man, an untouchable, came from the crowd. He shouted at Nehru some terrible insult and Nehru smiled at him, unaffected. His minister said, 'You are the Prime Minister of India. How can you let this man get away with such an insult? Why do you not react?' But Nehru said, 'What do you expect from a dog?'

"Similarly, we cannot expect more from people than what they are. Jesus Christ taught us forgiveness for this reason."

Poem nods.

"All of astrology is taking what is *here*," he points to a chart on the table, "and applying it to what is *here*," he points to Poem. "And doing your very best to help that person. If he is running exalted planet, you don't have to say or do anything, just thank you and have a nice day. Success will find him. If he is running debilitated or combust planet, it is a very difficult time. You can say this and he will know what you are talking. But unless you can help this person, to tell him his fate is useless. Better to not mention it."

"I found myself giving solutions from the opposite house like you said."

"This is good. The opposite opposes and is therefore the solution. It marks an axis of polarity. We see this most clearly in the 1/7 house axis.

"The 1st is you, the 7th is another. When *you* are troubled, where do you go? To another. When you have troubles with others, where do you go? Back to yourself, you see? Let's try one more. 2nd/8th house axis.

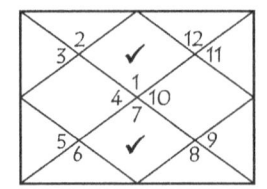

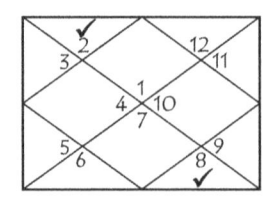

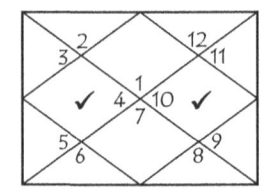

"When you have trouble with your assets, where do you go? To your partner's assets. When you have trouble with your family, where do you go? To your partner's family, or assets, or words of comfort. In both cases the solution to your problem is in your partner's 2nd house, which is *your* 8th, you see? Partner could be spouse, colleague, good friend, even lender. Similarly, if you have problems with your *partner's* family or assets, you will have to find refuge in your own. The nature of the solution is determined by the sign and planets involved. Let's try another easy one, 4/10 axis. If you have trouble with career, make peace at home; if you have trouble at home, make peace with your career."

"It's amazing, Mantriji, the symmetry of concepts in astrology, how it's based on opposites and like, relative musical keys."

"Beautiful what you are saying. There are still other things you can do to remedy difficult karma in the chart but this will come with time and experience. We will discuss. Remember, this is a metaphysical subject. There are no absolutes and yet, everything is predictable."

"One guy asked if everything is Fate and I said we still have freewill. Then he asked what about randomness and I thought the only thing that could create randomness is consciousness. But even consciousness has its cause and effect."

"That's right. Everything is karma, cause and effect. There is no randomness. Randomness defies law. Science relies on laws. Therefore randomness is unscientific. Can you name me anything, any noun or verb or adjective, anything that does not have a cause?"

Poem thinks. It is a Zen and possibly trick question.

"Tell me, why did you ask this question?"

"I was curious."

"Why are you curious?"

"Because I'm uncertain."

"Why are you uncertain?"

"I guess because my education is incomplete."

"Why?"

"Because… it's impossible to know everything."

"Why is this impossible?"

"Because to know everything would mean you have complete knowledge."

"Why is this not possible?"

"Because only a *supreme* being can have complete knowledge."

"Ahah! We are back to God, first principle, prime mover, the thing which is absolute and unknowable."

Poem shakes his head, "I don't know. That seems awfully reductive. Let's try that again."

Mantri brushes a pen so it falls to the floor. "Look what happened, what caused this?"

"You decided to make a point."

"Ahh… Think for a moment why I dropped this pen. What *caused* this?"

"I think you are a man who knows a great deal and you like to teach."

Mantri loves this answer. "And what is behind this?"

Poem thinks. "Probably from teaching others you learn yourself, plus there is the personal satisfaction and let's face it, you have to make a living."

"These are several causes but I guarantee if you deconstruct any of these, you will eventually and even rather quickly work your way back to the first cause, or God. Why do I need to make money?"

"Because we live in a monetary system and you need to pay rent."

"Ahh. And what is the cause of this?"

"Endless greed," Poem laughs. Thinking about it he says, "I guess people who don't grow food have to get it from people who do, and so what can they give the farmer, a gift, legal advice? They have to give him something he can use. So if everyone agrees that money means something then the farmer can get paid in something he can use elsewhere. You're giving him a promise."

"And what is the cause for this?"

"For the promise?"

"Doesn't matter."

"Yeah right, uh… It's a promise for gold really, or it used to be."

"Why gold?"

"Because gold is a metallic manifestation of the Sun."

"Very good. And the Sun?"

"The Sun takes us back to God—I see what you mean."

"Gold is money because it is the Sun. The Sun is the source of our world and vitality. It is the Godhead through which the Almighty flows."

"It's like teleology because things are connected to higher octaves of themselves."

"Ahh, this is good one." Mantri is enjoying the discussion. "But there is no randomness, only ignorance of the cause."

"And yet," Poem raises his finger. "Quantum theory, which is the basis of modern physics, is indeterminate. How do you reconcile that? The universe is not classical, it's jazz!"

Mantri laughs.

"Science is supposed to be certain, yet it's only probable, like improvised music. But who's the player?"

"Beautiful what you are saying," Mantri bobbles his head. "Even if we do not know the cause, doesn't mean there isn't one. Sometimes it is impossible to see the player, the invisible hand. How do you see an abstraction or an ideal? You cannot hold it in your hand and yet people march into battle over an ideal. Jesus Christ and Buddha showed the world how evolved beings behave and still today people shoot one another over the difference between oranges and tangerines. This is why the best we can do is give expression somehow to the things we will never fully understand, whether through music, through astrology, through love. Those who 'get it' attain enlightenment but the rest must keep working, must keep striving. This man is a theologian, this man is an astrophysicist; it is all the same."

"Well, Mantriji, I think I want to be an astrologer."

Mantri sizes him up, wondering if he knows what he is saying. "You *are* an astrologer. The question is what *kind* of astrologer? To be a *good* astrologer is not easy. You must work hard, study, practice." He picks up a book from the table, "Deconstructing is easy, but prediction is hard. It takes siddhi."

"You mean, uh... a miraculous ability?"

"It is miraculous, but it is also earned and requires great effort and devotion, sacrifice! This is not, how you say, 'Rock Star program.' One must be free of all vice, all doubt. One must be knowledgeable in the scriptures and in the sciences. To be an astrologer is to be a mystic," he bobbles his head, "and this requires courage and compassion, focus, and the ability to withstand the ignorance of others."

"What about tobacco?"

"Smoking is very difficult, I know myself, but if one can overcome smoking, if one has the will to beat this addiction, then one has the strength to learn astrology."

"You smoked?"

"Ho! Like chimney."

Poem can't believe it.

"I was young man too, Poem. Troublemaker," he grins proudly.

Poem feels closer to him, knowing that he was a rough boy, pumping weights, getting into fights, sitting in jail overnight, smoking, and here he is half a century later, a man of knowledge, wisdom and illumination.

"So what do you think, Mantriji, is the most important thing an astrologer should know?"

"To never give advice that is not asked."

Poem flashes to a number of times in his life when attempts to help others were perceived as offences. "This is good advice. I could have used it years ago."

"Understand, people make their own truth and do not want *the* truth until they are ready. Similarly, if you tell someone he does not have freewill, that his fate is in the planets, that he is a mere conduit to forces he doesn't understand, do not be surprised if this man resists your attempts to 'enlighten' him."

"Again, very good advice," he bows to his teacher.

"The world is mathematical, Poem, and it is the aim of astrology to understand the math of karma. As you say, this quantum theory is based on probability, yet science relies on certainty. Science is not coincidence, it is cause and effect. But when the cause is unknown we must say a series of coincidences makes a law. Just as we have the planets which are known predictable forces, we have the human who is free according to his awareness, and so our predictions can be only so precise, sometimes amazingly so, but at other times not so much," he flutters his right hand.

"Humans are machines, yes, but they are *aware* machines, and this awareness makes astrology a tricky business. It is the purpose of astrology to bring awareness, to apply an opposing force when necessary, and you must instruct the person this way. Make hay when sun shines and prepare for the rain they don't see below the horizon. Just remember, good advice does not expect thanks because very difficult to prove a negative. They will not come back if nothing happens. Only if something happens will they call you." He gives Poem a grandfatherly look, "But if your intention is pure and it is to help others, then there is no worry. You will make mistakes and you will do well and by God's grace you will help," he sticks his hand out like on a bible. "Metaphor brings meaning to phenomena, so if you know how to tell good story, put in *their* terms, song and dance. I hear you speak; you like jokes and stories, this is good. Certain things can be learned only through parable.

"Never tell the person they have debilitated, or fallen, or combust planet, even if this is so. Use kind words. To them 'fallen' is a bad word and people are fatalistic. Just discuss the situation without using this word. Debilitated planets still have some distinction by their being debilitated. It is not a normal position so it will produce 'un-conventional' results. Many great people have debilitated planets."

"Albert Einstein had debilitated Mercury and he was a genius!"

"He was a genius because his Mercury took him somewhere *outside*. He was allowed to think what others could not, even to this day. For him this debility occurs in his 10th house of career and so he was able to make an occupation from it, as you have fallen Mercury in your 7th and you are able to make relationships from it, from this unconventional, poetic mind."

Mantri looks tired.

"Wow. I feel like you're finally giving me Astrology 101."

"That's right. Always be rooted in the fundamentals and you will never go wrong." He picks up a book, "We will continue with Phala Deepika, one verse at a time. You must memorize and really eat what is going on here," he puts his hand on the book. "By mastering this work you will develop siddhi and you can be a great astrologer but you must put into practice or it won't come. You *have it*, Poem! You only have to want it. Saturn makes you aloof, detached, a philosophical mind, but action is better than inaction. Go to places where there are people and just offer free readings. Say, 'Hello, my name is Poem. I am a student of astrology. Will you tell me your time of birth?' Like this. You will meet people and you will get clients. It will force you to develop yourself. Just dress nicely, clean, and speak politely, put people at ease. You will learn a great deal and they will spread the word."

It sounds like a lot. Poem feels enthusiastic and overwhelmed.

"Last thing, most important thing, hardest thing," Mantri clenches his fist. "Be objective. People always give advice based on their own agenda, based on this idea that if you were more like them, this would make you perfect. But this is wrong. You must always put the client first, even if they cannot pay you, just help them. Do not help you. Help *them*. This is very important."

"Okay, Mantriji."

"Everything you learn must be applied to the real world. The scripture will say 'buffalo,' but you know it is a van or boat. The scripture will say 'king,' but we know today it is a manager or boss. The scripture will say 'jewellery,' but this means assets like stocks and bonds. Whatever you do, whatever you read, whatever you speak, must always be put into the context of a human being. And the intention must be love."

"Well, this should be interesting." Poem looks out the window then at Mantri, "Thank you, Sir, for everything. I mean… for everything. I'm sorry I can donate only so much," he pulls out his wallet.

"It is all right, Poem. When you devote yourself to others, you attain your own salvation."

"Maybe *that* should be rule number one."

"That's right," Mantri smiles. He leans back in his chair, looking like he could use a nap. "See you Wednesday, Poem. Don't forget food," he points to the plastic bag on the counter with prasad inside.

"Thank you, Sir." Poem gets up and bows to his wonderful Master. "See you Wednesday."

9 SATSANG

It is a ripe spring day. Blueness abounds. The fresh heat is liberating and people are all around. Traffic is relaxed on Christie as Poem drives past the busy baseball diamonds on his way to Vidya, a yoga studio where Mantri teaches twice a week to a class of mostly female yoga practitioners. The subject is Yoga Sutras with Sanskrit recitation, translation and illumination by Sri Mantriji, the 'real deal' from New Delhi. Most attendees take it seriously, some are even holier-than-thou. Poem once asked Mantri about this attitude and he said, "They are young and mistake judgement for enlightenment. It is easy to be dismissive and call it detached. But they are trying. It does not matter where you are in life so much as in what *direction* you are pointing."

It's been over a year since Poem's first Psychic Night. The agency asked him back for the next one and the next one and now it's a regular gig. He's doing private readings as well and it has deepened his interest in Jyotish, and by extension Vedanta.

He is now running a small supplements business in the west end for a friend, has a company car and a nice one-bedroom flat overlooking hardwood trees. He studies with Mantri three times a week and in lieu of university where he studied philosophy, he now attends satsang where he studies universe-ity.

Ria wants more and more to quit her job, sell the condo and take off travelling, while Poem wants more and more to stay in Toronto to pursue his studies. He's getting along with his family, his job makes him okay money, and satsang is his inoculation from an insane world.

He turns onto the bushy residential street where he finds easy parking and walks to the yoga studio. Leaving his shoes in the foyer he enters the lobby where a few people are milling about. He sees Carmela. "Hey…!"

Happy to see each other, they hug. It's been a while. "Since when do you come to satsang?" she's impressed. "Look at you."

"Yeah," he smiles. "Funny how things work out."

"How are your studies with Mantriji?"

"Pretty good. I mean, it's a lot, but I'm picking up Sanskrit now and coming out to satsang, as you can see."

"I see…! I think it's really funny how Mantriji showed up early that day just as you were getting ready to leave. He never does that, never!"

"Yeah… He's amazing."

"You know, Poem, he may come off all humble and even shy when you first meet him, like he's an ordinary man, but once you spend any time with him, like really talk to him, you realize that he *is* a Master." She looks through the glass door, "He just has this energy of understanding and wisdom, I don't know how else to describe it. You know he's known all over the world, right? Especially when it comes to Jyotish. We're very lucky to have him."

"I'm beginning to see that. Like the people who travel all the way from the States just to meet him or they hope to study with him, or sometimes, one woman came just to get a blessing! I guess Robert and Hart's books made him world famous."

"Plus, his brother was well known in India."

"That's right. He told me. Listen, Carmela, I just wanna really thank you for introducing me to him, I mean, I know I resisted and everything but, it really changed my life."

"I *see!*" she beams. "But don't thank me, Poem. Thank the universe. When the student is ready, the teacher will appear. He doesn't take on just anyone, y'know. He has to believe in you, never forget that." She looks around then says confidentially, "He adores you, Poem."

"I adore him too. He says I'm like a son to him and I can't believe it, like how many sons could he have? Am I really the only one he's ever said this to?"

"You have a very different relationship with him. You didn't seek him out. It just happened and you didn't even realize who he was. Everyone else kisses his ass because they want something, but you're more of a friend the way he talks about you. I think he's tired of disciples. They're wearing him down."

"I can see that. You know he has tinnitus and can't sleep."

"Yeah, I've been helping him to get in to see some specialists. I don't know how he teaches on so little sleep."

An entourage of students appears outside the door. They enter with a leaner Mantri who looks tired but radiant in his gold/beige kurta, smiling graciously and happy to see Poem. He removes his shoes and is *very* happy to see 'Carmel.' It's been a while since she attended satsang. They exchange greetings and he walks with her as everyone follows, smiling, the centre buzzing with activity like it's a holiday.

Poem follows them into the large main studio where Mantri sits in front of a table draped in pearl white cloth, a large pillar candle, flowers and a bowl of red mangoes. He unpacks books from his knapsack as everyone settles into rows of yoga chairs. Herbal tea is poured and served with small plates of fruit and pastries. Mantri patiently flips through his books, fielding questions from the front row, while people get their blankets, books, pens and pads in order. He looks up over his reading glasses for any new people, nodding and smiling as students arrive. Gradually everyone finds their spot and quiets down. Mantri waits for their silence and cues one of them to begin. A young woman in lotus position, eyes closed, begins to chant and everyone follows in monotone unison:

> "Om… Yogena chittasya padena vacham malam sharirasya cha vaidyakena…"

It is the invocation of Patañjali, author of the Yoga Sutras, father to Yoga, sage of spiritual illumination. Poem is in the back row still trying to memorize it with one eye on the text. He likes listening to the class and often attends just to be part of the choir. To him it's the rap version of a Gregorian chant.

> "Om… shanti, shanti, shanti-hee."

There is quiet for a moment before Mantri begins, "Does anyone know why we're here?" He scans the room and no one answers. It is always this way. Invariably one of the same three people, or perhaps a newbie, will answer or Mantri will single one out for interrogation.

"We are here to try and attain liberation," a regular says.

"And what does this mean?"

"To escape the cycle of death and rebirths."

"That's right. And why do we want this?"

"To end suffering?"

"Very good. And what is the root of suffering?"

"Desire."

"That is true. But according to this book, where does this desire come from? Why do you desire this and not that? Why when two babies are born they are not the same, they already have character, different desires, just ask anyone," he looks at Janine holding her toddler and she nods. "This baby is not a blank slate. She is born with personality already. What some see as *development* of character is actually the *revealing* of character that is already there."

"Sounds like astrology," Poem mumbles to Andrea sitting next to him.

"At the root of this character are subliminal impressions—Patañjali calls this 'Samskara'—and these lead us to suffering. Please read," he nods to a student who recites a short verse in Sanskrit which Mantri deconstructs etymologically. The student then reads the author's prosaic translation:

> "Attachment is *that* (modification) which follows remembrance of pleasure."

"Ahh... It is very simple. Pleasure leads to desire and this leads to emotional attachment. A modification of the mind is when an impression is made, a samskara, because you enjoyed it and now you are stuck. Here's how it works. I've lived in this country nearly 40 years and never did I eat chocolate. I did not even think about it. Now this woman," he points to Janine with her daughter. "See this little baby girl? She likes chocolate so I buy these, what you call, 'chocolate chips,' and I give just little dose when she is around," he motions putting it into her mouth. "Just so she can enjoy my company. Last week I ate one of these chips and now look here, it is nine o'clock Thursday night and oh God, where am I? At Loblaws, lining up at the cashier buying chocolate, a man of my age." The class laughs. "So you see, this baby girl has samskara for chocolate but I did not. But through *her*," he twists his hand, "*I* got the samskara and now *I* am on the chocolate program. Just like that. Nine o'clock at night in Loblaws looking for more chocolate." The class is giddy with laughter.

"See here, what started as a sensation has become a seed. And this seed grows so that something you were not even aware of is now something you can't live without." He scans the class above his reading glasses, "Very important to regulate your thoughts. We must take care of the body, yes, but we must pay particular attention to our thoughts because it is not the *activity* that kills us, it is what it does to our minds," he points to his head. "Amazing this concept. This is why it is very important with whom you mix. If you want music samskara, mix with musicians; if you want yoga samskara, go to the yoga studio; if you have money samskara, go to the bank, to Bay Street. If you have chocolate samskara, you go to this baby here," he points and the class giggles along. "You want to be with people who have some quality and ability in that which you wish to learn— are you getting this?" he looks at a young woman in the front row who blushes.

"As you sow, so shall you reap. When you go to the park, you will see a trail where many people have walked. This is karma. They could have walked anywhere, but one came and a second followed and everyone is walking the same path because it is now cut into the woods and easy to see. It seems foolish to go any other way. It is not easy to change habits. Why do we do satsang? It is to meet with good people, similar minds, who want to learn more about higher things and to aim their behaviour towards spiritual illumination, to study what Patañjali wrote about this, knowing he was more illuminated than us. What is this world we live in that we are so removed from reality?"

The class is silent with just the murmur of traffic outside.

"There is this material world," he knocks on the table, "we perceive with our senses, but there is a subtler world made of ideas and abstractions without which this table would not exist. Ideas have no form until we manifest it, and yet the idea can be ever-present. But it could remain in consciousness and not in form. In all my years I have never seen dogs play poker, yet the idea exists. They have paintings!" The class laughs. "You may dream of success but until you manifest it, it remains only a dream, a concept. Real, yes, but only to the dreamer."

Poem looks around. Everyone's perfectly still, either sitting up or leaning back into their chairs. Only Janine, rocking and restraining her child, makes a sound.

"We are unconcerned with the world as it is out there," he looks out the long storefront window, "with our jobs and day to day survival. We are interested in the world in here," he points to his chest. "Understand, the deeper we go *here*, the farther our consciousness goes out *there*," he sweeps his hand. "But what is it that holds us back?"

No one offers an answer.

"To get close to the truth, we must let go and yet, letting go is the hardest thing to do. We're so attached to our lives, to our egos. We find identity in our ego, and yet it is because of ego that we suffer. And it seems the more we learn, the more confused we become because we know only what we get through our senses, and yet our senses are in duality, *maya!*" he looks at Poem. "The truth is imperishable, it is non dual. As long as we are in this physical form, relying on sound/colour/touch/taste/smell and trapped in ego, we will never completely get to the truth. Remember, an important theme in the Gita is to work *not* for the fruit of your labours. Just think how this goes against the whole of Western thinking. We *want* to be recognized *and* rewarded. The whole of civilization is backwards and we call it progress."

The sound of a car vibrating noisily with hip hop stops in front, rattling the window pane before driving off.

"We live in complete illusion from the truth. Instead of the spirit, we idealize people and the body as pure, but it is not pure. No person, no body, can be pure. Just go to the hospital and you will see what I am saying. This man writes poems about his beloved, how pure she is, like snow, like an unsmelled flower; her vagina is a rose." The class shrieks with embarrassed laughter. "But tell me what would this woman smell like after one week of no bathing? He would see very quickly that she is not pure, that she is a human being, an animal, an impermanent vessel for something that *is* permanent. Which part he is in love with he will soon see," he chuckles and there is groaning in the room.

"People are too caught up in the sex program. Even when they say they are doing it for health, it is usually because they want more sex. This woman is going to yoga class all the time, climbing stairs at the gym. She says it's for peace of mind," he feigns meditating. "But she is doing 'buns of steel' program, making that ass smaller. For a year she is going, all this time and money. Now she has an eight hundred dollar ass." The girls squeal with laughter while some look shocked. Mantri is having a good time.

"This book," he holds up the Sutras, "is useless if you don't put into practice. Because you are here does not mean anything. If you do not *practice*, this book is waste of time. A drunk out in the street has more spirituality than you because you are caught up in yoga pants and not the yoga, you fuss over the candle and not the intent, you have *beautiful* bindi but the inner eye is asleep. We are always moving but in what direction? Instead of still, we are busy; instead of fulfilled, we are always seeking. Very difficult for people to be still. I will tell you one story."

The class mumbles in anticipation.

"A famous guru in India was trying to demonstrate to one of his students the difficulty of being still, of stilling the mind. They walk past a house being built by workmen when the teacher has an idea. He approaches the foreman and asks how much he is paying these men to work all day in the hot sun? The foreman replies that the men are being paid 10 rupees each a day. The guru says to him, 'I am doing an experiment and I need several men to help me. Tell your workers I will pay them 20 rupees a day each if they agree to come to my place and do nothing but sit still all day. They can have a shady spot and all they need to do is just sit there.'

"The foreman feels he can let go of a few men for the purpose of this 'experiment' and the next day several show up at the door of this guru. The teacher tells them all they have to do is sit still, don't move. Just find a comfortable place and don't do anything. 'My student will bring you water, food, whatever you need, but do not do a thing, just sit.' The men all happily agreed, thinking they were now on Easy Street."

There's murmuring in the class.

"Do you know what? Not a single one of these men lasted, not even half a day. They all one after the other started to scratch, fidget, move around. They could not handle sitting still so they all returned to the construction site to toil in the afternoon sun. It is easier for them to do backbreaking work than to do nothing at all, even for twice the pay! This is how restless our minds are. It costs us dearly and we call it 'productivity,' how you say, 'multitasking,' but towards what? More stuff, more attachment, more suffering. No. Humans cannot be still because the mind is restless and the mind wants to do. It wants things and it wants to become, to be active in the external world. The internal world is not good enough. There is not enough stimulation. People would rather do backbreaking work than be still and this is how they break their backs. What does this man say?" He cues a student who reads the purport in the book having to do with desire, pleasure, and leaving impressions on the mind.

She finishes and Mantri waits before saying, "Suffering is the result of attachment, and this attachment is due to karma which must be exhausted. But it is tricky to overcome this karma because planning to overcome it may lead to more suffering because it makes us attached to the goal. And rarely do things turn out the way we plan, so we are setting ourselves up for disappointment. The only way to dispel suffering is to understand the true nature of your existence. Remember, the higher-self, or 'the knower,' is not the experiencer. The *ego* experiences but the higher-self asks 'Who am I?' The closer we get to the higher-self, the thinner it gets until it is just ether or nothing at all and our consciousness pervades the whole universe. We become one, eternal, ubiquitous, and it is the end of suffering."

One of the newbies says, "I heard that identity breaks down at the level of electrons and that time does not exist inside the realm of light. Is what you're telling us to do is go into the light? Is that where we'll find our true Self and eternity?"

Mantri looks puzzled by her question. "There is light and there is darkness, and they are at either extreme," he points. "There are then two directions you can go. My advice is to go towards the light." The class laughs. "It is that simple. Einstein said that things travelling at the speed of light have no mass. What happens? They lose their identity and become universal. By vibrating at the same frequency as light, we can relate to the whole, to anything, everything! The light is in us. The human has the potential to *embody* the light, to raise ourselves to the level of Godhead, to *not* be at the mercy of what is animal in us.

"In astrology, this is the Aquarian pouring out in no particular direction. It is a universal flow and this is why Aquarians embody friendship, humanity, and universal love. But because they love many," he warns, "they are resented by those who want to possess them."

There is some chatting at this comment and Mantri waits till it abates.

"Similarly, to be in service is to embody the will of God, to be the 'grace of God' to another in fact. Service is the only thing that can take us to God because there is no ego in service, and when we do for others we are in a state of grace. Ego *will not* be in service to others because ego is busy serving itself, indulging its own sound/colour/touch/taste/smell. Similarly, so long as someone continues to become something, he cannot return to his original state. He is in fact moving away from it. He thinks he needs to become something, like a doctor, or accountant, or delivery man, but in doing so he becomes even more entrenched in the body, in the Self, in the ego."

Poem raises his hand, "Seems to me that what we're talking about is self-annihilation."

"It is not annihilation, it is becoming universal. When you feel compassion for another, do you lose your being or do you expand it?"

Another student raises her hand, "You broaden it by including others, and then by experiencing *their* life, you are able to relate to *them* and feel empathy. But the empathy is in *you,* so I think yes, it strengthens your 'being' to help someone."

"Right. It strengthens your *well-being* and yet… by helping another, you lose yourself. That is, you gain the world by permeating it with expanded consciousness. But yes, you do lose your ego in the process and this is good because you will lose your ego anyway when you die. Better to be whole than nothing, and by serving others you make your own death less painful. When you are in complete service, you transcend your ego and there is no death, there is only being. Are you getting this?" he looks at the front row.

"There are all kinds of things you can do to change your life. Some are more effective than others. Some people say if you move the couch from here to there, you will be more prosperous." The class laughs. "Move the plant here," he points, "and your sex life will improve. Understand that it is our intelligence or 'buddhi' which gives rise to ego and our sense of individuation, and that the intellect is above mind where our memories are stored, where we have these kleśas or *affliction*s of the mind.

"Kleśas are the result of karma from past lives and we have the ability to destroy them by applying intelligence and awareness, which are the potential controllers of the mind. When someone is in their mind, they are emotional, they think with their heart; when they are in the intellect, they are rational, they think with their brain. But some say 'kindness' is intelligence of the heart. It is not measuring facts and duality. It is a feeling intelligence. Does this make it any less valid?"

A few people shake their heads.

"The heart says by changing one thing, you change everything, but when we apply awareness to fix a problem or overcome a habit, we are strengthening the discriminating faculty of our intellect in order to know what to do to change our behaviour, to destroy these kleśas. Remember, to understand samskara is to *do* what you *don't do* and don't do what you do. It is to think and act 'rationally.'"

He is momentarily distracted by the gurgling baby bobbing around her mother. "Think of it this way. If you make a hundred loafs out of one defective bread pan, each and every loaf will be imperfect. Some will take a knife and attempt to correct every loaf individually and others will fix the pan. When we get to the root of our consciousness, our 'being' in the world, and make the adjustment at *this* level, then we fix the pan. Until then, everything we do, all our actions, decisions, relationships, come out flawed because of one fundamental error in our perception that may not even be the result of this lifetime. This is why we study astrology, to understand our existence and to discern on *this* level of awareness. Some people say there is no difference between intellect and mind, between spirit and soul. Some people do not even acknowledge a soul. I say what kind of discernment is this? Six billion people on this Earth believe in God and you dismiss it because there's no photograph?" The class laughs. "He says there is no force, no intelligence in the world beyond human; there is nothing but our senses and the biology of the brain. And he can look up at the sky on the clearest night and still see nothing. I say what kind of scientist are *you* if you do not thrill in the mystery of your own being?"

The class reacts with some chatter. Mantri looks in his book and waits. "If we want to change our course in life but everything is mechanical, where does change come from? Euclid said creativity violates a closed system. We see this in nature as an urge to do something, and it may take several generations before it manifests into a *genetic* mutation, but the urge is in the awareness, the buddhi of the animal. The mutation will be a response to the impulse so that the idea always precedes the action, even if the idea is itself mechanical. Human beings have the ability to act right away to affect change, whether to ourselves or to our environment. We can evolve with a single thought! Animals cannot. But it begins with awareness."

Mantri surveys the class to see if everyone is following. It's usually 50/50. His favourite recourse is to say, "Poem, you're a philosopher. What do you think of what we are talking? Will it help you find a better job?"

Poem laughs. "To have this knowledge will not help me find a better job, Mantriji. In fact, it may turn me off completely! But if I use this knowledge to sufficiently strengthen my mind, perhaps then I can go around hypnotizing people into giving me money."

There is laughter and Mantri says, "That's right. But until you are aware of these fundamental flaws in yourself—things you may not see right now—you will continue to see that the results do not match your intention and it is these kleśas that are at the root. We can use astrology to bring awareness to the cause, then we use our intelligence and *will* to change our behaviour, to override or exhaust undesirable karma. For those who remain ignorant of these distinctions, they can go to the psychiatrist, to the pharmacist, to the support group, but unless they are in touch with this concept, they will not and cannot heal themselves. The intellect brings discernment to the mind the way a human rides a horse. They are separate but they can work together and at times they may seem like one. But for those with no discernment, who are not in touch with this higher-self, or even the concept, they operate from the ego and it is difficult for them to relate to or even believe in transcendence. Transcendent beauty, transcendent love. 'What are these things?' he will ask."

Mantri surveys the class and summarizes, "We are here to develop discernment with the aim of identifying and shedding these kleśas so that we can get off this cycle of death and rebirths, so that we can attain Samadhi, or universal consciousness. It is only through our actions that we can do this. Talking won't do. This book here is useless if you don't put into practice. The whole of life is based on the will to know because if we are not aware, how do we know what to work towards?"

A student raises her hand and he acknowledges her. "I think it is our natural state to want Samadhi," she says. "And it is true that the veils, or kleśas, muddy up the light, but as long as we can see even just a little of this light then we can at least have a glimpse of our true nobility as human beings."

"Beautiful what you are saying. We do have the urge for perfection but it is muddied up by our senses, our memories, our attachment to that which does not bring happiness. But I say put being into being and not into ignorance. It is in the reconciling of contradictions that we find truth."

There is a collective sigh as people feel full and are noticeably restless.

"This is our purpose in being here, to help one another and remind each other of the greater goal. Whatever happens out there, it comes and it goes, but the one eternal thing is this," he puts his hand on his solar plexus, "This has been the witness through it all. It was here when I was a child, it was here when I was a young man, it was here when I was a lawyer, it was here when I was an astrologer, it is here still and I am an old man," he laughs. "This awareness, this 'I' is beyond time, it never ages, it is the constant in the cycle of rebirths. It never suffers; it is beyond duality, beyond comparison. When you strip away everything, you will find it because it simply is. This is what we are striving for, to be centred at this level of awareness, to look out from the watchtower, to survey with unbiased reason, detachment, and love. This is what we are learning here. If you have learned something else, you are not doing it right. Any questions?"

Sometimes there are questions, sometimes what questions could there be when the ultimate goal is to still the intellect? Everyone's good. He nods to the young lady who led the opening chant and in a full-throated, slightly out of tune voice, she begins the closing mantra and the class follows in martial unison. Poem looks around, surveying this young group of urban disciples. They love everything yoga, everything India, anything that doesn't smell of that mad corrupt world outside where ideas matter only if you can sell them. They sit in their postures, next to empty mugs, cupcake paper and grape stems, facing their beloved guru as he imbues their effort with spirit. Through him they learn Sanskrit, through him the Sutras and Gita are illumined, through him the light of India is revealed. Poem watches Mantri radiate a silhouette glow that balloons up against the back wall, undulating to the flowing group mantra. He is the filament to this bright blue bulb, filling the front of the room, humble, magical, difficult and wise, the centre of a community looking for their heavenly father, their illumined host, their benefic 9th house. Together they end with, "Ommm… shanti, shanti, shanti-hee."

"Thank you," Mantri bows.

People begin moving, stretching, getting up, talking, a few sit there contemplating. Poem watches the commotion, wondering how anyone can be so chatty after such profound words. He watches Mantri. People approach him reverently, asking questions, bringing gifts, envelopes, the community box makes its rounds and Poem puts in another 20. Everyone seems happy, inspired, there is love here, even among the snoots.

Poem eats his fruit which is now prasad, having been imbued with the rays of his Master. He pockets the cookie, slowly gets up and acknowledges some people. Feeling content, he quietly drops off his plate, heads to the foyer and puts on his shoes. Stepping outside he stares up at the early evening sky. Beyond that blue sea above are endless worlds stretching forever, the closest one an infinity away. Just contemplating it lifts him for it simply is, like rainfall to a cat. Satsang is where the Master recites words of scripture and elucidates their meaning into an atmosphere of love, for certain things can be understood only through the heart. Satsang is a dance with the divine, like cajoling a snake out of its hole, and when it comes it takes you beyond even thought to a place of sublime contemplation and oneness with God.

What a sweet space.

10 BUGS

It is one of those days when you wish it would just rain already. November's cold greyness casts its purgatorial pall, long faces come and go, while Poem and Sonia stand out front smoking with their Doppio Longs.

"I can't believe this is the only joy I have left in the world," Poem holds up his white Starbucks.

"I know," Sonia laments.

They both feel down and out, in the same boat, heading for winter, hating their jobs, working for a gay princess who turned out to be a fraud, and stuck in the middle of the worst economic downturn in two generations. Add to that Poem and Ria broke up, she sold her condo and took off to India indefinitely.

Poem's been running the supplements business for two years and just about everything that was promised to him when he started has evaporated. Marvin, the owner, is always too busy making vacation plans to do anything. He hired Poem under the pretense of a partnership to grow the business, profit share, to build a future here. It was all sunshine till Poem discovered he had to do all the work. He would have left long ago if it weren't for the recession. Now he's hanging on mostly for the car.

"Man, I fucking hate this job," Poem flicks his butt at the ashtray and scratches his wrist. Sonia drops hers into the can and the two enter the building with cups in hand.

Sonia got close to Poem and lived with Ria for a while before moving out west where she lost everything in a business venture. It turned her into a smoker and she eventually bounced back to Toronto to work for Poem, packing vitamins and preparing gift packages. She makes extra cash doing healings on the side but is struggling financially like so many avatars. She is one of the most evolved people Poem has ever known but like an artist she too is at the mercy of an unfeeling world.

They enter the apartment, into the sanitized smell of coated minerals, and head to their separate rooms and duties: Poem running the office, Sonia filling and labeling plastic jars. He gets back to emails and sees a new one from Marvin. He is ordering Poem to insert a few words into the attached Word document with instructions on where exactly to put them into the text. This is typical Marvin stupidity. Poem responds:

In the time it took you to write this to me, you could have done it yourself.

He grins and sends it off knowing it'll only infuriate him but he can't help it. When it comes to Marvin these days, Poem has a bug up his ass. To make it worse, Marvin would really like to be that bug. "I probably shouldn't have sent that," he sighs.

Poem is in a difficult Ketu sub-period and it's been this way for a couple months. He scratches his wrist and reads the next email. Sonia walks in sounding perturbed, "Those two *special* deliveries I had to rush have been sitting there since last week. Is Marvin picking them up or what?"

"He said he would stop by three times now. Man, he avoids this place like the plague."

"That's cuz it represents work to him and he thinks he's an aristocrat."

"Well, he's sorta useless like one. See this pile." He glides his chair over to the stack of folders next to the label maker. "He came in three weeks ago on some new diet or program, deciding he was gonna finally get it together. I said great! It lasted an hour. He had some appointment all of a sudden and that was that. He left the pile right here, for three weeks! I keep reminding him and he's always got some excuse, his health, his niece, some latest treatment, or he's meeting his travel agent. I'm waiting for the day when he says, 'I've fallen and I can't get out of bed!'"

Sonia laughs.

"I think it's about time I moves them aside." He stacks them into the bottom of the closet, noticeably scratching his wrist. Sonia asks him what's up with that and he says, "I got a mosquito bite or something."

"In November?"

"It could be a spider bite."

"Lemme see," she grabs his arms and examines it. "There's three bites here."

"Yeah, I noticed that. Weird, huh?"

"Could be an allergic reaction. Is it red because you're rubbing it? Do you have it anywhere else?"

"I did have a couple here," he rubs his pinkie. "Last week. I don't know what to make of it but it sure is itchy." He rubs it, feeling agitated, and Sonia tells him to stop, he'll just irritate it. "How are you doing with orders?"

"It's busy," she says. "Is Emily coming?"

"I called but she can't. Her grandmother died again."

"Wow, that's like three grandmothers."

"Yeah, I thought she ran out. Listen, I'll help you in production. Just make me a list and let me get through all this," he points to his emails. "But I can't stay late cuz I'm seeing Mantriji at 5:30."

"Oh yeah? Is he better?"

"I hope so. He never cancels like that. I'll see tonight but he sounded different on the phone."

"Well, I wish you a good lesson."

"Thanks, Sonia."

Mantri's health has been deteriorating for over a year. He has a relentless case of tinnitus that prevents him from sleeping. He's been to specialists and as far as Seattle looking for a cure but he's exhausted, getting by on medication, and losing weight. He cancelled their two lessons last week, saying he had conflicting appointments and would be in touch. For Poem it's symptomatic of how his own life's been going.

It started well in May when he began a Mercury sub-period and was offered his first musical gig in four years. This was followed by another and a collaboration, then a possible monthly gig in Niagara on the Lake. He wrote his first song in several years, made excellent progress in his studies with Mantri, the business (including him) was being courted by a rival company, he had a satisfying affair with Ria before she left, and was experimenting with a freaky yoga instructor ever since. Yes, things were looking good, that is, until September 2009 when Saturn entered Virgo.

In India roughly every two and a half years, a large nationwide festival marks the passing of Saturn, the great malefic, from one sign into the next. This time it went from Leo into Virgo, a friendlier sign. "There will be dancing in the streets," Mantri declared.

Leo signifies kings, gold, politics and the speculative urge, while Saturn signifies hardship, outcasts and darkness. Saturn has been in Leo since July 2007, presiding over the fall of Western economies and the election of the first black American President. In Virgo, Saturn creates the impetus to discriminate and organize, to try and put things right, to consolidate, to feed the poor, to serve in promoting the good. But for Poem, Saturn in Virgo, his lagna, means an endless series of obstacles and delays. Gigs got postponed then cancelled, the sale of the business is on hold, Ria is gone, the yoga instructor got possessive, Mantri even cancelled lessons. Everything that looked good started looking bad, and Poem, restless and agitated, has since developed the urge to jump out of his skin. He loves astrology but is finding the more he does, the further he has to go, like a sunset you chase and can never get to. His salvation here is smoke breaks with jolts of caffeine, like a suburban wife speedball. He knows he is peaking, moody, miserable, on edge. He wants to be something else but this comes out instead.

He gets through emails and paperwork and helps Sonia in production. At five he heads out, feeling another day of too much caffeine and cigarettes, and his wrist is raw from rubbing it. He lights up another smoke.

Out front of Mantri's building he parks, collects his stuff, and makes it to his door, which is uncharacteristically shut. He knocks, enters and whoa! The main room is almost bare. The bookshelf is naked. There are no clothes or towels, the mattress is gone; just cardboard boxes and bulging garbage bags. He wonders if he's in the right place. He walks in and sees Mantri standing next to the table, looking like he just ate a tofu canary.

"Are you moving out?"

Mantri laughs. "No. Just doing a little spring cleaning."

"In November?"

"That's right," his gravely voice sounds dubious. "Come," he waves Poem in.

Poem walks curiously through the boxes of books, cleaning supplies and laundry-stuffed garbage bags. He takes off his jacket and sits at the table.

Mantri sniffs at the air, "Did you smoke?"

Poem nods wearily and Mantri looks concerned, "Are you okay, Poem?"

"No, not really. I'm pissed off with my job, Mantriji. I feel like I'm gonna jump outta my head. I need a friggin vacation, man, or something, just to get away from this shit."

"Is it busy? Is he not paying you?"

"It's not that. I'm just so bored and tired of working for this complete moron."

"Poem, I will tell you a little story about peace of mind. You see, there was a certain married couple who had everything but somehow no peace of mind. They were worried all the time, fighting over little things, so they decided to see their guru, thinking he could help.

"When they met him, they explained they had everything they wanted, their children were grown, they had good friends, and so on. But for some reason they felt that true peace was lacking so they asked him what to do. The guru thought a while and said, 'What you need is to get a chicken and let it run free in your house. Then come back and see me next week.'

"The couple was confused, but knowing their guru is a wise man of mysterious ways, they agreed to do so and returned the next week. The guru asked them how's it going and they respond, 'Well, Sir. The chicken is running everywhere, leaving feathers and droppings all over the place. Its clucking keeps us up at night. It certainly has not brought us peace of mind.'

"'Ahh,' the guru says. 'What you must do now is get a pigeon. When you find this bird, let him fly freely in the house, then come back next week and tell me how it went.'

"The couple follows the guru's advice and get now a pigeon. The next week they return and the guru says, 'How's it going?'

"They respond, 'Great honourable, Sir. We have added the pigeon as you advised but to tell you the truth, we still have no peace of mind. In fact it is worse. The chicken runs around stinking up the place, feathers everywhere, and now the pigeon flies from room to room shitting on our furniture. Please advise us.'

"The venerable sage orders them to find a squirrel and let it run free in the house, then come back next week and tell him how it went. The couple look at him discouraged, but knowing the guru is the face of God, they find a squirrel, capture it, and let it free inside the house. The next week they return and the guru asks how's it going?

"'Well, Sir, the chicken runs around fighting the squirrel. The squirrel is getting into the garbage, eating our furniture. The pigeon shits like there's no tomorrow and our house smells like a barn. Sir, though we respect and honour your advanced age and wisdom, we cannot see how this will bring us peace of mind.'

"'Ahh,' the guru says. 'What you must do now is *remove* the chicken. Just eat it if you wish and come back next week and tell me how it went.'

"The couple is relieved and agrees to do so. They return the next week and the guru says, 'How's it going?'

"'Well, it is much better than last week; a little quieter, no clucking, but the squirrel still chases the pigeon and the pigeon still shits everywhere. We still have no peace of mind.' The guru orders them to now remove the pigeon. They happily thank him and say they will return next week.

"The following week they visit and he asks, 'How's it going?' They respond, 'Well, most noble Sir. We have removed the pigeon as you advised and yes, things are very much quieter. There is no longer fighting and shrieking in the house but the squirrel still runs everywhere, we don't know where it is, whether in the garbage or eating our furniture. We respect your opinion, Master. Please tell us what to do.

"The guru orders them to now remove the squirrel and come see him next week. They do so and when they return he asks, 'How's it going?'

"'WE HAVE FOUND PEACE OF MIND!!'" Mantri raises his arms in adulation.

Poem laughs. "Did that really happen?"

"It happens all the time, Poem. People are always going away to lose themselves to this or that, here and there. They go on vacation and get into all kinds of nonsense, have an affair, not realizing that true peace comes not from, how you say, 'shenanigans,' but from returning safely home to where you can finally rest."

"So in other words, there's no reason to leave your house."

"There are only two reasons to ever leave your home: to increase your 'being' or your 'prosperity.'"

"I remember." He sees Mantri's puffy eyes and dry lips. "How are you, Sir? How are *you* feeling?"

"Not good," he looks down.

"Did you see a doctor last week?"

"There is nothing that can be done."

"There's always something that can be done. We just have to find it. Are you being taken care of?"

"When you see my bathroom clean, it means I am good."

In the seven years Poem has known Mantri, he always has some woman, usually a student, who comes by to clean his apartment. He remembers him saying:

> *"If we are to understand astrology in a sophisticated way, we have to first understand that men and women* **fundamentally** *see the world differently. I can go a year without cleaning my bathroom because I am a man, I live here alone. But as soon as one of my female students sees it after only a month, she insists on cleaning it for me. She won't even use the toilet until the entire bathroom is clean."*

"Didn't you say you know what to do but you just don't want to do it?"

"I am fine, Poem. It is God's will," he looks up. "How are you? How is this Ketu antra you are feeling? Ketu in 2nd house, man," he wags his finger, "Watch what you say."

"I'm finding that a little hard, Mantriji. I'm just so pissed at work right now and it's spilling into my personal life. I can't believe I work for this moron! I used to work for a respectable politician."

"The biggest stress for an honourable man is to work for a dishonourable man."

"Well I didn't see you last week, Sir, but I did a little experiment. Every morning for about two weeks, I was waking up feeling totally ill. My lungs were aching, my stomach felt like a rock, and it didn't matter how much I smoked or didn't smoke the night before. I felt awful in the mornings, like I was dying or something. I didn't even swim. So I decided last week to take Friday off. I said fuck it, I ain't going to work, and you know what? I woke up that morning totally fine. No stomach pain, lungs normal. Here I thought I was dying and the whole thing was psychosomatic!"

"Tsk tsk tsk," Mantri clicks his palette. "Business is for money people,

Poem. You like ideas, justice, relationships. You are not 'bottom line guy,' no. This anger is dangerous. It is eating you. Stomach is anger, lungs is fear. You are part of an eye for eye culture out there which only perpetuates violence against one another. You must guard against any anger or cruelty because anger is like fire: it grows so long as there is fuel for it to burn. The boss yells at you at work, you call the wife and next thing you know, you are arguing on the phone. She was fine till you called. Now she is taking it out on her son who wonders where this anger came from. It catches him off guard and makes *him* angry. The husband is not even sure why he got mad with his wife, but now the son is suffering and takes it out on his girlfriend who takes it out on her mother, and now the mother of the girlfriend is making her whole family suffer, and so on. So you see, this boss—who is a dick—is causing misery, not just in his employees but in a whole string of people who are connected and who are all unknowingly feeling the wrath of one man's boss. It is the same with war. People are killed or worse, crippled, and they have to go an entire lifetime with no leg or arm or eyesight is gone. Their family suffers. If he has children, *they* suffer. It affects their upbringing, mental state and view of the world, creating their *own* sense of injustice which can carry on for generations.

"Your mother was born in Poland in the war. She suffered tremendously from what you told me. We can see it in your chart. She was orphaned so she came here. She is all her life going on about money and security, a good job. Her son is smart man, but her fear, her desperation, is passed onto him, and despite all he has going for him, he eats this fear and it is very hard to succeed if one does not take a chance. He may come to resent life, and if he were to have children, *they* would inherit this seed of resentment."

"Wow. You make it sound so hard," he scratches his wrist.

"This is karma, Poem. People do not know their actions. They act but they know not what they affect. They are ignorant, asleep. If they knew the extent of their actions and the great wheel of suffering that continues even generations down the line, they would think, they might even stop, but no. People are not aware of their actions. They are selfish and call themselves altruistic."

"Yeah right, like getting a receipt for charity."

"That's right. This man wants *credit* for his charity."

"And yet, isn't real charity supposed to be anonymous?"

"Charity *is* anonymous. What we have today…" he shakes his head. "Most people who say they are charitable, they seek only to glorify themselves."

"I heard about this one guy, Mantriji, in the news. He's president of some fundraiser for a big hospital downtown and apparently he got a five million dollar bonus raising money for—get this, *charity*!"

"Tsk tsk tsk," Mantri shakes his head.

"This idiot is raising money for charity thinking he's doing good in the world but five million of what everyone gave goes just to his bonus!"

"Tsk tsk tsk."

"And you know what he said?" Poem assumes an official sounding voice, "'Well, I raised more money than anyone else. I *tripled* donations.' Meanwhile, how many people do you think it takes to donate five million dollars? And *they* think they're helping kids with cancer but in fact it's going to this guy's yacht and escort service!"

"This is the way it is, Poem."

"And they still call it charity?! They have the nerve to ask you in line at the supermarket, 'Wanna donate to charity?'"

"No, Poem. This is ignorance. This man thinks he is doing good but only because he is blind. He is glorifying himself thinking he is helping others. His motivation is clear. Any 'charitable' man would say thank you and return the money. To make this kind of bonus means he's already making good money. No, this is not charity. This is a thief. No different than stealing from orphans. He probably has Rahu in his lagna or with lord of the 6th."

"Why Rahu?"

"Rahu is insatiable. He can justify anything. He says he is helping others, but really he is helping himself."

"It's amazing. How much harder do you think he works than the average person to justify that money? Meanwhile, people are doing real charity for nothing because there's no money in real charity."

"Very hard to make money off good deeds."

"Is that why it's so hard to make a living off astrology?"

"You can make money from astrology, but most cases people who do astrology are motivated not by money but by the desire to understand and help others. People who like to own things and have big titles, these people are not interested in studying astrology. They like hearing about themselves, but to study, to master, to apply to help others? No. They are too busy with the tally sheet in their head. How much is this worth? What's the return on this? You do not get rich on the path of righteousness."

"I heard this one guy, this white guru on YouTube. He said it's wrong to make money off Jyotish because it's a spiritual practice and anyone who charges for it is somehow a crook."

"This is total bullshit. B.V. Raman and Krishnamurti were both great astrologers and pious men and they made plenty of money on their craft, writing books, teaching, the Ramans have their own magazine. Bullshit what this man is saying. How does one eat, live, create, educate, raise a family sometimes. All this takes money. This man has no money problems to say such a thing. Probably his father is rich or he married some fat woman."

"But I kind of understand what he's saying, like in an ideal world."

"The world is not ideal, Poem. Success has more to do with ego than talent. If you don't put yourself out there, doesn't matter how talented you are, how good you are, you just won't succeed. You are a Saturn man. Some people are handed success, but you, you must work for it. You cannot sit around wondering how an ideal world should be, comparing yourself to others. You must first love yourself before you love another. You are a diamond, Poem. You just haven't been discovered yet."

"I just see how I pursued music all those years, Mantriji. I was so pure in my motivation. I put my *soul* into it and what did I get? Just a whole lot of dead ends and broken promises," he looks down in disbelief. "I can't believe I didn't make it," he shakes his head. "And then I see people I grew up with starting families, owning a house or a business. They have some sense of accomplishment. Compared to them I'm just a gypsy and then I think, man, has my life been a failure?"

"This is wrong thinking, Poem. You will never win the comparison game. Saturn is transiting your lagna so you feel, how you say, 'low down,' self-critical. It will pass."

"Look, if it wasn't for money, Mantriji, I wouldn't have a problem. I just can't seem to get practical in that sphere of my life, my 2nd house. I went from music to philosophy to friggin astrology like I'm determined *not* to make a living! I'm putting all my time, identity, everything into astrology now, and I've been studying with you for *seven years!* Now I'm realizing the more I know, the deeper I have to go, and sometimes it feels like a bottomless hole. And yet, I keep pouring myself into it and for what?! People want you to fix their life for 20 bucks!" He rubs his wrist and Mantri says,

"Are you okay?"

Poem shows him the rash and Mantri looks alarmed.

"My whole life, Mantriji, I spent in this ethereal realm, letting my heart be the guide. Just like they tell ya, every English teacher: 'Follow your heart!' But when I look back, I see so many missed opportunities because I was distracted with philosophy and astrology and this whole cosmology thing—what the fuck?! I just wanna make a decent living! I just wanna stop worrying about my future! I just wanna stop feeling like I chose a bridge too far! And then I see these friggin morons making all kinds of money doing things that mean nothing! I mean, what's more useless than a stockbroker, and yet, they make all the money!! What the fuck?!"

Mantri leans back as Poem lets it fly, "And then the questions, holy shit, talk about pressure?! These people come for a reading thinking you're God and they're ready to act on whatever you say. I had one woman wanna know if her husband's having an affair. I look at his chart and he's running

Rahu in the 7th house!"

"Tsk tsk tsk."

"And I gotta be the one to tell her?!"

Mantri sighs, remembering his own struggles, why he left astrology, the inherent pressure to always be right.

"I mean, who's an astrologer these days? Who even makes a living off astrology?"

"There are all kinds of people in the world, Poem, including writers and astrologers, and you are one. I think you should teach astrology."

"Sure I can teach, Mantriji, but how much am I gonna make doing that? Again, I should be looking for *real* work. What am I doing this for? Who am I saving? Why are the things I love ruining me?! I HATE MY LIFE!!" He stops, realizing he just popped. He takes a long deep breath and Mantri looks concerned for him. "Sorry, Mantriji. It's been a bad couple weeks."

Mantri rocks in his chair, looking uncomfortable, and locks his fingers together. "Poem…" he says with the tone to listen carefully. "Let us take a break."

"What do you mean?"

"Let's just take a break for a couple weeks. Cool off. I will call you. You just need to… take a break for a while."

Poem is stunned. In the seven years he's been coming here, Mantri never suggested a break. He always lauded Poem's dedication to show up each and every week. Poem looks around the bare room apprehensively, "Are you going to India, Mantriji?"

He smiles. "I will let you know."

"Why can't you just tell me?"

"I don't know yet." He gets up from the table and disappears into the spare room and returns with a cardboard box that he hands to Poem. It is filled with a dozen or so antique hard cover books. "I am cleaning house. Time for something new."

Poem is bewildered, "What's the occasion?"

"I must concentrate on Gita program now. Final liberation."

"No more Jyotish?"

"We will see."

Poem doesn't know what to say. His stomach is in his throat like dealing with a sudden breakup. He examines the books: Star Lore, Medical Astrology, Ashtakavarga System of Prediction, Events & Nativities, Astrology and Jyotirvidya, Cornerstones of Astrology, Esoteric Astrology… "Wow!" he holds up the Esoteric Astrology, "I always wanted to read this one. Thanks, Mantriji. This is amazing!"

Mantri smiles. "We will take a little break and see how it goes. You have lots of reading to do now. Don't forget to complete your book and master this Raman program. *Master* it and you will have siddhi."

Everything seems weird, like something's going on and Poem's not in the loop, like listening to Jimi Hendrix through only the left speaker. He thanks Mantri and sees by his posture that it's time to leave. He puts the books back into the box and offers a donation but Mantri resists, this time for real, and Poem has to pick up his twenty dollar bill.

"Well, Sir..." he feels guilty for his hasty Ketu-esque words. "I guess I will see you at satsang then. Sorry I got so pissed off."

"It's all right. You have lots to read now, Poem. I just ask one thing. When you go, please go down these stairs here," he points around, indicating the south stairwell. "Do not go down the elevator through the front, okay?"

"Sure, Mantriji, whatever you say." He hesitates. "I guess that's it." He gets up, puts on his coat, picks up the box and looks around. The room is barren and Mantri looks worn. He smiles gratefully at his old Master. "Thank you, Mantriji, for everything you've taught me. I'll call you in a couple weeks, okay?"

"That's right, Poem. Thank you. Namaste," his grainy voice sounds tired.

"Namaste, Sir."

Poem walks to the door, biting his lower lip, feeling weird. He steps out into the hall with Mantri following to make sure he goes the right way. Poem looks back to see him watching as he rounds the corner to the stairs. He thinks to call Carmela. *She's close to him. I wonder if she knows what's going on.* He drives leisurely, thinking about his visit, about Mantri's apartment, everything in bags. Mantri looked like he was about to skip town.

Back at his place, Poem goes through the books. They are old, worn, and full of character. He organizes them nicely on his bedroom shelf and stands back to admire his new collection. "Wow... Mantriji's books." He basks in their glory and calls Carmela. "Hey, it's Poem."

She's surprised to hear from him.

"Yeah, yeah, how are you?"

She gets into it as Poem sits, then lies on his bed. "I'm just gonna put you on speaker phone."

"Can you hear me?" she says.

"I hear you just fine. The reason I'm calling is because I was just at Mantriji's. I don't know if you know what's going on but all his stuff is in boxes and bags, like he's moving to Vegas or something."

"What did he tell you?"

"That he's spring cleaning."

"Yeah, Poem," she says doubtfully. *"I'm not supposed to say anything because he's really embarrassed and only a couple people know. He hasn't been taking care of himself because he's so tired all the time. We try to help him keep the place clean but it's*

not easy. You've seen how his bathroom gets."

"Ho yeah."

"The new Super has been giving him a hard time because his neighbour complained that he feeds the squirrels and he had pigeons living on his balcony and it's driving some tenants crazy. So this new guy made him clean it up and promise to not feed the squirrels. Those squirrels are his friends, Poem!"

"I know."

"But this latest thing is the craziest. He has no idea where they came from."

"What're you talking about?"

"Bed bugs."

"What?!"

"Yeah. Please don't tell anyone, Poem. It's so embarrassing. He thinks he got them from his neighbour but the Super is blaming him! He thinks because he's old and Indian."

"Are you serious?!"

"Plus, Mantriji's been living in that building for 30 years. You know how much they could raise the rent if he moves out? The guy's being a real asshole, Poem, pushing him around, threatening to evict him for bugs. I wouldn't be surprised if this was a set up."

Poem can't believe it. "He's like 73 years old and this guy's hustling him?!"

"Oh yeah…! Please don't tell anyone. Mantriji is taking it as a sign that he should leave, go back to India. He thinks he's gonna die soon because he sees no end to the tinnitus or his suffering."

"Man, I can't believe this!"

"Spend whatever time you can with him now because he may be leaving soon."

"Oh shit," he cups his head. "He just suggested we take a break from lessons."

"He's not supposed to have people in the apartment. His Super is trying to quarantine him."

"I wonder if that's why he had me leave through the side entrance."

"Probably. The energy there is really weird right now and it's bugging everyone."

"Hmm… Thanks, Carmela. I really appreciate you telling me. Will you be at satsang this weekend?"

"I will definitely be at satsang this weekend."

"Great. I'll talk to you then. Thanks again."

"Just between you and me, Poem."

"I promise." He hangs up, takes a deep breath and examines his wrist, "Are these bites or is this a heat rash? How would I get a heat rash here?"

He looks at Mantri's books on the shelf and picks out Behari's colourful hardcopy edition of 'Esoteric Astrology,' which looks utterly fascinating. He lies on his bed and examines the pasted cover and cotton spine with some weird spots on the inner pastedown. There's more on the bottom edge. *I wonder what that could be?* He holds it up and suddenly out of the spine wriggles a pitch black insect about the size of a pea. "What?!" He shakes the book down and the little monster falls onto his bed. *What bloody putrid evil thing is this?!* It wriggles on its back and he smacks the book down!! "What the hell is that?!"

He lifts the book and it is still squirming, a tiny round reptile-looking thing, with stubbly legs and an evil head. He smacks it three more times until it is broken and oozing black fluid. He grabs a tissue and picks it up. *Is this a bed bug?* "It's friggin huge!" He's never seen an insect like this before. It looks like some primordial demon from another world. "This is what sucks your blood at night?!" He is thoroughly grossed out. He buries it into a tissue and dumps it into the toilet, feeling the itch on his wrist. "Holy shit!" it dawns on him. "I have bed bugs! HOLY SHIT!!"

He rushes to get all Mantri's books off the shelf, back into the box and out into the cold of his fifth floor balcony. "Holy shit!" he looks at his wrist. "I got bedbugs from Mantriji! What the fuck is this?!" He sits on the bed with his head in his hands. He saw Mantri's apartment, everything in bags. "Oh God."

Esoteric Astrology. 8th house! I pick up this book and look what I found, this secret that lived with my Master.

He frantically drags his futon mattress out into the cold night and kicks the box of books aside. He slams the balcony door shut then stands there looking out the window at his infested bed, his heart racing. *What just happened?!*

He reflects on his visit, on the day, on the last two months. *Why do I have to know that Saturn is in my lagna?*

It only complicates things, forces him to think. He scratches his wrist, wondering how he's going to sleep, where these bugs are, how to get rid of them, whether it's too late to unlearn what he knows.

"This is starting to bug me," he stares out the window, "This is really *bugging me*!"

He puts his hot hands onto the cold glass and mournfully sighs, "What have I done with my life?"

11 NAMASTE

"Hey, Ash. I'm here."
Poem shuts his phone and waits in his idling car out front. It's been three months since he last visited Mantri. He's been attending satsang, working on his book, doing readings, getting by with the business, still no news on the sale. He finally quit smoking to everyone's delight, with Sonia's help, and three days from hell. In it he had to confront Monique buying a house with her new boyfriend, that he never saw Maya again, and that Mantri seemed to be slipping away. Smoking was the thing that helped him bury his issues inside under so many layers of tar, but he could no longer cushion the hurt. He just could not take any more smoke. His hand wanted to but his lungs said no and he was forced through the fire to be reborn, to transcend 15 years of karma. He feels lighter now, less nervy, less of a pariah, and it all came down to a simple change in psychology, the one thing we think is in our control. He sits there relaxed when he would ordinarily have a smoke.

Ashwini emerges from his house and approaches the car. "Hey, Poem," he climbs in. "Thanks again for the ride. My Jag's been giving me nothing but problems lately."

"Must be rough."

"You don't know," he sighs.

Ashwini is a bright, nervy nuclear physicist in his mid-fifties. He wears glasses and has short curly hair. Born in India he became a scientist earning five degrees at UofT before settling into a comfortable position at the Pickering nuclear plant. He was diagnosed with leukemia while still in his thirties and after exhausting Western medicine looking for a cure, he turned to his roots in India travelling there to study Ayurveda. He first encountered Jyotish, like so many people, with a simple reading that challenged his notions of fate and freewill. He returned to Toronto with a suitcase of books, tracked down Mantriji, whom he'd heard of, and spent the next nine years studying astrology while battling cancer and working at the power plant. Now retired he does free readings out of personal interest and to meet women. He has lately been in and out of remission.

"How are you feeling?" Poem looks him up and down.

"Okay, Poem, okay. How 'bout you? Any chickies?"

Poem winces at the antiquated word. "Oh you know, Ash. Beatin' 'em off with a stick."

"Well, as long as they're beating you off too, eh?"

They laugh and Poem puts the car into drive. "Sad day, huh?"

"Depends on how you look at it. I may go visit him in Delhi once he settles in."

"Wow, I'd like to do that."

"Maybe we'll go together."

"Sounds good." They shake hands.

"Turn here."

"Sure, Ash." They merge onto Quebec Ave. "Y'know, it's weird that Mantriji, the one we look to for the answers, couldn't fix himself."

"He *is* fixing himself, Poem, but it means going back to India. He told me he didn't want to but he feels he no longer has a choice. His karma is pulling him back."

"Man, I'm really gonna miss him."

"You studied seven years, right? You're lucky. Some people he wouldn't even take their calls."

Poem smiles at his privileged position. "So what did you get from it, Ash? I mean, I know you were looking for a cure."

"Jyotish is not a cure thing so much as an understanding thing. It's through understanding that you figure out a cure. That's why they use it in Ayurveda, to verify their diagnosis."

"It's interesting how they still use palmistry and astrology in India, whereas I think Western doctors would laugh at this."

"That's because in the West we treat the body, but in India they treat the soul. It's a much older, wiser culture, Poem. People talk about *American* exceptionalism? What about *Indian* exceptionalism? No other culture like it and it really is global now."

"Did you tell your colleagues you studied astrology?"

"Are you kidding?!"

"But you're a scientist. Don't they trust your judgement?"

"Scientists are people, Poem, and they can be complete ignoramuses, believe me. They know math and they know physics but they don't know everything because there are no scientific answers to metaphysical questions. Inference just isn't proof—turn here." He watches Poem make the corner and puts his hand on the dash, "And ultimately the difference between science and religion is the difference between a particle and a wave. *How* you look at it determines what you see."

"Good point."

"Besides, most scientists, when you get a few drinks into them, believe me, they're into this stuff. They just don't admit it publicly. But people get into science because they're curious, Poem, because they wanna know the unknown. You don't get into science to be a skeptic. It's just a tool we use to cut off excessive speculation. But as far as I can see, there are two types of people in the world: those who ask questions and those who don't. I'm in the science camp because I have a lot of questions."

"Maybe the people with no questions already know it because they have faith."

This makes Ashwini think. "Mantri once told me it was *faith* that leads to understanding but I disagreed. I thought it led to ignorance or dogma. But he said there are two types of knowledge: the material and the spiritual. And one can know the material from the spiritual but no way can you know the spiritual from the material. So yeah, the truth is in our hearts and we just rely on our brains to somehow express it." He cranes his head towards some girls on the street, "So what did you get from it? What're you gonna ask him?"

"Well, it changed my life, man," he looks at him. "And I figure I learned a whole new language. So now I'm literate in English, music, *and* astrology. And I guess I agree with Jung and Plato in that there are certain universal archetypes like 'mother,' 'heart,' 'chair,' 'door,' whatever, that manifest in all kinds of ways, but *they* are the building blocks of perception the way an alphabet is to language. I mean, think about it, our intellectual understanding of the world is built mostly on 26 letters that combine endlessly to indicate, and in some cases *create*, just about every abstraction we have!"

Ashwini nods along.

"I mean, astrology is really just a system of divination that uses archetypes to understand and predict human behaviour."

"I like your level of intercourse."

"But you know, Ash, the more I understand and really *feel* astrology, the more it registers like music to me, like it's the same thing, this ethereal language that communicates but is not linguistic. The abstractions are completely different, like colours blended, or notes harmonized. Pythagoras called it the 'music of the spheres' and I've come to really understand that astrology *is* music and what I ultimately want to do is compose with the stars, to be unrestrained by material science or immaterial religion and to expand outward and embrace the whole, to be one and beautiful and to kiss the face of God." He turns to Ash, "For who am I if not a piece of this God?"

"Beautiful. Turn here."

Poem turns onto Raglan Ave. "I personally think Mantriji's head is buzzing with all the petty annoyances of his students who are always asking him what to do or fawning over him like he's Leonardo DiCaprio. Either way, you can kill a man with praise."

"There's a spot. You're right, Poem. What did you say about theatre directors?"

"Oh, because they're not interested in anyone's 'opinion,' they have a tendency to go deaf."

"Right. Well, maybe gurus develop buzzing because they don't wanna hear anymore. You know, the whole time I was studying astrology, part of me was trying to disprove it."

Poem stares at him before turning off the motor. "Okay so, I'm seeing him first and I'll see you—where you gonna wait, in the lobby?"

"Naw, I'm gonna go check out the babes on St. Clair. Just call me when you're done. It's a five minute walk."

"All right." They exit the car and Poem walks into the building as Ashwini heads south. He calls up and gets buzzed in. Coming out of the elevator he sees Jim, a long-time student of Mantri's, standing there with his hands on his face, sobbing. "Hey Jim."

"Hi Poem. God, it's so sad he's leaving us."

Poem puts a hand on his shoulder, feeling himself become emotional, "Yeah… Are you okay?"

"Yeah I'm fine, Poem," he suddenly comes out of it. "I have money so I'm good." He walks into the gaping elevator, says goodbye and the doors quickly shut. Poem is startled like he just hit a wall. He turns and knocks on Mantri's door before entering.

Inside, the apartment is more barren than before with just three suitcases and a travelling trunk. He was expecting the old furnished flat somehow. The ambiguity of it hits him and he realizes it's over. He takes a deep breath, walks into the creaky void and sees Mantri standing next to the clean kitchen table with just two chairs and a knapsack. He is smiling, looking thin, happy to see him.

"Hi, Mantriji, Namaste," Poem approaches and bows reverentially.

"Namaste, Poem. How are you?" They shake hands. The white board is gone with just a rectangular patch of dark yellow wall.

"Very sad, Mantriji. Today is our last day," his voice is choked.

"It is all right," Mantri reassures him. The two men sit in their usual spots, this time without books or paper, just Mantri's knapsack. Poem surveys the stark room with its few odds, like the broken down set for Mantri's cancelled TV show. He looks at his dear old teacher who says, "I have found that you cannot change one thing without changing everything, so I have decided to go to India to prepare myself for the final stage of life."

Poem's eyes well with tears and his sinuses want to cry. Mantri sees this and says, "It's all right, Poem. Everything is changing, always. To keep things still leads only to ill health. I told you so many times the solution is in the opposite house, so I must now listen to my own advice and fix my health by going into the 12th," he points to an imaginary chart. "Final Liberation," he raises his hand.

Poem is awestruck by his attitude, feeling boxed-in compared to him.

"How is work?"

Poem gives him a look that says it doesn't matter. "I've learned, Mantriji, that when it comes to business, a lot of people feel they have a license to lie. And if you want to do really well, you have to be good to some very bad people."

"Ahh," Mantri sighs, sounding satisfied. "I'm so glad, Poem, you finally realize that most people are bullshit. But I will tell you a story. You see, one time, Pundit Nehru, Prime Minister of India, had a rival, what you call 'thorn in his side,' a certain dissident who was always accusing him and his government of corruption. He was quite vocal and determined to make trouble so one day Nehru's advisor asked Nehru what to do with such a man. Nehru said to give him a comfortable government job. The advisor protested, saying why reward him, but Nehru told him to do it anyway. The dissident accepted the job and they never heard from him again."

Poem laughs.

"You can pacify people and that is about all you can do. People are funny. They tell lies all the time and say they are searching for truth. But I have found there are only two things on this Earth that people will lie for: money and sex. That's it. How is this expression, 'All is fair—"

"In love and war?"

"That's it. And there are only two ways to get rich in this world: inherit it or steal it. People spend the whole of their lives stealing from one another and call it business. How can this man be worth 10 billion dollars? Can anyone *earn* 10 billion dollars?"

Poem nods, listening to Mantri's grainy but commanding voice.

"But I have found most evolved people are not on the money program. They are looking for something else. They may have money from luck of birth or through some natural acumen, but they are not *after* money the way people here are."

"Money's like cocaine: when you see someone *really* into it, it's kind of gross."

"But money in itself is not bad. It is just that people have made money into God. People used to do anything, *everything,* for God, for some higher purpose or calling, but this has been replaced by money because there is no faith anymore. With money you know what you have; with God, you may, you may not. But people want to be convinced there is something more. They will pay good money to be convinced there is something more. But when they are *unconvinced*, they turn to money to lose themselves to a godless world."

"Because they ultimately want to believe in God."

"They *do* believe in God, but do they *know* God? This is the question."

"Good point."

"People worship money and they will worship *you* if you have money. But they will curse you if you don't. You see this man?" he motions generally. "This man works for the post office carrying the mail, and yet, he is one of the wisest men in this city. If people knew what he knows, they would beg him to teach them. But to everyone who sees him, he is just an ordinary man, a letter carrier.

"Now *this* man," he thumb-points behind him, "drives a Mercedes-Benz to work and when he gets there, people say 'Yes Sir' and 'Thank you,' not because they like him but because he makes a lot of money and has a big title. But what does he do? Talks on the phone, moves things around on the computer, makes decisions based not on wisdom but on his education, his conditioning, the way a dog is trained. Really, he is doing nothing and he knows even less, yet he will speak quite forcefully on matters he knows very little about.

"Now this man delivering the mail *does* something. He is in service. He may be smart, wise, talented, but he does not want to answer to a dick boss and would rather reflect on philosophy than speculate on the stock market. He knows the market is an invention, invented by humans. It doesn't mean anything. It is not nature, it is not the cosmos. It is a game set up to make the winners rich. He is soft-spoken, polite, unassuming, practically Jesus Christ, and yet when people look at him they see a mailman. They dismiss him because of his uniform, but when you compare these two men against each other, the postman is miles ahead of the stockbroker. In fact, the stockbroker keeps falling back because he is continuously seduced by his wealth. His main hardship is whether he will live up to his father's expectations."

"Helpless like a rich man's child."

"That's right. Things are rarely how they appear on the surface and we should not use money to measure one's worth. What is anything worth? I have seen, Poem, that you can inspire people's passions. This is worth much more than money. You cannot buy this. But somehow you have it in your head that you cannot make money from this, but this is nonsense. You are tall, good shoulders, good-looking man, intellectual man, you can talk, this is your country, you should be prospering, but instead you are talking philosophy, justice. Where did you get this justice idea? This will not make you rich unless you run for politics. Where did you get this idea that there should be justice?"

"I just…"

"Mars in Libra in 2nd house. You feel it is your duty to speak the truth. Libra is the scales, and justice is weighing things, like in commerce. When one is a merchant or lawyer or judge, he is weighing the good and bad, the profit and loss, the commodity and its value, so that money can be made. This is why the rich can buy justice because lawyers themselves want to be rich. You cannot get rich by defending the poor, no matter how righteous the cause."

"But there are good lawyers."

"There are, but how many? How many lawyers will do it for nothing? No. People become lawyers because they want status, money, they want to be important, they want respect, they want their parents to love them. This man became a lawyer because his father made him. So now he lives off the misfortunes of others. You would have made a good lawyer, Poem, but instead you became a poet. This is not easy. Poetry is the highest, most difficult thing."

"And the lowest paid profession."

"That's right. But I must tell you one thing so that you understand your burden and your worth. One time, a father had two rocks he needed to move and two sons to help him. One rock was large and very difficult; the other was smaller, easy to move. He assigned the larger rock to his eldest son who afterwards complained, 'You must love me the least to have burdened me with the heavier task.' But the father said, 'No. I have more *faith* in you.'"

Poem reflects on this as Mantri watches him. "Similarly, you have chosen this path because you have the strength and courage to walk it. Most people go with the flow, get regular jobs, live life, how you say, 'by the numbers,' and they may become very successful in the vein of normal life, but what new thing did he do? Is it just more of the same? You are a creator doing the Creator's work, by making things, poems, songs, ideas; I see how you like to compose. Do not underestimate how noble your life is that you live it in poetry and song. Sometimes people live their entire lives totally wrong because of preconceived notions, but you found this imagination and ability to inspire. This is like possessing gold. Imagination is more important than knowledge. Those who create, not just copy, these people are like little suns, like diamonds glimmering in the depths, beyond the reach of surface riders. You are a diamond, Poem, unseen by a blind world, but a precious diamond, undiscovered, un-owned. Do not short sell yourself."

Poem deflates into his chair and looks out the window, "I know you said never give advice that is not asked but what about people, like family, that you know well, and you *know* their chart, and you want to help but they just don't wanna hear it?"

"There is an expression that says 'a boy cannot be doctor in his own village.' This is because they will always see him as the little boy that was. Even if he is right, even if he is an expert, even if he speaks the undeniable truth, it is very hard for people who are familiar with him to overcome their bias that here is this little boy; we used to change his diapers and now he is telling us what to do? No. Family or no family, most people live in the past and you can enlighten them only so much before they rebel. But I have learned, Poem, the most *important* thing in this life is to let go. Just let it go," he flicks his fingers. "There is no good or bad in the world, it is only us who make it so. Nothing matters as much as you believe it does. The path to liberation is not in what you get but what you leave behind. This I say because you are just like a son..." he becomes emotional and Poem's heart sinks. "All good health, all good things, freedom, love, eternal life, all come to those who are able to let go. It is only attachment, mental, physical, emotional attachment, that imprisons us. Nothing else. We are our own wardens."

The two men are silent when Poem says, "People are always looking for the one way, the *right* way to enlightenment, to heaven, but there isn't any one right way, right?"

"No. There are many roads and one must travel the one best suited for him. You are a thinker. Devotion will not satisfy you. You need answers, even if they are speculations. You would rather have some theory than some faith. For others, answers, logical, rational, intellectual answers, will not do. They may grasp it but they are bhakti people. They need to *connect*, to feel the *pulse* of the Creator. They understand the music but not the words."

"Can I become more devotional?"

"Anything is possible, Poem, but your own experience of life should tell you whether you want this. What do you spend your time doing? Would you rather be in devotional service praying to an altar, cleaning houses for free, chanting Hare Krishna, helping the poor? If this is you, then there are many places you can go to do this. But I know you and you would rather play music or write poetry or study the universe, which *is* a form of devotion, so why bother with *this* devotion if your intent to play music is pure? You can chant all you want. You will not be satisfied until you connect with your heart and overcome all the conditionings of the mind. Until then you will rely on knowledge, intellectual knowledge, to feed your soul."

"But you know, Mantriji, I do like bhakti, that is, I like seeing it and being around when it's going on, but I just don't have the urge to be *in it*, you know? Like, I like *watching* football but I don't wanna play the game."

"You cannot truly understand Krishna consciousness or the equivalent higher order without bhakti, and bhakti is not a spectator sport. What you have in your head cannot become understanding unless you have the 'being' for it to be *transformed*. Then you can be enlightened. But until then you can be only an inspired philosopher, a poet in search of his heart. Sometimes a man finds what he wants and starts weeping because the search is over. He was not looking to find but looking to look," he laughs. "But I see that you do have a strong devotional nature. You have been coming to me seven years, every week. You are a profound astrologer and still do not see it. You have mastered this music-making years ago, composing. This is not easy, this is a gift, and yet, you do not prosper from it," he shakes his head. "How did you master these things? This is all devotion, bhakti to the gyan program. You are a devotee of knowledge, Poem. When you put this into your heart, you will be a god on this Earth."

This is all so profound, the wise encouraging words of his teacher, his sublime father and mystical sage, his guide and cohort in philosophy, his usher to the Gita, illuminator of the Sutras, his source of bad jokes, his springboard of ideas, his bi-weekly inoculation, his inspiration, his wise preceptor and friend, his enlightener during darkness, his explainer of subtleties and unseen connections. He has come to see Mantri's life, the hub of a community, the light of an extended family, the sun to so many eclectic worlds. Who is this magic man? It's like all familiarity has slipped away and Mantri is again a complete mystery, a fount of profound musings penetrating into the source, into the essence of what makes us real, alive, cognitive beings able to step back even from ourselves.

"You know, Mantriji, I used to think I was an artist seeking a spiritual path, but now I see that I am a spiritualist seeking artistic expression. I guess after everything I've learned about the planets and their influence on human affairs, after learning all these subtle and profound laws and permutations of karma, all this incredible analysis and understanding the metaphysical source of someone's personality, destiny and probabilities, I don't know. I wonder sometimes. Is it better to know? To know these things, or does it just stifle every move? Do we analyse to death everything that happens, knowing it has a cause and effect, or are we best to just dismiss it all as meaningless random events and good luck to you."

Mantri thinks a moment. "Is it better to know? This is a good question. I say there is light in this direction and darkness in that direction and my advice is to go where the light is," he smiles. "When we broaden ourselves, when we understand things in a BIG way, then we find comfort in truth because with truth there is no rude awakening. With truth, there simply is. I know you long time, Poem, but not just now, from before, before even this life. We are family from long ago and who knows, you may have been my father in a previous life. I tell you one thing…" he opens the knapsack and shuffles through some papers inside. "Ahh," he pulls out a blue envelope. "This card you gave to me three years ago," he slides it out. "I get cards, notes, all the time, but I never keep anything. But this card…"

Poem recognizes the birthday card. Mantri opens it and reads aloud,

Thank you, Mantriji, for your guidance and light.
You are my spiritual father and dearest friend.

He puts the card down, touched by the sentiment. "Friend," he says. "You wrote that I am your dearest friend. No one has expressed this to me in a long time, in so heartfelt a way. You have shown your devotion to learning and to friendship and for this I say thank you, Poem," he bows Namaste. "When we do this gesture, it means we acknowledge the divine in another. And so I say to you, Poem, that truly you have won my heart. And where you go, part of me will always be with you as it was with my teacher and his teacher before him." He offers Namaste again and Poem does the same, choked with emotion. They smile at one another. "I must see someone now."

"I know. Ashwini. I'll let him know."

"Ahh, good. You'll be at Vidya?"

"Of course."

"Good. I have just one last thing for you." He gets up and walks to the counter where there is a white plastic bag with a Styrofoam container inside: prasad from the temple. Poem can't believe it.

"Thank you, Sir. See you at Vidya."

"Namaste." Mantri stands.

Poem picks up the bag and saunters out, looking one last time at the apartment, no longer Mantri's. *He lived here thirty years. Can you imagine the good fortune of those moving in? They are inheriting the energetic lair of a genuine Master.*

He steps out into the hall and phones Ashwini who's already in the lobby. Poem takes the stairs down and outside into the lot, rounds the building, puts the food in the car then goes for a little walk. Coming back to the row of apartments along Raglan Ave, he wonders about all the everyday lives stacked one on top of another. How many masters live among them? He gets to the lobby of Mantri's building where he waits for Ashwini and the two men reflect on their individual meetings and years of study with Mantri. They have an hour before satsang so they head to an Indian restaurant on Bloor to continue their favourite topic: science playing God while denying his existence.

They end up running late to Vidya where they see people entering the side door. The foyer is piled with shoes and the lobby is buzzing with students, young and old, some faces Poem hasn't seen in years. It's a good-looking crowd and Ashwini is happy to be here. "Is there usually this many babes?" They shuffle in their socks into the main studio packed with disciples. Mantri is sitting in front of his table with a lit candle, fruits and papers. A line of people greet him individually, donating envelopes, chocolates and charms; he has parting words for everyone. Onlookers sit in rows of yoga chairs, some on spare blankets, gabbing, smiling, a few children run around. Plates of fruit and pastries are being passed, tea is poured; the room is festive with anticipation and farewells. All kinds of students, former and present, private and public, are here to pay their respect, say goodbye, good luck and maybe see you in New Delhi. It is a moving scene. Poem stands in the entranceway, watching as people come and go into the lobby and main room. He sees Carmela approaching him. "Hey, how are *you* faring?"

"I'm sad," she droops. "But we're so lucky to have had him, Poem. Where else outside of India are you gonna find a man like him, the real deal, who lived here," she looks around, "apparently for the purpose of touching all these lives. I think he is the greatest man I have ever known, but don't tell him I said that," she elbows him.

"I know what you mean."

"How about you, Poem? I know he became like a father to you."

"Yeah… I'm gonna miss him. It's amazing to know someone like him; I'm still learning from it. Funny how it ended with bugs forcing me out. But I see how it was symptomatic of all the things that were bugging both of us at the time, and like father like son, I think I was the only one he infected," he laughs. "I now feel honoured in a strange way. But yes, it forced a change and probably a much needed disruption and cleanse in my life. I never felt so vulnerable, to go to bed not knowing whether something was gonna be eating me."

"Gross."

"I remember at the time I had this dream that this huge bug the size of a cello had me down and was sucking my blood, it was friggin disgusting. By evening I started developing bites and realized that was no dream! I had witnessed in my sleep, with pinprick local consciousness, this demon creature shredding my skin for the blood. It was horrible."

Carmela winces.

"And if Mantriji's experience was anything like mine, I can see why he took it as a sign to go, that something evil was afoot."

"Were they hard to get rid of?"

"No, but it was a lot of work. And I must say that aside from that big one I found in the book…"

She sticks her tongue out in disgust.

"I never did see another, not even dead. I even considered maybe I just had sympathy bites for my teacher, like stigmata."

She laughs and Poem notices a bodacious, middle-aged Indian woman enter the side door.

"Hey, there's Prema," Carmela says.

"Prema?" he recognizes the name.

"Mantriji's sister! I'll be back." She darts off into the main room, leaving Poem to watch this curvaceous woman slide off her high-heeled boots and slink inside. He heard that Mantri has a sister but they've never met. She looks at him through incredibly green eyes and he nearly tips over.

"Are you Prema?"

"Yes I am," she smiles flirtatiously. "And you?" her accent is lovely.

"I'm Poem. Nice to meet you, Prema."

"Oh you're Poem?! Yes, Mantri talks about you. Nice to meet you too," she shakes his hand warmly.

"Are you Mantriji's sister?"

She rolls her eyes. "He says that but we're not related. I've just known him a long time."

This is not at all what he expected when he heard Mantri had a sister. This mature goddess was surely a sex symbol in her time. She's a sex symbol now! Who is this mysterious, full-figured deity, with flowing wild hair, gypsy scarf and silver-hoop earrings? Her striking, magnetic eyes are like pools of hot springs begging him in. "What do you do, Prema?"

"I sell carpets."

"Are they flying carpets?"

She laughs. "No, just regular carpets."

"Oh. Are you on the spiritual path too?"

"Not like he is."

"Are you sad he's leaving?"

She reflects, "I see how happy he is to be going, so yes, I am sad for myself but happy for him."

Carmela returns and the two beautiful ladies greet one another, talking like old friends. Poem watches, in awe of it all, by Mantri's huge life and all the things he doesn't know, that he will never know about this brilliant and very human man. Prema tells Poem it was nice to meet him and she slinks inside. He watches her, shaking his head.

"I remember the day you two met," Carmela says. "I can't believe that was seven years ago, Poem. You really took it up big time. Everyone knew you were his favourite and it seemed like such an unlikely match, you know, the guru and the gangster," she laughs. "I bet you learned a lot from him."

"He changed my life."

"Any regrets?"

"Hmm..." he thinks a moment. "I should have went for the money?"

She laughs and he beams a huge smile. "I can't help it," he says. "I'm just made this way."

She gives him a knowing look and the two head into the main room and sit among the students settled in. Mantri is chatting with people in the front row. Everyone is friendly today, even the uppity ones. There are smiles all around and for the first time Poem feels among family.

Mantri sits quietly at his table, eyes closed, collecting his thoughts. It's the class's cue to settle down. There is no announcement, everyone simply knows. In the sudden tranquility, Mantri opens his eyes and cues a woman in the front row. She begins a powerful solo mantra to the Bhagavad Gita and the class is still, listening to the Sanskrit phonetics, feeling the meter and purpose of their call. Everyone joins in on the Om shanti part and after a brief silence, Mantri holds up the Gita and says,

"In this book, Krishna tells Arjuna that this time too will pass, and similarly, all things must pass. I want to thank everyone for coming today. Today is a special day for me, for today I get to go home."

There is already sobbing and the atmosphere turns sad and restless.

"It is all right," he assures everyone. "I have been here over thirty years and I have taught many students in many places. I have known many people from many walks of life. What I see is people are hungry for truth, but what is truth? I remember someone said if you want to lose your faith, make friends with a priest." There is laughter. "Similarly, we should not look to anyone for the answers because everyone here already has the answers within. This is not feel-good New Age program I am talking. This is the atma of your existence, the fundamental core of your being. This is the same as Brahma, which is the all-pervading Holy Absolute, without attribute, the one true thing that links us all like beads in a mala.

"You see, what happens is people are restless and they have so much to choose from. They think what they were born into is no good. They want a change. But if you are digging a well, looking for water, you must dig deep, you must remain in one place. If you start digging and someone says another spot is better and you start digging there and someone else tells you *this* spot is better and you start digging *there*, you will never find water. You will just have a bunch of shallow wells.

"What is preventing us from sticking with one thing is our changeability. We are changeable because we don't know our dharma. As soon as we discover our true selves, we discover our permanence and life becomes easy, all decisions are made. But without dharma, very difficult, always changing. Even if your dharma is to be a servant, better a happy servant than a miserable boss, for when you are not in dharma then you are in misery. But when you live your dharma, you become virtuous," he pats his chest, "regardless of what you do. Virtue has nothing to do with ideology. It is about character and being true to yourself. Virtue comes from an intelligent heart."

There is muffled sobbing and blowing of noses.

"Some say we are just animals here to reproduce, but I say our duty is to serve and seek the Truth. Schools today no longer educate the heart with music and the arts; they are programming human machines to 'produce' within a system. So much of what you think is yours is just conventional thinking," he twirls crazy to his head, "but this does not suit you. It only suits the ones who run the machine. You may find comfort in convention the way one finds comfort in sleep, and if that is the case then this program," he picks up the Gita, "is not for you. We study this book not to be comfortable but to make ourselves *uncomfortable* and alert, to see the world as it is. To be conventional is not honest, it is merely conforming, like water, and this only works against dharma. For all our actions, all our intentions, all our efforts must be done deliberately, with awareness, if we are to know ourselves, if we are to *free* ourselves, if we are to fulfill our dharma. But it takes work and discipline and a broad mind to understand and conceptualize our connection to the cosmos." He smiles. "Some say we know more about the surface of the Moon than we do the bottom of the sea, but this is because we are outward looking, away from ourselves, not understanding that when we look at the night sky, we are looking at ourselves from the inside.

"When people don't know truth, it is easy for them to fall to superstitions and fatalism like astrology. We see that it works, but how much better off would we be without astrology? When people try to master something, they sometimes do more harm than good because *until* they master it, they are not perfect. So every person they help along the way is helped imperfectly. But this is how it is. This is why it is always best to trust the divine hand when rendering judgement," he raises his arms in praise. "All my life I have been surrounded by astrologers. This man is an astrologer," he points to various students, "*This* man is an astrologer. This lady is a gifted astrologer. This lady here is a learned astrologer." He points to Poem, "This man is a *profound* astrologer."

Poem is secretly delighted and bows. He understands now that astrology is not in the razzle-dazzle but in the understanding of and helping others.

"This is my samskara, to be with those who seek meaning in the light of the stars. This Jyoti program is light, and light is in the heart. To be a Jyotishi is to live from the heart and to reflect the divine light the way a diamond reflects the Sun, and to have faith that it will always show us the way."

The class is silent and Mantri points his finger, "We must seek to rise above planetary influences, to liberate ourselves from this maya, this material realm, to be one and eternal, self-determining and whole. When we put too much in others, we lose ourselves." He surveys the class: different ages, races, disciplines and nationalities. All with one thing in common, that he touched them with Vedanta, with the Sutras, with Jyotish. The inspiration he passed to his early students has sired Jyotishis all around the world. Now he sits there regally, weak with age, strong in spirit, a shepherd about to leave his flock.

"Sometimes," he extends his hand, "when you try to point to something, people will *not* look at what you are pointing to, but like a dog they will look at your finger. They will see the pointer but not the pointed." The class laughs. "It is like Jesus Christ; he tried to show us the way but instead they made him into a God. He is pointing to a higher reality and everyone's looking at his finger," he twists his hand. "You must learn to do this yourself, to not depend on others, to stand by your own convictions and understanding.

"In this place of maya, of worldly illusions and sensual pleasures, it is easy to confuse things, to be fearful of things that are not what they appear to be. This is how it works." He clears his phlegmatic throat. "This man needed to go into the forest one dark night because of this, what you call, 'outhouse program.'" The class laughs. "But when he got to just the edge of the wood he saw a snake in the grass and was afraid to go any further. He left and came back but the snake was still there and he had to go badly. His brother came carrying a flashlight and saw the man standing there in agony with his legs crossed. He asked him what he was doing. The man said he would like to use the outhouse but he is afraid of a big snake waiting on the edge of the wood. The brother asked him where it was and the man pointed, so the brother went to investigate and returned shortly holding a long piece of rope. 'Is this what you're afraid of?' he asked. The man now felt ashamed for his mistake, for he thought the rope was a snake."

There is a collective sigh to yet another variation on a well-known parable.

"Similarly, we look at the world and see not what is but what we want to see. Sometimes we see the rope and not the snake and we get bitten. Other times we see the snake and not the rope and we stifle ourselves. The deciding factor, according to me, is light. Under the light of knowledge, he would have seen the rope, but in the darkness of ignorance it is difficult to tell. The world needs more light and in this case the brother is a Jyotishi for having dispelled the darkness."

He surveys the class, looking every one of them in the eye, then looking at the Gita he says, "We have learned many times that there are two paths you can walk in life. You can walk the path of pleasure or you may walk the path of liberation. But I have been around a long time and if you ask me, there is only one thing that truly matters in this world, and that is L-O-V-E: Love. We may seek pleasure and that is okay; Krishna is a loving man," he blinks coyly and a few girls laugh. "But desire can prevent you from seeing love, true *unconditional* love."

He takes off his reading glasses. "I was asked once to choose, do I want love or do I want wisdom or do I want material wealth? I chose love because wisdom does not guarantee love or wealth. And wealth does not guarantee wisdom or love. But *through* love one can gain wisdom *and* wealth."

Poem sees Mantri's shadow on the back wall expand and flicker into a marine blue auric shine that pulsates like a psychedelic lightshow. It radiates warmth and love, surrounding Mantri in a ring of otherworldly splendour. His body glows, his face beams, his energy field seems to crackle. Poem looks about the room to see everyone transfixed by the shiny words of their Master. Mantri cues a woman in the front row who reads:

"Fear not, Arjuna, for what is not real never was and never will be.
What is real always was and cannot be destroyed."

Mantri nods, allowing time for the verse to sink in. "I have found that all suffering comes down to three things: attachment, desire, and fear. Understand that fear is the *opposite* of love. When you fear, it is because you have lost your faith, and faith comes from the heart. I tell you it is all Love. Everything comes down to Love. What Krishna tells Arjuna here is very simple. There is and there is not, and so long as we are rooted in what is, then no matter what we do, or where we go, or whom we are with, or whom we might miss, we are always at home."

Poem feels his heart rise into his throat, filling his chest with euphoric hope. The top of his head feels like it is broadcasting light. Seeing his teacher in front, knowing he is leaving, it hits him, this feeling in his heart. He is knock-down, head-over-heels in love with this man, the way a teenaged girl has a high school crush. Poem's lungs seem to exhale a silvery thread of rotating blossoms that illuminate only Mantri and him as the rest of the room becomes a group silhouette, a dark universe to binary suns, disciples of light and love, father and son.

Mantri asks if there are any questions. Several people raise their hands—an unusual occurrence—and when he calls on them, they thank him profusely, lavish him with praise, and wish him well with his new life in New Delhi. Mantri beams effulgently, taking in the loving, encouraging words of his students who are deliberately protracting their last satsang together. With every question and answer, the group grows restless and giddy until Mantri looks at his watch and says, "If that is all, then let us complete this program." He cues a young lady in the front row who starts to chant and the class follows.

"Om asya sri argala stotra mantrasya visnur ṛṣih…"

Poem listens to the choir of Sanskrit voices chanting 'Praise that Unfastens the Bolt,' an invocation to the Great Goddess of the Chandi Paṭh. It is loose and soulful and even the novices join in, reading off their neighbour's page, singing the last sacred hymn. It ends with, "Shanti, shanti,

shanti-hee."

There is a long profound silence before Mantri says thank you and the class ends.

Poem sits back and watches the students break, piling their blankets and plates, stretching, stacking booklets and cups. A crowd gathers around Mantri and people stand aside as the owners of the studio, a lovely Scandinavian couple, present him with their personal dedications. There is smiling and picture-taking and a grateful and overwhelmed Mantri chuckles along benevolently, shaking hands, kissing children, accepting the occasional awkward hug. He is touched, everyone can see. He nods to his young assistants who help him collect his stuff and they form into an entourage that clears a path. Everyone walks out to the lobby and there is crying among the ladies. The owners are especially sorry to lose a genuine guru. Both sadness and elation reign as Mantri slowly makes his way through the lobby and out the foyer. Everyone wishes him well as Poem follows him out into the cool late afternoon. Carmela asks if she can hitch a ride and Ashwini enthusiastically invites her along. Andrea joins them as well. Everyone gets into their respective rides and a four car convoy makes its way up to Eglinton, to Allen Road, to the 401 and onto Pearson International Airport.

Poem is mostly silent as the others go on about Mantri with personal anecdotes and speculations on whether he'll be able to endure an Indian summer. They've known him almost 20 years. There is laughter and tears, discussion of the sutras, planets, and hopes for the future. They are optimistically heading into the oblivion of their teacher's permanent absence and it feels right in a transformative way. It feels like something lifting.

At the airport they park and rendezvous with the others, meeting in front of the Air India counter, a dozen or so people. Poem is not familiar with everyone so introductions are given. They are all former students of Mantri who have since gone their way. Mantri jokingly introduces one middle-aged woman as his 'future life girlfriend' and everyone laughs, revelling in their teacher's buoyant joy to be going home. They see him through the line, chatting, keeping company, showing support; this 74 year old Master heading back to the country of his birth after 40 years of passing it onto the West. He is returning to the source, to be fed and not the feeder, to no longer be needed or depleted, to suckle at the bosom of Mother India, his childhood home, and to walk the streets of his rambunctious youth.

Bags checked in, he has his ticket and passport in hand, everything is done for him; his connection waits in New Delhi. They walk him over to the gate, to the frontier line between Toronto and the rest of his life, the departure lounge for all time. He turns to look at them, solitary and bewildered, this handsome babe of a man against the ultra modern Terminal 3, an anachronism of wisdom in this world of technology. This man of ancient India in his kurta and winter parka, moving stiffly, looking tired and content. He embodies a distant time when humans were in harmony with the Earth, with the cosmos, and with Truth. How stark, these airport lights, this glass-skinned steel-ribbed cathedral of international travel with its procedures and modern marvels. Here stands a sage in the belly of a technological whale, willingly swallowed so he can return home.

Mantri tells Prema how much he fears flying and Prema suggests he break his vow of no alcohol. "Just for today," she says. "Think of it as medicine."

"That's right," he mumbles. "Under the right circumstance, anything can be medicine."

Two women greeters at the gate welcome him. Poem steps forward and says to them, "This man is the most illuminated human being I know. If you help him, you will surely be doing God's work."

They smile and seeing it in Mantri's kind face, one nods and offers to show him the way. Mantri winks at Poem to confirm his good luck with the ladies and everyone seems relieved. He stops, gives one last look and bows a heartfelt Namaste. His students bow back, "Namaste."

He is ushered into the Departure lounge and they watch as he disappears into the crowd, like a diamond dropped into the sea. In some ways it feels like the end of the world. Everyone looks at everyone else and they solemnly walk back to their cars, some already making dinner plans. Poem feels a sudden lightness enter his heart, an internal sense of newness and rebirth. He realizes this is not the end but the beginning. He stops, turns around and bows one last time, "Thank you, Mantriji. See you in the next life."

EPILOGUE: GURU LOKA

"Here's the problem," Poem looks at the client's chart. "Transiting Saturn afflicts your natal Venus."

She knew there was something wrong with her Venus.

They are in Poem's sunny apartment at the kitchen table next to a whiteboard. Posters of Hindu deities adorn the walls. He proceeds to weave the various significations of the woman's chart into a simple, cohesive, even poetic exposition of current life issues relating mostly to her 10th house.

She listens and sighs, "Well, you were right last time."

"What did I say?"

"That my sister would get a promotion."

"Oh?" He looks at the chart, "That's good."

"It's great because now I can hit her up for that loan you promised."

"Riiight," he doesn't remember. "But I can see right here," he taps the 11th, "why that would happen!" he laughs. "Let me put it this way: your younger sister's good fortune is potentially *your* gain."

Poem has quit his job to work on his book. He's doing readings, has a couple students, not enough to make a living but it's okay. By helping others, you attain your own salvation.

"You know that ritual thing you told me to do?" the client says. "Where I fill a glass with shower water before I bathe and put it in the garden."

"It's to develop a ceremonial relationship with water."

"Well," she twists her face. "I sort of did it my own way: instead of fetching the glass after my shower and pouring the water back into the tub like you said, I just poured it into the garden on my way out to work."

"Well, you did it, how you say, 'lazily.' But better to do something imperfectly than not at all. Strength comes through effort."

"But you know what happened? After pouring the water into that same spot, after only a week I noticed it unearthed a small silver-hoop earring, which I must have lost gardening in the spring."

Poem sits back, intrigued.

"My sister gave me these," she touches an earring, "for my birthday. I pretty much lost one the very next day." She looks down and smiles like a witness to magic. "Finding it reminded me how lucky I am to have her, how much I love her, that like these earrings, we belong together."

"You have Moon in the 3rd. Moon rules silver while sitting in the house of younger sibling."

"Hmm. Well I phoned her up and told her the story. We got to talking and… we mended our relationship. She didn't know I lost the earring, only that she never saw me wear them. It may sound petty but it's actually pretty important, the little things."

"Moon is very sensitive and sometimes vain. She didn't feel appreciated."

"That's exactly what she said."

Poem nods.

"So what's this about my Venus?"

"Well… Saturn is your obstacle right now, but *it will* lift. Just give it a couple years. This is a good time for you to help others while planning ahead. Just avoid expectations. Something will work out, something you don't see now, but work towards it so when it *does* take off, you're better situated on higher ground."

"Hmm," she looks at the minimalistic chart, wondering how Poem does it. "Do you really think it's all in the planets?"

"I think the planets are like people you have to appease, like a cranky grandma who just needs some attention. They're really the most fundamental archetypes in our world and each planet's influence extends throughout. To know how to use these planetary frequencies is helpful when approaching life spiritually. After all, the stars impel, they do not compel. We still have freewill."

She smiles then gives him a skeptical look, "What if I don't believe the same things you do?"

"You can believe what you want to believe. I *know* the mind is powerful. And there is strength in believing, there is no strength in not believing."

"What if I just believe in myself?"

"It's good to believe in yourself. Everything is karma so very important to know your dharma. When you find what you're meant to do, there is no resistance."

She gives him a long look of consideration. "You're very wise, you know."

He smiles. "I had a good teacher."

APPENDIX 1: SANSKRIT, UNFAMILIAR NAMES, WORDS & TERMS

Antra	In the dasa system, the third level down; sub-period of a bhukti
A priori	Philosophical term: something existing in the mind prior to personal experience with it
Ascendant	The astrological sign on the eastern horizon at any given moment; referred to as 'the lagna'
Astral light	The unseen vibrant colours of the spiritual world
Atma	Individuated spirit; the soul
Ayurveda	An ancient Indian holistic tradition of healing
Benefic	A positive influencing planet
Bhagavad-Gita	A famous ancient Indian scripture
Bhakti	Active devotion
Bhukti	In the dasa system, the second level down; sub-period of a dasa
Bindi	Ornament worn on the forehead to signify a third eye
Bobbitt	John Wayne Bobbitt was a philanderer whose girlfriend famously cut off his penis
Book of Tables	Tables of Houses: used to determine the degree of an ascendant (lagna); based on latitude
Braha	James Braha, an author and Western practitioner of Jyotish
Brahma	The Creator: one of the trinity of Gods in Hindu philosophy
Brahmin	The educated, religious cast of India, or of any culture
Buddhi	The intellect; Mercury
Chandi Paṭh	A book of chants to the Goddess; 'Paṭh' is pronounced 'Pat'
Chart	Astrological chart; the natal chart
Dasa	In the dasa system, the first level; a major period; a period of time. Pronounced 'dasha'
Dasa lord	Planet that rules a particular dasa; i.e. Saturn dasa
Dasa sequence	The fixed sequence of planets in the Vimshottari dasa system
Dasa system	A system of timing used in Jyotish; there are several dasa systems
Deposited	When a planet is placed in a particular house, it is said to be 'deposited' in that house
Dharma	Life purpose
Doppio Long	Double espresso you get at Starbucks
Dual sign	Signs with a dual nature: Gemini, Virgo, Sagittarius, Pisces
EI	Employment Insurance
Ephemeris	A record of the daily motion of the planets
Fallen	When a planet is debilitated (weak); the opposite of exalted or strong
Ghee	Clarified butter used widely in India
Gita	Bhagavad-Gita
Gap-shap	Gossip
Guna	Mode of behaviour; quality or attribute of which there are three: Tamas, Rajas, Sattva
Guru	Spiritual teacher; Jupiter
Gyan	Jñana (pronounced 'Gyan' by some): knowledge
Hart	Hart de Fouw, an early student of Mantri's who has authored books on Jyotish
Helen Keller	A famous author and advocate who overcame blindness and deafness in order to communicate

House	A fixed portion of the sky; a state of being; there are 12 houses in astrology
Jyoti	Light, brightness
Jyotish	The science of light; Vedic astrology; pronounced "Jo-tish"
Jyotishi	A practitioner of Jyotish; an astrologer
Karaka	Natural indicator; each planet is a karaka (indicator) for certain things
Karma	The law of cause and effect
Ketu	South node of the Moon; bottom half of the serpent
Kleśa	A mental affliction of the mind carried over from a previous life
Krishna	The Supreme Lord in Hindu philosophy
Krishnamurti	Professor K.S. Krishnamurti; famous Indian astrologer and author
Kshatriya	The warrior in the caste system
Kurta	Traditional Indian-style men's shirt
Lagna	The ascendant of an astrological chart; considered your astrological sign in Jyotish
Lagnesh	The planet ruling the lagna; lord of the lagna
Loka	World, plane of existence, parallel universe
Lord	The ruler of an astrological house
Lord of lagna	Ascendant ruler; ruler of the 1st house; lagnesh
Malefic	A negative influencing planet
Manas	Mind
Mantra	A Sanskrit phrase repeated for a desired effect; incantation
Mantri(ji)	Mantri means 'counsellor;' 'ji' suffix is added as a term of respect, like 'Sir'
Masala Dosa	Crepe stuffed with spiced potato
Maya	Illusion
Mrigashira	The 5th Nakshatra: a dear's head; indicates Mars dasa
Mula	The 19th Nakshatra: the root; ruled by Nriti, goddess of destruction
Nakshatra	Lunar Mansion; there are 27 lunar mansions
Namaste	A gesture of respect done with hands in prayer position and a slight bow. It means 'I acknowledge the divine in you'
Natal chart	Astrological birth chart
Native	The subject of an astrological chart; client
Natural Zodiac	Aries lagna because the numbers of the signs match the numbers of the houses
Nodes	Rahu/Ketu: points where the orbit of the Moon cross the ecliptic; considered shadow planets
Papa Grows Funk	New Orleans funk band
Patañjali	Sage and author of the Yoga Sutras
Phala Deepika	13th Century Sanskrit scripture on Jyotish
PLED-C	Parkdale Liberty Economic Development Corporation; pronounced 'Pled-C'
Prakriti	Material world
Prasad	Blessed food from the temple or as a result of satsang; food imbued with spirit
Prashna	Horary astrology; using the chart of the moment to understand an event or make a prediction
Precession	Precession of the Equinoxes; a 26,000 year Earth cycle (wobble) in relation to the stars
Rahu	North node of the Moon; top half of the serpent

Rajas	One of the three Gunas; it signifies passion, action, energy…
Raman	Dr B.V. Raman; famous Indian astrologer and author
Rishi	Master; teacher; sage
Rising sign	The sign on the eastern horizon; the ascendant, lagna, 1st house
River Djallon	A mythical river in Africa that joins *all* rivers, symbolizing a common source
Robert Svoboda	An early student of Mantri's who has authored several books on Jyotish
Running	To experience the effects of a particular planet during its dasa
Samskara	Subliminal impressions
Satsang	Meeting of good people to discuss scripture and truth; led by a guru
Sattva	One of the three Gunas; it signifies illumination, purity, goodness…
Shakti	Strength
Shanti	Peace
Shiva	The Destroyer; one of the trinity of Gods in Hindu philosophy
Shudra	Servant caste
Siddhi	Miraculous ability or skill
Sidereal Zodiac	To do with the stars; the actual position of planets against the stars; not the Tropical zodiac
Sivananda	Famous guru in India
Solar plexus	Located between the rib cage and naval, it signifies power and will
Sri	Blessed or Holy; prefix to a personal name, i.e. Sri Mantriji
Sutra	A verse of scripture; aphorism
Svabhava	Fundamental Nature
TA	Teaching Assistant
Tantra	The oldest known writings of India on rituals and various spiritual disciplines
Tamas	One of the three Gunas; it signifies inertia, darkness, laziness…
Tapas:	Austerity
TO	Toronto, Ontario
Transit	When a planet is traversing a particular sign
Tropical Zodiac	Symbolic zodiac; precedes 1° every 72 years; it is currently 24° off the Sidereal Zodiac
UofT	University of Toronto
Vasana	Desire from a previous life; unfinished business
Vata	Air element
Vedas	The ancient treatises of India
Vedanta	The culture and study of the Vedas
Vidya	Vidya Institute, where Mantri taught classes (satsang); Vidya means 'knowledge'
Vishnu	The Preserver; one of the trinity of Gods in Hindu philosophy
Vimshottari	The most widely used dasa system in Jyotish
Die Walküre	A famous opera by Richard Wagner; known widely for its 'Flight of the Valkyrie'
Yoga Sutras	The prime ancient treatise of Yoga, authored by Patañjali

APPENDIX 2: NATAL CHARTS

The natal chart consists of 12 houses and 12 signs. The houses are fixed, that is, the top diamond is always the 1st house followed counter clockwise by the 2nd house, 3rd house, 4th house, and so on. The numbers in the chart refer to the signs and not the houses. The first example is Aries lagna, known as the Natural Zodiac because the numbers of the signs and houses coincide. Taurus lagna has '2' in the 1st house indicating the second sign of the zodiac, Taurus.

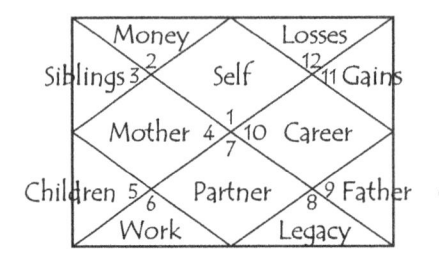

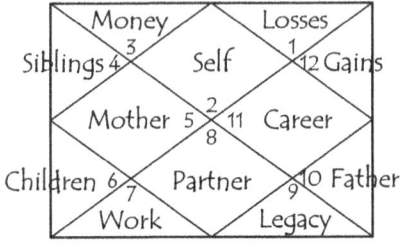

```
┌─────────────────────────┐   ┌─────────────────────────┐
│       Money  │  Losses  │   │       Money  │  Losses  │
│          2   │   12     │   │          3   │    1     │
│ Siblings 3 × Self × 11 Gains │ Siblings 4 × Self × 12 Gains │
│       Mother 4 × 10 Career   │       Mother 5 × 11 Career   │
│              1                │              2                │
│              7                │              8                │
│ Children 5 × 9 Father        │ Children 6 × 10 Father       │
│          6   │   8           │          7   │   9           │
│       Work   │  Legacy       │       Work   │  Legacy       │
└─────────────────────────┘   └─────────────────────────┘
```

If the 1st house has 6 inside, this signifies Virgo lagna because Virgo is the sixth sign of the zodiac. 10 in the 1st house would be Capricorn lagna because it is the tenth sign of the zodiac, and so on. In the above examples, we see that for Aries lagna, Scorpio (the eighth sign) rules the 8th house of legacy, whereas for Taurus lagna, Sagittarius (the ninth sign) rules the 8th house, thus the native's' experience of 8th house matters will differ accordingly.

Signs are designated by their number. Planets are designated by their first two initials.

1. Aries	Su Sun
2. Taurus	Mo Moon
3. Gemini	Ma Mars
4. Cancer	Me Mercury
5. Leo	Ju Jupiter
6. Virgo	Ve Venus
7. Libra	Sa Saturn
8. Scorpio	Ra Rahu
9. Sagittarius	Ke Ketu
10. Capricorn	
11. Aquarius	
12. Pisces	

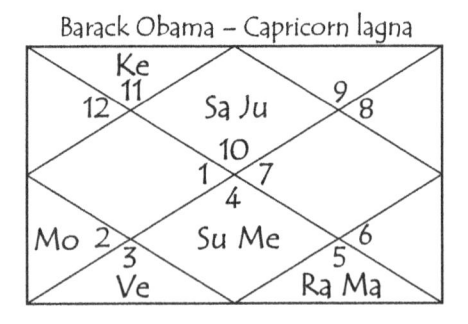

Barack Obama – Capricorn lagna

```
┌─────────────────────────────┐
│         Ke                  │
│         11                  │
│    12 ×  Sa Ju  ×  9        │
│                    8        │
│              10             │
│           1 × 7             │
│              4              │
│   Mo 2 ×  Su Me  ×  6       │
│       3              5      │
│         Ve       Ra Ma      │
└─────────────────────────────┘
```

Planetary significations (karakas):

Sun	Soul, father, authorities…
Moon	Mind, mother, happiness…
Mars	Force, strength, conflict…
Mercury	Intellect, speech, skill…
Jupiter	Wealth, luck, knowledge…
Venus	Love, harmony, comforts…
Saturn	Hardship, obstacles, experience…
Rahu	Serpent's head, insatiable, ambitious…
Ketu	Serpent's tail, mystical, outcast…

APPENDIX 3: JYOTISH vs. WESTERN ASTROLOGY

The main difference between Western astrology and Jyotish are the two zodiacs. Western astrology uses the Tropical zodiac which is based on the seasons. It is a symbolic zodiac because the signs are projected onto the sky rather than being fixed to the stars. Jyotish uses the Sidereal zodiac which is fixed to the actual stars that make up the signs.

Because the Tropical zodiac is Earth-centered, it always aligns with the seasons, therefore the Sun always enters Aries on March 21st, the Spring equinox. Because the Sidereal zodiac is star-based, it is subject to the Precession of the Equinoxes, a slight wobble in the Earth's rotation around the Sun with a periodicity of roughly 26,000 years. This means the Sidereal zodiac shifts one degree of arc (of 360 degrees arc), or one full day, every 72 years. Currently the Sun enters Aries not on March 21 but on April 13. In 72 years from now the Sun will enter Aries on April 14; add another 72 years and it will be April 15, and so on. The two zodiacs were last aligned somewhere around 300AD. The Precession of the Equinoxes is what defines the great astrological epochs; i.e. 'Age of Aquarius.'

Because of the difference between these two zodiacs (currently 24 degrees apart), planets in the first two thirds of a sign in Western astrology are placed in the preceding sign in Jyotish. Example: someone born August 4th considers himself to be a Leo. In the Tropical zodiac his Sun is 12 degrees Leo, but in the Sidereal zodiac it's actually 19 degrees Cancer. This may cause some initial consternation to the novice but keep in mind that the Sun is only one part of an astrological chart. Besides, in Jyotish 'your sign' is the one rising on the ascendant at the time of your birth (your lagna); it is not your Sun-sign like in Western astrology.

APPENDIX 4: PROVERBS

There are many proverbs quoted in this book, i.e. 'when the student is ready, the teacher will appear,' that are part of the vernacular of spiritual teachers and seekers. Many are variations on scripture (Bhagavad Gita, the Bible, etc.) and many are difficult to attribute. Mantri would recite these truisms freely and I do so as well. What follows are quotes I use without attribution in the text, which I can attribute here:

The genie joke at the beginning of Act 1 was told to me by Timothy Stock, Professor of Philosophy at the University of Toronto. I don't know where he got it from.

"To be loyal to one would be to deny all the rest." From Mozart's opera <u>Don Giovanni</u>; libretto by Lorenzo da Ponte.

"I don't know where you got your education from, but I suggest you demand a refund." Lifted from <u>Murphy Brown</u>, an American TV sitcom; I'm not sure if this is the exact quote; I heard it many years ago.

"…it's not guns that kill, right? It's people who kill."
  "It is bullets that kill…" Paraphrasing a routine by comedian Chris Rock

Martha at the Angelic Center in Act 2 quotes a number of proverbs during the reading, i.e. "He who pays the piper calls the tune." Few of these I can attribute because they are from remote times, however, "In the dark a tick is worse than I tiger," I lifted from <u>Meetings With Remarkable Men</u> by G.I. Gurdjieff

"How can we agree on objective truths when everyone's having a subjective experience?" Paraphrasing Soren Kierkegaard

"Worse than broke—I owe money." Paraphrasing a joke by Louis C.K.

"A man is satisfied not by the quantity of food but by the absence of greed." From <u>Meetings With Remarkable Men</u> by G.I. Gurdjieff

"Happy is he who sees not his unhappiness." From <u>Meetings With Remarkable Men</u> by G.I. Gurdjieff

"The more laws you create, the more criminals you make." I believe this comes from Lao Tzu.

"You cannot step into the same river twice." Heraclitus

"Where's there a machine that has no purpose?" Arthur M. Young

"Mind is the matrix of matter." Max Plank

"Helpless like a rich man's child." From <u>Temporary Like Achilles</u> by Bob Dylan

"The stars impel, they do not compel." This astrological adage is attributed to Shakespeare.

ABOUT THE AUTHOR

Gregory Brozek is a poet, writer, composer and philosopher with a Bachelor of Fine Arts in music. He spent his early adult life as a guitarist, prolific songwriter and band leader, performing under the name Adi Poem, all the while investigating world religions and the Human Potential Movement, in particular the works of Gurdjieff and Ouspensky. He met master astrologer Mantriji in 2002 and spent the next seven years studying Jyotish with him while, among other things, running a business and working in municipal politics. An avid swimmer and long-time tutor of Music and English, he started practicing and teaching Jyotish in 2007.

Email: adipoem@gmail.com

Made in the USA
Coppell, TX
04 May 2025

48990607R10194